SAFE FROM HARM

KATE
SERINE

sourcebooks
casablanca

Published by Sourcebooks Casablanca, an imprint of Sourcebooks, Inc.
P.O. Box 4410, Naperville, Illinois 60567-4410
(630) 961-3900
Fax: (630) 961-2168
www.sourcebooks.com

Printed and bound in Canada.
MBP 10 9 8 7 6 5 4 3 2 1

For my dear friend R. G., and all other first responders who have given their lives in the line of duty.

Chapter 1

DEPUTY GABE DAWSON PULLED INTO THE PARKING LOT of Moe's Diner, habit and finely honed instinct allowing him to take in at a glance the cars parked out front. There were the two guys—mechanics from the adjacent garage—smoking cigarettes at the corner of the building, shooting the shit on their break. And the three construction workers with mud-caked boots just coming out of the diner with their to-go orders in a plain white plastic bag. A businesswoman in a power suit was texting furiously as she hurried down the sidewalk in three-inch heels. And a couple strolled toward their car, gazing at each other with wide smiles on their faces as they held hands.

Moe's was certainly hopping with activity, the restaurant's reputation making it one of the most popular lunch spots in the county. The fifties-themed burger joint hadn't changed much in the decades since it'd started serving up milk shakes to the teenagers who'd come there back in the day to listen to their favorite records on the jukebox and sit knee to knee with their sweethearts, sipping a soda with two straws while they gazed at each other all moony-eyed. It was like something out of a freaking Norman Rockwell painting.

Too bad the neighborhood around the diner had pretty much gone to shit in the last ten years or so. Now, Moe's was right in the middle of a region with one of the highest crime rates in the entire county. You wouldn't catch any teenagers in there now unless they were high and looking for some cheap eats to curb the munchies.

These days, the typical clientele mostly consisted of people who worked in the area and couldn't take one more day of eating at the handful of fast food restaurants or at the pizza place, which, on its third owner in five years, had been on the Board of Health's shit list more than once. The diner was also known to be one of the favorite lunch spots for law enforcement who patrolled the area.

Bart "Moe" Morrison appreciated having the extra police presence around to deter the criminal elements and riffraff that had driven so many other businesses out over the years. He'd worked damned hard to keep the diner his father had started in 1958 alive and wasn't about to let his old man down.

Gabe sure as hell could understand *that*. His own father was Sheriff of Fairfield County, Indiana, as had been *his* father before him and *his* father before him... and on down the line. Law enforcement was in the Dawson family's blood. As Mac Dawson reminded his four sons often, the Dawsons had been the law in the county since before it even *was* a county, and they had an obligation to carry on the family legacy. But with his dad and grandfather having had long, distinguished careers, Gabe had a lot to live up to.

Which was one of the reasons he requested to be assigned to this particular area as often as possible. He wasn't going to make a name for himself sitting on his ass in Amish country or dealing with the occasional pissed-off neighbor in the suburbs. He needed to be where the action was, where he could actually make a difference and protect the community.

But even in this section of the county there were uneventful days, and this had promised to be one of them. He knew he should be grateful he hadn't had to deal with a break-in or a shooting or domestic dispute, but he hadn't had a single call, which made the day drag on.

Gabe sighed as he pulled into a parking spot and called in to dispatch, letting them know he was going to be out of service for lunch. He was just getting out of his department Tahoe when a squad car for the local police department pulled in a couple of spaces down from his.

"Well, I'd *thought* this place was going to hell," Gabe drawled as he sidled up to the driver's open window, "but now that you're here, I have proof."

Officer Chris Andrews laughed as he got out of his car. "Fuck off, Dawson. Let me know when you want to leave the sheriff's department and come work for a *real* police force."

Gabe returned his laugh and extended his hand to his friend. "What the hell are you doing here, Chris? I thought Jessica went into labor yesterday."

Chris grunted. "Yeah, change of plans."

"False alarm?"

Chris nodded on a sigh. "*Again*. I swear, you'd think we'd know the real deal by now."

Gabe chuckled as they headed into the diner together. "What is this anyway? Kid number fifteen or something?"

Chris rolled his eyes and shook his head. "*Three*, dumbass."

Gabe feigned a look of surprise. "Seriously? I thought it had to be more than that. It seems like you two are popping out kids all the time."

"Piss off," Chris shot back, snagging one of the only empty tables in the diner. "You're just jealous. You'll change your mind one of these days. When you meet the right woman."

Gabe grunted, glancing around a little. He hated having his back to the door. Not being able to see the entire room at once made him twitchy. "Yeah right. How long have you known me, Chris?"

Chris laughed good-naturedly. "Hey, it could happen—even to a loser like you."

Gabe chuckled. "If I recall, you had a reputation of your own once upon a time, Andrews."

"That was in high school, you dick. I wizened up."

Gabe lifted a brow at his best friend. "Oh yeah? I can think of a few dumbass moves since then. Need a few reminders? 'Cause I remember 'em all, dude."

"God, no!" Chris said with a grin. "It's a wonder we even survived with some of the stupid shit we used to pull. If your dad had had any idea of what we were up to, he'd have kicked our asses all over the county."

"No shit. He…" Gabe's words died on his lips when he suddenly caught a glimpse of a stunning titian-haired woman sitting a few tables away. "I'll be damned. What's *she* doing here?"

Chris twisted around in his seat. "Elle McCoy? Dunno. I'm sure they let her out of the prosecutor's office now and then." He turned back around, then a slow, shit-eating grin spread over his face. "No way."

"What?" Gabe demanded, dragging his gaze away

from where the county's deputy prosecutor was chatting with some douchebag in a suit.

"You've got the hots for Elle," Chris drawled.

"Whatever," Gabe scoffed, although he had to admit it didn't sound very convincing. Probably because he was lying out his ass. "She can't stand me. And she's more than happy to tell me to fuck off at every opportunity."

"I always knew she was wicked smart," Chris mused with a grin.

"Yeah, well, she was smart enough to pink-slip you," Gabe shot back, still irked all these years later that his best friend had ended up going out with Elle her entire senior year before they'd called it quits. Even worse was that it was his own damned fault Chris and Elle had dated because he'd actually suggested Chris ask her out. It pissed him off even more that in spite of their breakup, Chris and Elle had stayed friends all these years, while *he'd* rarely even received a civil word from her.

"So, what are you saying? Jessica's an idiot for marrying me?"

"An *idiot*?" Gabe scoffed. "Hell no! The woman's a *saint* to put up with your ass."

"Well, it's gonna take another saint to handle you, that's for damned sure," Chris assured him. "And I don't know that you'll find another woman like Jessica."

Gabe glanced back to where Elle and the Suit were sitting to see them pushing back from the table. The guy didn't even pull out her chair. God, what an asshat. She could do so much better. She *deserved* so much better.

When she suddenly glanced over their way and smiled, offering a little wave in greeting, he jerked his chin, belatedly realizing she'd been waving at Chris.

"Shit," Gabe muttered under his breath, feeling like a moron when Elle noticed him. But, much to his surprise, she and douche-suit made their way over to his and Chris's table.

"Hey, Chris," she greeted with a friendly smile. But when she turned toward Gabe, her gorgeous green eyes danced with light, and she raised a brow as if in silent challenge. "Dawson."

He allowed a slow grin to curve his mouth and leaned back in the chair, resting his forearms on his gun belt as he drawled in a low voice, "McCoy."

She flushed a little as their gazes held, but then her chin went up a notch and she turned her attention back to Chris. "How's Jessica? Any news?"

Chris's gaze was darting between Gabe and Elle, and he had to smother a grin when he replied, "Soon. I'll let her know you asked about her."

"So who's your friend?" Gabe asked, jerking his chin toward the stiff who looked extremely bored to be having a conversation with two cops.

"Oh, sorry!" Elle replied as if suddenly remembering the guy was even there. "Chet, this is Officer Chris Andrews and Deputy Gabe Dawson."

Jesus, seriously? Chet?

Gabe stood and extended his hand, not surprised at all when Chet's grip was pathetic and clammy. "What brings you slumming to this part of town, *Chet*?"

Chet gave him a tense smile, his gaze darting around nervously, like he was afraid he'd catch a mean case of the clap just by being in a place that didn't take reservations a month in advance. "Well, Elle suggested we dine in this...*unique* establishment. I believe she called it a 'cultural icon' of the county. And how could I refuse one of her little whims?" He placed his hand on the small of Elle's back and gave her a look that made Gabe's jaw tighten with disgust. "She's so delightful that way."

God, what a fucking tool.

"Uh-huh." Gabe blinked at the guy. What the hell did Elle *possibly* see in that guy? "So where you kids off to now? Too early for the opera, I guess."

Chet looked down his nose at Gabe as he said, "I'm heading back to the office to close a multimillion dollar deal before calling it a day and heading to the gym. And how about you, sport? Have you met your doughnut quota today?"

As much as Gabe would've loved to clock the condescending little prick, he settled for giving him a cock-eyed grin, refusing to rise to the bait. "Not yet, *champ*. But the day's still young. There just might be a cruller in my future."

"Chet, would you mind going out and starting the car?" Elle interjected, dismissing the guy before Gabe could get in another jab. "It's such a hot day…"

"Sure thing, babe. Don't be long."

As soon as he was gone, Gabe shook his head. "*Babe?* Wow. Gotta hand it to you, Elle, he's a whole new level of asshat."

"See you later, Chris," Elle said, pointedly ignoring Gabe's remark before turning on her heel and striding toward the door.

Gabe muttered a curse under his breath, then cast a glance at his friend. "I'll be right back, Chris. Order somethin' for me, will ya?"

He didn't wait for a response before hurrying after

Elle and catching her just as she was pushing open the door. "Here," he said, holding it open for her. "Let me get that."

She huffed and turned toward him, giving him a perplexed look. "I don't get you, Dawson." She sighed. "One minute you're a total jackass with the social graces of an ape, and the next you're a complete gentleman."

He leaned his shoulder against the doorframe and offered her a grin. "What can I say? I'm a total enigma."

She rolled her eyes, but her mouth hitched up slightly in one corner. "Yeah, right."

"You know what I think?" he asked.

She blinked at him, her sarcasm in every bat of her lovely eyes as she said, "Oh, do tell. This should be enlightening."

He leaned slightly toward her. "I think that deep down you actually really like me and that this whole 'kiss my ass, you suck, Gabe' attitude is just an act to disguise your true feelings."

He didn't miss the way her cheeks flushed even as she turned her eyes up to the ceiling, as if considering his words. Then she shook her head. "Nope. Pretty sure it's for real."

"Nah," he drawled, leaning in just a little closer. "I know you, McCoy."

She raised a single brow, and there was no mistaking the challenge this time around. He had the sneaking suspicion she enjoyed their little sparring matches as much as he did. "Dawson," she said, closing the gap just enough to make him hold his breath in anticipation, "the only thing you know about me is my measurements."

Ouch.

He straightened, clutching his chest as if she'd struck him. "Knife to the heart, McCoy. Knife to the heart."

She patted his chest with mock sympathy. "Be strong, Dawson. I'm sure any pain you're suffering at my rejection will be short-lived."

"Let me take you out for a drink tonight at Mulaney's," he suggested. "Give me the chance to turn on the ol' Dawson charm."

"I've never known you to be without a date on a Friday night," she said, her tone a little wary. "Hit a dry spell?"

He shrugged. "Was just keeping the night open for you."

"Sorry to disappoint," she said. "But don't worry—I doubt you'll have *any* trouble finding some bubble-headed badge bunny who'll fall for that famous 'charm' of yours."

Ah, hell, she's even gone with the finger quotes.

Gabe chuckled, but before he could say another word, she offered him a teasing grin and followed the douche-suit outside, leaving Gabe standing in the doorway smiling like an idiot.

God, if she only knew how she slayed him with every rejection. The woman was torture. Absolute torture.

As soon as Gabe returned to their table, Chris whistled. "Damn, man, you weren't kidding. I've had convicts look at me with more love than that. What the hell did you do to piss Elle off?"

Gabe shook his head. "Got me."

At that moment, their waitress, Debbie—no wait, *Deirdre*—finally came up to their table wearing a pissed off look and a blouse that was just a little too tight for her ample bosom. "Well, hi, *Gabe*," she said,

setting down a glass of water in front of Chris so hard
that it sloshed out onto the Formica table. "I haven't
seen you in here in a while. Or, you know, anywhere
else for that matter."

Gabe sent a quick glance Chris's way just in time to
catch the amused look on his face. "Uh, yeah. I've been
working another area of the county lately."

She gave him a tight smile and slammed his glass
down. "I'll bet."

Gabe cleared his throat. "So, uh…how ya been?"

She tilted her head to one side, giving him a dirty look.
"Like you care." She then turned to Chris and offered
him a bright smile. "What can I get you, Officer?"

Chris gave his order, all the while smothering a
smile—the bastard—but when Gabe started to give his,
Deirdre turned away in a huff, blond ponytail swinging,
and marched angrily back to the kitchen.

"What the hell?" Gabe muttered, lifting his arms to
his sides.

"Well, you're just making friends everywhere," Chris
taunted. "Probably just as well. I don't know that I'd eat
anything she serves you if I were you. She looks like
she'd like to see you gargling broken glass. Dare I ask
what you did to piss *her* off? Or are you clueless on this
one, too?"

Oh, no, *that* one Gabe knew.

"Let's just say I was more of a gentleman than she
expected and leave it at that," Gabe grumbled, pushing
back from the table. "I'm going to go see if I can just put
in an order at the counter. Back in a sec."

Gabe strode toward the counter, glancing out the
expanse of windows that lined the front of the diner

as he went, his pulse kicking up when he saw a man making his way in from the parking lot. The guy had his hands shoved into his pockets, his shoulders hunched over, and his baseball cap pulled down over sandy-brown hair, his eyes cast down at the pavement. Not exactly anything out of the ordinary, but something about the guy seemed *off*.

Gabe's internal shit-storm alarm went into over-drive—a persistent gnawing at his gut that was enough to make him glance over his shoulder to track the move-ment of the guy as he came into the restaurant and took a seat at the counter.

"How ya doing?" Gabe said with a jerk of his chin.

The guy's eyes darted toward him, then away again, but he didn't say anything, just clasped his hands in front of him and tried to a little too hard to stare straight ahead.

"You been in here before?" Gabe asked, keeping his tone conversational. "Their BLTs are awesome, in case you're wondering what to order."

The guy sent another glance Gabe's way, looking oddly uncomfortable to be receiving any attention. His voice cracked a little when he muttered, "Thanks."

Yep, something was up. That was for damned sure.

Gabe regarded him for a minute longer, giving him the once-over, looking for any bulges that might indicate a weapon. Unfortunately, he couldn't just frisk a guy without any cause. He didn't look high or drunk. He wasn't being belligerent. He just looked nervous as hell. No crime in that.

Still, there was something about him that Gabe didn't like one damned bit. When the guy pulled out his phone and started texting, Gabe received the message loud and clear. Obviously, he wasn't interested in a conversation.

"Enjoy your lunch," Gabe said, abandoning his own lunch order. He headed back to the table where Chris sat, already enjoying his chicken salad.

"What's up with that guy?" Chris asked, jerking his head almost imperceptibly toward the man at the counter.

He shook his head. "Dunno, but something's making him jumpy." A beep suddenly sounded in his earpiece, sounding a low-battery warning. "Shit, my radio's going dead. I'm gonna run out and grab another battery from the car."

Gabe headed to his car, casually strolling past the guy's red pickup truck, glancing into the cab and the bed as he went. Nothing unusual or suspicious in plain sight, damn it all to hell. He had half a mind to run the guy's plates, see if there was an outstanding warrant or suspended license or something that would be making the guy so jumpy.

But he tamped down his paranoia as he got into his SUV to switch out his radio battery. The guy could be jumpy for any number of reasons. Maybe cops just made him nervous. It happened. It was probably fine. That's what he kept telling himself, in spite of the nagging suspicion eating away at him.

He was sitting in the front seat of his Tahoe, testing the new battery in his radio, when a beat-up blue Ford pickup pulled in. The driver parked a few spots down and had barely put the POS truck into park before he jumped out and went charging into the diner.

What the fuck?

Gabe launched from his Tahoe, speaking urgently

into the radio mic at his shoulder as he rushed toward the door. "Dispatch, car three."

The radio crackled as dispatch responded. "Car three, go 'head."

"I have a 10-37 at Moe's Diner on—" A sudden rapid popping sound and terrified screams made Gabe's gut clench. *Shit*. "Shots fired! Going in!"

Gabe didn't wait for a response before drawing his weapon and rushing forward. He threw open the door, assessing the situation at a glance. The restaurant patrons were on the floor, huddled under tables. What he didn't see was the shooter. Or Chris.

Deirdre was crouched nearby, hugging an elderly woman who was sobbing hysterically, and pointed toward the kitchen. Gabe gave her a terse nod and hurried that way, taking a quick peek through the round window in the door before easing it open.

"Where'd he go?" Gabe whispered to the man in a hairnet that was huddled next to a supply shelf.

The guy gestured toward a door that led to a storage room. "B-back door."

Gabe hurried to the storage room and the back door that led to the employee parking lot behind the diner. The second guy he'd seen enter the restaurant was nowhere to be found, but the shifty guy who'd been sitting at the counter was trying to haul ass, but he was limping.

"Stop!" Gabe roared. "Sheriff's department!"

The guy stumbled a couple of steps forward, but then stopped, wisely raising his hands and dropping to his knees. Gabe rushed toward him, keeping an eye out for the other guy, relieved to hear approaching sirens. He quickly patted down and cuffed the son of a bitch as he read him his Miranda rights.

"My name's Billy Monroe," the guy said in a rush. "It's not me you want. I didn't shoot anyone!"

"Maybe you missed the 'remain silent' part," Gabe spat as he hauled the guy to his feet.

"I swear!" Billy insisted, his words tumbling out. "I was supposed to do this mission with him, but I didn't."

Gabe frowned at his words. *Mission? What the...?*

"I'm not a killer, man," Billy continued. "It was my cousin, Derrick Monroe. I'll tell you what you need to know. You gotta believe me—I didn't do this. But I need a doctor. I think I got hit by a ricochet or somethin'."

Gabe didn't respond. He was too busy running the name Derrick Monroe through his head. *Why the hell was it so familiar?*

He'd just led Billy around to the front of the building when the other cars arrived. His brother Tom was the first to come rushing forward. "You okay?"

"Yeah, I'm good," Gabe assured him. "You see the other guy?"

Tom shook his head.

"How about Chris Andrews?" Gabe panted. "He come out yet?"

Tom frowned. "Chris? He's here?"

Gabe's stomach sank, and suddenly he remembered why the name Derrick Monroe had sounded so familiar. It was because Derrick was the son of Jeb Monroe, a local farmer whose antigovernment rants—which specifically included anticop tirades—had begun to gain an impressive following on social media. They'd received an alert on Derrick just a few days before based on some comments he'd made online, comments that had included a declaration that the only good cop was a dead cop.

He shoved his suspect into Tom's hands and ran back into the diner. "Chris!"

"Deputy!" someone called out. "Over here!"

He rushed toward the sound of the voice. It was one of the other waitresses. She was on her knees next to Chris, where he lay on the ground among shattered glass and plates and other debris that littered the floor, pressing a bussing towel to his neck. Chris gurgled, gasping for air, choking on his own blood, his eyes silently pleading with Gabe.

"Ah, Jesus, Chris," Gabe ground out, dropping down beside him and taking over for the waitress, glancing toward the door to see the paramedics hurrying inside. "Hold on, buddy. Help's comin'. Just hold on…"

⁓⁓⁓

Gabe sat in the corner of Mulaney's pub, his head in his hands. His broad shoulders, normally held erect and proud, were hunched, his dejection a palpable force in the room as Elle approached.

He reached out for his beer, but it evaded his grasp with a harsh scrape of glass on wood. "What the hell do you want?" he growled, slowly lifting his gaze to meet hers. It seemed to take him a moment to completely focus.

"I'm cutting you off," she said, easing down into the chair next to him. "How many have you had anyway?"

He shrugged. "Dunno. Lost track. Not enough, however many it is." He pulled a hand down his face. "You know I can still hear the shots? I can still see Chris on the ground, bleeding out."

She reached out and grasped his forearm, giving it a comforting squeeze, not sure what else to do to help him. "Gabe—"

"And I can still hear Jessica's screams," he interrupted, squeezing his eyes shut as if trying to block the sound in his head. "When the doctor told her Chris hadn't made it, she lost it. I just... Yeah." He shook his head, banishing the words that had been on his lips. "So, if it's all the same to you, honey, I'll keep going until that particular memory is washed clean."

Then he gave her his trademark grin and gently took the bottle from her, lifting it briefly in salute before chugging it down.

Elle glanced around, noticing some of the other patrons were staring, trying to figure out what the hell was wrong with the drunk in the corner. She sent an angry glare their way, and they abruptly averted their gazes. When she turned her attention back to Gabe, she leaned in a little and smoothed her hand along his arm. "Gabe, it's time to go."

"You don't work here," he grumbled.

"True, but I'm half owner," she admitted. "And I'm not letting you drink yourself to death. Chris's murder wasn't your fault."

"The hell it wasn't," he snapped. "I should've been in there with Chris. I *had* been in there just two minutes before. If I'd *been* there when that asshole went in—"

"You'd probably be dead, too," she interrupted, the horror of that possibility making her stomach roll with dread. She had to give herself a mental shake before she could continue. "Derrick Monroe went in that diner to kill a cop. It didn't matter *which* cop. Chris just happened to be the one he chose."

Gabe ran his hand over his hair. "D'you know Jessica went into labor when she found out? Gave birth to their baby girl."

Elle nodded.

"Yeah?" He lifted his brows at her, then laughed. "Hell, what am I saying? Of course you know. You know everything."

She stared at him for a long moment, wondering where the hell that was coming from. But then she shook her head, willing to cut him a little slack under the circumstances. "We'll explore that bullshit comment later," she assured him. "But you might be interested to know Billy Monroe gave me enough to get a warrant for his cousin. And he's agreed to testify against Derrick. I'm going to put that son of a bitch away for what he's done, Gabe. I promise. I want you to know that."

"Why?" he countered.

She frowned at him. "Sorry? Why, what?"

"Why are you suddenly being *nice* to me?" he asked. "Normally, you avoid me like the fucking plague."

"I'm just trying to be a friend," she told him truthfully, not willing to go into why she'd kept him at arms' length all these years, why she'd refused to let him get past her defenses despite all his advances. Why bother? Nothing she could say would make a difference. He wouldn't change. So why should she?

He grunted. "Yeah, well, my friends have a way of meeting untimely ends, so you might as well save yourself the trouble."

She pushed back from the table and stood, extending her hand to him, her heart twisting with pity. "C'mon, Dawson. Let me take you home. You're going to have one hell of a hangover tomorrow."

He turned his aqua gaze up at her, studying her through lashes that were far too long and thick to be wasted on a man. "Shouldn't you be on a date with douche-suit?"

She frowned, confused. "With *who*?"

He shook his head. "Mr. Multimillion-Dollar Deal. The asshole."

She sighed. "He's not an asshole."

He gave her a pointed look, clearly conveying his opinion on the matter.

"Okay, fine. He's an asshole," she admitted. She'd already determined *that* without Gabe's input. It'd been abundantly clear Chet was not the guy for her when he'd acted completely put out by the fact that she needed to go deal with a suspect in the murder of a cop. "But that's not why I bailed on my date with him."

He lifted his head, squinting as if trying to focus. "Yeah? Then why did you?"

"Because your brother Tom called me and said you'd told him to go to hell when he tried to take you home," she confessed. "And then your brother Joe called to tell me you'd told him to fuck off and leave you alone. And then the bartender called and told me he didn't feel comfortable telling a cop to leave. And, seeing as how my aunt Charlotte is out of town and can't come in here to kick your ass out of our bar, they thought maybe I could manage it."

Gabe blinked at her for a long moment, then finally

said, "I'm sure I'd be able to come up with an appropriately sarcastic remark if I wasn't so shitfaced right now.
I'll have to owe you one."

She extended her hand. "Then you should probably
take me up on that offer to drive you home. Maybe
you'll think of something on the way."

<hr>

Gabe was out cold in the front seat of Elle's Accord,
his forehead pressed against the passenger window as
he snored softly. She glanced over at him, sympathy at
what he must be going through softening the heart she
kept trying to harden where he was concerned. He'd
looked so forlorn, so lost and alone at the bar when
she'd walked in, it was all she could do not to wrap
her arms around him and hold him close, offering what
solace she could.

She sighed and ran her hand through her thick, red
curls. She hated to see him this way. It was far easier to
pretend she couldn't stand him when he was the usual
cocky, swaggering jerk he'd been when she'd met him
back in high school. She'd come to town to live with her
aunt Charlotte after the death of her parents and sisters,
and had been hard-pressed to keep from drooling like
an idiot when the handsome teenage boy had shown up
on her aunt's doorstep, having been sent by his father to
help move Elle in.

But he'd barely noticed *her* that day. Or ever, really.

Hardly surprising. With a sexy, dimpled smile that
turned girls into giggling puddles of goo, Gabe had
dated a different cheerleader every week, leaving a trail
of broken hearts a mile long.

And her? Well, she'd been the awkward, too-skinny, freckle-faced, flat-chested brainiac with untamable, frizzy, red hair who'd adored him.

So, yeah…suffice it to say, he hadn't asked *her* to prom.

And yet it was his name more often than not that had appeared in her journal, circled with little hearts. And when she received a bouquet of wildflowers once from a secret admirer after one particularly disappointing day, she liked to imagine a certain boy with dimples was behind it. She'd been at every one of his football games, cheering him on in the one year of school they'd shared. She'd sat beside her aunt at his graduation ceremony, trying to suppress the heat that rose to her cheeks when they called his name or when she'd given him a congratulatory hug at his open house.

She'd replayed that hug in her mind every night that summer before going to sleep, hating the fact that she was stuck in high school for three more years. And although she'd never admit it to anyone, it was the same dimpled smile on her mind more often than not when she drifted off to sleep now. And wildflowers were still her favorite.

But it was common knowledge that Gabe Dawson was a player. He'd never given her a second thought when they were younger, but he certainly noticed her now that she had curves and could fill out a sweater quite nicely, thank you very much.

He'd been coming onto her mercilessly for the last couple of years, trying to use that same old tired act on *her* that had worked on everyone else all his life. And normally she could keep her guard up and ignore the way her stomach fluttered every time she saw him, could ignore how her pulse hammered when she heard his voice. She knew better than to give in to her longings, knew that it could only lead to trouble.

But in moments like this one, when he allowed a rare glimpse of vulnerability, she was undone. And all the defenses she'd built up over the years came crumbling down in an instant.

She sent another glance his way, her heart aching for the pain he had to be feeling at the loss of his best friend, pain she knew she'd be feeling as well once she allowed it in. She'd been so caught up in dealing with all the legal aspects of the case, she hadn't taken a moment to truly grieve for her friend, hadn't let the horrible truth really sink in yet.

But now her heart constricted painfully and tears choked her, making it impossible for her to ignore the pain any longer. She tried to hold back the tears, but they fell anyway, blurring her vision and making it difficult to see the road. Thankfully, Gabe's house wasn't far.

She pulled into the driveway of his modest brick ranch and sat for a moment with her forehead pressed against the steering wheel, letting the sobs overtake her. But after a moment of indulging her sorrow, she abruptly pushed away from the wheel and shook her head.

"No," she sniffed. "Not now."

In spite of her declaration, the tears continued to slip to her cheeks as fast as she could swipe them away. Finally, with a sharp curse, she threw open her car door and strode around to open the door for Gabe.

"C'mon," she murmured, trying to pull him to his feet. He mumbled something incoherent but managed to stand and wrap his arm around her shoulders. When they reached his front door, she asked, "Where are your keys?"

When he didn't answer, she huffed and slipped her hand into his pocket, imagining the smart-ass remarks he'd be throwing at her at that moment had he been aware of what was going on. But then a throaty groan rumbled up from his chest and her eyes snapped up to his face and caught his grin.

Warmth flooded her cheeks as her fingers closed around his keys and she yanked them out. "Let's just get you inside, shall we?"

It only took a moment to find his bedroom, but without the lights on, she stumbled and they fell in a tangle onto his bed, his arms going around her and pulling her into the curve of his body as he rolled onto his back, so that she was half on top of him.

Her breath caught on a gasp when she found herself peering down into his eyes, open now and studying her intently. "You're crying," he whispered.

She swallowed hard, damning the tenderness in his voice and how it flooded her with warmth. "I'm fine," she insisted. But when his hand came up to gently caress her cheek and wipe away her tears, her shoulders shook on a sob, proving she was a liar.

Gabe's arms came around her, pulling her closer. She buried her face in his chest and allowed the tears to come as he silently smoothed her hair. When her tears began to subside, she lifted her head from his chest to thank him, but as she peered down at him and her gaze locked with his, the words died on her tongue.

His hand slid into her hair and he slowly drew her in

to press his lips firmly against hers. For a moment, she melted into his kiss, electrified by the intimate caress of his tongue as it teased her lips. Then with a jolt, she came to her senses and shoved against his chest, pushing him back enough to break the kiss. But his hand was still at the nape of her neck, and her lips hovered dangerously close to his. Even in his drunken state, the brief kiss had been warm and sensual, and awakened something in her she'd just as soon not recognize.

"Elle," he whispered, his gaze searching hers. "Unless you want me to kiss you again, you should probably go."

He was right. She should go. She should. Staying would be a very, very bad idea. They were both grief-stricken, vulnerable. Letting things go any further would be a colossal mistake. And Gabe was a ladies' man. Always had been. God knows who would've ended up in his arms that night had she not shown up when she did. She was just a warm body when he needed someone to hold. That's all this was. She meant nothing to him. She was just another conquest. And for all she knew, he wouldn't even remember her having been there come morning.

"You're drunk, Gabe," she reminded him. "You don't know what you're doing."

His gaze was so intense, she had to suppress a shudder. "I know exactly what I'm doing," he assured her, his voice going deeper. "Do you?"

Every logical thought told her to get up right now and go. But before she quite realized what she was doing, she leaned in, brushing her lips against his...

Chapter 2

One year later…

"YOU ARE AN IRREDEEMABLE *JACKASS*!"

Gabe grinned and crossed his arms over his chest as he regarded the deputy prosecutor who was glaring at him with such fury, any other man might've withered under her irate gaze. But not him. *Hell* no. Because Elle McCoy was vibrant and fiery even when he *wasn't* on her shit list—but when she was pissed at him? Well, then she was just goddamned adorable. And he couldn't help acting like a frigging ten-year-old, goading her just to see those almond-shaped emerald eyes of hers flash.

"Irredeemable?" Gabe taunted, giving her the dimpled smile he knew had a way of vanishing the panties of every woman he'd ever wanted—except her. "Don't you mean *irresistible?*"

Elle's eyes narrowed at him, her glare growing more furious, if that was even possible. She snatched up the yellow legal pad from the table and shoved it into her sleek leather briefcase. "No, Dawson, I *don't*," she hissed in that slightly husky voice that made the criminals she prosecuted know she meant business. "You're damned lucky I was able to convict this asshole without his cousin's testimony."

Gabe's swagger faltered ever so slightly. Elle was

convinced he'd hooked up with the girlfriend of a key witness on the case she'd been working her ass off on. He hadn't known the woman's connection to the case when she'd offered him a ride home from Mulaney's one night. But she sure as hell had known who *he* was. And even though nothing had happened between them, she'd lied to her boyfriend, telling him all about a one-night stand with the deputy investigating his family for the murder of a damned good cop—and Gabe's best friend.

Billy Monroe had gone apeshit—big shocker there. And when he'd finished threatening to relieve Gabe of his manhood and force him to ingest it in spite of Gabe's attempt to explain that nothing had happened, that he'd only gotten a ride home from Chelsea, Billy had clammed up, refusing to cooperate and offer any testimony on his waste-of-space cousin.

Fortunately, Elle had still managed to persuade a jury to convict Derrick Monroe of murder even without his cousin's testimony. But that didn't make Gabe feel like any less of an asshole for screwing things up to begin with. He knew Elle had fought tooth and nail for this conviction, and he owed her. Big time.

He cast a quick glance around the nearly empty courtroom, then took a step toward her, closing the distance between them. He gently took hold of her elbow. "I'm sorry, Elle," he told her, his voice low. "I really am. I fu—" He caught himself and sent another glance around the room before sighing. "I screwed up. I know that. Let me take you to dinner, make it up to you."

Her even gaze met and held his, but there was no forgiveness there. Hell, if he was being honest, she'd been even colder and more distant with him in the last year—since Chris's death—than she'd ever been.

He'd thought maybe things were improving. Elle had been so concerned for him the day Chris died, dragging his sloppy-drunk ass home before he'd done something colossally stupid. But the rest of the night after that was kind of a haze. He thought *maybe* he'd kissed her, but hell, he'd been dreaming of her for so long, longing to taste her soft lips, that kiss and the resulting unbelievable make-out session could've just been a figment of his imagination. And she sure as shit wasn't giving him any vibes to the contrary...

"Dinner?" she scoffed. "Are you *kidding* me? You think dinner is going to make up for nearly losing this case?"

He closed his eyes for a moment on a sigh. "No, Elle. I don't. I know nothing I can do or say is going to make a difference, but it won't stop me from trying. I'm sorry as hell. I don't know how many times I have to say it before you believe me."

Elle's chin trembled a little as she said, "That son of a bitch Monroe ambushed one of my friends—one of *your* friends, Gabe. He walked into the diner where you and Chris were eating lunch and shot him three times—just because he was a cop. And Monroe nearly got away with it because you couldn't keep your dick in your pants." She jerked her arm out of his grasp. "*Sorry* doesn't cut it."

Before Gabe could stop her, Elle had taken a few angry strides away, her heels clicking purposefully on the floor in a very clear message that echoed the ramrod straight line of her back and dismissive angle of her chin. But he jogged to catch up and cut in front of her, blocking her path. "Then what will?"

She huffed and gave him an exasperated look. "*What?*"

"What do I have to do to make it up to you?" he pressed. "We have to work together, Elle. You can't be mad at me forever."

"Bet me." She shouldered her way past him, storming out of the courtroom.

Gabe heaved another sigh and ran a hand over the blond spikes of his high-and-tight before following, determined to win her over and insinuate himself back into her good graces. He just didn't have any frigging clue how to go about it...

Damn Gabe Dawson and his arrogance!

Nothing ever changed.

Well, she had news for Fairfield County's golden boy. She wasn't buying what he was selling. And she'd be damned if she was going to be just another notch on Gabe Dawson's belt. She'd leave that role to the badge bunnies who threw themselves constantly at the handsome deputy.

Fortunately, he didn't seem to recall the night of Chris's death, when she'd taken him home and had been stupid enough to find herself in his arms in the best make-out session of her life. She could only imagine what it'd be like when he was completely sober. And she *had* imagined ever since. Often. Which seriously pissed her off.

Elle huffed in disgust as she stormed away from Gabe, not sure if she was angrier with him or with herself. To think she'd ever found him even *remotely* attractive! Clearly, she'd been just like every other girl who'd been taken in by that sexy smile and those aqua eyes that sparkled with mischief. Thank God she'd come to her senses before things had gone too far.

She'd had a lapse in judgment that night, that was all. And the way he'd been since then just confirmed she'd been right to put the brakes on. So no matter how many dimpled smiles he threw her way, she wasn't about to let him off the hook for jeopardizing her case because he couldn't keep it in his pants.

"Elle! Wait up!"

She increased her pace, lifting her chin higher, determined to make it very clear what he could do with his apologies and dinner invitations.

But her pace faltered when she reached the courthouse doors that led out to the steps where reporters were waiting. She hated dealing with the media, hated having to give a statement about her success or failure. Her stomach twisted into knots, and for a brief moment, she entertained the idea of waiting for Gabe to catch up and join her as she addressed the press. He had a way with the public, could charm them all with that confident, commanding air of his that had them all eating out of his hand.

But then she set her jaw and shoved open the doors, determined to meet them all head-on. She'd worked too damned hard to get where she was to hand over the reins because of her distaste for dealing with reporters. She'd never once backed down from a challenge—she sure as hell wasn't about to start now.

The moment she reached the courthouse steps, the

reporters moved in en masse, shouting their questions all at once, trying to be heard over the others in their throng. She held up her hand in a request for silence and opened her mouth to give the statement she'd rehearsed in her head when she suddenly caught sight of a face in the crowd that sent a shiver down her spine.

Mark Monroe, the brother of the man they'd just convicted, stood a few feet behind the reporters, his face twisted into a furious mask of hatred. He'd been implicated in the murder with his brother as an accessory after the fact, but they'd had insufficient evidence to charge him. He'd been popping up periodically ever since, glaring daggers at her, his demeanor vaguely threatening but never crossing a line that could give her a reason to go to the police. He wasn't the first angry family member she'd ever had to deal with, and he certainly wouldn't be the last.

Still, there was something in the man's expression this time that made her glad of the crowd of reporters surrounding her. The fact that he was wearing an old jacket in spite of the oppressive summer heat momentarily set off alarms in her head until she remembered it was the same jacket he'd worn every day in court. Nothing to be worried about. It was over. The trial was over. And finally she could sleep well, knowing she'd put Chris's killer behind bars.

Donning a genuine smile, she dragged her gaze away from his and back to the dozen or so faces eagerly awaiting her statement. But even as she began talking, she could feel the weight of Mark Monroe's gaze on her, felt the heat of his anger that prickled her skin in vague but persistent warning.

—⁓—

Gabe didn't know why in the hell it bothered him so much that Elle thought he was a first-class loser. But it did. It rankled him like nothing else ever had. He normally didn't give a shit what anyone thought. If someone had a problem with him, he was more than happy to offer a cordial invitation to kiss his ass.

But when Elle had given him that pointed look of disdain that could turn even the most hardened criminal into a quivering mass of *fucked-up*, the foundation of his normally unshakable confidence was left a little cracked. The woman had a way of bringing him to his knees without even trying. She always had—although she didn't know it.

He'd been completely knocked on his ass the first day he'd seen her. She'd been just an awkward teenage girl who still hadn't even come into her full beauty, but he could see it there, could sense the strength and intelligence in her intense gaze. He'd felt like she was the only one who could see right through him, past all the bullshit. And it'd scared the hell out of him. At eighteen, he hadn't known how to handle someone getting past his cocky teenage facade. So he'd avoided her, all but ignored her—at least, publicly.

But that wasn't an option now. Their careers threw them together on a regular basis, whether they liked it or not. And her effect on him had turned out to be exactly what he'd anticipated. But instead of being afraid of Elle getting too close to the person he truly was, Gabe had been surprised to discover he craved it. He *wanted* her to see that side of him no one else had access to, that vulnerable part of him he kept safely locked away.

What the hell was that *all about?*

"Where's the fire?"

Gabe's head snapped toward the direction of his older brother's voice. Tom was leaning against the railing of the mezzanine that overlooked the courthouse's massive marble foyer. The courthouse was one of only two buildings in Fairfield County that could boast being mentioned in architectural magazines for the beauty of its design. While it all seemed a little over the top to Gabe and made him afraid to even frigging sneeze for fear of knocking over an overpriced bust of some long-dead president, Tom seemed right at home among all the stateliness.

But then nothing ever seemed to rattle his brother. The guy was annoyingly levelheaded, which made him pretty much the last person Gabe wanted to see just then. If he said a word about his frustrations, Tom would offer some kind of sage advice that Gabe knew he'd be better off taking but wouldn't because it came from his brother.

"Hey," Gabe muttered, jerking his chin at Tom in greeting. "Need to catch up with Elle."

Tom nodded, falling into step beside him. "Ah."

"What the hell is that supposed to mean?" Gabe snapped as they jogged down the steps to the main floor.

Tom shrugged. "Nothing. Should it?"

And here we go…

Gabe groaned before he could catch himself. "I'm not in the mood to be analyzed, Tommy." He pushed through the revolving door, rolling his eyes when Tom ambled into the next open slot as the door came around. "Seriously, Bro. Not a good time."

"What's your problem?" Tom demanded. "I just came by to talk to Judge Pettigrew and heard about the verdict on the Monroe case. Thought I'd see how you were doing."

Gabe caught sight of Elle standing just a few feet away on the courthouse steps, giving a statement to reporters, and headed in that direction. "I'm fine, Tom," he called over his shoulder. "Everything's just fine."

He heard his brother calling after him but continued forward, not interested in a lecture just then. When the reporters saw him approaching, their attention suddenly shifted to him and they rushed forward, shoving microphones into his face.

"Deputy Dawson!" they called over the top of each other, competing for a sound bite.

He paused long enough to mutter the appropriate statement that he'd written the night before, explaining how happy he was that justice had been served. He'd intended to say more, but when he saw Elle slipping away, he wrapped it up with a hasty "thank you" and squeezed through the crush of press to get to her.

"Now, about dinner," he said as he fell into step beside her. "Should I pick you up at seven?"

She halted abruptly and turned toward him, her cheeks flushed with anger, but then her eyes suddenly went wide. "Gun!"

Gabe reflexively went for the weapon at his hip as he turned, simultaneously shoving Elle behind him to shield her with his body as he drew. But he wasn't fast enough. He heard the repeated crack of the assailant's gun at the same moment as pain exploded in his chest, the sound of the gunfire reaching him a split-second behind the actual impact.

What the fuck?

For a fraction of a second, he was confused by the sudden blow that stole his breath. But then the truth hit him, as sure as the bullets that had nailed him in the chest. A wave of panic and fear washed over him, but he shoved it away and managed to raise his weapon, returning fire at the bastard who'd gotten the drop on him. And there was no question who that bastard was.

Mark Monroe.

Gabe's ears filled with the screams of the reporters and others on the courthouse steps, panicked as they raced for cover. He heard his brother Tom's ragged scream of fury. More shots were exchanged as the sidewalk came rushing up on him.

Then there was silence.

It took him a few seconds to realize he lay on the steps, staring up at the clouds as they drifted overhead. For a moment, he wondered if he was dead, but then he saw Elle's beautiful face peering down at him, her brows drawn together in concern. She was taking his face in her hands, saying something. He wasn't really listening. All he could focus on was the blood trickling down her cheek from a wound on her forehead. A fury like none he'd ever experienced filled him at that moment.

Monroe had hurt her. That sick, cop-hating asshole had hurt her. Pissed as hell and ready to knock some heads, he shoved up, trying to get to his feet, but Elle pressed him back down.

"I'm fine," he ground out, pushing back and attempting to get up. "I'm fine. Wearing my vest."

"You're *not* fine, dammit!" she snapped, her voice shrill, panicked as she snatched the silk scarf from around her neck. "Jesus, Gabe—be still!"

This brought Gabe up short. Elle didn't panic. Not ever. She was too tough. Too strong.

Shit. Not good.

He collapsed back onto the concrete, the edges of his vision beginning to blur. But he was coherent enough to know she was tying the scarf around his leg. Like a tourniquet.

Well, hell...

Chapter 3

ELLE'S HEART WAS IN HER THROAT. SEEING GABE lying there, his leg bleeding, his face growing visibly pale, rattled her more than she cared to admit. And yet in spite of his own injury, he kept frowning at her with what looked like concern.

"You're hurt," he mumbled.

She shook her head. "No, no, I'm fine, Gabe. Just be still. I—"

He reached up and touched her forehead with such surprising tenderness it stilled her breath, but when his fingers came away covered in blood, her breath returned to her in a gasp. Her own fingers were covered in blood from trying to staunch the flow from Gabe's leg, so she wiped the inside of her wrist against her head, wincing with pain, though her own touch had been nearly as gentle as Gabe's had been.

Her eyes widened when she looked at her wrist and saw blood there.

What the heck?

In the next moment, hands grasped her upper arms and pulled her back, away from Gabe.

"No!" she cried out, reaching for him, but then she saw the paramedics crouched down beside him and turned to see who'd drawn her away.

"Oh good," Gabe mumbled with a grin. "The cavalry has arrived…"

One of the paramedics laughed, sounding relieved to Elle's ears. "Hang in there, Dawson. We gotcha."

"Let's get your head looked at," Gabe's brother Tom was saying, his arm going around her shoulders and leading her to where several police cars were waiting, their lights flashing. The rapidly alternating red and blue made her wince now that her adrenaline was beginning to taper off and one hell of a headache was coming on.

She reluctantly nodded, then cast a look over her shoulder to see the paramedics loading Gabe onto a gurney.

"He'll be okay," Tom assured her, but Elle could hear the note of concern in his voice. He'd seen the amount of blood Gabe had lost. He knew they were racing against time. "Now, c'mon. We need to get your head checked out. Looks like you might need some stitches."

Elle was only vaguely aware of the paramedics inspecting her head wound. She winced when they wrapped it well enough for her to be transported to the hospital, and she was pretty much in a daze as the ER staff cleaned and stitched the laceration just below her hairline, where the bullet had grazed her.

If Mark Monroe's aim had been any better, she'd be lying dead in the morgue instead of sitting in the tiny exam room that smelled of rubbing alcohol and disinfectant, waiting for a ride home. Elle blinked away tears as she realized how close she'd come to dying that day, how close *Gabe* had come to dying. Just the thought of it made her physically sick, and she put a hand to her mouth, searching desperately for a bedpan or bowl.

Luckily, a nurse popped her head in at that moment, offering her a smile, distracting her from her churning stomach. "Your aunt is here to take you home, Ms. McCoy."

Even before the nurse had finished speaking, Aunt Charlotte was pushing into the room and enveloping Elle in her motherly embrace. "Oh, my sweet girl," Charlotte murmured into Elle's hair. "When I heard what'd happened at the courthouse…"

Elle managed to swallow the bile that burned her throat and sniff back her tears before being released from her aunt's embrace. "I'm okay," she assured her, not quite sure if her words were true. "I'll be fine."

Charlotte put her at arms' length and searched her face, determined to do her own assessment. She must've been satisfied with what she saw because she gave Elle a curt nod and turned to the nurse. "Is she free to go home?"

The nurse handed Charlotte a handful of papers that Elle had signed and vaguely understood to be her discharge papers and instructions for wound care. "As far as we're concerned, but I believe Sheriff Dawson wants to speak with her."

Charlotte frowned. "Mac? Where is he?"

"Waiting for his son to get out of surgery," the nurse explained.

Elle slid off of the bed. "Let's go."

"Mac can wait," Charlotte said, her irritation evident.

Elle didn't care what kind of tension might be brewing between Charlotte and her old friend and one-time high school sweetheart, Mac Dawson. That could wait. All she cared about was getting an update on Gabe.

She turned to the nurse. "Show me where they're waiting."

When Elle arrived in the family waiting room with her aunt reluctantly in tow, she wasn't surprised at all to see the entire Dawson family there. Tom paced the room, his normally unflappable calm clearly overridden by concern for his brother. Their younger brothers, Joe and Kyle, sat in the row of chairs, their respective girlfriends gripping their hands, offering the men their love and support.

Their venerable patriarch, Sheriff Mac Dawson, stood at the window, arms crossed over his chest, his back to all of them. Mac had a gruff, severe demeanor even on a good day, but the scowl on his face was fierce when he glanced over his shoulder to see who had entered.

"How's Gabe?" Elle asked, her voice tight with apprehension.

"They removed the bullet from his leg," Tom told her. "Luckily, Monroe didn't hit an artery or the bone."

Elle closed her eyes for a moment and breathed a huge sigh of relief. "Thank God."

"How are *you*?" Joe asked, gesturing toward her head.

She forced a grin. "I'll have a scar, but nothing—"

Elle's words died on her lips as all three Dawson brothers suddenly stiffened, on alert, their expressions deadly. The hair on the back of her neck rose in warning, and she spun around to see a tall, gangly man with a tanned face lined with creases that told the story of his many years working in the sun. Unfortunately, she knew him all too well.

"What the hell are you doing here?" Tom demanded, his hands fisted at his sides.

Jeb Monroe held out his hands in a placating gesture.

"Just came to identify my boy's body," he replied. "And I heard what had happened to one of yours."

"Like you had nothing to do with it," Joe snapped.

Jeb nodded. "I figured you'd assume that, given our…history. I didn't know what Mark had planned. But I'm sure the idea of his brother being locked away by your government was more than he could bear."

Elle couldn't suppress the little grunt of disgust that slipped out, drawing Jeb's attention to her. But she didn't look away from his offended gaze. The son of a bitch had everything to do with what had occurred that day, she was sure of it. He'd been preaching his hatred for years. And he'd filled the heads of his sons and other family members and acquaintances with the same vitriol.

"The bloodshed today is on *your* hands," Elle hissed. "You might not have stood on the steps and pulled the trigger, but it's all on you."

Jeb's eyes flashed with anger. "I wouldn't expect *you* to understand, Ms. McCoy. You are the very tool—"

"I think it'd be best if you left, Jeb," a deep, rumbling voice said, cutting through Monroe's words. Everyone turned their attention to the sheriff, who still stared out the window. Without turning, he continued, "My boys have showed a great deal of restraint since you entered the room, but I'm afraid I lack their self-control. And if you don't turn around and walk out of this room right now, I will be forced to disrespect your grief by explaining to you none too politely exactly what I think about what happened today."

Jeb's eyes narrowed at the sheriff's back. "Well, I expect we've *both* got a few things to say, Mac. We never *have* finished the conversation we started all those years back. But as I see I'm not welcome here, I guess I'll just save what's on my mind for a later time."

Mac's voice was little more than a growl when he replied, "You do that."

As soon as Monroe had gone, Tom shook his head, looking like he wanted to spit acid. "That son of a bitch. He's even crazier now than he's always been."

"What the hell was he talking about when he said you'd never finished a conversation years back?" Joe asked. "What conversation?"

Mac cast his steely gaze around the room, lighting on Charlotte and Elle for a long moment, as if weighing the prudence of talking openly in front of them. He finally turned his attention to his son. "The Monroe family's farmland used to be much more extensive, but about ten years ago, Jeb's father got into some financial trouble after several years of bad crops. He defaulted on loans and owed hundreds of thousands of dollars to the IRS. In order to pay off some of his debts, he was forced to sell some of his best land to developers. A few weeks later, he suffered a massive heart attack while working in the fields and died before paramedics could reach him."

"What's that have to do with you?" Charlotte asked. "If anything, you'd think Jeb's problem would be with the IRS for leaving old Buck Monroe no choice but to sell his land."

Mac sent her a sidelong glance, trying a little too hard not to acknowledge whatever was going on between them in Elle's opinion. "I served Buck with the papers. Thought I should do it myself since I'd known him for so long. But Jeb saw it as me taking the government's side. He blamed me for his father's ruin—guilt by association. He blamed the government for not valuing farmers. He blamed the paramedics for not getting there sooner when Buck had his heart attack. Jeb already held some extreme opinions at that point, but with his father gone, there was no one else who could talk any sense into him. We had rather heated words."

Elle could imagine. She'd known Mac Dawson for a long time, but had never really *known* him. There weren't many people who intimidated the hell out of Elle—not anymore. But Mac was among them. The only person she'd ever seen break through that tough exterior was her aunt. And on *that* topic, Charlotte was just as tight-lipped as the object of her affection.

"So, basically," Tom interjected, bringing Elle out of her musings, "he blamed everyone else for anything and everything horrible that ever happened to him or his family, and began posting his antigovernment rants online."

"How is it he's not on your watch list?" Joe demanded of his brother Kyle. "Shouldn't the FBI be keeping an eye on this guy?"

Kyle crossed his arms over his chest. "Oh, we're aware of guys like this, trust me. But our resources tend to be focused more on foreign terrorists or the organized groups who have huge followings and are stirring up trouble on a large scale—not these lone-wolf types of domestic terrorists. They're hard to track and can spring up literally anywhere—cities, towns, rural areas—without warning. These guys can be even more danger-ous and unpredictable than organized cells."

"Well, Monroe's certainly not acting alone,"

Tom told him. "His brothers have totally bought into his bullshit. And so have his kids, obviously. Who knows how many other friends and family he's swayed to his beliefs. But we can't pin anything on *him* personally."

Elle couldn't agree more. Too bad the patriarch of the Monroe clan had been careful to veil himself behind layers of plausible deniability from a legal standpoint. But anyone who knew the man also knew his radical views on the government and what he considered to be the tyranny of law enforcement. He believed men should make their own laws as dictated only by the word and letter of the Bible—most specifically, the eye-for-an-eye style of justice in the Old Testament.

Elle had heard his views on this particular subject more times than she cared to recall while she was building the case against his son. He'd been more than happy to offer up an anti-*everything* sermon at any opportunity. But he'd never crossed a line, had never been threatening. In every instance, he'd merely been exercising his First Amendment rights—according to him.

"Social media has given him a whole new audience for spreading his conspiracy theories and rallying others to his cause," she interjected into the conversation. "His following is growing. The disenchantment with the government and all their infighting is making it easier for him to recruit."

"Fan-fucking-tastic," Joe murmured, slipping his arm around his fiancée's shoulders and pulling her in close, tucking her under his chin. "That's *exactly* what we need."

Elle glanced away, suddenly feeling like an intruder

on the family's time together. She turned to Charlotte, the only family she had left, the loss of her parents and siblings a sharp pang in the center of her chest.

"Let's go," she whispered. "I feel like I'm just in the way. I'll check in with Mac later and answer any questions he has for me."

Charlotte's auburn brows drew together in a frown. "Alright, honey. If that's what you want."

Elle nodded quickly and slipped out into the hallway without saying good-bye, her eyes lighting on a spritely doctor with unruly, wavy, bobbed hair. "Hi, I'm looking for a patient who was in surgery for a gunshot wound to the leg. Deputy Gabe Dawson."

The doctor started at Elle's direct approach, then giggled. "Oh jeez. Sorry! Little jumpy. This is what happens when they let me out of the operating room." She laughed again, her hazel eyes sparkling. She looked at Elle expectantly as if waiting for her to say something. Then she shook her head and closed her eyes for a moment. "Sorry. You asked me about a patient."

Elle grinned. "Gabe Dawson."

The doctor turned on her heel and took a few bouncy little steps before motioning for Elle and Charlotte to follow her. Charlotte sent an amused look Elle's way, brows lifted in a silent question. Elle shrugged and followed the quirky doctor.

A moment later, they were standing at the nurse's station. "Here you go," the doctor said, gesturing vaguely toward the woman behind the desk. "Wanda can help you."

"Thanks!" Elle called when she noticed the doctor was already walking away.

"Well, she's an odd little thing," Charlotte said with a laugh.

"Oh, that girl is *completely* crazy," Wanda shot back with a shake of her elaborate network of crimson-dyed braids. "But she's a good surgeon, so they keep her around."

"Who is she?" Elle asked.

Wanda clacked on the keyboard with long, gold-lacquered nails. "Dr. Isabel Morales. Now, who are you looking for, baby?"

"Gabe Dawson," Elle murmured, frowning at Dr. Morales's back, wondering why the woman's name sounded so familiar.

The nurse made a few rapid keystrokes, then gave a curt nod. "Looks like he's in recovery. Gonna be a little while before he can have visitors. You can go sit in the family waiting room."

"Oh, no," Elle said in a rush, shaking her head. "I'm not family. I'm just…" She paused, not quite sure how to categorize their relationship. *Girlfriend* certainly wasn't an option, considering he didn't remember anything that had happened between them and had moved on with a vengeance. And *reluctant colleague* seemed kind of impersonal and catty considering how he'd thrown himself in front of her to protect her from harm. She probably owed him at least that dinner he'd offered now that he'd taken a bullet for her. She forced a smile when she saw Wanda giving her an expectant look. "A friend. I'm just a friend."

Wanda pursed her lips. "Mmm-hmm."

Elle glanced at her aunt, then back at the nurse. "No. Really. I wouldn't even call it a friendship. He's kind of an ass. I mean, okay, he's really good-looking and all, don't get me wrong, and he does have his moments now and then, but there's nothing going on—"

Wanda turned back to her monitor. "Mmm-hmm."

Elle huffed a little and turned to her aunt, giving her an exasperated look.

"C'mon, sweet girl," Charlotte said with a grin, steering Elle away from the desk and toward the elevators. "Let's get you home. I imagine Mac and the boys'll be wanting to see Gabe when he first wakes up. You can stop by tomorrow to check on him."

"Why are you grinning?" Elle protested as the elevator doors opened and they stepped inside. "You know he gets on my last nerve! Like there'd ever be anything going on between *us*. I can barely stand to be in the same room as him. His ego makes things a little crowded."

Charlotte made no effort at all to smother her grin. "Mmm-mmm."

Elle gave her a sardonic look. "*Et tu*, Charlotte?"

Charlotte laughed and gave her niece a gentle squeeze around the shoulders. "I seem to remember you didn't always find Gabe Dawson so repugnant. In fact, as I recall, a certain freckle-faced teenager had a mighty big crush on him back in the day."

Elle sniffed dismissively. "Well, that teenager grew up," she mumbled. "Unfortunately, the object of her affection did not."

"Anything you want to tell me, honey?" Charlotte asked.

Elle glanced at her aunt but quickly averted her gaze, not liking how perceptive the woman sometimes was. "No. Why?"

Charlotte gave Elle's shoulders a squeeze. "You just seem to be pretty concerned for the well-being of a man you insist you despise."

Elle shrugged, trying to appear indifferent to Charlotte's words. "I'd be just as concerned about anyone else I work with."

But even as she spoke the words, Elle studied her reflection in the mirror, grateful that she'd only have a small scar at her hairline to show for what had happened that day. Thanks to Gabe.

And a small—*very* small—part of her began to wonder if maybe she'd misjudged him all these years. If maybe there was something more to Gabe Dawson than she'd been willing to see...

Chapter 4

THE FIRST FACE GABE SAW WHEN HE AWOKE WAS HIS brother Tom's, his brows drawn together in an uncharacteristically dark frown. "Hey, man, how ya doin'?"

"Livin' the dream," Gabe mumbled, his mouth feeling like it was full of cotton. "You alright? How's Elle? She was bleeding. Is she okay?"

"I'm fine," Tom assured him. "And Elle will be okay. She needed some stitches but was otherwise unharmed. She came by asking about you before Charlotte took her home. She looked pretty worried."

Gabe blinked a little through the lingering fog of anesthesia. "She did? I'll be damned."

"You saved her life, Son. I'm sure she's grateful."

Gabe's gaze swung toward the sound of his father's voice to see him wearing the same expression as Tom. *Shit*. Seeing those two visibly worried about him rattled him down to his bones.

"It was Mark Monroe," Gabe rasped. "That son of a bitch—"

"Is dead," Tom finished, his gaze dropping. That look told Gabe everything he needed to know. Tom had taken the bastard down and had no doubt saved numerous lives, including Gabe's. But that didn't make it any easier on Tom. In all the years Tom had been a deputy, he'd never even had to draw his weapon. Until today. "You don't have to worry about him."

"Yeah," Gabe murmured, the spike of fear he'd experienced in that moment on the steps rushing back on him and making his heart race. The tempo of the beeping monitors near his head gave him away, bringing in a fierce-looking nurse with numerous loops of crimson braids.

"Alright, now," she said, shooing Tom out of her way. "I told you all that you needed to let him rest." She patted Gabe on the shoulder. "Don't worry, baby, I'll take good care of you. You go on and get some sleep now."

"Where're Joe and Kyle?" Gabe asked, the room beginning to spin a little from whatever it was they were giving him for pain.

"Nurse Ratched here wouldn't let us all come in," Tom told him, sending the nurse an irritated glance. "They're out in the hallway with Sadie and Abby."

Gabe wasn't too out of it to notice the tightness in his brother's tone when he mentioned the women. Probably because his own wife's name was noticeably absent. It'd been three years since Tom's wife, Carly, had been killed in the line of duty as a DEA agent. And the murderer—a drug lord from Chicago—was serving a life sentence thanks to Tom's tireless efforts to put the bastard away. But Gabe knew Carly's loss still weighed heavily on his brother. Tom's already solemn and intense personality had become doubly so since losing the woman he loved.

"Oh my goodness!"

Everyone's attention darted to the door, where a woman with unruly, dark, bobbed hair and polka dot scrubs was standing.

"Isn't this a busy place!" she said with a little giggle. "How's the patient? Oh, hey, *hi*!"

Gabe forced himself to focus on the pixie-like face of the doctor who'd come in and was now maneuvering around to the side of the bed where Tom stood.

"Uh, hi," Tom muttered, looking a little embarrassed by her sudden appearance.

The doctor grabbed Tom's hand and pumped it vigorously. "It's so good to see you again! I didn't realize—oh, *Dawson*! You two are related, right?"

"Gabe's my brother," Tom said, looking like he wanted to sink into the floor. "Nice to see you again, Isabel."

Was Tom actually blushing? The fuck?

Gabe was way too out of it to try to puzzle through how Tom was acquainted with his doctor—whoever the hell she was—and why her presence was enough to fluster him. But it was definitely something he planned to ask about when the fog cleared.

"Dr. Morales?" the nurse prompted.

The doctor was still shaking Tom's hand, grinning like crazy, then suddenly seemed to realize what she was doing and dropped his hand with a little laugh. "I'd better take a look at your brother. See how my handiwork is doing. But maybe we could grab coffee later? Catch up?"

Tom ducked his head a little and glanced at the other occupants of the room. "Uh, yeah. Sure." Then he coughed, clearing his throat, and turned his attention back to his brother. "I'll check back on you later, Bro."

His father patted Gabe lightly on the shoulder, his normally stoic expression cracking a bit with emotion. But the Old Man covered it well—as usual—and just gave Gabe a curt nod before turning and leaving the room.

"Well, that wasn't awkward at all," the nurse said, sharing a glance with Gabe.

Dr. Morales washed her hands and grabbed a couple of latex gloves from a box hanging on the wall. "I haven't seen Tom in years, Wanda," she said rather wistfully. "Not since the incident in the ER." But before the doctor could explain what she was talking about, she gave Gabe a bright smile. "So, how are you feeling, Deputy Dawson?"

"Like I got shot," Gabe drawled, sleep creeping in as the nurse moved the sheet off of his leg so that the doctor could take a look. "How 'bout you?"

As sleep dragged him under, he heard the doctor's giggle, heard her say something in reply, but he couldn't quite make it out and was too tired to bother trying...

———

It was dark when Gabe awoke for the second time. At least, it felt like he was awake, but he wasn't quite sure. The edges of his vision were blurry and the room seemed to swim a little. His body felt light, almost like he was floating—or maybe just threatening to. For a brief, panicked moment, he wondered if he was dead, if the floating sensation was his soul drifting away. But then the dull pain in his leg made him realize he was still very much alive.

He sighed, relieved, and was letting his lids close again when he realized he was not alone in the room.

His eyes snapped open, his senses suddenly alert as he battled through the fog of sleep and painkillers to try to figure out who the hell was in there with him. He tried to sit up. Couldn't. His body, so light just a moment before, now seemed to weigh a ton and wouldn't respond to his command.

"Who's there?" he managed to croak out, his throat dry and scratchy, making the question sound more like a growl.

The shadows in the room shifted a little and a figure slowly moved into the small pool of light cast by the various monitors. And he recognized the face immediately. His pulse quickened in a mixture of fear and anger, but still his body wouldn't respond. The monitors began to beep like crazy again, but Nurse Wanda didn't barge in this time. He was alone. With the father of the man who'd tried to kill him.

"Get the fuck out," Gabe spat.

Jeb Monroe *tsked* and shook his head. "Such vulgarity," he drawled, sounding to Gabe's ears as if he was under water. "Guess I shouldn't be surprised to hear such language from a dirty pig who will lie down with any whore."

"Nurse!" Gabe yelled as he reached for the call button, keeping his gaze locked on the crazy son of a bitch walking toward him. His fingers fumbled, his body not cooperating as a result of the pain meds, and the device tumbled from the edge of the bed.

Monroe's hand lashed out, and he grasped Gabe by the throat, but not tight enough to choke him or leave any marks. The slippery bastard was far too smart for that. "The nurse just left the desk to attend to another patient down the hall, so I thought now would be a good time for us to chat."

"There'll be security footage of you entering my room," Gabe warned.

Monroe's brows lifted casually as if he was unconcerned. "True. But last time I checked, it wasn't a crime
to visit a man in the hospital."

Gabe narrowed his eyes. "What the hell do you
want, Monroe?"

He leaned in, his breath rank as he hissed, "You got
my boy killed."

"He got *himself* killed," Gabe shot back. "And it's
on your head, Monroe. I'm guessing he was just following orders."

Monroe chuckled darkly. "Orders? What orders?"

Gabe's eyes narrowed. "Yours. You sent him to take
out Elle McCoy, didn't you?"

Monroe grinned. "Now why would I ever do such a
thing, Deputy Dawson? I'm a peace-loving man who
just wants his government to keep its promises and stop
imposing its tyrannical laws on God-fearing citizens. I
encourage nonviolent civil disobedience. Like Thoreau."

Gabe scoffed. "Right. That's *exactly* who you remind
me of."

"Don't believe me?" Monroe said, arching his brow.
"My views are right there on my website. You can't
prove I believe otherwise, Deputy. And you know it."

"Why the hell did you come here?" Gabe hissed, his
fury at the truth of Monroe's words raging in his veins.

"Just wanted to say that I forgive you," Monroe said.

Gabe stared at the man, wondering what the hell his
angle was. "What?"

Monroe's grin grew, the lights from the monitors
casting his face in shadow, giving him an even more sinister look than usual. "Make no mistake, Deputy, there
will be a reckoning for what occurred today, for the

promising young life that was taken. But it won't come from me. So whenever anyone asks, I will tell them I forgave you, just as the good Lord commands us."

"Your son opened fire on innocent people at the courthouse," Gabe reminded him. "There was only one way it could've ended. You *wanted* him to die today, to become a martyr for your cause."

Monroe's eyes flashed with anger. "We're all required to make sacrifices in war."

"The only war you're involved in is the one going on in your own twisted mind," Gabe insisted.

"Oh, no," Monroe said, shaking his head. "You're wrong. There's been a war brewing for decades, brought on by the sins of this country, of our government. 'When new gods were chosen, then war was in the gates.' One day, you will have to decide which side you're on, Deputy Dawson. The side of our government? Or the side of all that is righteous?"

Gabe met his gaze without flinching. "You threatening me, Monroe?"

Monroe chuckled and slowly drew away, releasing Gabe's throat. "Of course not, Deputy. I don't make threats."

Gabe kept his gaze fixed on Monroe as the man sauntered toward the door, but he didn't look back to gauge Gabe's reaction or to offer a parting shot. He strode from the room with a casual gait, completely unconcerned with getting caught.

The moment Gabe heard the door close, he collapsed against the pillows and heaved a sigh of relief. But it wasn't over. He knew that for damned sure. He could see it in Monroe's eyes—fuck all his bullshit talk about forgiveness. Gabe knew better than to believe any of that.

The son of a bitch. He'd come to taunt Gabe, to assure Gabe he'd pay for his son's death, to keep him looking over his shoulder, waiting for the attack that might never even come.

But as fucked up as Gabe's situation was, suddenly he was more concerned about Elle. He hadn't been the target that day. God knew he was in the Monroes' crosshairs just because he was a deputy; he'd accepted that risk on the day he'd been sworn in. And he had put himself at risk on more than one occasion since, determined to make a name for himself among the storied men in his family who'd come before him. But Elle hadn't signed up for this shit.

He ran a hand down his face, wiping away the last of the fog from his pain meds. There'd be no resting now. He glanced up at the clock on the wall. Two a.m. It was going to be one helluva long night…

Gabe started awake, throwing off the covers and bolting to his feet. Pain shot up and down his leg as soon as he made contact with the floor, making him groan through clenched teeth and follow it up with a juicy curse.

"Mother*fu*—"

"I'll just come back later."

His gaze shot up to see Elle standing inside the doorway, gorgeous eyes wide, her peaches-and-cream skin flushed an alluring shade of pink that deepened as he gaped at her. When she dropped her gaze, turning first left, then right, as if forgetting where the door was, he suddenly realized his bare ass was hanging out of the back of his hospital gown giving her quite an eyeful.

"No, that's okay," he said in a rush. "Come on in."

He straightened quickly, wincing with the sudden movement, belatedly realizing his wound apparently hadn't affected other areas of his anatomy and he was sporting some serious morning wood, which was pitching one helluva tent beneath the thin cotton gown.

He cursed again and dropped down on the bed, throwing the blanket over his lower body in one quick motion and trying unsuccessfully to suppress another groan. He squeezed his eyes shut for a second until the wave of agony passed. When he opened them again, he was surprised to see Elle standing before him, her gaze searching his face.

"Are you okay?" she asked, her hand coming up to cup his jaw. The gentle warmth of her palm sent a chill through him, making him shudder. Her hand immediately dropped away at the response, mistakenly thinking her touch was unwanted when, in fact, he desperately craved it. "I'll get the nurse."

When she reached for the call button hanging near the head of the bed, he gently grasped her wrist and drew her hand away. "Leave it. I'm fine."

She swallowed and dropped her gaze briefly to their hands, looking like she wanted to bolt and rid herself of his touch. He almost released her, saddened that she found the contact so unwanted. But then he felt her pulse quicken beneath his fingertips.

So maybe it wasn't revulsion she was feeling after all…

When her gaze drifted back up to his, he decided to

test his new theory and let his thumb slowly smooth over her skin. "How are *you*?" he asked softly.

She gave him a tremulous smile and, God help him, he damned near dragged her into his arms and kissed her. But he managed to restrain himself as she said, "Shaken up a bit. But no lasting harm."

He narrowed his eyes at that, not believing her for a second. "You sure about that, honey?"

"I'll be okay," she assured him, nodding a little, her lips pressed together as if she was trying to convince herself of the truth of her words. "It's just..." She sighed. "I almost died yesterday."

There it was. The truth they both needed to face. Elle was no fool. Hell, she was brilliant as far as he was concerned. She must've known as certainly as he did how close they'd both come to losing their lives the previous day. So there was no denying her words, no use trying to convince her she was mistaken.

"Yeah," he said, still caressing her pulse point. "You sleep at all last night?"

She shook her head, her eyes beginning to glisten with unshed tears. "No. All I could see when I closed my eyes was—" Her words broke off when her voice hitched with emotion.

Ah hell.

He slipped his hand into the thick waves of hair at the base of her neck and pulled her toward him. Every inch of him—especially those hidden under the blanket— longed to kiss her lips, but at the last moment, he pressed his lips to her forehead in a lingering kiss.

He didn't know what to say to make her feel better. It wasn't like that time when Todd Jenkins had broken up with her a week before the homecoming dance and Gabe had hinted to Chris that maybe *he* should ask her. Or the time her biggest rival was made editor of the school yearbook and he'd broken into her locker before school to leave her flowers (anonymously, of course). Or the time he'd given Aaron Maguire a fat lip when that asshole had gotten a little grabby with Elle in spite of her saying no loud and clear. Or the time he'd driven two hours to the college she was attending to fix her car on the sly because her aunt Charlotte had mentioned that it wasn't running and Elle refused to ask for the money to fix it.

He'd been secretly looking out for Elle for as long as he had known her, never letting on that he was the one, never asking for anything in return. Knowing she was safe and happy was enough. But he was at a loss on how to comfort her this time, when they were very literally face to face.

He'd never known how to deal with a woman when she was upset. He supposed he got that from his father, who wasn't exactly the most nurturing guy. Normally, Gabe bailed when things got serious enough with a woman that she was actually sharing *emotions*. Okay, to be honest, he usually bailed way before that. But seeing Elle looking lost and afraid brought out a protective urge in him that he'd never really experienced with anyone else—not to this extent, anyway.

He could lie and say she'd be fine in a few days. But the truth was, it might be something that haunted her far longer. God knew he had plenty of nightmares—some of them walked and talked and dropped by for a visit in his hospital room in the middle of the night.

Elle's hand came up to rest lightly on his chest, and he felt her breath quicken as tension began to build in the air between them. "Thank you for saving my life," she whispered. She pulled back enough that their faces were just inches apart. And for a moment, he thought *she* might actually kiss *him*. The look in her eyes told him she was considering it, which shocked the hell out of him.

But as he leaned in to close the gap, his hospital door opened. "Good mornin', baby!"

Elle started and stumbled back a few feet as the nurse, Wanda, came in pushing a cart filled with flowers, balloons, and plush animals holding little stuffed hearts.

"What the hell?" Gabe muttered irritably, pissed off at the intrusion.

Nurse Wanda parked the cart at the end of his bed and began to unload the various deliveries onto every flat surface in the room. "Looks like you have a few admirers," she said, giving him a knowing grin. Then she turned her attention to Elle. "How are you, honey?"

Elle looked a little uncomfortable as she took in all the crap from his well-wishers.

"I'm good. Thanks, Wanda."

"Oooh, look at this one," Wanda said, holding up a ridiculously sweet-looking teddy bear with huge, teardrop-shaped eyes. She lifted the card and read aloud, "Get well soon, sweetums. Smooches, Beth."

Gabe frowned. *Beth? Who the hell was Beth?*

Wanda picked up a vase of some kind of blue flowers and read, "To my little snookie-ookums. Feel better. Hugs and kisses, Amy."

Okay, so Amy he remembered. She was the college

student who'd picked him up at Mulaney's a month or so ago when they'd gotten together to welcome his brother Kyle back to town. God, he'd gotten totally shit-faced that night. Fortunately, he'd only made out with the hot little blond. But apparently it'd been enough to make an impression on her.

"Oh, and look at this one—"

"Thanks, Wanda," he interrupted, casting a glance at Elle, embarrassed by the ridiculous sentiments being lavished on him. Not that he wasn't grateful people cared enough to send flowers and shit, but *snookie-ookums*? What the fuck was that about?

"I'll leave you alone to go through all your..." Elle's words trailed off as she gestured toward Wanda's cart, a look of mild disgust and disappointment on her face. Then she forced a tight smile and handed him the little bouquet of wildflowers he hadn't noticed she was carrying—wildflowers that were remarkably similar to the ones he'd left in her locker back in high school. "Take care, Gabe."

"Elle," he said, his stomach sinking at the thought of her leaving so soon. "Please don't go. I—"

"I'll see you soon."

Before he could say another word, she turned on her heel and practically fled the room.

"Did you have a good visit with your friend?" Wanda asked as she absently moved some of the arrangements around to make room for more. "She's a pretty little thing."

"Yeah," Gabe said, staring at the closed door, hoping she'd come back in. "Yeah, she is."

"Was awfully worried about you last night, too," Wanda told him.

This brought his gaze back to her. "Yeah?"

"Mmm-hmm." Her lips curved up in a little smile. "And I'm guessing she wouldn't call you her *snookie-ookums*."

He actually chuckled a little, wincing at the pain in his ribs where one of Monroe's bullets had struck his vest. "No. I'm sure she wouldn't. She prefers *jackass*."

Chapter 5

IT'D BEEN A MISTAKE TO VISIT GABE. ELLE HAD KNOWN it the moment she'd walked in only to see his perfect ass peeking out of his hospital gown. Then, when he'd turned around... Good Lord.

She once more pushed away the images of the two of them going at it like rabbits that had flooded her mind when she'd caught a glimpse of his erection. No wonder women were constantly throwing themselves at him.

And to think she'd been *this close* to breaking her own promise to not be one of them. She was pretty sure he'd been about to kiss her again when they'd been interrupted by Wanda and her cartful of crap from Gabe's previous—or, hell, *current* for all she knew—conquests.

She gave herself a quick mental shake as she strode toward her black Honda Accord, but her steps faltered when she got closer and one of her tires was flat. Her embarrassment from her visit with Gabe was replaced by fury. "Are you freaking *kidding* me?"

She quickly did a mental map of all the places she'd gone that morning, wondering if she'd driven through a construction zone or over any road debris, but when she was within a couple of feet of her car, she noticed it wasn't just a flat tire. A jagged scratch ran the length of her door where someone had keyed the paint job.

Clearly not an accident.

"Son of a bitch!"

It was like the universe was trying to smack her upside the head to clue her in that allowing herself to get even a little close to Gabe was a mistake. Clearly, she shouldn't have gone to the hospital that day. The only bigger sign would've had to be in flashing neon, for crying out loud.

She heaved a sigh and fished her phone out of her pocket to call a tow truck. Then she phoned her Aunt Charlotte, leaving her a message to fill her in, leaving out the part about seeing Gabe half-naked and nearly kissing him.

She'd just hung up when a Fairfield County sheriff's car pulled up behind her. "Hey, Elle. Need some help?"

She turned to see Gabe's younger brother Joe. "Hey. No thanks. Tow truck's on the way. But thanks. Are you still on duty?"

Joe didn't bother suppressing a smile. "Just got off. Thought I'd stop in and see my brother for a few minutes before I meet up with Sadie. She's having her ultrasound today. Have you seen her?"

Elle shook her head, sorry to have missed Joe's fiancée. She'd always liked Joe—he was a sweetheart and clearly adored Sadie, who had been the love of his life since they were all kids. Joe had nearly been killed while on deployment in Afghanistan and then had nearly lost Sadie when a crazy ex-boyfriend had stalked and threatened to kill her—and might have followed through had Joe not been there. Elle had definitely been glad to prosecute that asshole and make sure he served time for his crimes.

Seeing Joe and Sadie so happy together now, seeing their joy as Sadie's pregnancy progressed, Elle couldn't help but be reminded of the family she'd once had, the joy that had filled her home growing up until all that had been so cruelly wrenched away. She prayed Joe and Sadie always had the love and happiness they had now—they certainly deserved it.

"Elle?"

She started, realizing that he'd been talking to her. "Sorry," she said with a little laugh. "I was distracted. Been kinda crazy, you know."

He nodded. "Yeah, I do. If you need to talk to anyone about what you're going through... Well, I've been there."

He'd had his battle with post-traumatic stress disorder after he'd returned from the war. She could only imagine the kind of hell he'd experienced and what it had cost him to learn to cope.

"Thanks, Joe," she told him sincerely. "I'll definitely keep that in mind. Good luck with the ultrasound. And give Sadie my best."

He gave her a terse nod that seemed to be a trademark of the Dawson men and offered a wave as he drove off. While Elle waited for the tow truck to arrive, she tried not to dwell on the dark memories that haunted her and instead tried to focus on something positive—like the date she had coming up later in the week with an investment banker who had jokingly offered to take her to dinner in a little seaside spot in southern California after a short plane ride on his private jet. At least, she'd thought he was joking. But maybe not.

Any woman would've been flattered to receive such an offer. And she *had* been. At the time. But every time she tried to picture Brad's face, all she could see was Gabe Dawson. God, what the hell was wrong with her? Was she seriously so swept up by his heroism the previous day that she was now willing to overlook all his flaws?

The number of goodies being delivered to him was a none-too-subtle reminder of what was in store for her if she hooked up with Gabe Dawson. Because that's exactly what it would be. A hook-up.

Fortunately, the tow truck didn't take long to arrive and she was soon distracted from her brooding by a massive man in a mechanic's jumpsuit with sweat stains under his arms. He was chomping on the stub of a cigar when he rolled up and continued to do so even after she was riding with him in the cab of his truck.

An hour later, when he finally came out from his workshop to talk to her about her tire, she was glad to see he'd ditched the cigar. "Found the problem," he said, wiping the grime from his hands with a rag as he made his way behind the counter.

"Road debris?" she asked, hoping there was a way that the flat tire and keyed paint could be blamed on something other than someone intentionally vandalizing her car.

He grunted. "Not unless you hit a guy with a tactical knife."

She jerked a little at his words. "You're sure?"

"Your tire was slashed, Ms. McCoy," he informed her. "Whoever did this made damned sure it couldn't be repaired. And the scratch on the paint's pretty deep. Then there's the brakes—"

"The brakes?" Elle interrupted. "What was wrong with the brakes?"

"Been tampered with," he told her. "I think you might want to give the police a call."

Tom rose to his feet and put his hands on his hips, frowning as he continued to study Elle's tire. "We can try to get a print, I guess," he said, "but I doubt we'll find any except for your mechanic's."

She caught the guarded glance he sent her way and could tell he was thinking the same thing she was. Considering the events of the previous day, it was all a little too coincidental. This wasn't a random act of vandalism. Whoever had done this had specifically targeted her car. Had targeted *her*. Unfortunately, she had a pretty damned good idea who might want to leave her a very pointed message.

"I'll see if we can get anything from the hospital security tapes," Tom continued. "Maybe one of the cameras caught something."

She nodded. "Thanks, Tom."

"You need a ride home?"

She shook her head. "No. I'm good. I'll give Aunt Charlotte a call if Al can't get my new tires on today."

He jotted down something in his little black notebook and stowed it in his shirt pocket, giving her a sidelong glance. "You doin' okay?"

"Oh, yeah, sure, fine," she stammered too eagerly. "Yep. I'm good. Just pissed about my tires."

But he didn't return her forced smile. Instead, he narrowed his eyes a little, studying her.

Unnerved by his scrutiny, she grasped at some other—*any* other—topic to divert his attention. "How are you doing? Did you ever go out with that EMT? What was her name...Lindsey?"

He flinched a little at her question but recovered quickly. "No."

The sudden tension in his expression told her more than he probably realized. Clearly, she'd chosen the wrong topic to get Tom talking. Fortunately, she was rescued from the awkward silence by his cell phone ringing. He snatched it from the clip on his belt and answered with a terse, "Dawson."

Elle turned away to give him some privacy but came to an abrupt halt when she saw the man watching her from the pickup truck parked across the street from the mechanic's. He looked familiar. But as her mind raced, trying to figure out how she knew the driver, the truck slowly pulled away from the curb and drove off. Not exactly the hallmark of a person trying to avoid being seen, but then, maybe he'd wanted her to see him, wanted her to know he was watching.

Goose bumps prickled her flesh at the thought that it might be the same man who had so viciously slashed her tires. Worse, she finally realized where she'd seen him before. She could've sworn that it was one of the Monroes sitting in the driver's seat. One of Jeb's sons. At least that's what she suspected. She couldn't be certain, but she knew she had seen him in the courtroom during the trial, sitting with the other family members and looking nervous, as if he were on trial himself.

She heaved a sigh and turned back to her ruined tires, frowning at how the rubber had been shredded with such savagery, and wrapped her arms around her torso, suddenly cold in spite of the summer heat.

"I gotta go."

Tom's announcement was so abrupt, Elle started at

the sound of his voice. She cleared her heart from her throat with a cough before asking, "Everything okay?"

"That was Gabe," he explained. "He wants us to come back to the hospital. Something about Jeb Monroe paying him a visit."

She nodded and headed for his Tahoe. "Okay, then. Let's go."

"By *us* I meant us Dawsons," Tom called after her. "I wasn't—"

She whirled around to face him, cutting him off. "I'm not letting you Dawson boys sideline me just because I don't have a badge," she snapped. "I was there yesterday, Tom. Remember? And it's because of me that Gabe is lying in that hospital bed now."

Tom gave her a sympathetic look. "We put our lives on the line every day, Elle," he told her. "We knew the risks when we chose this career. You can't blame yourself for what happened to Gabe."

"I'm not blaming myself," she insisted. "I'm stating the facts. And here's another fact for you—I'm going to nail that bastard Jeb Monroe to the wall when we prove he's behind this."

—⁓—

Jeb Monroe slid the sharpening stone slowly along the blade of his hunting knife, studying the gleaming edge of the steel, searching for any pits that needed to be ground out. It was the fourth such knife he'd sharpened that day. And it was completely unnecessary—he kept his weapons in immaculate condition, as his father had taught him. But it helped relieve the ache that had settled in the center of his chest.

Mark is dead.

The horrible truth echoed over and over again in the cavernous depth of his soul. His eldest son. His right hand. The man who would've inherited the farmland that had been passed down in their family since the first Monroes had settled there over two hundred years before.

He heaved a sorrowful sigh. He had three other sons who would be eager to carry on the family name, the family legacy. But they weren't Mark. Weren't his courageous, brave boy who'd been willing to give his life in the fight for freedom against a tyrannical government.

The hole his absence left could never be filled. But Jeb was damned well going to try. The first steps toward filling that hole had already been put in place with his visit to that bastard Gabe Dawson.

The arrogant pretty boy had thought he was untouchable because of who his father was. But Mark had proved otherwise. Now that little shit was scared. Jeb had seen it in his eyes. He'd seen that look before, in the eyes of other men who'd looked into the face of death and had seen their sins staring back at them. Gabe Dawson was no different. And the pretty little whore who had prosecuted his son Derrick would pay her own price. He'd sent his son Jeremy to deliver *that* message.

Jeb slid the stone down the edge of the blade again, the soft scraping oddly comforting.

Oh yes, they'd pay for their transgressions. No one oppressed the Monroes—not the federal agents who had tried to keep his people from running booze during Prohibition, not truant officers who'd tried to make his father send him to school, not the IRS agent who'd darkened his doorstep to try and force him to pay his taxes a year ago.

Most of them had been run off and had eventually given up, seeing they were no match for the Monroes. Only the IRS agent had refused to heed Jeb's warnings. And now that agent of evil was buried fifty miles west of their property in a little patch of woods. But he wouldn't be so subtle with the Dawsons. He wanted them to know what was coming, to live in fear, to know whose hand delivered final justice.

Movement in the corner of his eye brought his gaze up briefly, and he saw his only daughter entering the kitchen as quietly as possible so as not to disturb him.

"How's your mother?" he asked, startling the girl.

Sandra set the plate of uneaten food on the countertop and swiped at her eyes quickly before turning to face him. She'd been crying. His baby girl had been crying. He had to clench his jaw to keep from going into a rage at the thought of the pain his son's death was causing his family. Especially his sweet girl.

"She hasn't stopped crying," Sandra told him, her chin trembling. "And I can't get her to eat anything."

Jeb returned his attention to the knife. "Leave her be for a while," he advised. "She'll be alright."

The room was so quiet that, for a moment, Jeb thought his daughter had left, but then he heard her cough a little, clearing her throat, and he glanced up to see her chewing her bottom lip.

"What is it, Sandra?" he prompted.

"I was just wondering…" she began, pausing for a moment as if considering her words. Finally she continued, "I was just wondering if we're doing the right thing."

Jeb's hands halted, midswipe. "I beg your pardon?"

"Mark tried to kill that lawyer," Sandra pointed out. "He tried to kill that deputy. What did you think would happen? What did *any* of you think would happen?"

Jeb narrowed his eyes at his daughter. "I will thank you to adjust your tone, girl. You don't speak to me that way. I'd hate to smack the smart mouth off you today of all days, but I will."

She shrank into herself a little, dropping her gaze. "I'm sorry, sir. I just…I just don't want anything to happen to you or the boys. What if you die, too?"

"Then I will die a martyr for freedom," Jeb told her, having made peace with that fact long ago. "I will not be subjugated by the laws of tyrants, handing over my hard-earned money to them just so they can give it away to everyone else who sticks their hands out, begging for what they didn't earn. And I will not allow my family to be ruled by the police who enforce an illegal government's tyrannical laws."

"Yes, sir," Sandra mumbled.

"What's that?" he snapped. "Didn't hear you, girl."

"Yes, sir," she replied, louder this time, visibly trembling in fear. "I was wrong to question you."

He turned his attention back to his knife and rubbed his thumb across the edge of the blade, testing the sharpness. It was perfect for tearing the heart out of a deer. Or a pig. And he'd take a great deal of pleasure when he ripped out Mac Dawson's heart the same way his own heart had been torn from his chest when he'd seen his boy lying on that gurney with a sheet over his face.

"'Vengeance is mine,'" Jeb quoted, "'and recompense, for the time when their foot shall slip; for the day of their calamity is at hand…'" He raised his eyes to his daughter, giving her an expectant look, waiting for her to finish the verse from the only authority he recognized.

She swallowed hard, her face pale as she added, "'And their doom comes swiftly.'"

Chapter 6

"WHAT THE HELL IS *SHE* DOING HERE?"

"Well, hello to you, too," Elle snapped, her eyes flashing in indignation. "Glad to see you're feeling well enough to be back to your usual asshole self."

As much as he enjoyed seeing those emerald eyes spark, he wasn't particularly happy to be on the receiving end this time. In fact, he felt like a total ass for clearly offending her, when in actuality, seeing her had made his heart leap up into his throat and choke off his breath. He'd been thinking about her nonstop since her visit earlier in the day, wishing like hell that she hadn't witnessed the delivery of all the shit from his various lady friends.

In fact, he'd had Wanda give all the stuffed animals to the kids in the children's ward and the flowers to some of the patients who didn't have anyone to send them anything at all. The only thing he'd kept was Elle's bouquet, which was in a vase on the little table across from his bed where he could see them easily.

"Sorry," Tom said, interrupting his thoughts. "She insisted on coming."

Elle crossed her arms over what Gabe liked to imagine were perfect breasts and gave him a defiant look, daring him to kick her out. He couldn't help the amused grin that tugged on his mouth. "Well, I learned a long time ago I'm no match for Elle's stubbornness."

And then he winked at her.

Her arms dropped just a little and her expression did an interesting little dance, going from defiant to surprised to confused. If he wasn't mistaken, that was a little flush of color rising to her cheeks.

Well, isn't that interesting?

Unfortunately, he didn't have a chance to offer another flirtatious comment about her reaction before the door opened and his younger brothers entered, jerking their chins in greeting.

"What's up?" Kyle asked, shoving his hands into his pants pockets and waiting for Gabe to fill them in. "You getting out of here soon or what?"

It still threw Gabe to see his FBI agent baby brother looking all grown-up and businesslike in his standard dark suit and tie. But he was damned proud of Kyle, and for all their differences over the years, he was glad to have him home again.

"Couple of days," Gabe told him, "but that's not what I wanted to talk to you guys about." He sent a glance Elle's way. "I got a visit from Jeb Monroe last night."

"That son of a bitch has a hell of a lot of nerve," Joe spat.

"What did he want?" Tom demanded, talking at the same time.

"He wanted to deliver a message," Gabe informed them. "To let me know this isn't over. From what I gathered, we'd better watch our backs."

Kyle cursed under his breath. "Did he make any specific threats? Anything we can bring him in on?"

Gabe shook his head. "Of course not. He's a slippery son of a bitch. He's not going to put himself at risk."

"He wants us to live in fear," Elle chimed in. "It's the same crap I've been dealing with since we arrested Derrick after Chris's death."

Gabe's attention snapped to her. "What are you talking about? Were you receiving threats before yesterday?"

She suddenly looked a little less defiant, almost contrite as she cast her gaze around the room at the four brothers. "I couldn't prove who the threats were coming from," she said, her tone apologetic. "Local PD checked into it for me, but there was nothing really to go on. You can't charge someone if you don't know who to charge. You know that, Tom."

"You should've come to *us*, Elle," Tom insisted. "We could've at least brought the Monroes in again for questioning."

"So he could deny everything as usual? I get threats now and then from the families of people I prosecute," Elle told him. "Hell, sometimes they come from the general public—people who don't even *know* the defendant. It's usually nothing."

"Well, it wasn't *nothing* this time," Tom spat. "Gabe could've been killed. What the hell were you thinking?"

"Back off, Tom," Gabe interjected, sitting up straighter in his hospital bed.

"I screwed up," Elle said, edging back a little from Tom's anger. "I know that. I should've taken the threats more seriously."

"Damn right you should've," Tom fired back.

"I said back off, Tommy!" Gabe shouted, stabbing a finger in Tom's direction. What the hell was Tom's damage anyway? It wasn't like him to lose his cool in *any* situation—he certainly wasn't usually so short with people. If anything, Tom was normally way too forgiving and understanding, in Gabe's opinion.

Tom's jaw tightened, but he just shook his head and ran a hand through his dark hair, mumbling something under his breath.

Gabe met Elle's gaze and held it for a moment. "She couldn't have known this would happen. None of us could've known it would happen. What's important right now is taking the threats seriously from here on out. I just want you all to watch your backs."

Joe rubbed the back of his neck, not bothering to hide his concern. "Damn it."

Gabe knew exactly where his thoughts were going. He was thinking of his pregnant fiancée and how to keep her safe when he wasn't around. It wasn't that long ago that he'd almost lost Sadie to her psychotic ex-boyfriend who'd held a gun under her chin.

"I'll send out another law enforcement awareness bulletin," Tom told them, "make sure everyone knows that if they see the Monroes to approach them with caution. And we'll put a deputy on Gabe's door while he's here."

"This shit is becoming far too common," Kyle said. "If it's not the Monroes, it's someone else. When the hell did *we* become the enemy?"

"Unfortunately, it's the jerks and assholes abusing power—or *perceived* to be abusing power—who get all the press," Elle replied. She turned her gaze on Gabe, something in her expression warming the center of him when she added, "And everyone takes it for granted that you're always there, protecting us."

There was a long pause in the conversation until one of his brothers cleared his throat, causing Elle to glance away guiltily. When Gabe looked toward the sound, he found Kyle trying to smother a smile.

"So…" his baby brother said with a significant glance between Elle and Gabe, "I think I'm going to head out. Joe, you comin'?"

Joe, the shithead, was grinning too. "Yeah, I'm right behind ya. You need anything, Bro, let me know."

Only Tom was looking sullen, his brows furrowed. "Elle, you want me to give you a lift back to the garage to get your car?"

"Your car?" Gabe repeated. "What's wrong with your car?"

She gave Tom a chastising look. "My tire was slashed when I left the hospital earlier," she explained, leaving out the rest of the details about the extent of the vandalism and earning a sidelong glance from Tom. "I called Tom to report the incident and asked him to take a look."

Gabe felt a spike of irrational jealousy at the thought of his elder brother coming to Elle's aid while he was stuck in a hospital bed. "That right?" he drawled, knowing even as he said it that he was being a jackass. But still…

"Thanks, Tom," Elle said. "Could you give me a few minutes with Gabe and then I'll be ready to go?"

Tom gave her a terse nod and slipped out into the hallway.

"What the hell is going on with him?" Gabe mumbled.

"He's worried about you," Elle said. "And everyone else. Tom carries the weight of the world on his shoulders."

That green-eyed monster reared its head again and

he clenched his jaw, suddenly wanting to clock his brother simply because Elle seemed to have a decent read on the guy. "You know Tom pretty well."

Elle shrugged. "I guess so. We've worked together a long time. He's a good guy."

Gabe grunted, not able to deny what she was saying. His brother had been his hero since they were kids. He'd worshipped Tom when they were growing up, had always tried to keep up, to measure up. And once again, it seemed like he was playing catch-up with Tom.

"Well, you'd better get going," he grumbled. "Don't want you to miss your ride."

She took a few steps forward, coming to the side of his bed. "I'm going. But first, I wanted to make one thing very clear to you, Gabe Dawson."

"Yeah?" he said. "What's that?"

She narrowed her eyes and leaned over him, caging him with her arms on either side of his head. "Don't you ever again treat me like I'm some delicate flower who can't handle the truth."

Damn.

Having her that close was tempting as hell. For the first time, he noticed she had tiny flecks of gold in her eyes and a few more freckles on the bridge of her nose than he'd realized. God, she was beautiful—stunning, really. He had to muster all his willpower not to drag her into his arms and kiss the full lips that were currently pursed in irritation. But he forced himself to meet her gaze and lifted a single brow.

"Oh, I know you're no delicate flower," he said, his voice going deeper, betraying the effect of her nearness and giving his words a weight he hadn't intended.

Her cheeks went a little pink, but she didn't back away. "We're in this together, whether we like it or not. And I'm not going to be kept in the dark just because I'm not a cop."

"Oh, I don't know," he said, not bothering to suppress the grin tugging at his mouth. "You might like being in the dark with me, Elle."

She blinked, her mouth opening and closing as if she wanted to say something more but was clearly speechless. Then she pressed her lips together and gave him a frustrated look. "You know what I meant, Gabe."

At this, the little devil on his shoulder got the better of him, and he chuckled, letting his gaze drop down to those gorgeous lips. "Yeah, I know what you meant, Elle. Doesn't change what *I* meant."

When she didn't immediately pull away at his advance, he took a chance and reached up, gently taking hold of her chin and guiding her lips down to his. But before he could make contact, she suddenly broke away from his tender grasp and straightened, staring down at him with a look of confusion and panic in her eyes.

Okay, well, that wasn't exactly the reaction he'd been hoping for…

"I have to go," she breathed. But she didn't take a single step. "I really… I should go."

He met her gaze, waiting, wondering at her next move. "You sure?"

She licked her lips, looking as if she was truly torn between going and staying. But then she lifted her chin, giving him that defiant look he'd grown so used to seeing from her. "Yes, I'm absolutely positive."

Without another word, she turned on her heel and

strode toward the door without so much as a glance over her shoulder.

But the little exchange was enough to offer Gabe the encouragement he needed. Maybe the brilliant, beautiful, iron-willed woman wasn't quite as unaffected by him as she wanted him to believe.

———

"You okay?"

Elle waved away Tom's concern as she strode down the hallway toward the exit. "Yep. Fine. Let's go."

It was all she could do not to demand that Tom get his ass moving. Did he seriously always have to walk so damned slowly? Of course, the rational side of her wondered why in the world she was practically sprinting down the hall. It wasn't like Gabe was going to come running after her, pull her into his arms, and kiss her breathless.

She came to an abrupt halt as the image of such an encounter filled her head, sending a sudden spike of desire through her veins.

Dear God. I nearly kissed him. Again.

Or, more accurately, had almost allowed *him* to kiss *her*. What had she been thinking?

But as soon as the question crossed her mind, she knew the answer. She'd been thinking how much she longed to feel his lips on hers again, how much she longed to feel his strong arms around her, and wondering what the harm really could be in giving in.

The problem was, she knew all too well that one kiss wasn't where it would end with Gabe Dawson. Not that she worried he would seduce her into doing anything she wasn't willing to do. For all his womanizing, Gabe was always described as a gentleman. Heck, if he hadn't been, he certainly wouldn't have had all his ex-whatevers sending him gifts in the hospital. And he'd proven just how much of a gentleman he could be that night a year ago. He'd let her take the lead, only going as far as she was comfortable with. And when things had become truly hot and heavy and they were lying together on his bed, half-naked, he'd slowed it down, backing off.

Oh, no. It wasn't Gabe she didn't trust. Quite the contrary. *She* was the one she worried about. She wasn't a one-night-stand kind of girl. And as nice as it might've been to give in to Gabe's advances, she wasn't going to fall into bed with him just to satisfy her curiosity.

"Hi again!"

Recognizing the chipper voice of the quirky doctor she'd met the day before, Elle spun around, ready to politely explain that as much as she'd like to chat, she really couldn't stay, only to find the doctor offering Tom a friendly grin and enthusiastic wave. Tom looked like a trapped animal who would very happily gnaw off his own foot if it meant he could escape.

"Hi, Isa," he muttered. Then he sent a pleading look Elle's way. "This is Elle McCoy. She's—"

Isabel flashed Elle her pixie grin. "Hi! How are you? How's the head healing?"

"It's doing okay," Elle assured her. Then she frowned a little, looking back and forth between Tom and Isabel. "We were just here visiting Tom's brother."

"I thought that might be the case," the doctor said, her grin not diminishing. "I was so surprised when I ran into Tom yesterday! I didn't make the connection between him and my patient."

Elle's brows went up at this. "You knew Tom already?"

She nodded. "Oh yeah! We met ages ago. He's my knight in shining armor."

Elle blinked a couple of times in disbelief, then turned a questioning gaze on Tom. "Really? How so?"

"It's not important," Tom mumbled. "It was nothing."

"Nothing?" Isabel said with a laugh. "Are you kidding? He doesn't give himself enough credit. He saved my life."

Elle now understood perfectly. Of all the Dawson brothers, Tom was the most humble—almost to a fault. Isabel was absolutely correct that he didn't give himself enough credit. But that still didn't quite explain Tom's reaction to the woman. Elle couldn't help but wonder if there was more to the story.

Fortunately for Tom, Isabel's cell phone beeped, distracting her. She took the phone from the clip at her waist and checked the screen. "Sorry, have to get to surgery. It was great seeing you both again!"

Tom mumbled something indistinguishable, then turned and headed for the nearest exit.

"What was that all about?" Elle asked, glad to turn the conversation away from Tom's inquisitiveness and distract him from asking *her* any additional questions.

"I told you, it's not important," Tom said. "She's exaggerating."

Elle laughed. "Liar. What happened?"

He sent an irritated look her way. "A few years ago, a woman and her daughter were brought in with severe injuries. They'd been beaten by the woman's boyfriend. The girl was in a coma and wasn't expected to make it. The woman had internal bleeding and required emergency surgery. I was called in to investigate and get a statement from Isa, who'd been the surgeon working on the wife, when the guy burst in and went apeshit. He shot two security guards and took Isa hostage, demanding access to his wife or he'd kill the doctor. I managed to negotiate her release and apprehend the suspect."

"I remember that story!" Elle said, now understanding why the doctor's name had sounded familiar. They lived in a largely rural county comprised of several small towns and cities, but violence and crime weren't just problems for the big city. If they were, Elle wouldn't have had a job. Meth houses were popping up in suburbia all over the country; drugs were a growing problem, regardless of socioeconomics. And domestic violence *certainly* knew no boundaries. Elle had counseled women from *all* walks of life who'd been the victims of violence. "He received the maximum sentence, if I'm not mistaken."

Tom fished his keys from his pocket as they stepped out into the summer sunshine and headed toward his Tahoe. "Unfortunately, that won't bring back his victims. The girl died two days later and her mother only hung in there for a while longer."

"And that's it with Dr. Morales?" Elle prompted, studying Tom's closed-off expression. "Or is there more to the story?"

He shrugged. "We had coffee a couple of times."

"When?" Elle asked.

He cleared his throat. "In the months after the incident."

Elle's stomach sank. "You cheated on your wife?"

"God no!" he practically shouted. "I'd never do that.

We just chatted over coffee a couple of times during the investigation. That's *all* it was. But I could talk to Isa about things I couldn't talk to Carly about. That was a wake-up call about my marriage, so I decided to really focus on what was important and fix what was broken between Carly and me. She was everything to me, Elle. It was killing me that we were falling apart."

"I'm sorry, Tom," Elle said, suddenly feeling like an insensitive bitch for pressing him. "It's none of my business."

He shook his head as he opened her door for her. "It's okay. I just wish Carly and I had been able to work things out before…"

Elle grasped the edge of the door. "Before she was killed."

He sighed and briefly massaged the back of his neck. "Apparently, she'd been planning to leave me, Elle. I was served with divorce papers two days after her death. Losing her was devastating enough, but finding out she hadn't been in love with me anymore when I'd been trying so hard to fix things…"

Elle gave Tom a sympathetic look. "Then what's the harm in spending a little time with a certain doctor who clearly has a crush on you? It's been three years, Tom."

He looked down, avoiding her gaze, waiting for her to get in so he could close her door. Obviously, he had said all he was going to on the matter. Taking the hint, Elle climbed inside and turned her thoughts back to what had nearly happened in the hospital room with Gabe—and began to feel like a complete hypocrite. Here she was, urging Tom to take advantage of a little companionship to stave off the loneliness, and yet she

was fighting the sexual tension between her and Gabe
at every turn.

But she shook her head, pushing away that kind of
rationalizing. No, it was better if she and Gabe kept
things completely professional, completely platonic.
Any other possibility, as enticing as it might be—as
enticing as she knew from experience it *would* be—
wasn't an option.

Chapter 7

"YOU OKAY?"

Gabe hobbled toward his living room on his crutches, taking a moment to navigate between the brown leather recliner and end table to get to his comfy-as-hell overstuffed couch before answering his brother. "Yeah, I'm good."

Joe followed him into the room, hovering and fussing like a goddamned mother hen, plumping pillows, lining up all the remotes on the coffee table so they'd be within easy reach. It was driving Gabe fucking crazy. All he wanted to do was just stretch out on the couch and doze off while watching ESPN, but his younger brother had insisted on hanging out with him on his first day back home.

"You sure?" Joe pressed as Gabe eased down onto the couch, wincing with the pain.

Gabe gave Joe an irritated look. "Dude. I'm fine. How many times I gotta say it?"

Joe folded his arms over his chest and stared down his nose at him from where he stood. "Until I'm sure you're not lying out your ass."

Gabe's brows lifted. "Okay, then. Truth? I'm irritated as fuck with you at the moment, but other than that, I'm good."

Joe grunted. "Yeah? How'd you sleep last night?"

Gabe looked away, clenching his jaw so tightly he could feel the muscle ticking with the strain.

"That's what I thought," Joe replied as he sat in the recliner and eased it back, the smug little shit.

After the silence had stretched on for several seconds, Gabe finally heaved a harsh sigh and turned his gaze back to his brother, not surprised at all to see Joe studying him. "It's not like what you went through in Afghanistan," Gabe assured him. "This is totally different, Joey."

"You were shot, Gabe," Joe reminded him—as if he needed it. "You could've died. A guy doesn't go through something like that without it affecting him."

Gabe reached forward and snatched the remote from the coffee table, turning on the TV and upping the volume, hoping his brother might take the hint. But Joe didn't budge.

"Didn't say it didn't affect me," he admitted after a moment. "I'm pissed as hell at that fucker Monroe. I'm pissed Tom had to pull his weapon and use it for the first time in his entire career. I'm pissed Elle was half an inch away from getting her fucking head blown off. And I'm pissed I took three to the chest and one to the leg and could've ended up like my best friend did a year ago." He turned and pegged Joe with a hard look. "So, yeah, Joey, getting shot by some son of a bitch with an ax to grind about us locking up his cop-murdering bastard of a brother has affected me. But I'll deal. And it'd be a hell of a lot easier if I didn't have you talking over *SportsCenter*."

Joe shook his head with a bitter laugh and slammed the recliner's foot rest back down. "You know what? Fuck you, Gabe. I'm just trying to help you get through this. But, hey—you don't want my help? Fine." He shoved to his feet. "I'm outta here."

Gabe pulled a hand down his face, immediately feeling like a total piece of shit. Maybe Elle had been right. Maybe he *was* an irredeemable jackass. "Joe!" he called after his brother as Joe strode toward the door. "Joey! Dude, I'm sorry! I just—"

The front door slammed, cutting him off.

He let his head drop back against the sofa cushions and closed his eyes. Awesome. His brother the war hero had tried to be there for him, had tried to let him know he understood what Gabe might be going through, and Gabe had pretty much just told him to go fuck himself.

Yeah, Elle was definitely onto something with the whole jackass thing...

Speaking of Elle, he wondered how *she* was doing. He'd never seen her so rattled as when he'd come to visit him in the hospital. The look in her eyes when she'd voiced the truth—that she'd almost died—had sent a chill through his entire body, and not just because of the calm accuracy of her observation. The hollow look in her eyes, the recognition of her own fleeting mortality, concerned him.

If there was anyone Joe should've been following around like a freaking puppy and attempting to psycho-analyze, it was Elle.

Gabe put his life on the line every day. He assumed a certain amount of risk. He knew one day he might not come home. That day could be thirty years from now. It could be tomorrow. But it was different for Elle. Even though she dealt with criminals on a daily basis, saw the effects of their crimes on their lives and the lives of others, and was no doubt jaded by her experiences, it wasn't the same. There was no way it *could* be the same.

Not really. At least, that's how it was *supposed* to be. She was supposed to be one of the blissfully ignorant citizens he was sworn to protect from those kinds of attacks.

But he'd failed. That son of a bitch had come way too close to killing Elle on Gabe's watch—and it was that truth more than his own close call that he was having a hard time dealing with. Because his focus had been on getting into Elle's pants instead of what was going on around him. So when he looked into her eyes and saw that empty, hollow fear, he had to accept that he was just as much to blame for putting it there as Mark Monroe was.

He pulled his hands down his face, then groaned a string of curses before reaching for his phone and dialing his brother.

"What?" Joe answered.

Gabe took a deep breath and let it out slowly. "I'm sorry, Bro. I know you're trying to help."

"There's no shame in being shaken up, Gabe," Joe assured him. "But I'm here for ya, man. You know that, right? I've been there. I just..." He sighed. "I don't want to see you go through what I did."

"I know. And I appreciate that."

"You might be my big brother," Joe continued, "but I worry about you. Don't take this the wrong way, but you haven't been the same since Chris's murder."

Gabe grunted and randomly flipped through the channels on TV, suddenly deciding *SportsCenter* wasn't all that interesting after all. "None of us have, Joe. You can't tell me you don't worry about not making it back home to Sadie when you start every shift."

"No, I don't," Joe said without hesitation. "You know why? I can't think about that when I'm doing my job.

I can't think about it at all. I go to work each day with the attitude that I'm coming home that night. Otherwise, I make bullshit mistakes that could get me or someone else killed." He paused for a moment then added, "But that doesn't mean I don't have nightmares about someone taking me out like they did Chris. Or that I don't worry about what would happen to Sadie and our baby if something happens to me. Hell, *that's* the shit that keeps me up at night, man."

Gabe let that hang in the air for a moment, caught somewhere between gratitude and sorrow that he didn't have a wife and family to worry about him—and that he didn't have to worry *about*. He knew damned well the reason he never stayed in a relationship long was that he didn't want that kind of worry hanging over him, didn't want to experience the pain of that kind of loss— pain he'd witnessed when his father had been forced to watch Gabe's mother slowly fade away in spite of all his efforts to save her. And yet Gabe envied Joe, and now his youngest brother, Kyle, for having exactly what he'd always tried to avoid.

Because at that moment, he couldn't think of anything he wanted more than to hold a certain woman with fiery-red hair, kiss her full lips, and hear her moan with need, and make love to her all night long and confirm that, in spite of Mark Monroe's efforts, they were both very much alive.

"Gabe? You okay, Bro?"

Gabe actually had to think that one over. *Shit*. He wasn't quite sure anymore. But he said, "Yeah. Yeah, I'm good."

"Well, you need anything, call me," Joe insisted.

"Sadie and I are just down the road. And if she finds out you needed something and didn't ask, she'll kick your ass. You know she will."

Gabe chuckled. Sadie had been like a little sister to the Dawson boys while growing up and had needed to knock some sense into them more than once over the years. "Oh, I have no doubt. Hey, Joe?"

"Yeah?"

"I love ya, man. Stay safe."

"Ah, hell," Joe muttered. "Now I'm *really* worried. You're getting all sentimental and shit."

Gabe laughed. "Fuck off."

"Back atchya, Bro."

Gabe was still smiling when he hung up and settled back against the cushions, letting his eyes close as the oh-so-snappy dialogue of some sci-fi movie with shitty special effects droned on, lulling him into a blissfully dreamless sleep.

Elle sat in the driveway for a long moment, wondering what the hell she was doing. She should be home, working on…*something*. She certainly had cases waiting on her to get to them. But she couldn't concentrate, couldn't focus on the work. The words swam before her eyes, making her head ache.

She'd tried to run errands to keep her mind off of things, to keep from reliving the horrors of Gabe being shot, of the sight of his blood on the courthouse steps, the look in his eyes when he was so worried and concerned for her, unaware of his own peril. And that, inevitably, led to thoughts of the night she'd spent in his arms and the hurt and disappointment that had followed when he'd failed to ever mention it. But that didn't keep her from remembering the commanding tenderness of his kisses.

She gave herself a mental shake and glanced around, looking over her shoulder for the hundredth time that day. She couldn't quite shake the feeling she was being watched, that someone was staring at her even now, tracking her every movement. The hair on the back of her neck prickled in warning, but there was no one. The only other person out during the sweltering Indiana summer heat was a man watering his lawn a few houses down.

She shuddered and shrugged her shoulders a few times, trying to rid herself of the feeling. She was being paranoid. Understandable under the circumstances. And, of course, if someone was watching her, sitting in her car in Gabe's driveway for a half hour was probably starting to look a little suspicious.

She heaved a determined sigh and shoved open the car door, grabbing the bag of takeout from the passenger's seat before she lost her nerve, and strode to Gabe's front door, knocking firmly.

Still unable to shake the uncomfortable feeling making the base of her spine tickle with apprehension, she cast another look around her surroundings, narrowing her eyes as she scoped out the cars parked along the street. Nothing.

"Get a grip, Elle," she murmured. "It's nothing. You're totally overreact—"

"Elle?"

A startled cry escaped her lips before she could check it, and the bag she was carrying dropped to the concrete porch with an ominous, wet *thunk*. She whirled around with wide eyes to see Gabe standing in his doorway with the aid of crutches, his aqua eyes studying her a little warily.

"Jesus!" she breathed. "You scared the crap out of me, Gabe."

His blond brows came together in a confused frown. "Um…sorry?"

She snatched up the bag and carefully slipped past him, throwing another uneasy glance over her shoulder as she went inside. "I brought you dinner. Where's your kitchen?"

He gestured vaguely with a jerk of his chin. "That way."

"I hope you like Italian," she called as she hurried to the other room, hoping he didn't notice the warmth of humiliation flooding her cheeks. "I wasn't sure. But I took a chance."

She set the bag on the kitchen counter, which she noted was surprisingly clean for a bachelor pad, and rummaged through his cabinets, finding an equally surprising assortment of pots, pans, dishes, and cooking accessories.

"Elle?"

She turned to see Gabe hobbling in on his crutches. "So, do you prefer lasagna or veal piccata?" she asked. "I'm good with either."

He shook his head a little, still looking bemused. "What are you doing here?"

She went still, her stomach sinking, and closed her eyes, suddenly feeling like a total idiot. "Oh my God. You probably have someone coming over. I didn't even think… I'm *so* sorry! I should've called first."

Now experiencing a whole new level of humiliation, she made for the door, hoping to make a quick exit. But he stepped into the center of the doorway in front of her, blocking her path just as she attempted to plow through, and she slammed into him, nearly knocking him on his ass. With a startled cry, her arms reflexively went around his waist, pulling him forward to keep him on his feet.

When she looked up at him, an apology on her lips, he was grinning down at her, his handsome face disconcertingly close to hers. "No one's coming over, Elle," he assured her, the sound of her name on his lips somehow as intimate as a lover's caress. "Just you and me."

She suddenly became very aware of the sculpted muscle beneath his shirt where her hands rested on his back and had the almost inescapable urge to let her fingertips go exploring. "Oh," she managed, wondering what the hell had happened to her language skills.

His head tilted slightly to one side as he scrutinized her. "You okay?"

She took a step back, needing to put a little distance between them to quiet her pounding heart. "I just… I thought you might like some dinner. That's all."

His lopsided, dimpled grin grew. "I've been trying to get you to have dinner with me for years. You think I'm going to turn you down now?"

She couldn't help returning his smile. "Yeah, well, getting shot to get me here was a bit extreme, don't you think? Flowers might've been a less painful way to go."

He leaned a shoulder against the doorframe. "Nah. Flowers are far too prosaic for someone like you. At least, not any ordinary flowers. Everybody gets those."

She sent him a cautious look, wondering what cheesy come-on he was teeing up. "Uh-huh. And what kind of flowers would you give me?"

He held her gaze for a moment. "Wildflowers."

Her breath caught in her chest. Was it possible that he really *had* been the boy who'd left them in her locker? Had her silly teenage fantasy been accurate after all? No. It was just a coincidence that he'd selected wildflowers—most likely because that's what she'd brought him in the hospital. But still, she had to ask, "And why's that?"

He shoved off the doorframe and hobbled forward on his crutches, opening one of the cabinets Elle hadn't gotten to yet and revealing a stack of simple, white plates. "Because they're honest and unpredictable and thrive no matter where they're planted."

She was a little breathless when she replied, "And what does that mean?"

"It means you're one of the most incredible women I've ever known, Elle," he told her. "And you can see through my bullshit like nobody else. Clearly, I'm going to need to up my game to make any headway."

Elle tried to cover her happiness at the compliment by giving him a saucy glance as she stood on her tiptoes to reach the plates and sashayed past him to set them on the table. "Yeah, well, don't get any ideas, hotshot. This is just dinner. Nothing else."

When she turned around to grab the food, she was surprised to find him close behind her, his smile laced with mischief. "You're perfectly safe with me. I swear I won't try a thing." He winked and added, "Unless you want me to."

She gave him a wry look, hoping he couldn't tell how damnably hard her heart was pounding when he looked at her that way. "Fat chance, Dawson."

He shrugged with an exaggerated sigh. "Suit yourself."

She laughed a little as she swept her hair up and pulled it into a haphazard ponytail, trying to tame the thick waves with the rubber band she kept handy on her wrist. "Go sit down," she said, shooing him away. "I'll handle this."

She turned away and began dishing up the food, but she could feel the weight of Gabe's heated stare, the sensation warming her skin and making her restless in ways she didn't want to acknowledge. And when she finally turned and caught his gaze, she was surprised to see not the usual playfulness and mischief sparkling in his eyes but what she could've sworn was loneliness.

"Everything okay?" she asked. "You look pale. You really should sit down and rest your leg."

"Why'd you really come here?" he asked, ignoring her concern. "If you'd just wanted to drop off dinner to help me out, you would've only brought enough for one."

She maneuvered around him to set the plates on the table, giving her time to consider his question. For a moment, she thought about giving him some flippant, bullshit answer, but instead, she sighed and wrapped her arms around her torso, hugging herself to try to banish the cold fear that had penetrated to her bones.

"I didn't want to be alone tonight," she admitted, keeping her back to him, too humiliated to face him as she said it. "All I can see when I close my eyes is Mark Monroe's face, so twisted and so full of hatred. I just..." She heaved a frustrated sigh. "You're the only one who can understand, Gabe. I didn't know who else to talk to."

She started when she felt his hand on her shoulder but didn't resist when he gently turned her around to face him. "I'm here," he assured her, smoothing his hand along her arm. "Anytime you need me."

She studied his face for a long moment, his harshly chiseled features even more fierce when he was so close. "What do I do now?" she asked. "I send victims to get counseling, to help them work through the trauma. Hell, I even volunteer as a counselor myself! Yet I can't bring myself to go. I need to know what I can do to get that bastard out of my head, Gabe, what I can do to stop feeling so afraid."

He gently grasped her chin. "You help me bring down that son of a bitch Jeb Monroe and put him away for good."

She pressed her lips together in a determined line. "When do we start?"

Chapter 8

JEB MONROE SAT IN HIS PICKUP TRUCK, WATCHING THE deputy's house through narrowed eyes, his blood boiling with hatred. Every ounce of him wanted to rush the porch, kick open the front door, and deliver a powerful message to Mac Dawson about grief and retribution. The son of a bitch had stolen Jeb's father's farm on behalf of the government, had taken from Jeb what was rightfully his. And then he'd sent his favorite deputy, his own son, to arrest Derrick in the very home where Mac had darkened the doorstep years before, adding insult to injury.

The Dawson boy carried himself with the same arrogant swagger, the same self-righteous, blind devotion to the government as his father. They were instruments of evil. And Jeb had been selected by God himself to rid the world of such evil. He'd heard the Voice telling him what he must do. And he would obey.

Jeb took a long, deep breath and let it out slowly, reining in his ire, forcing it down to a low simmer. He needed to bide his time, wait until the perfect moment to exact his vengeance. Then he'd strike. He'd rip out Mac Dawson's heart.

The sheriff needed to understand what it felt like to lose a favorite son, needed to feel the pain that tore at Jeb's chest with savage claws, shredding every ounce of him until he felt like nothing more than a hollow shell of a man.

Jeb's cell phone rang on the seat next to him. Without turning his gaze away from Gabe Dawson's house, he snatched the device from his seat and barked, "Go ahead."

"I have the information you requested, sir."

Jeb's jaw tightened at the sound of his son Jeremy's voice. "Well, I'm waiting."

Jeremy cleared his throat nervously. "Tom Dawson's wife, Carly, was DEA, but she was killed three years ago in an undercover operation. But your cousin at the courthouse told me she'd been filing for divorce when she was killed. Maybe he has someone else."

Jeb grunted. "Scratch her off the list. What about the others?"

"Joe Dawson's fiancée, Sadie Keaton, is an English teacher at the high school," Jeremy informed him.

"Asterisk her," Jeb ordered. "She'd be easy enough to get to."

There was a slight hesitation before Jeremy added, "But she's pregnant—about five months along."

"I said asterisk her," Jeb hissed.

Jeremy cleared his throat, clearly uncomfortable with Jeb's order, but the boy was young, inexperienced. He didn't understand that every war required sacrifices. "Yes, sir."

"And the others?"

"It looks like Kyle Dawson is living with his girl-friend, Deputy Abby Morrow."

Jeb considered this one for a moment. "Leave them off the list," he decided. "I don't want to draw the FBI's attention any more than necessary. If Kyle Dawson's anything like his father, he's already stepped up their surveillance. I don't want to give them any reason to move in sooner."

"Yes, sir."

"And Gabe Dawson?" Jeb prompted.

"Unattached at the moment," Jeremy told him. "He has no shortage of women on the hook, but he's not with any of them."

Jeb grunted in disgust. "Doesn't appear that way. That whore attorney is at his house as we speak."

"But everyone says she can't stand him."

"I don't give a shit what everyone *says*," Jeb hissed. "She's probably spreading her legs for him right now. You want to argue with me some more, boy?"

"Of course not, sir," Jeremy mumbled.

"I want her taken out," Jeb spat. "She's the reason Derrick is in prison and why Mark is dead. The fact that she's no doubt fucking Gabe Dawson is just a bonus."

"Who should we do first, sir?"

Jeb sighed, mulling it over. "No one yet. I want them living in fear, knowing we're coming. I want them to spend every moment worrying about when we're going to strike, wondering when death will be visited upon them. I want them to know that they're powerless to stop us."

"Yes, sir."

Jeb grinned, pleased by his son's loyalty. "I want you to stay on Elle McCoy," he decided. "She already saw you watching her. I want her to feel your presence. I want her looking over her shoulder everywhere she goes. Do this well, boy, and I'll give her to you."

"*Give* her to me?"

"That's right," Jeb said. "If she's going to act like a

whore, we'll treat her like a whore. And when we're done with her, I'll let you be the one to put a bullet in her head."

Jeb hung up on his son, tossed his phone onto the seat beside him, and snatched up the little present he'd prepared to welcome Deputy Dawson home.

———

"Will you be okay here tonight on your own?" Elle asked as she strolled toward his front door, clearly moving slowly so he could keep up with her on his crutches.

He slid a meaningful sidelong glance toward her. "You offering to stay?"

She rolled her eyes, but he could see a hint of pink rising in her cheeks. God, he loved making her blush like that. The fact that he could bring a flush to the cheeks of a woman like Elle made his chest swell with pride. The only thing better would be making her flush with desire as he made love to her.

A sudden, vague image of her arching off his bed in ecstasy made his cock go rock hard, making him seriously fucking glad he was wearing his shirt untucked for once so she couldn't see the effect she had on him. God, she had to be beautiful in the throes of passion. What he wouldn't give to watch as rapture played out over her features, to hear her scream his name, to feel her nails digging into his skin...

"Do you ever stop?" she teased, leaning against the doorframe.

He shook his head, and his voice was rough with desire when he answered, "Not where you're concerned."

She turned toward him when they reached his front door and regarded him for a long moment. "Why?"

Her question took him off guard. "Huh?"

She tilted her head to one side, far more adorable than she realized. "Why are you so interested in me, Gabe? You can have any woman you want."

He scoffed. "Not true. My reputation has been greatly exaggerated. Right now, there's only woman I want."

She rolled her eyes. "Fine, for argument's sake, let's pretend that's true."

Pretend? What the hell?

Did she really buy into all the rumors about him sleeping with anything with a pulse? His false reputation had been haunting him since high school. Okay, his fault for not refuting the rumors, but what teenage guy wouldn't want everyone to think he was a god in bed? And, now that he knew better, he was too old to give a shit what people thought.

"Why would you want to keep pursuing someone who has pushed you away over and over again?" she continued. "I mean, what's so special about me?"

He reached up and tugged at a curl that had come loose from her ponytail. "How long do you have?"

She grinned and patted him lightly on his chest, just above the bruises from the shots he'd taken, but he managed to keep from wincing. "Ah, so *that* must be the famous Dawson charm you keep mentioning…"

He leaned on his crutches, bending forward, close enough to kiss her. "Is it working?"

She shoved away from the doorframe and straightened to her full height, bringing her lips even closer to his. Her mouth curved into a sensual smile as she searched his face. Then she stepped closer, her arm slipping around his waist as she leaned into him, her breasts pressing into his chest as she put her lips close to his ear and whispered, "Not even a little, Romeo."

With that, she stepped back and winked at him before opening the door and sending a wave at him over her shoulder as she strolled toward her car.

Oh, she was good…

He had seen the mischief in her eyes after she'd whispered in his ear. She knew exactly what she did to him with every word, every touch, and she was enjoying it. And, hell—truth be told, so was he.

He chuckled, shaking his head as he watched her pull away.

He was still grinning when her car turned off his street, but his grin faded when he caught a glimpse of something hanging from the plant hook at the corner of his porch. Frowning, he hobbled toward it, his stomach clenching when he saw what it was.

A noose made of twine hung from the hook. And hanging in the noose was a voodoo-style stick figure that looked like something his brother Kyle had probably encountered when he'd done a stint with the FBI office down in New Orleans. But encountering one in Northern Indiana was somehow even more chilling.

Gabe's head snapped up, his senses on high alert as he scanned his surroundings. Seeing nothing out of the ordinary, he snatched the hanging man from the hook and fished his phone out of his pocket, dialing Elle, waiting impatiently for her to answer.

"Hey there," she finally answered after the eighth ring. "What's—"

"Are you okay?" he blurted, cutting her off.

"Yes, I'm fine," she assured him, her tone wary.

"I've literally gone only two minutes down the street. I don't think—"

"Check your rearview mirror," he interrupted again, his eyes narrowing as he scrutinized the cars and houses around him once more. "Tell me if there's anyone behind you."

"No," she said, her voice a little shaky. "There's no one. What the hell is going on, Dawson? You're scaring the shit out of me!"

"While you were here, someone dropped off a little welcome-home present for me." He tucked his phone between his jaw and shoulder and maneuvered back into his house, not eager to hang out on the porch, exposed to anyone who might be watching, and locked his front door.

"Present?" Elle repeated. "What kind of present?"

Gabe glanced down at the crude form in his hand. "A stick figure in a noose."

"Jesus," she breathed. "Do you think it was Monroe?"

Gabe grunted. "That'd be my guess."

"He's just being an asshole," she assured him, although her tone sounded a little unsure. "He's trying to get into your head."

Gabe made his way to the living room and lowered himself onto the sofa before responding. "Maybe. But I'd feel better if you weren't at home alone tonight. Can Charlotte come over?"

"I'm a grown woman," Elle reminded him—as if she needed to. He was all too aware of the fact that she was all grown up. And all woman. "I won't ask my aunt to babysit me. Besides, Monroe wouldn't care if Charlotte's there with me or not."

He ran a hand over his hair, frustrated with his helplessness. Had he not been laid up with his leg, he would've hopped right into his car and driven to her house the minute he'd seen the damned stickman hanging there. "Well, could you go over to her house?"

"For how long, Gabe?" she asked. "I can't let Monroe uproot my entire life until we finally catch him doing something criminal and put him away. We can't prove he's the one who left the hanging man, right?"

"Quit thinking like an attorney for one damned minute," he shot back. "To hell with *proving* anything. I'm worried about your *safety*, Elle."

There was a slight pause then a very quiet, "Thank you. For worrying about me."

Gabe's throat suddenly felt constricted with anxiety for her. He wished he could invite her back to his house so he could keep an eye on her, but that was out of the question. Considering what she thought of him and his reputation, odds were she'd see it as another come-on instead of his genuine concern for her well-being.

They were both silent for a long moment before Gabe finally cleared his throat and said, "I know you can't just put your life on hold, Elle. But I'd feel a lot better if I knew you had someone with you. Hell, what about the newest douche-suit? What's he doing? Could he come stay with you?"

He heard her exasperated sigh, but her voice sounded slightly amused when she said, "I really wish you wouldn't refer to the guys I date that way. Not all of them even wear *suits*. But I tell you what. I'll see if I can stay at Aunt Charlotte's house tonight."

Gabe closed his eyes and let his head fall back against

the sofa pillows. "Good. I'll sleep a hell of a lot better. But promise me you'll call 911 and then me if anything strange happens."

"I promise." Another long moment of silence stretched out between them. Finally, Elle asked tentatively, "Gabe? Are you still there?"

"Yep," he replied. "I'm here. I'll stay on the line as long as you want."

"This is ridiculous, right?" she said with a nervous laugh. "I mean, we can't let this bastard scare us into being paranoid at every turn. I'm already jumpy. I felt like someone was watching me all day everywhere I went, and now—"

Gabe's eyes snapped open at this. "You did? Why didn't you say anything?"

She sighed. "I just... I felt like I was overreacting, considering what we've been through. And you have enough to deal with right now without worrying about me."

He shook his head. Damn, the woman could be exasperating. "You want to be partners in this, in bringing Monroe down? Then you don't keep anything back from me. I'm letting you in, Elle."

Shit, that was an understatement.

The fact that he was so worried about her—not just as any cop would be about someone who was at risk, but as a man who cared about her more than he liked to admit—was testament to just how much he'd already let her in.

After a moment, he heard her finally clear her throat. "I'm at home," she announced. "I'll give Aunt Charlotte a call and then head over there."

He didn't like the fact that she was home alone even

for as long as it took to put a bag together and call Charlotte, but she was right. She couldn't live in fear every moment. That would be giving Monroe exactly what he wanted.

"Call me when you get to Charlotte's, will ya?" he asked. "So I know you're okay."

"I will," she promised. "And, Gabe?"

"Yeah?"

"Be careful." There was a slight pause before she added quietly, "I worry about you, too."

Before he could respond, she hung up, leaving him sitting there in stunned silence at her admission. After a moment, he pulled the phone away from his ear and stared at it, wondering if he'd heard her right.

Chapter 9

"Thanks, Aunt Charlotte."

Charlotte pressed a kiss to the top of Elle's head and set the mug of hot chocolate in front of her on the table. "Anytime, baby girl. You know you're always welcome here. I'm more concerned by the fact that Gabe thinks you shouldn't be staying alone. Maybe you should stay here for a while."

Elle waved away her aunt's words. "We've both been through a lot. He's just being overly cautious."

Charlotte pursed her lips. "If Gabe's worried, there's a damn good reason to be. And seeing as how my security system here is better than the one you have at your house, you're safer here. Besides, Mac sends extra patrols around to check in on me."

Elle's brows lifted. "He does?"

Charlotte's lips curved into an amused smile. "He thinks I don't know. But ever since the break-in down the street a few years ago, he's been encouraging me to move to a better neighborhood."

"This neighborhood has one of the lowest incidents of crime in the county," Elle reminded her. "Plus, you have fantastic neighbors who keep an eye on each other's houses and a great crime-watch program—not that there's really been much to report over the years. Where does he think you'd be *any* safer?"

"I doubt he'd think I was safe enough if I were

right next door to him," Charlotte told her with a wink. "Maybe being overly cautious when it comes to the people they care about runs in the Dawson family."

"Yeah, well, I think it's rubbing off on you, Aunt Charlotte."

"If I didn't love you, I wouldn't worry." She paused, as if struggling with whether she could continue with the words that Elle could plainly see were right on the tip of her tongue. But her aunt was never one to keep her opinions to herself, so Elle wasn't entirely surprised when Charlotte added, "Maybe you should reconsider that job offer."

Elle bristled, wishing she'd never told her aunt about the opportunity she'd been offered just a few days before the shooting. She'd been surprised when her friend Cassandra had offered her the position of executive director at the local nonprofit that helped women and children rebuild their lives after experiencing violent crimes. Elle had volunteered there since it had opened several years before and had seen it grow from a handful of people to a thriving organization that made a difference in a lot of lives. But she'd made a promise to herself years before that she'd become an attorney. And giving that up somehow seemed like a betrayal. "Charlotte—"

"Hear me out," her aunt insisted. "I just want you to be safe and happy, Elle. This is not the first time you've been threatened."

"No, it isn't," she agreed. "But I can't live in fear every time I'm assigned a case. The odds of anything ever happening—"

"Clearly don't mean a damned thing," Charlotte

pointed out, taking a seat across from her. "Mark Monroe proved that, didn't he?"

Elle sighed, really having no way to refute her aunt's argument. "You of all people should understand why I went into this profession. My family's killer did so little time he practically *walked*. I don't want that to happen to other families."

Charlotte reached across the table and squeezed her hand. "Baby, you've done a lot of good for the people of this county; there's no disputing that. But helping the women and children of this area when they need someone most would still be honoring your family's legacy."

She was right, of course. The woman had had a way of reasoning Elle into a corner in every single argument they'd ever had. Elle had a feeling Charlotte would've been a terror in the courtroom had she chosen to go into law.

"But if I take another job, I want it to be because I feel like it's where I can do the most good," Elle told her. "I don't want it to be because I'm scared to do my current one."

Charlotte's expression softened. "I can certainly respect that, baby girl. You remind me so much of your mom sometimes. She was never one to back down from a challenge."

Elle grinning. "Runs in the family."

"Will you just promise me you'll reconsider the position?" Charlotte pressed. "Will you at least think about it some more?"

"Fine," Elle said, relenting. "I'll consider it. But I'm not making any promises."

"Fair enough." Charlotte took a sip from her own

mug and her eyes sparkled, giving Elle a heads-up that the conversation was about to lighten. "So…back to Gabe Dawson."

"He's just a friend," Elle insisted. "Barely even that, really."

Charlotte grinned at her. "Mmm-hmm."

Elle groaned. "Would you stop doing that?"

Charlotte chuckled. "Sure. As soon as you stop denying what's going on between you two."

Elle sighed and gave her aunt with an understanding look. "Look, I know you worry about me and want me to eventually have a relationship that lasts more than a couple of months, but Gabe Dawson isn't the guy for me."

Charlotte leaned back in her chair, scrutinizing Elle with eyes the same shade of green as hers. "Want to know what I think?"

Elle's lips twitched with amusement as she blew across the top of her hot chocolate. "I learned a long time ago that you're going to tell me anyway, no matter how I answer that question."

Charlotte winked at her. "You always were a smart girl."

"Another trait that runs in the family," Elle replied. "So this sage wisdom is…?"

Charlotte pressed her lips together for a moment before answering, "I think Gabe is a lot like his daddy. Mac had more than his fair share of pretty young women on his arm when we were younger. I'd love to say I was his only high school sweetheart, but that would be a lie. I was just the last. Mac was quite the charmer back in the day. Still is."

Elle's brows lifted. "Mac? He doesn't exactly strike me as the romantic type."

Charlotte leaned forward, resting her chin on her hand, a dreamy expression coming into her eyes. "You'd be surprised. Oh, it's a side he doesn't show to many, that's for sure. But I would've married that man in a heartbeat had he asked."

"But then he met Gabe's mom," Elle supplied.

Charlotte nodded. "Theresa was the kind of woman Mac needed at that time of his life. I would've made a terrible cop's wife back then. I was far too reckless and headstrong, and valued my independence and freedom way too much to settle down and raise a family."

Now it was Elle's turn to scrutinize. "And now? What if Mac were to waltz in here and sweep you off your feet?"

Charlotte laughed. "First of all, Mac wouldn't *waltz* anywhere. He'd kick in the door and barge right on in. And he wouldn't take no for an answer if I turned him down. He's persistent, that man."

Elle shook her head. "Charlotte Mulaney, I think you're just as much in love with Mac Dawson as you ever were. Does he know?"

Charlotte flushed to the roots of her hair. "He knows I care about him. When you've known each other as long as we have, some things just don't need to be said."

"Sure they do," Elle argued. "Does he feel the same way?"

Charlotte's expression clouded over for a moment before she forced a smile. "Oh, I'm sure he does, in his way. We never stopped being the best of friends, and we enjoy our time together. But I don't know that he'll ever get over losing Theresa."

"She's been gone a long time," Elle pointed out. "Maybe he just doesn't know how to tell you what he really feels."

Charlotte laughed outright at this. "Oh, don't be so sure. Mac has always known how to woo a girl. But we're a little old for flowers and poetry at this point."

"Mac? A poet?" Elle said, finding such a thing hard to believe.

Charlotte's smile widened. "Someday I'll drag out my memory box and show you a few of the verses he wrote for me."

Elle shook her head. "Wow. I stand corrected."

"My point is, I see the same qualities in Gabe," Charlotte continued. "Of all the boys, he's probably the most romantic. And by that, I don't mean the other boys don't know how to treat the women they love and make them feel special. I can tell that just by looking at how Joe and Sadie and Kyle and Abby are together. But Gabe…" She took a deep breath and let it out slowly. "I think Gabe has an idealized vision of what love is supposed to be like. He saw how much Mac adored Theresa, saw everything he did to be there for her, to be the rock for their family when she was sick. I think he won't settle for any less of a steadfast love."

Elle scoffed as she took a sip of her cocoa. "You wouldn't know it by how quickly he goes through women."

Charlotte wagged a finger at her niece. "That's where you've got it wrong, baby girl. Gabe doesn't move on quickly because he's fickle. He moves on because he realizes she's not the one."

Elle tucked away that little bit of intel to muse over later. Her aunt was one of the most insightful women

Elle had ever known, but she was also biased when it came to the Dawson men. She'd been a surrogate aunt to them their entire lives, especially after their mother had died. And her affection for Mac certainly made her more lenient when it came to the foibles of his offspring. But the jury was definitely still out for Elle.

"And what about you?" she asked her aunt, eager to divert the subject away from her own interactions with the Dawson clan. "Do you ever regret that you never married and had children of your own?"

Charlotte shook her head. "Not in the least. You're every bit a daughter to me as if I'd given birth to you myself. And as for marriage…" Here she paused and sighed. "Well, everything turned out as it was meant to." She rose and came around to Elle, taking her face in her hands. "And I'm sure it will for you, too—whatever path you choose."

Elle grinned as her aunt pressed a kiss to her forehead. "Thanks, Charlotte. I don't know what I'd do without you."

Charlotte pulled a face. "Oh, you'd do just fine. You're a fighter, Elle. You always have been. And you'll get through this mess with that son of a bitch Jeb Monroe, too. And as far as Gabe goes? Well, *I* certainly feel better knowing that he's watching over you."

Gabe jolted awake and glanced around the living room, wondering what it was that had awakened him so suddenly from his favorite dream for the past year or so—the one where he and Elle were tangled together on his bed, half-naked and straining toward each other, desperately wanting each other but holding back.

His frustration at being interrupted was only dampened by the adrenaline pumping in his veins as his fight-or-flight mode kicked in. Even though his sofa wasn't directly across from the windows or his front door, Gabe suddenly felt very exposed. He moved silently, grasping the Glock he'd set on the sofa next to him after talking to Elle and ensuring she'd made it safely to Charlotte's.

He'd locked his doors and set his alarm before dozing off on the couch, but something had brought him out of a deep sleep—and the dream. But as he sat there, listening intently for another sound, he didn't hear anything.

He cursed under his breath and managed to get to his feet, grabbing one of his crutches as he limped to the window and peeked through the blinds. The neighborhood was quiet. Nobody was out and about at this late hour.

"Come on," he muttered. "Where the hell are you, you son of a bitch?"

After a few moments, he made his way through the rest of the house, checking the doors, peering outside through other windows to get a different vantage point. But nothing seemed out of the ordinary. Shit, for all he knew, just the normal pops and creaks of a fifty-year-old house settling could've been what he'd heard.

He heaved a relieved sigh and checked his watch.

Three a.m.

Christ, it was going to be a long night if every little noise was going to have him on edge like this. But now that he was completely awake, sleep was out of the question. He made his way to his office and powered on his laptop.

An hour later, he'd checked both his work and personal email, and had caught up on the news he'd missed while in the hospital, but the adrenaline-infused tension still had every muscle in his body taut and ready for a fight.

He heaved a frustrated sigh.

Hell, he might as well make use of the time if he wasn't going to be going back to sleep. Besides, some of his best investigating was done on sleepless nights just like this one, when his thoughts wouldn't stop churning, trying to connect the dots that would help him solve the most stubborn cases.

He brought up a browser and, after a couple of minutes, found his way to Jeb Monroe's blog. If he was gonna bring the bastard down, the first thing he needed to do was really get into his head. The antigovernment tirades on his blog were a good place to start.

Four hours later, Gabe jolted awake again. Not because of a suspicious noise this time, but because his head had slipped from where he'd been resting it against his fist and he'd nailed his forehead on his keyboard.

Nice.

Gabe pulled a hand down his face, wondering how long he'd dozed off while reading Monroe's blog. He'd managed to get through dozens of posts before he'd run out of steam, but it was enough to have him shaking his head in disbelief.

The man was completely delusional. He'd read his fair share of rants about the government and law enforcement—some of them even well supported by evidence and incredibly persuasive. He could see how people already frustrated and discontent could buy into what these groups were saying. But Monroe… The guy was a fucking nutjob. And the people following him and leaving comments were just as crazy.

The bullshit he was spewing was so far beyond a run-of-the-mill conspiracy theory that Gabe half expected to see the guy walking down the street with a foil hat one of these days. But his followers were bordering on the fanatical. Given a few more years to recruit, Jeb Monroe could easily reach cult status.

Gabe yawned and stretched, then got to his feet and grabbed one of his crutches, intending to make his way to his bedroom and collapse onto the bed when his doorbell rang.

He frowned and glanced at his watch again. It was just past seven o'clock. Who the hell would be dropping by at this time of morning?

Gabe grabbed his gun from the desk, where he'd set it the night before, and tucked it into the waistband of his pants at the small of his back before heading to his front door. He carefully peered through the peephole and let out a relieved sigh. He quickly disengaged his alarm and unlocked the door.

"Tom?" he said, surprised to find his brother standing on his doorstep. "What are you doing here?"

Tom gestured with the cardboard drink carrier he had in his hand. "Brought you coffee. Thought you might need it."

"Uh, yeah," Gabe said. "Thanks. I didn't sleep much last night."

Tom grunted. "Figured as much."

Gabe stepped aside. "Come on in. Have you had any breakfast?"

"Nah," Tom said, heading for the kitchen. "I'll make you something. What'll it be? Cocoa Puffs or Froot Loops?"

Gabe chuckled. "I see your culinary skills haven't improved since we were kids."

Tom gave him a hint of a grin, which was about all anyone got out of the guy these days. "Yeah, well, I never claimed to be a god in the kitchen."

"So many comebacks, so little time, Bro," Gabe said, shaking his head. "I'm going to take pity on your sorry ass because you brought me coffee and let that one go unanswered."

Tom sent a wry glance over his shoulder as he grabbed cereal bowls from the cabinet. "You *must* be tired. You've never missed the chance to be a smart-ass."

Gabe eased down into a chair and scrubbed his face with his hands. "I was reading through Jeb Monroe's blog. That guy scares the shit out of me, I don't mind admitting."

"You and me both." Tom set a bowl in front of Gabe and took the seat across from him.

Elle's seat.

Gabe pushed that thought away as soon as it occurred. One dinner didn't mean anything. She'd needed someone to talk to. That was all it was—and probably a little pity thrown in for good measure.

He forced his thoughts back to his brother, who was wolfing down his cereal like a man on a mission. Tom wasn't especially communicative anyway, but he was particularly closed off that morning.

"How you holdin' up?" Gabe asked.

This brought Tom's head up. "I'm fine. Why?"

"You killed a man," Gabe said. "That's not something you just shrug off, Tom."

Tom swallowed slowly, then took a gulp of his coffee before he finally managed to meet Gabe's gaze. "I'm dealing."

"I don't think I ever said thank you for saving my ass," Gabe said.

Tom shrugged and managed another half grin. "I've been saving your ass for thirty-six years. Just add this one to the grand total. Now, eat your cereal, loser. I have to get to work."

Gabe lifted his spoon in mock salute, then scooped a spoonful of cereal into his mouth, sending a covert glance Tom's way as he ate. If the dark circles under his brother's eyes were any indication, he hadn't slept much better than Gabe.

Of course, he had a feeling Tom's sleeplessness had started before the shooting of Mark Monroe. But he wasn't going to bring up the subject of Tom's deceased wife. His brother would come to him if he wanted to talk. That's the way it'd always been. But that didn't mean he couldn't be there for him when it came to the shooting.

"Mark Monroe knew what he was doing when he showed up at the courthouse," Gabe said around a mouthful of cereal. "You know that, right?"

Tom nodded. "Yeah."

"And you know if you hadn't taken him down, he could've killed who knows how many innocent people," Gabe continued.

Tom finished off his cereal and got to his feet to take his bowl to the sink. "That's not the part that gives me nightmares, Gabe." He braced his arms on the counter, his head hanging between his shoulders for a moment before he straightened and ran a hand over his dark hair in frustration. "You know, it never used to worry me that we were all in law enforcement. I mean, we've heard the lectures since we were kids about carrying on the Dawson legacy, making our family proud, protecting and serving the community. But after what happened…"

Gabe stared at his brother for a moment, taking in what he'd said. "We all knew what this job could cost us," he said. "The Old Man lost our uncle to a hopped-up junkie in a routine traffic stop. And Carly…" His words trailed off at the heartbreaking look Tom sent his way. "My point is, it could happen to any of us."

"But knowing that and watching it play out are two different things," Tom said. "Seeing that fucker take aim at you…" Tom paused and shook his head. "In my nightmares I didn't stop him in time, Gabe."

Gabe's stomach sank as the full extent of what his brother was going through hit him. "Shit, Bro. I'm sorry. I had no idea."

Tom shook his head. "It's not you. I gotta deal with this. It's not like you, Joe, and Kyle are gonna give up your careers. At least you'll be a desk jockey for a while when you get back, so—"

"What?" Gabe interrupted. "You're parking me?"

"Isa said—"

"Isa?" Gabe asked, cutting him off. "Who the fuck is Isa?"

"Dr. Isabel Morales," Tom explained. "Your surgeon. She said you'd be on medical leave for a couple weeks and would then need to take it easy for a while until your leg is healed."

"It's a flesh wound, Tom," Gabe shot back. "It's not even as bad as what Joe had to deal with when he was wounded in Afghanistan, for shit's sake!"

Tom crossed his arms, giving Gabe the look he always did when pulling rank—not just as the eldest Dawson brother, but as Gabe's boss in the sheriff's department as their father's executive deputy. "It's not up for discussion, Gabriel."

Gabe shoved his cereal bowl away from him, sloshing some of the remaining milk onto the tabletop. "You sound more and more like the Old Man every day," he muttered. "Since when do you call me *Gabriel*?"

"I already talked it over with Dad," Tom informed him, grabbing a paper towel from the roll and wiping up the milk. "You're taking a break, Gabe. It's not a punishment. It's for your own good."

Gabe scoffed. "Bullshit. It's for *your* own good, Tommy."

Tom heaved a frustrated sigh and clenched his jaw, the muscle in his cheek ticking from the strain. "Maybe. But I'm not going to let you get yourself killed. And I know that if I put you back on the road, the first thing you'd do is go after Monroe."

"Got news for you, Bro," Gabe said. "I'm going after Monroe regardless of whether I'm on the road or stuck behind a desk. He left me a present last night—a hanged man in a noose. If that's not an invitation to go kick his ass, then I don't know what is."

Tom's expression barely altered, but Gabe could see he was startled by the news. "You should've called me when you found it."

"Why?" Gabe asked. "So you could come racing over here to hover around like a mother hen? I figured it could wait until morning. There's nothing you could've done last night that I didn't already do unless you want to canvas the neighborhood to see if anyone saw anything. I wasn't quite up to pounding the pavement."

"I could've filed a report so we could have the incident on record," Tom snapped.

Gabe sighed. "Well, I'm telling you now. But there're no prints on anything, of course—already checked for that. Nothing tying Monroe to the damned thing. There never is."

Tom scrubbed a hand down his face, looking even more haggard than when he'd first arrived. "Shit."

Gabe grunted. "Tell me about it."

"Why's he targeting you, though?" Tom asked.

Gabe shrugged. "Maybe I'm just up first because Mark didn't finish me off? Or maybe it's because I was the one who arrested Derrick after Chris's murder."

Tom frowned. "Yeah, but I was the one who killed Mark. You'd think he'd be coming after me."

"Who says he's not?" Gabe replied.

"I'll give Kyle a call," Tom told him, "see if we can get some additional surveillance going from the FBI. Unless Monroe gives us something to bring him in on, there's not much else I can do."

Gabe leaned back in his chair and spread his hands. "Exactly why I didn't call you."

Tom regarded him for a long moment then finally

said, "If you turn up anything, you'll tell me? You won't go off half-cocked?"

Gabe raised his right hand. "My hand to God—if I go anywhere, I'm taking my whole cock."

"I'm serious, Gabe."

"So am I!" he shot back.

Tom laughed and snatched an orange from the counter, lobbing it at his brother.

Gabe dodged it easily and chuckled, "Nice throw, dickhead."

"Piss off," Tom laughed. "I'm taking it easy on you while you're recovering."

"Uh-huh," Gabe teased. "Sure."

"Oh, you wanna be a tough guy?" Tom darted forward, putting Gabe in a headlock and rubbing his knuckles on the top of Gabe's head. Tom released him abruptly and stumbled back with a laugh when Gabe punched him in the gut.

Gabe jabbed a finger at his brother. "You're lucky I can't kick your ass right now."

Tom shook his head, grinning. "Yeah, yeah. You can owe me one, Billy Badass." His phone chimed, drawing his attention. He checked it quickly and shoved it back into the case at his hip. "Gotta go. Duty calls."

"Everything okay?" Gabe asked.

"Same shit, different day," Tom assured him. "Call me if you need anything—or if you get any other presents from Monroe."

Gabe gave him a mocking salute. "Yes, sir."

"I mean it," Tom called over his shoulder as he headed out of the kitchen. "Don't be stupid."

Gabe sighed, then muttered, "Wouldn't dream of it."

Chapter 10

ELLE WAS EARLY.

She'd talked to Gabe nearly every day during the week since their dinner at his house, just a few minutes here and there to check in on him, see if he'd had any other problems with Monroe she might be able to work with. But it'd been quiet. For him anyway.

Even though she'd promised to keep him apprised of any uneasiness she'd felt, she wasn't about to tell him about every single paranoid moment she'd experienced. She was certain someone was following her. She could feel his gaze on her when she was loading groceries into her trunk. When she left the fitness center. When she left the office and was walking to her car…

But she'd only seen someone once. And that could've been just a coincidence. After all, Fairfield County wasn't exactly a bustling metropolis. Mostly comprised of farmland and factories with the occasional cluster of houses in a suburban neighborhood, the towns in Fairfield County epitomized small-town Midwest life. The fact that she'd seen Jeremy Monroe sitting in a corner booth sipping a cup of coffee while she was at lunch with her coworkers was hardly surprising. And really not even worth mentioning to Gabe.

At least, that's what she kept telling herself. Because otherwise she was going to go crazy.

And yet, she couldn't quite shake the feeling, even

now as she made her way to Gabe's house to go over some of the information he'd been gathering, that someone was trailing her. She'd checked her rearview mirror too many times to count, had tried to keep track of all the vehicles that were behind her between her house and Gabe's. But there were none that stood out.

Still, with paranoia adding to her eagerness to see Gabe—purely for the sake of information gathering, of course—she'd broken pretty much every traffic law possible. Lovely. Great idea for the deputy prosecutor to get caught in a serious traffic violation. That'd go over *really* well with her boss...

She sighed with relief when she turned into Gabe's driveway and practically sprinted to the front door, glancing over her shoulder as she waited for him to answer her knock. Her stomach began to twist into knots as the seconds dragged on, her uneasiness building. She knocked again, louder this time, glancing around again.

Come on, come on, come on...

Her heart began to pound, the blood flooding her ears. The birds chirping nearby suddenly sounded distorted, surreal. The sunlight was overly bright, blinding. Her chest heaved, her breath coming in gasps as fear surged in her veins.

He should've answered the door by now. Something was wrong. She knew it. Something was terribly wrong.

She punched the doorbell a couple of times then pounded on the door with her fist, trying the knob with her free hand. "Gabe! Answer the door! Gabe!"

She was bringing her fist up to pound on the door again when it suddenly swung open. Gabe stood in the doorway leaning on a walking cane, shirtless and barefoot, his jeans apparently hastily pulled on because they weren't yet buttoned. "Hey, I didn't—"

Without thinking, Elle threw her arms around his neck, hugging him tightly. "Thank God," she whispered. "I was so worried when you didn't answer the door."

His arm came around her, holding her close. "I'm fine," he assured her. "I was just getting out of the shower when I heard you pounding on the door. Took me a minute to get here."

Her hold on him eased a little as humiliation overrode her fear, and she pulled back, one arm still around his neck. She closed her eyes on a relieved sigh. But when she realized her other hand was resting lightly on his bare chest, her eyes snapped back open.

"Oh jeez," she said in a rush, pushing back to put some distance between her and one of the most amazing sets of pecs she'd seen in a seriously long time. But his arm around her waist tightened just enough to keep her from backing away.

"Hang on a sec," he said, his brows drawn together in a concerned frown as he searched her face. "What's really going on? This isn't just about me. Your heart is pounding like a rabbit's."

She swallowed hard, not about to tell him that, at least at that moment, her pounding heart had nothing to do with her fear and everything to do with the fact that her body was pressed against his.

"I thought someone was following me," she admitted. "I didn't see anyone—just felt like I was being watched. And then when you didn't answer the door…"

He released her and took hold of her hand, leading her into his office, where music was playing on the stereo. He grabbed a remote from the desk and adjusted the volume. "Sorry," he said. "Guess I forgot to turn it off before I got in the shower."

Is that Ray LaMontagne? Huh. Somehow she'd pegged him more as a country music kind of guy.

He hadn't been kidding about being an enigma. As she was quickly discovering, there were many things about Gabe she hadn't expected...

He gestured to the laptop on his desk. "Which one of the Monroes do you think it is?"

She brought her focus back to the investigation and narrowed her eyes, realizing he had photos of Jeb Monroe and his various family members and acquaintances open on the screen. "Where did you get these?"

"Kyle's pals at the FBI," he told her. "They're helping with some surveillance. I got these last night."

She pointed to a photo of a man she recognized. "He's one I've seen around a couple of times."

He blew out a harsh sigh. "That's Jeremy Monroe, one of Jeb's sons."

She pointed to another photo. "He's *definitely* the one who was following me the day after the shooting."

Gabe's brows lifted. "The one who slashed your tire?"

"I can't prove it," she admitted. "But it's a little too coincidental, don't you think?"

He sat down on the corner of his desk and crossed his arms over his chest, making his biceps bulge in a way that was most distracting. "How long?"

She dragged her gaze up to his eyes. "How long what?"

"How long have you been having this feeling?" he pressed. "You haven't mentioned anything when we've talked."

She felt warmth flooding her cheeks. "I didn't want to worry you just because I was being paranoid."

He gently took her hand and pulled her closer, until she was standing between his thighs. "I want you to tell me everything, especially when it's something that causes you to have a panic attack on my front porch."

She tried to avert her gaze, but he tenderly grasped her chin and forced her to look at him.

"Elle, you are the strongest woman I know. Nothing is going to change my opinion of you in that regard."

Elle's breath caught in her chest when he looked at her with such intense admiration. She'd noticed it before, had seen the respect in his eyes. But she hadn't realized until that moment how much it meant to her. He was right. One of the reasons she hadn't said anything was because she didn't want him to think any less of her. Why that mattered was a mystery. But it did.

"Okay," she said softly.

His thumb smoothed lightly over her jaw and his aqua gaze grew more intense. Just when she thought he might lean in and kiss her, he said softly, "I want you to come to me."

She shook her head, clearing the fog of desire that'd been building there, swamping her reason. "Sorry?"

"If you even suspect anything else is going on," he explained.

"Oh!" she said, laughing a little at her own presumptiveness. "I thought—" She bit off her words before it was too late to take them back. She'd honestly thought he was talking about wanting *her* to make the first move. She took a deep breath—and a step back.

He grinned, actually flushing a little, and glanced up

at her through golden lashes, giving her a look that was completely devastating.

"Did you think…?" He cleared his throat and fought to hide a smile. "Did you think I was going to kiss you just then?"

"Oh, no," she said, waving away his words. "No, of course not."

He got to his feet, bringing him back to within a breath away from her. "Would it be so bad?" he asked softly, his gaze searching hers.

She blinked at him, trying to pretend she had no idea what he was talking about. "What?"

"Kissing me," he murmured, the back of his finger caressing along the edge of her jaw, making her pulse trip over itself. "Would it be so horrible?"

Her hand came up to rest on his waist, and her lids drifted shut a moment. *Horrible?* Hell no. It would be sheer bliss—and something she'd craved ever since first tasting his lips. But she took a deep breath and let it out slowly, forcing herself to get a grip on her libido. "It's not a kiss that worries me," she told him, tired of denying what had happened between them and worrying about whether or not he remembered. She needed to get it off her chest. "It's what comes after—or, more accurately, what *doesn't*."

His brows drew together in a frown. "What's that supposed to mean?"

Well, since he asked…

"It means you only want me because you can't have me, Dawson," she said. "As soon as you get want you want, I wouldn't be any different from any of the other women you've had. You'll move right along to the next."

He cringed a little at her words. "No wonder you think I'm an irredeemable jackass." He laughed, the sound edged with bitterness, and shook his head, resuming his seat on the desk. "Don't worry about me trying to kiss you again. You've made it perfectly clear you wouldn't piss on me if I were on fire. I sure as shit can take a hint."

She gave him a sad smile. "The thing is, Gabe, you *have* kissed me. You were just too smashed to remember it."

His face went slack, his surprise impossible to disguise. "After Chris died," he murmured. "That happened."

"Yeah, it happened. And then…" She raised her arms out to the side. "Nothing."

"I thought it was a dream," he told her.

She laughed bitterly. "Oh, that's a good one. A dream? Nice try, Dawson." Then she blew out a frustrated sigh and held up a hand, cutting off whatever response he was about to give. "You know what? I think I'll just go. Just email me whatever you have."

"Elle—"

"I'll see you around, Gabe."

"Elle!" Gabe called. "Would you hold on for one goddamn minute?"

When she turned back to face him, she was surprised to see him standing right behind her. Before she could say a word, he grasped her around the waist and jerked her toward him, claiming her lips in a harsh, savage kiss.

Elle stiffened, taken aback, but then his hand came up to cradle the nape of her neck and his lips grew gentle, tender, stroking hers. The desire she'd fought against blossomed in the center of her, its warmth spreading through her body, filling her, overtaking all logic and reason. She kissed him back, pulling his bottom lip into her mouth, scraping it gently with her teeth, drawing a low moan from him as his kiss deepened.

Her arms slipped around his waist, her fingers splayed along his muscled back, and she leaned into him, fully surrendering to the strength of his arms, the sultry caress of his lips against hers. As their kiss slowly drew to a close, she kept her eyes closed for a moment, taking the time to try to bring her breathing under control.

Gabe pressed a kiss to her cheekbone, her temple, near her ear. "Jesus, Elle," he whispered, his breath feathering across her skin. "Kissing you is even better than I remembered."

She pulled back slightly, lifting her gaze to his. "But I thought you didn't remember."

He shook his head slowly, tucking her hair behind her ear as his gaze searched hers. "I thought what I remembered was just a dream—and that's no bullshit line. It's the truth. I was so out of it that night, I seriously thought maybe I'd just imagined everything that happened between us."

"Why didn't you say something?" she demanded. "Why didn't you bring it up?"

"Why didn't *you*?" he fired back without missing a beat. "Put yourself in my position. I was going to look like a total jackass no matter what I did. Asking about it because I wasn't sure if it'd happened would've pissed you off. Clearly. And if I'd said something and it *hadn't* happened, you would've thought I was off my fucking nut."

She had to admit, he had a good point. Why *hadn't* she said anything to him about it? "When you didn't say something, I thought what happened didn't mean anything to you."

He closed his eyes for a moment and rested his forehead against hers. "Oh, honey... You couldn't be more wrong," he murmured. "Do you have any idea how many times I've dreamed of kissing you, holding you?"

His lips found hers again in a slow kiss that stole her breath, and if she did not abruptly end the kiss, she had the distinct feeling she would yield to the desire that was burning in her veins.

Really hating to bring things to a grinding halt, Elle nonetheless gently eased out of his arms. "I'm sorry... I can't do this."

He looked confused by her sudden withdrawal. "You don't believe what happened between us meant something to me?"

"I believe you, Gabe," she admitted sincerely. "But think about it. You and I were both hurting, grief-stricken about losing Chris that night. We just needed someone. If it hadn't been me making out with you, it would've been someone else."

"That's not true," he argued, but she caught the note of uncertainty in his voice.

"Here we are again," she continued, "having gone through something that shook us both to our roots. I just... I don't know that I can trust this. And I've seen how you operate, Gabe. Women are constantly throwing themselves at you. I've seen you leave Mulaney's with more women than I can even count."

He crossed his arms over his chest, his posture

growing defensive. "Didn't realize you were counting. If I'd known, I would've given you a copy of the score-card I keep in my wallet, let you play along."

She closed her eyes, trying not to let his sarcasm get to her. He was hurt by her perception of him—that was clear. The knowledge that her words were hurting him made her stomach sink. She reached out and placed a hand on his arm, but the contact was a mistake. Hell—every contact with him was a mistake. She'd discovered that all too well.

She could deny her attraction to Gabe all she wanted, could lie to herself—to *him*—and pretend her heart didn't race every time he walked into a room, that her stomach didn't somersault whenever she heard his voice. But there was no denying how her fingers tingled the moment they touched his skin and how that simple contact sent heat lancing through her.

"It meant something to me, too," she said softly, let-ting her fingertips drift lightly along his forearm.

"Elle."

Her gaze snapped up to his. "Yeah?"

"You should probably go."

—◦◦◦—

Her hand instantly fell away, his reaction no doubt unex-pected. She probably thought he was being a petulant asshole, but he was actually trying his damnedest to be a gentleman. Because what he *wanted* to do was kiss the hell out of her again, sweep her off to his bed, and make love to her until they both passed out from sheer, blissful exhaustion.

"Okay," she said, backing away, her expression

conflicted. She held his gaze for a long moment as if she might say something more, but then turned and headed for the doorway.

"It's bullshit," Gabe called to her, not willing to let her walk out the door thinking he was a piece of shit manwhore.

She turned back, frowning. "What?"

"My reputation," he repeated. "How many women I've slept with. It's not what you'd think—not what I *let* people think even back in high school. And none of the women I *have* been with were one-night stands, contrary to popular belief."

"What about Chelsea Barton?" Elle demanded.

It actually took him a minute to figure out who the hell she was talking about. "Billy Monroe's girlfriend?"

Elle nodded.

He scoffed, shaking his head with a bitter laugh. "No, Elle," he said, "I really didn't sleep with her. She only said that to piss off Billy and to get back at me for turning her down. Yeah, she gave me a ride home from Mulaney's that night, but when she wanted to get busy, I turned her down. I wasn't interested."

Elle blinked at him for a moment. "But…why didn't you say something when Billy first backed out of testifying against his cousin for Chris's murder?"

"I tried to deny it, if you'll recall," he reminded her. "But given my reputation, you didn't buy it."

She closed her eyes on a sigh, her shoulders sagging. "Gabe—"

"My point is, Elle, I don't sleep with just any woman with a pulse," he continued, not willing to accept an apology now, not when he was hurt by her lack of faith and trust in him. "I never have. When I'm with a woman, it's because I care about her and I respect her. If either of those things is missing, it's a no-go, no matter what my dick has to say about it."

She stared at him for a long moment, maddeningly silent. She could see through him in so many ways and didn't give a good goddamn about his charm or his swagger or any of the other bullshit he dished out. That's what he loved so much about her. So why couldn't she accept *this* truth?

"I get it," she said, her chin lifting. "What you're saying is perfectly clear. Thanks for saving me from making a *huge* mistake."

He frowned, perplexed by her reaction, and went after her as she stormed toward the front door but wasn't able to keep up with her thanks to his leg.

Why the hell was she acting so pissed? He'd just explained he didn't sleep around, that he wasn't the total asshole she'd thought he was. Fucking hell, that's what he got for being a gentleman on the night they'd—

Shit.

She must've thought the reason he'd put the brakes on during their make-out session after Chris's death was because he didn't care enough about her to sleep with her when the truth was the exact opposite. Even though he'd been completely shit-faced, he would've had enough presence of mind to not ruin his shot with Elle by sleeping with her when he was wasted.

"Elle!" he called. "Elle, wait! I didn't mean—"

The slamming front door was the only response he received.

He heaved a sigh. "Way to go, genius. Gonna need a

crowbar to get your fucking foot outta your mouth this time around."

A moment later, his cell phone rang. To his surprise, it was Elle. "Elle," he said before she could speak, "when I said that—"

"Come outside," she interrupted, her tone even, serious.

He pulled open the front door and his stomach immediately sank. Spray-painted in white across her windshield was the word "WHORE."

Elle fixed him with a look so forlorn it broke his heart, but then she gestured toward his house. He came out onto the porch and turned around to see "DIE PIG" painted on his door. He disconnected the line and dialed his brother.

"Hey, Tommy." He seethed, anger making him grip his phone with white knuckles. "That promise you wanted me to make about not going after Monroe, cutting off his dick, and shoving it down his throat? Yeah, not sure I'm gonna be able to keep that one."

Chapter 11

"AND?"

"I did what you told me to, sir," Jeb's youngest son, Brian, told him, his eyes gleaming with a mission accomplished. His first. He was only thirteen, so he was green and inexperienced, not like his older brothers. But he'd be one hell of a soldier for the cause when he was a little older.

Monroe nodded. "Good. Good. It's a little risky tagging in daylight, but it makes a stronger point than sneaking around in the darkness like a coward."

"He knows we're not afraid of them," Brian said with a triumphant grin.

Jeb ruffled the boy's hair, smiling down at him. "That's right, Son. That's right. It's important to immediately establish dominance. If he knows we're the ones in control, he'll realize he's powerless. And being powerless makes a man afraid."

Brian nodded. "Yes, sir."

"You *sure* no one saw you?" he asked. "Someone shows up here looking for you, you know there'll be hell to pay."

Brian nodded again, more vehemently this time. "I didn't see anybody at all. And I did her car first, so nobody'd see it right away from the street."

Jeb frowned. "Her car? *She* was there?"

Brian glanced toward his brother Jeremy, as if asking permission to continue.

"She was parked in his driveway," Jeremy supplied. "I thought we might as well send her a message while we were there."

Jeb nodded his approval. "Glad to see you taking a little initiative. Finally."

Jeremy huffed and all but spat, "Thank you, sir."

Jeb eyed his sons, not liking Jeremy's attitude of late. He was eighteen, a man. His mother wanted to coddle him, keep him from fighting the cause as his older brothers had done. But Jeb had a legacy to maintain. He needed lieutenants in his army for freedom. And who better to count on than his own family?

It was time perhaps to initiate him into something more than petty vandalism. And he had just the job in mind.

———

Elle stood at a distance from Gabe, her arms wrapped around her torso in spite of the summer heat. She was chilled down to her marrow. It was bad enough to see her car vandalized, but the death threat on Gabe's door affected her even worse.

"You okay, baby girl?"

Elle dragged her gaze from the threat against Gabe and turned her attention to her aunt. Charlotte's auburn brows were drawn together in a concerned frown that made her look every bit of her sixty years. The stress of the situation was taking its toll on more than just Gabe and Elle. Their families were suffering, worried about their safety and well-being. But maybe that was the point.

"I'll be okay," Elle assured her, forcing a tentative smile. "It's just paint."

"This time," Charlotte fumed. "Did you get a look at who did it?"

Elle shook her head, wishing she'd stayed inside a little longer, enjoyed the warmth of Gabe's arms, the heat of his kiss, for a few moments more instead of storming out. Maybe then she wouldn't be so cold now.

The sound of a car pulling up brought both of them around to see Mac Dawson getting out of his Tahoe and striding toward his son. But Charlotte was already moving to intercept him. If Elle hadn't been so shaken by the events of that morning, she would've been amused to see her aunt going toe-to-toe with the sheriff, his imposing figure towering over hers but wearing an expression that looked a little intimidated by the fierce tilt of her chin.

"Douglas MacArthur Dawson," Charlotte said, hands on her hips, "what *the hell* is going on?"

"Well, Charlotte," he drawled, "that's what I'm here to find out."

She wagged a finger at him. "Don't you dare 'Well, Charlotte' me. It's the Monroes, and you damn well know it. I want that crazy son of a bitch arrested and behind bars where he can't hurt anyone else."

Mac heaved a patient sigh. "Charlotte, we have no proof it was Monroe or any of his kin. I can't arrest him or anyone one else without cause."

She shook her head. "There was a time when you weren't so by the book," she admonished. "You used to be more concerned about protecting victims than offending the criminals."

Mac ran a hand over his close-cropped gray hair and sent a glance toward Gabe and Tom, then Elle. "I'll bring him in for questioning," he relented. "But that's the best I can do, Charlie."

Elle's eyes widened slightly. *Charlie?* She'd never heard anyone but her mother call Charlotte by that name. She'd long suspected there was more between Mac and her aunt than just friendship, but there was something in the way Mac looked at Charlotte at that moment that spoke volumes. Instead of looking offended by being cornered by Charlotte, he looked like he enjoyed her fiery tirade. And Elle could've *sworn* she saw the formidable sheriff grin as he turned away.

Charlotte was positively triumphant as she came back to Elle, head held high. "Don't worry, honey. Mac will handle it. Now, let's get you back to my house. I think it's best if you stay another night or two."

Elle started to argue, but she realized she didn't really want to be alone that night. She felt a heaviness in the center of her chest and looked over her aunt's shoulder to see Gabe staring at her, his expression difficult to interpret. He looked as if he wanted to come to her, hold her. Or maybe that was just her projecting the desires weighing on her own heart.

———

"Gabe? Did you hear what I said?"

Gabe dragged his gaze away from Charlotte's car as it drove away, wishing he'd had the chance to talk to Elle for a few minutes before they'd left. But she hadn't made an effort to talk to him at all either, so maybe it was just as well.

He turned back to Tom, trying to focus on what he was saying. "Sorry, what?"

"I said, you need to bring Dad up to speed on what's been going on," he said. "We're going to bring Jeb Monroe in for questioning. And I'm going to send extra patrols around to keep an eye on your house."

This got Gabe's attention. "Good. Let's go pick up the bastard right now."

"You're not going anywhere," Tom informed him. "Unless it's to Joe and Sadie's while the team finishes processing the scene."

"Bullshit," Gabe spat. "I'm not just going to sit around on my ass while you guys talk to Monroe."

"You are on medical leave, Gabriel," Mac interjected. "And there's a reason for that. If you want to be fit for service later, you need to take care of yourself now. Is that clear?"

Gabe clenched his jaw, fighting back the urge to argue with his father. He knew arguing wouldn't do any good. Once the Old Man dug his heels in, it was over, and no amount of ranting, raving, or whining would make a damned bit of difference. All that would do was piss him off even more. That was a lesson he'd learned when they were all kids and was probably why he and Mac had the best relationship. His brothers saw it as kissing their dad's ass. Gabe saw it as picking his battles.

But he was having a hard time swallowing his protests this time around. "I think I can handle asking a few questions."

"So can your brother," Mac informed him.

Gabe's jaw tightened, and he suddenly felt like a ten-year-old kid again. "Dad—"

Mac gave him a stern look. "This is not up for discussion, Gabriel."

"Why?" he pressed. "I was shot in the leg, for Christ's sake!"

"Gabe," Tom warned. "Let it go, man. I'll handle it."

Let it go? Like hell.

"I'm not going to do nothing when I'm the one whose life is being threatened!"

Mac took a step forward, now nose to nose with Gabe. "It is exactly because your life is being threatened that I am keeping you out of this. I'm also not letting Tom question Jeb alone. I won't have the legitimacy of an investigation of this son of a bitch compromised or questioned."

"I'll give you a call after we talk to him," Tom assured him. "We're not gonna leave you in the dark, Gabe. You know that."

Yeah, he knew it. But being sidelined still pissed him off. Without another word, he went back into his house and slammed the door. He wasn't going to Joe and Sadie's just because some asshole had tagged his house. As soon as the vandalism was documented, he'd grab leftover paint from when he'd painted his garage a few months earlier and take care of it.

He was more concerned about the effect the event had had on Elle.

When he got back to his office, he tried to go over the info he'd planned to show her, but he couldn't concentrate. All he could think about was the way she felt in his arms, how yielding her soft lips had been, how her little moan of desire had sent a current of need down his spine and into his cock.

He leaned back in his chair with a groan and pressed the heels of his palms to his eyes, trying to banish the erotic images plaguing him. But it didn't do any good. He was on the verge of getting up to go take a cold shower when his cell phone rang, startling him.

Even more startling was the number he saw on the screen.

"I'm sorry," he said the moment she answered. "I'm an idiot."

Elle laughed on a sigh. "Let the record show that *you* said it, not me."

"So, you okay?" he asked, half holding his breath as he waited for an answer.

"I will be," she assured him. "I'm going to stay with my aunt for a couple of days, I think."

He cleared his throat, choosing his words carefully. "If, you know, you need someone to talk to, feel free to give me a call. Or stop by."

"I don't know that stopping by would be a good idea," she said.

His stomach sank. "No?"

"No," she affirmed.

"Mind if I ask why?"

"Because I'm a little worried what would happen if I stopped by," she admitted softly, her voice like a maddeningly sensual caress on his skin.

Holy shit. Was she saying…?

He honestly didn't even have a comeback for that one. If it'd been any other woman, he would've been able to come up with something appropriately seductive. But she left him speechless. The idea that she might be on board with where his thoughts were tending made his mouth suddenly go dry and his already-throbbing cock swell to the point of pain.

"I'll see you soon, Gabe."

He stared at his phone for a long moment after she'd hung up.

Holy. Hell.

Oh yeah. A cold shower was *definitely* in order…

———∿∿∿———

What *the hell* was she *doing*?

Elle knew as soon as she'd called Gabe that it was a mistake. She'd just stormed out of his house and now she was throwing out "do me" vibes? Okay, granted, she hadn't intended to throw out any vibes when she'd called. She'd just wanted to make sure he was doing okay after having his house vandalized.

But then she'd heard his voice, heard that deep rumble that made her shiver when the sound washed over her. She *wanted* him. Wanted him with an intensity that nearly sent her driving back over there. Luckily, until the authorities were finished processing her car for evidence she was without a vehicle of her own, and so she had to park her libido.

It was just as well. She needed to get a handle on this lust-fueled infatuation she had for Gabe. It couldn't end well. He'd all but told her that. Hadn't he? Or had she misunderstood?

Elle groaned and snatched up the files she'd been gathering from her office to take over to her aunt's house with the idea that working on some of her cases might help keep her mind off of Gabe and his heated kiss. With that in mind, she grabbed a couple of other file folders from their drawer and shoved them into her business tote for good measure. But when she turned to go, she paused. Taking a look around the confines of her office, the hair on the back of her neck stood on end.

Something was off. Nothing appeared to be missing or out of place, but she couldn't shake the feeling someone else had been there. But why? Anyone looking for information would've been disappointed—she took her laptop home with her every evening and her files were all locked securely in the filing cabinet.

Still, she did another sweep of the room to make sure that nothing was out of place. She shook her head. The only problem she could see was that her plant on the windowsill was looking pretty sad. Obviously, the office manager had failed to water it while she'd been working from home.

"Elle?"

Elle started, dropping her tote with a curse. "You scared the crap out of me!"

"Sorry, honey," her aunt said. "You were just taking so long I thought I'd come up and check on you. Everything okay?"

Elle's brows came together. "No," she confessed. "Something's wrong in here."

Charlotte took a stroll around the room, frowning as she searched for any sign of something off. "Everything looks okay to me, honey."

Elle shook her head. "I don't know... I just—" Her words died abruptly when she caught sight of a photo on her bookshelf that was slightly out of place.

Elle hurried to the photo and picked it up, tears coming to her eyes. It was her mother and father on their wedding day—one of her favorites. It usually sat directly in front a copy of the *Collected Works of*

William Shakespeare, but it had been moved, the slight disturbance in the light coating of dust on the shelf confirming her suspicions.

But why?

She set the frame aside and took out the book, leafing through it until she reached the page she sought. She heaved a huge sigh of relief when she saw the article she'd cut out of the newspaper years ago and had placed in the book for safekeeping.

Charlotte came to her side and peered down at the yellowed newspaper clipping. "Oh, honey," she whispered, putting an arm around Elle's shoulders and giving her a squeeze. "Why would someone want to steal the news story on your family's death?"

Elle had to swallow back the tears that choked her before she could say, "I doubt they did. No one knows I keep this here. I just wanted to make sure it was still here. And with that photograph being out of place...I just wanted to double-check."

Charlotte gave her another squeeze. "Well, then, it's probably nothing. I'm guessing someone was in your office while you were out and saw that picture of your mom and dad and how happy they were that day and just had to get a closer look."

Elle smiled. Thank God for Charlotte. She didn't know what she'd do without her aunt. "I'm just being paranoid." She placed the book back on the shelf and set her parents' wedding picture where it belonged, her fingertips lingering for a moment on the edge of the frame. "It's hard to believe next week is the anniversary."

"Why don't we go away next weekend?" Charlotte suggested. "It'd be good for you to get away for a little while. Maybe we can head up to Chicago, do a little shopping. I can ask Tony to run the bar while I'm out of town."

"Maybe," Elle hedged. "I'll let you know."

Charlotte gave her a look that clearly conveyed she knew Elle would decline the offer, but she didn't push. "Okay. Now, let's get outta here. I think we could use some time by the pool, don't you?"

The thought of lounging by her aunt's backyard pool sounded divine. "Add in a couple of mimosas and I'm in."

―∞―

Gabe's leg was hurting like a motherfucker. He'd been pacing for who knew how long, waiting to hear back from Tom about their chat with Jeb Monroe. He was torn between calling Joe and demanding he drive Gabe to the department in spite of their father's very clear instructions to keep the hell out of it, and the desire to call Elle back to see if she might be up for dinner again.

Unfortunately, he had a pretty good idea what the response would be in either case. But he couldn't continue to sit on his ass. It was driving him up a fucking wall. Finally, frustrated to the point of fury, he returned to his office and powered up his laptop.

He went back through the information Kyle had passed along and the different blog and social media posts he'd already read more times than he could count, trying to come up with anything incriminating he might've missed on a previous pass. But he came up with a big fat fucking nothing.

Then he turned his attention to the photos, trying to

put names and faces together. In addition to Monroe's children, Jeb's brothers were also a concern. David Monroe, Jeb's younger brother, wasn't quite as vocal a critic of the government and law enforcement as his brother was, but was more active in other groups that were already on various watch lists.

Then there was Jeb's youngest brother, James Monroe. He already knew that bastard well from their various encounters over the years, long before Jeb Monroe's bullshit vendetta against the Dawsons kicked up. He'd been out to James's house for too many domestic calls to count. Fortunately, James wasn't the brightest of the Monroe brothers and, aside from being an abusive asshole, usually just followed his other brothers' orders, from what Gabe could tell.

Yet at the moment, there was nothing Gabe could pin on any of them.

Gabe pulled his hand down his face to keep from putting his fist through his screen. "God *damn* it!"

His phone rang, and he snatched it up immediately. "What do you have?"

He heard his brother sigh and knew the answer was just going to piss him off before Tom even said, "Jack shit. Jeb did his usual song-and-dance number. We even brought in his son Jeremy and daughter, Sandra."

"Jeremy's the one who's been following Elle," Gabe told him. "She pointed him out from the photos Kyle gave us from the FBI surveillance."

"Yeah, well, he's just as good at being evasive as his father," Tom said.

"Of course he is," Gabe scoffed. "He's brainwashed those kids for years."

"I don't know," Tom drawled. "Sandra might not be buying into everything her dad has to say. I got the impression she was more afraid than loyal."

"What about Billy Monroe?" Gabe suggested. "Think we can try to get him to talk now that Derrick's trial is over?"

"Doubt the Monroes are sharing much with Billy these days," Tom said. "Jeb no doubt saw Billy's initial cooperation on Chris's murder as the ultimate betrayal. Even though Billy ended up reneging on testifying, he still gave us enough to cut a deal for himself."

"Let's make a trip over to Michigan City and have a chat," Gabe insisted.

"Can't," Tom informed him. "Billy got out last week. He's living on State Street in Nelliston."

Gabe grunted. "Nice neighborhood. He'll fit right in."

"No shit," Tom agreed. "I can see if he'd be willing to talk to us but can't make any promises. Might take some persuading."

"C'mon, Tommy, if anyone can get him to agree to talk to us again, it's you."

Gabe heard his brother snort. "Like I said, no promises."

"Thanks, Bro."

Gabe hung up and checked his watch. *Christ.* It was only half-past four. His head was swimming with all the bullshit he'd been reading and he couldn't take another damned minute of it. He had to figure out something else to do to make the time pass or he'd lose his fucking mind.

Before he could change his mind, he dialed Joe's number. "Hey, loser. You need to come entertain me."

Joe laughed. "That so? What'd you have in mind, asshat?"

"*Godfather* marathon?"

"I'll go one and two with you," Joe agreed, "but you're on your own for the third, Bro."

Gabe groaned. "Dude. Was three even an option?"

He tossed his phone onto the desk and blew out a harsh sigh. Hanging with Joe would keep him occupied for a while. But this sitting around "taking it easy" shit had to go…

Chapter 12

THREE WEEKS. IT'D BEEN THREE WEEKS SINCE HE'D buried his boy in the family cemetery at the edge of their property. For some fathers, that would be the end of things. But this was far from over. He'd been preparing for war for most of his life, and he wasn't going to back down now.

He wanted to make sure Gabe Dawson and Elle McCoy knew they would be the first casualties.

The whore was jumpy, glancing over her shoulder everywhere she went, always with friends or her aunt, Charlotte Mulaney, if she was out after dark. But it'd been a week since the boys had vandalized her car and the deputy's house, since Jeb and two of his children were brought in for questioning in the incident. They'd handled it just like they always had, as Jeb had trained them to do, and the police had had no choice but to let them go.

But to be on the safe side, he'd asked his brothers, David and James, to continue to keep an eye on the whore from a distance in the week since, reporting back on her routine. And, as usual, they'd taken care of their missions without question, providing Jeb with the intel he needed. Now he knew where she had her hair done, where she bought her groceries, where she liked to jog in the morning, what time she went to bed every night.

And Gabe Dawson? He was boring as hell. The man

was still laid up with his leg, unable to go much of anywhere without someone else hauling his ass around. But he'd soon be back to work, back enforcing the government's tyranny. Jeb would see to it he wouldn't do that much longer—or anything else for that matter.

He'd been waiting for the perfect time to deliver the next message. And today was the day to make his next move.

"Jeremy!" he called from his study, where he'd been writing his current blog post.

A moment later, his son entered the room, wiping his hands on a mechanic's rag. "The tractor's nearly fixed," he announced. "Brian should be able to mow later today."

"It can wait," Jeb told him. "I have another job for you."

"Yes, sir." He stowed the rag in the back pocket of his jeans. "What is it?"

"I want you to pay a visit to your cousin Billy, drop off a package."

Jeremy licked his lips, his gaze darting around the room at nothing in particular. "What kind of package?"

"What's it matter, boy?" Jeb demanded. "Your brother never questioned my orders. You want to be like *him*, a hero for the cause, or wind up a useless waste of space?"

Jeremy squared his shoulders, red creeping up his neck. Whether it was humiliation or anger turning him red as a beet, Jeb didn't care, so long as it was enough to make him do his duty. "What do you want me to deliver, sir?"

Jeb nodded his approval. "That's more like it." He

gestured toward the kitchen table. "It's a message to remind Billy what happens to traitors. He planned to sell out your brother Derrick, to give evidence against him in his trial."

"But he didn't," Jeremy pointed out. "He changed his mind."

"It doesn't matter!" Jeb roared. "He was unfaithful to the cause, unfaithful to his family. I cannot—*will not*—allow insubordination to go unpunished. Is that clear?"

Jeremy nodded. "Yes, sir."

"Make sure you leave it somewhere he can find it, but not where you'll be seen," Jeb continued. "If you fuck this up, I'll cut you loose, boy. Is that clear? I'm not going to let you drag me down because you're incompetent."

Jeremy's voice cracked with a little healthy fear as he replied, "Yes, sir."

Jeb gave him a terse nod. "Say the words with me now."

"'Blessed be the Lord, my rock, who trains my hands for war, and my fingers for battle,'" the boy said in unison with Jeb, as instructed.

"Go on, then." Jeb gestured to the doorway. "Don't disappointment me."

Gabe winced as he genuflected and crossed himself before entering the empty pew. It wasn't his usual way to spend a Saturday morning, but he'd been avoiding today's visit for a while now and couldn't really put it off any longer.

He pulled down the padded kneeler attached to the pew in front of him and gritted his teeth as he slid down onto his knees. It'd been three weeks since he'd been shot, but it'd most likely be a few more before he could really get around as he wanted to.

After he'd finally settled onto the kneeler, he slipped his Saint Michael medal from beneath his shirt and pressed a kiss to the silver before letting it rest against his chest. Before she'd died, his mother had given him and his brothers identical necklaces bearing the patron saint of police officers. He'd worn his every day since.

There'd never been any question Theresa Dawson's boys would go into law enforcement—the Dawson family history pretty much guaranteed it. Gabe's father and grandfather had had reputations that'd gained them the kind of notoriety that got their names in newspapers and history books—and on shit lists. And Theresa wanted to make sure her boys were protected after she was gone.

Gabe had never been particularly devout and hadn't been to Mass in years—in fact, the last time he'd gone had probably been Kyle's confirmation. But after the close call on the courthouse steps, he couldn't shake the feeling that his mother had been watching over him— just as she'd promised she would. And it was time he'd kept his promise to *her* to get his ass to church now and then.

As he knelt there, offering up a prayer of thanks that was long overdue, he tried not to remember the day she'd made her promise, tried to keep her voice from invading his head and bringing back all the pain he'd tried to suppress for years. Too bad it didn't work.

It was almost as if she were there beside him, smoothing his hair, the lilac-scented perfume she'd worn wrapping around him, a sensory hug that was a poor substitute for the real thing but was comforting nonetheless. He felt someone join him on the bench and the scent grew stronger. Startled, half expecting to see the ghost of his mother there beside him, his head snapped up.

But it wasn't Theresa Dawson kneeling beside him.

"Dad?" he whispered. "What are you doing here?"

His father sent a glance his way but then returned his gaze to the crucifix at the front of the church. "Promised your mother I would come to pray for you boys every week," he murmured. "And I have."

It was then that Gabe noticed that his father gently grasped one of his mother's old handkerchiefs in his fingers instead of a rosary. The delicate cloth still held the scent of her perfume.

"I didn't know," Gabe said softly.

His father took a deep breath and let it out slowly. "Well, it was between her and me. Didn't see the need to talk to you boys about it."

That Gabe could believe. The Old Man didn't talk much about anything, let alone the wife he'd buried years before. Maybe if Mac had been a little more open about what he'd gone through in the years since, the relationship between him and Kyle might not have been pretty much nonexistent until Kyle had returned to town and they'd been forced to deal with shit. They still had a way to go toward repairing things, but Gabe was relieved as hell to finally see the Old Man making an effort.

"What?" Mac grumbled.

Realizing he was staring, Gabe looked away. "Nothing. Sorry, sir."

They knelt in silence for several minutes more before Mac reached over and clasped Gabe on the shoulder in the closest thing to a hug Gabe had received from him since he was a teenager. Then, in a move that would've made Gabe keel over in shock had he not been kneeling, his father put his hand on the side of Gabe's head and pulled him close to press a kiss to his hair. Without a word, he rose and left the pew, leaving Gabe kneeling there with his mouth agape.

But Gabe didn't have any time to mull over what the hell had just happened before his phone began to vibrate. He glanced down to see Tom's number. He instinctively started to answer it, but the many lectures they'd received from their father every Sunday before Mass, including a very specific outline of what would happen to each and every one of Mac Dawson's sons if they *dared* to be disruptive in church and disrespect their mother, the priest, and God himself made Gabe send it to voice mail. He resumed his prayer, but a few seconds later, the phone began vibrating again. With a sigh, Gabe crossed himself, rose, and left the church before answering the phone so as not to disturb any of the other parishioners who were still praying.

"Hey, Bro, what's up?" Before Tom could answer, he went on in a rush, "You'll never guess who I just bumped into at the church. The Old Man. I guess he goes every week—"

"I'm coming to pick you up," Tom interrupted.

"I'm fine," Gabe assured him. "Doc Morales cleared me to drive yesterday during my follow-up visit."

"Then meet me at Elle's house."

Panic squeezed Gabe's lungs and he picked up the

pace, damning his leg for not fully cooperating with his need for haste. "Why? What's wrong? Is she okay?"

"That's what I want to make sure of," Tom told him. "I can't get in touch with her. I already have a car in route. How far are you from her house?"

"Five minutes, tops," he said, suppressing a groan as he jumped behind the wheel of his 1970 Dodge Charger that he and his brothers had lovingly restored when they were teenagers. He normally used his beat-up pickup truck when he was tooling around town while off-duty, but the truck's clutch was tricky and would've been hell on his leg, but he was damned glad to have the extra horsepower at the moment. "Just so you know, I don't plan on sticking to the speed limit."

"No worries," Tom assured him. "You might even get there before the cars that've already been dispatched."

"So you gonna tell me what the hell happened?" Gabe demanded over the growl of the Charger's engine as he started her up.

"Billy Monroe is dead," Tom informed him.

Gabe's stomach sank. His mouth was dry when he asked, "What? How?"

He heard Tom's muffled curse and something about a turn signal. Apparently, he was en route to Elle's house as well. A moment later, his brother replied, "Explosion this morning. Took out his house and part of the neighbor's. The neighbors weren't home, but Billy wasn't so lucky."

"You're sure he was home?" Gabe said.

"Positive. The guys from Station Eleven got the fire put out and found his body inside. Well, part of it anyway."

Gabe breathed a harsh curse. "You think it was

Monroe? Do you think he found out Billy was supposed to come in tomorrow to give a statement?"

"If I was a betting man, that'd be what I'd put my money on," Tom admitted. "But I'd also bet that there's no way in hell we'll be able to prove it."

"Gotta be him," Gabe agreed. "There was no way he was gonna let Billy get away with turning against the family. He's not a 'forgive and forget' kind of guy."

"How close are you now?" Tom asked.

Gabe narrowed his eyes, glancing at the small green street signs that zipped past him as he sped toward her house. "Couple more blocks," he said, his heart racing faster the closer he got. Just then he saw the entrance to her subdivision and slowed slightly to take the turn. "Turning onto her street right now."

He didn't wait for his brother to respond before hanging up. He screeched to a halt outside her house and grabbed his service weapon from under the seat where he'd stowed it. He quickly checked the clip before getting out of the car and approaching the house, his Glock at the ready. When he got to her front door, he stood to one side and knocked loudly.

"Elle!" he called, his heart hammering. He pounded again on the door. "Elle, you okay?"

He was just about ready to kick open the fucking door when he heard the dead bolt turn and the door swung open to reveal Elle standing there in cutoff shorts, a T-shirt, and bare feet, her hair pulled back into a ponytail, tiny red spiral curls having slipped out to frame her face.

"Gabe?" she said, frowning. Her gaze darted over his shoulder to the other cars arriving, including Tom's. "What the hell...?"

"You okay?" Gabe panted, the pain in his leg cutting right through him now that his adrenaline was beginning to ebb.

"Yeah, I'm fine," she said, pushing open the screen door and coming out onto the porch with him. "Can't say the same about you. You look like shit."

He attempted a grin. "Aww, honey, you say the sweetest things."

"Elle okay?" Tom yelled.

Gabe nodded, shifting his weight off of his aching leg. "Yeah, she's good."

When Tom turned away to deal with the other arriving deputies, Elle pulled open the screen door and pegged Gabe with a no-nonsense look. "So," she said, "would you like to come in? And by that I mean, 'Get your ass inside and explain what the hell is going on.'"

"How could I refuse such a kind request?" Gabe mumbled, limping past her. "But we'll have to wait for Tom. I only know the CliffsNotes version."

A few minutes later, he was sitting in Elle's kitchen with a cup of coffee, trying to keep his hand from shaking as he lifted the cup to his lips. Gabe wasn't sure if it was the pain affecting him or his fear for Elle's safety. Either way, he wasn't going anywhere in the near future.

As soon as Tom joined them, looking a little drained and out of sorts himself, he filled them in on Billy Monroe, not sparing any of the gory details. Elle dropped into the chair next to Gabe's and shook her head.

"Poor Billy," she murmured. It was only then Gabe realized she'd been crying before they'd arrived, her eyes still a little red and puffy.

"I got this, Tom," Gabe said, jerking his chin toward

Elle. "I'm going to need to stick around for a few before I drive home anyway. I'll keep Elle company for a little while, check the place out, make sure she'll be fine before I leave." He glanced at Elle, "As long as that's okay with you."

She blinked at him for a moment as if trying to figure out a response. Finally, she shrugged. "Uh…yeah. Sure. I guess that's fine."

Gabe stayed at the table while she escorted Tom to the door but started to get up when she came back into the kitchen.

She motioned for him to sit back down. "I appreciate you guys racing here to check in on me, but as you can see, I'm fine."

"Why didn't you answer when Tom called you?" he asked, taking another sip of his coffee. He offered her a wry grin. "Could've saved you the hassle of us barging in."

"I'd turned my ringer off," she said softly, her voice catching a little. "I was going through some pictures and didn't exactly feel like talking to anyone."

He frowned at her a little. "Not happy memories, I take it?"

She attempted a smile that he supposed was meant to be brave, but her chin trembled a little when she explained, "It's the anniversary of my family's death."

Gabe cursed under his breath, feeling like a total ass. "I'm sorry, Elle. I didn't know." He drained the last of his coffee and got to his feet. "I'll take a quick look at the perimeter on my way out."

"Gabe!" she called after him as he limped toward her front door. "Gabe, wait!" She took a step toward him, her hand reaching out as if she might touch him, but then she let her arm fall back to her side. "Please...don't go."

Gabe held her gaze for a long moment, trying to determine if her offer was sincere or if she was just being polite. Even though he was still on the fence, he gave her a terse nod and took a step toward her, wincing a little.

"Here," she said, taking hold of his arm and pulling it around her shoulders. "Is that better?"

He gulped, willing his body not to respond to the nearness of her, to the warmth of her arm wrapped around his waist, and cleared his throat a little before peering down into that enchanting, emerald gaze.

Holy hell.

Having her this close, pressed against his side, lending him her strength, felt a hell of a lot better than he cared to admit. Reflexively, his arm tightened around her shoulders, bringing her in closer.

Chapter 13

ELLE'S HEART HAMMERED IN HER CHEST, MAKING IT hard for her to breathe. Or maybe the difficulty breathing had something to do with the intensity of a certain aqua gaze boring into hers. Or the hard muscles of his chest beneath her fingertips where her hand lightly rested. Or *maybe* it had something to do with the fact that she could feel *his* heart hammering, too.

Oh God. Not good. Not good at all.

Why, oh why had she bailed on that shopping trip with her aunt?

She'd witnessed Gabe putting the moves on women over the years and had lost track of how many times she'd rolled her eyes in those moments, wondering how the silly, giggling bubbleheads could fall for such a transparent act.

But as their gazes locked, what she saw there wasn't the usual cocky self-assuredness she was used to seeing in his eyes. If she'd had to hazard a guess, she'd say he actually looked...torn. Or tortured. And unlike the tired come-ons she was used to, the uncertainty she saw now that he'd let his guard down was dangerously close to completely disarming her defenses again.

When that gaze flicked down to her lips, her breath caught, and the small shudder of anticipation, of longing, for the kiss that seemed to be just moments away no doubt completely betrayed the sudden and unexpected fantasies of where such a kiss would lead if she gave in. The heat she felt creeping into her cheeks made her drag her gaze away from his mouth before she gave into temptation.

To her immense relief, when she took a step forward, he followed, allowing her to lead him into the living room, where her photo albums and loose photos were scattered across the sofa, coffee table and floor.

She slipped out from under his arm and hastily began to clear a spot for him on the sofa. "Sorry. Let me just get these out of the way."

"Is this you?"

Her head snapped up to see Gabe holding a picture of a little girl with red pigtails and a lopsided grin standing on a beach on a bright summer day. "No," she said, looking away so he wouldn't see the tears that sprung to her eyes. "That's my sister Eve. That picture is from our family vacation to Sanibel when she was ten."

"She was a cutie," he said, easing down onto the sofa. "You two look a lot alike. Is this your other sister?"

Elle glanced up at the photo he held out for her to see. "Yes. That's Erin at her First Communion. She died a month later."

"I'm sorry." Gabe's voice was so gentle, Elle had to swallow past the tears to keep from completely breaking down. "I know what it was like when we almost lost Joe after he was wounded in Afghanistan. I can't imagine what you went through—what you still go through."

"Thanks." Elle set the photos she'd gathered on the coffee table and took a seat next to him on the sofa. "I'd like to say it gets easier every year, but it doesn't."

Gabe leaned forward, sifting through the pictures a

little before pulling one from the stack and turning to Elle with a grin. "Now, this one I know is you."

Elle grimaced before she could catch herself. The picture of a gawky, gangly teenager with unruly red hair was definitely her. She snatched it from his grasp with a little laugh. "Yeah, let's just forget that period of my life ever happened."

"Are you kidding me?" he said, reclining against the pillows and draping one arm casually over the back of the sofa. "You were adorable."

"Liar," she laughed. "Thank God I grew into my legs."

Gabe gave Elle's legs the once-over slowly, his gaze as soft and sensual as a lover's caress, then grinned. "I thought they were great even back then, but I certainly won't complain now."

"Uh-huh. Right…" she drawled, trying to ignore the way his gaze sent white-hot heat zipping through her veins. "So what you're saying is dating all those cheerleaders back in high school was just a front, and in actuality, you were secretly into girls who looked like flamingos? Gee, Gabe, who knew?"

Gabe shrugged. "Oh yeah, I'm full of surprises."

She gave him a wry grin. "So I'm learning."

He chuckled but quickly sobered, his expression becoming serious as his gaze traveled over her face. "You really have no idea how beautiful you are, do you?"

His praise was so obviously sincere that Elle looked away before he could see her blushing. "If you want to see someone really beautiful," she said, sifting through the pictures to avoid acknowledging his compliment, "take a look at this woman."

Gabe took the picture she held out and whistled appreciatively. "Damn."

"That's my mom," she told him, curling up beside him on the couch and leaning against his shoulder to better see the photo. Her mother's smile was so vibrant, her eyes so full of happiness, it was almost like she was looking back at Elle from the photograph, sharing an inside joke.

"She was gorgeous," Gabe agreed. "You can tell she and your aunt Charlotte are sisters. And that she's your mom. You have her smile."

"She was the kind of woman who took over the room when she walked in," Elle told him wistfully. "Made everything brighter, more beautiful. My dad used to say that the sun shone brighter when his Evelyn smiled."

"It sounds like she was a pretty incredible person," Gabe mused. "I'm sorry I didn't get the chance to know her."

Elle sighed and gently took the photo from his grasp, gazing at it for a long moment before taking a deep, shaky breath as a few more tears escaped. A moment later, she felt Gabe's fingers clasp hers in a comforting squeeze. It was then Elle realized she'd rested her head on his shoulder while gazing at the photo. Embarrassed for quite literally crying on his shoulder, she abruptly sat up and wiped at her eyes.

"I'm sorry," she muttered. "You didn't come here to listen to me cry about my family."

"No," he admitted. "I didn't. But I'm glad I'm here." He reached up and wiped at the tears that stubbornly continued to flow down her cheeks. "And I'll stay as long as you'd like."

Elle turned her gaze down to where his other hand still tenderly clasped hers. Part of her wanted him to stay, enjoyed the way he caressed the back of her hand, loved the way his deep voice soothed her. But part of her was terrified of what might happen if he did.

She wasn't naive. She fully realized that she was in an emotionally vulnerable place at the moment and that the longer he sat there, being so damnably sensitive and sincere, the more likely it was that she was going to find herself in his arms again—and this time she had a feeling neither of them would be holding back.

And yet…

She settled back against his shoulder and twined her fingers with his. "It was a car accident," she began after a few moments of companionable silence. "I was supposed to be with them, but I'd been at the library with my friend Stacy doing research for a school project and had lost track of time. When I realized what time it was, I called my mom and told her to go on without me, that I'd just have Stacy's mom drop me off at the restaurant where we were supposed to be having dinner for my dad's birthday."

Gabe's thumb continued to smooth over her skin, but he didn't say a word.

She paused, remembering every detail about that day down to what she'd been wearing, what kind of car Stacy's mom had been driving when they came upon the traffic jam, the way her stomach had dropped when they finally made it past the wreckage of an automobile that was barely recognizable as the same kind of car her parents drove.

"I saw the wreckage," she finally continued. "They

were working on the car with the jaws of life as the police officer directed us past the scene. I didn't realize it was my parents' car until I saw a shoe on the pavement that looked like the ones Eve always insisted on wearing. They were hot-pink Mary Janes." Elle laughed a little, but unshed tears distorted the sound. "Nobody wore hot-pink Mary Janes. Especially not a redhead."

"Jesus," Gabe breathed.

Elle blew out a long, bracing breath. "I started screaming," she told him. "It was so loud and frantic, Stacy's mom pulled over and one of the police officers came racing over to see what the hell was going on. They told me they were trying to get my dad out of the car. He lived for a couple of days—long enough for me to say good-bye. They wouldn't let me see my mom or sisters. I never got to say good-bye to them. Not even at the funeral. I'm told it was better that way."

"Did they ever figure out what had caused the accident?" he asked.

"Yeah," she told him, not bothering to check her bitterness. "A guy hopped up on cocaine had plowed into them with his pickup truck. He walked away without a scratch. He was convicted, of course, but got out in a year. He killed my entire family and only served one *fucking* year. Where's the justice in that?"

"I don't know, honey," Gabe admitted. "Sounds shitty to me."

"That's why I became a prosecutor," she told him. "I wanted to do everything I could to put bastards like him behind bars."

"I'm sure your family would be proud of you," he told her. "You do one hell of a job—even in spite of irredeemable jackasses who nearly ruined one of your cases."

Elle laughed, glad for a little levity, but her laughter died on a sob. She squeezed her eyes shut, trying to hold back the additional tears that threatened to break forth now that she was actually talking about that horrific time in her life. She'd refused to talk about any of it after coming to live with Charlotte, had sat with the grief counselor for hours of therapy, willing to talk about anything and everything except that time. But not today. For some reason, she *wanted* to tell Gabe her story, to make him understand why she was the way she was. Why it even mattered that he understand she couldn't say. But it did.

And when he shifted, putting an arm around her and pulling her close against him, she didn't resist. Instead, she wrapped her arms around his torso, buried her face in his chest, and let the tears come.

She had no idea how long she cried, how long he silently held her, smoothing a hand up and down her back, soothing her. At one point, his arms tightened around her and he pressed a kiss to the top of her head. Unfortunately, his kindness caused her to cry harder.

Sometime later, when her tears had finally subsided, she took a deep breath and let it out slowly. It was only then that she realized the room had grown darker, cast in shadow now that the morning sunlight was no longer streaming through her bay window.

"What time is it?" she asked, abruptly sitting up.

Gabe checked his watch. "About two."

Her eyes went wide. "Oh, Gabe—I'm so sorry. I've kept you here way too long. I can't imagine sitting here with me for a couple of hours while I sniffled all over your shirt was quite what you had in mind for your day." She brushed at a damp spot on his shoulder where her tears still hadn't dried.

He lifted her chin with the edge of his hand. "I wouldn't have wanted to be anywhere else." But as if to contradict his words, his stomach grumbled, making them both chuckle. "Okay, so maybe I could've used some lunch. But you needed somebody to listen, and, hey, I have ears."

Elle laughed, wiping away the last of her tears, and got to her feet. "Thanks, Gabe. For being here."

"Ah," he said, pushing up from the sofa with a knowing grin. "I guess this is where you say, 'And by that, I mean, get the hell out now.'"

Elle's shoulders sagged when she realized how ungrateful she sounded. "Oh God—I'm sorry. That's not what I meant—"

He held up a hand, halting her words. "How about you let me take you to lunch and we call it even?"

She glanced down at her clothes. "I'm a mess, Gabe. I can't go anywhere looking like this."

"Sure you can," he said, giving her that dimpled smile that made her insides flutter no matter how hard she fought it. "I know just the place."

————

Gabe chanced a glance at Elle in the seat beside him, the air from the open windows of the Charger whipping loose curls about and freeing more of their comrades from the confines of her ponytail holder, giving her a reckless, wild look he found damned alluring.

Elle was a beautiful woman whose appearance was impeccable every single day when she was working, giving her a very intense, powerful presence. So seeing her a little disheveled and windblown got his blood pumping to all the *wrong* places.

She'd been worried about not being dressed appropriately to go anywhere for lunch, but in a white T-shirt that hugged her curves and cut-offs that showed off her long, shapely legs, she was gorgeous, in his opinion. As much as he was aching to feel her in his arms again, the last thing he wanted to do was come onto her like a total asshole when she was dealing with some seriously heavy emotional shit.

"So, where are we going?" she asked, frowning as she glanced around.

"Just be patient," he insisted, sending a grin her way. "It's okay to let someone else take the lead now and then, Elle."

"I'm not a control freak," she informed him. "I let other people take the lead all the time."

He glanced over at her, giving her a disbelieving look that made her laugh.

"Okay, okay. Fine! I'm a control freak. Happy now?"

He nodded. "Yeah." He was more than a little astonished to find that he actually *was* happy. For the first time since Chris's death, really. He'd had some moments of happiness, he guessed—and almost every one of them involved the incredible woman at his side.

But even those moments, as amazing as they'd been, and as often as he'd relived them in his mind, were nothing to what he felt just then with Elle at his side, grinning as she smoothed her curls back and closed her eyes, then turned her face into the wind. Knowing he'd been able to relieve her sorrow and suffering, even if for just a little while, made him feel like he could take on the whole goddamned world and come out on top.

He was actually disappointed when their destination came into view and he had to park the Charger. But then Elle's eyes opened, and she laughed and turned toward him, grinning from ear to ear, her green eyes sparkling with delight.

"You're kidding me!" she cried, gesturing toward the entrance to the county fairgrounds. "You can't go in there. You can barely walk."

"Hey, if there's a foot-long chili dog and a lemonade shakeup in it for me, I can manage a little hike around the fairgrounds." He got out of the car and came around to open her door. "Now, c'mon. You could use a little fun today, am I right?"

She seemed to hesitate for a moment, then nodded and hopped out. "But be prepared, I fully intend to kick your ass on the midway."

A few minutes later, they were settling onto a bench side by side with chili dogs and lemonade, the music from a nearby country music concert drowning out the conversations of those at the adjacent tables and giving him an excuse to lean toward Elle when he asked, "How's your lunch?"

She turned her head to answer and flushed when her nose nearly brushed against his. But she didn't back away before she said, "Delicious. Thank you."

When she still didn't pull back, Gabe's pulse began to race, and it was all he could do not to lean in just another inch and capture those full lips that were turned up in a sultry grin. But he forced himself to draw away and turn his attention back to his food. He was finally managing to break through her defenses. He sure as hell didn't want to ruin it by moving too fast. He wanted to savor every moment, every look, every caress.

And today was about her. He hadn't been joking when he'd said she needed to have a little fun. He knew the dark mood he always found himself in on the anniversary of his mother's death, and if there was anything he could do to spare Elle that kind of sorrow, he was glad to do it. It was worth it just to see her smile, hear her laugh.

As soon as they finished eating, they headed toward the midway where Elle made good on her threat to completely trounce him at the ring toss. But he paid her back by totally killing it at the shooting gallery — in spite of her efforts to throw off his shots by blowing in his ear. Which he had to admit, he didn't mind one damned bit.

"So how are you holding up?" she asked as they shared a bag of cotton candy, the sugar crystals clinging to her lips, tempting as hell.

He forced himself to look away and focus on where he was walking after he nearly plowed into a woman pushing a stroller. "I'm okay," he lied. His leg had gone from sore to throbbing, but he wasn't about to call it a day just yet.

Of course, she saw right through him. "Liar," she said with a laugh. "We should get you home."

"I'm fine," he insisted. "Besides, you haven't gone on any of the carnival rides."

Her brows shot up at this. "Are you serious? We're hardly teenagers, Gabe."

"So what?" he countered. "There's nothing that says grown men and women can't act like kids now and then." He gestured to an elderly couple climbing aboard the Ferris wheel. "They have at least a *couple* of years on us, don't you think?"

She grimaced a little. "The truth is, I'm afraid of heights. If I get stuck at the top of that thing, I'll have a total panic attack."

He gave her a disbelieving look. "You? Afraid? Don't believe it."

She shook her head, casting a nervous glance toward the Ferris wheel. "Believe it. I'm terrified."

"Would it help if I held your hand?" he asked, reaching tentatively for her fingertips. When he looked up from her hand, he was surprised to see her chest heaving with short, shallow breaths. He took a step closer, frowning with concern. "Hey, it's okay. We don't have to go if you're that scared."

She shook her head, her cheeks flooding with color. "No, it's not that. I, uh…" She pulled her fingertips from his grasp and took a step back, forcing a smile. "Let's go. I'll be fine."

"You sure?"

She shook her head with a tremulous little laugh. "No. Not at all. But I have to conquer this fear sometime, right?"

―∿―

A moment later, they were sitting in the Ferris wheel car, swaying gently as it stopped to allow others to board.

"Okay, I was wrong," she said, squeezing her eyes shut. "This was a bad idea. A really, *really* bad idea. I think I'm going to throw up."

"Oh God, don't do that," Gabe pleaded. "The poor kids beneath us will be traumatized for life."

She actually laughed a little, then took a deep breath and forced her eyes open. And immediately regretted it. "Oh crap. We're not even at the top yet."

"Hey," Gabe said softly. "Look at me." When she turned her head slowly toward him, finally meeting his soothing gaze, he gently grasped her chin. "I'm not going to let anything happen to you, Elle. I swear it."

Elle's stomach flipped end over end at the intensity of his promise. "I believe you."

His thumb smoothed lightly over her skin and his gaze dropped down to her lips. But as his head dipped ever so slightly toward hers, the jolt of the Ferris wheel made her gasp and he pulled back.

"I'm sorry, honey," he said. "I'll flag the guy down and let him know we want to get off."

She shook her head. "No. I can do this." Then, impulsively, she reached for his hand, twining her fingers with his, and found it did help to know he was there beside her, that he had sworn to keep her safe.

She was just about to tell him so when she suddenly caught sight of a familiar face. One of Jeb Monroe's sons—Jeremy—was standing across from the Ferris wheel, his arms crossed over his chest as he leaned against a low fence post, staring up at her.

"Oh God," she whispered, her skin prickling with fear that had nothing to do with heights. "He's here."

"Who?" Gabe asked, following her line of sight.

"Jeremy Monroe."

"I'm sure he was probably just visiting the fair and happened to see us up here," Gabe assured her, but she could feel the tension in his muscles and knew he wasn't as unconcerned as he appeared.

When she gave him an irritated look, he raised her hand to his lips and pressed a lingering kiss to her palm that sent a jolt of desire through her body. "I think you're trying to distract me, Gabe Dawson."

He winked at her. "Is it working?"

She rolled her eyes and turned her attention back to where Jeremy Monroe had been watching them, but he was gone, having vanished into the crowds milling around the midway.

"I made you a promise, Elle," Gabe reminded her, caressing her skin in a maddeningly sensual motion. "I'll do whatever necessary to keep you safe."

She turned to meet his gaze, the heat she saw there practically searing her skin. Or maybe that was just the warmth spreading through her body, a fire that burned so intensely Elle worried she might spontaneously combust if she didn't soon get some relief.

Chapter 14

"They're at the fair."

"The fair?" Jeb repeated, not quite sure he'd heard his son correctly.

"Yes, sir," Jeremy assured him. "Looks to me like they're on a date."

Jeb Monroe shook his head. He *knew* the deputy and that whore were fucking each other. Well, all the more reason to provide her with a little reminder of how fleeting life could be. She'd clearly forgotten what it was like to mourn a lost family member. But *he* remembered, remembered every day.

"Do you have the items I gave you?" he demanded of his son.

"Yes, sir."

"Well, then, why the hell are you on the phone with me, boy?" Jeb raged. "Get your ass moving and complete your mission."

"Yes, sir."

Jeb hung up and turned to storm from his study but came to an abrupt halt when he saw his wife standing in the doorway, her eyes swollen and puffy. "What do you want?" he sighed. He'd grown tired of her continued uselessness. If she was going to mourn their son, she needed to channel her grief and do something productive—like exacting justice on those who'd taken him from them—instead of wallowing around the house, looking like hell.

"Where's Jeremy?" she demanded. "Where is my son?"

"He's doing his duty. Which is more than I can say for you." He looked her up and down, his expression twisting with disgust at how she'd let herself go. "When was the last time you bothered to make yourself presentable?"

She clenched her fists at her sides and lifted her chin at an angle he didn't altogether care for. "What are you making Jeremy do for you? What is this 'mission' you've sent him on?"

"If I'd wanted you to know, I would've already told you," he growled, charging forward and grabbing her by the arm, shoving her through the doorway. "If you want to see justice for our boys, you'll let me handle it and not question my judgment."

He slammed the door to his study and turned back to his computer. He generally wasn't a fan of the Internet, didn't trust it. Too many idiots voicing their ignorant opinions or spreading rumors and lies. But he had to admit it came in handy now and then, and had proven to be a useful tool for sharing his vision.

Jeb grinned as he scrolled through the newspaper article he'd printed and had given to Jeremy to deliver. Elle McCoy once knew what it was like to lose those she cared about. It was too bad she'd forgotten what that felt like, the emptiness such a loss leaves in one's soul. Well, she'd soon remember. He wanted her to suffer for a while before he took his final revenge upon her. And this little bit of news was exactly what he needed to make that suffering complete. It seemed that when he managed to take what mattered most from Mac Dawson, the loss would touch more than one heart...

—᠕᠕—

"Thanks for today," Elle said as she and Gabe headed back through the midway. "I appreciate you keeping my mind off of things."

Gabe shrugged but grinned down at her. "Least I could do."

She sent a sidelong glance his way. His limp was more pronounced than it'd been earlier that day. She'd suggested leaving several times, but he'd been determined that she have a good time to keep her mind off the anniversary of her family's car accident.

"Even so, I appreciate it," she told him, slipping her hand into his. "It means a lot to me."

He nudged her playfully with his shoulder. "Then my job here is done."

God, she hoped not...

He'd been a perfect gentleman the entire day—coming to her rescue when he'd thought she was in danger, listening patiently and holding her for hours while she grieved her family, whisking her away to the fair to relieve some of her sorrow and bring a little happiness to her heavy heart. The most he'd done was kiss her hand a few times.

And it was driving her crazy. The time for being sweet and gentlemanly was over. She wanted him. Desperately and dangerously. The realization socked her so hard in the gut, her breath caught in her chest. She'd been fighting the sexual tension, not willing to let her heart get broken again. But Gabe was no longer the boy he'd been when he'd unknowingly trampled a teenage girl's fragile heart. He was a man—and a far kinder, more caring one than she'd allowed herself to see before now.

She wanted to feel those amazing lips on hers, wanted his hands on her skin, wanted to feel him inside her.

But she knew there was no way he was going to make the first move this time. Not after the horrible and hurtful things she'd said to him the last time he'd tried. If she could take back her words, she would, but as her Aunt Charlotte always said, that horse was out of the barn. She'd have to eat a little humble pie and make the first move.

Elle cleared her throat. "So..." she said, trying to sound nonchalant, "aside from the appearance of the son of a homicidal separatist and me nearly yakking on the Ferris wheel, not bad, as far as first dates go."

He peered down at her from out of the corner of his eye, lifting a single brow, and gave her one of his cockeyed grins. "Was this a date then?"

She felt her cheeks growing warm and would've edged away from him to put a little respectable distance between them had he not released her hand to drape an arm around her shoulders and pull her closer against him.

Emboldened, she slid her arm around his waist and forced her tone to be casual and lighthearted when she replied, "I think this qualifies."

"Well then, Ms. McCoy," he said, "I should probably get you home before we break curfew."

She laughed. "I can't imagine a little thing like a curfew ever mattered to you in the least, Dawson."

He lifted *both* brows at her this time. "Oh yeah? I'll have you know I made it a point to always get my dates home no later than five minutes before their curfews." He shrugged, qualifying his accomplishment a bit as he added, "That made it a lot easier to convince the parents to let me hang out with their daughters after they'd gone to bed…"

Elle shook her head on a sigh, trying to keep her mind from wandering to what might happen once he got *her* home. "Do you ever *not* get what you want, Dawson?"

"That remains to be seen." He turned his eyes down to her, giving her a look so heavy with meaning Elle's pulse kicked into high gear.

The fact that he hadn't answered her question with his trademark arrogance told her he was still keeping his distance, waiting for her to give the green light. As they approached his Charger, her heart hammered in her chest.

C'mon, Elle, c'mon. Make a move. This isn't high school… You know he wants you. Show him you want him, too.

Gabe opened the door for her and turned to hand her in, but instead of sliding into the passenger seat, Elle impulsively threw her arms around his neck and kissed him hard on the mouth. She felt his initial surprise in the hard line of his mouth, but it lasted only a split second before his arms came around her, pulling her into the curve of his body so tightly that she was pulled up onto her toes.

She teased his mouth with the tip of her tongue. His lips parted on a groan and his tongue plunged deep, stroking hers with rhythmic insistence. The kiss was savage, hungry. His hands slid down, gripping her bottom and pressing her against him. She ground her hips against his, another moan of need escaping her before she could check it.

He abruptly broke their kiss. "Jesus, Elle," he practically growled. "You're killin' me here."

Holding his gaze, she slid her hand between them, over the rock-hard bulge beneath his zipper. "Then we'd better get home. Now."

His eyes snapped shut and he shuddered, cursing a blue streak. "Get in."

It wasn't a request.

Without a word, she hopped into the car, not entirely surprised when he seemed to make it around to the drivers' side within seconds. His lips were pressed together in a harsh line as he started up the car and threw it into reverse.

Elle watched him intently as they drove. He kept his eyes on the road, his hands gripping the steering wheel so hard his knuckles were white. "Gabe? Is everything alright?"

When the grim line of his mouth turned down in a frown and he remained silent, she reached over and placed her hand on his thigh. He flinched at her touch and she saw him swallow hard.

"Gabe?" she prompted. "Are you okay?"

Was he okay? Was he okay?

He was in fucking agony! *Shit.* His cock was pounding like a fucking drum. The twenty-minute drive back to her house was going to be sheer torture unless he could get rid of the raging boner pressing against his zipper. But he sure as shit wasn't going to tell her the thought of burying himself balls deep in her sweet heat was making his hands tremble and his mouth dry.

He was *nervous*, for fuck's sake. What the hell was *that* all about? He hadn't been this jacked up the night Suzanne Parsons had talked him into handing over his virginity at Tracy Wilkins's seventeenth birthday party, when they'd stolen away to the barn's hayloft. Okay, so she hadn't exactly had to twist his arm, but *still*.

He shifted in his seat to try to relieve some of the ache and finally chanced a glance at Elle. "Yeah, I'm good."

She gave him her "bullshit" look. "Liar."

He quickly looked back to the road and eased off the accelerator, suddenly realizing he was going about twenty-five miles per hour over the speed limit. He risked letting go of the steering wheel with one hand to wipe some perspiration at his hairline. "I'm..." He paused, not sure what to say.

She withdrew her hand from his thigh and pulled back, her spine stiffening a little, as if she was offended. "Sorry," she said stiffly. "I shouldn't have come on so strong. It's not like me to be that forward. I just thought..." Her words trailed off and she heaved a harsh sigh. "I just thought..."

What the hell? She thought he was having second thoughts because she'd made the first move?

"Jesus, Elle—are you kidding me?" he managed, his voice shot to shit. "That was sexy as hell. *Everything* about you is sexy as hell. I'm hangin' on by a thread here just sitting beside you."

Her voice was little more than a whisper when she said, "Oh."

Now that he'd started the ball rolling, though, he

couldn't shut the hell up. "Seeing you in those cutoffs all day has been torture. All I've been able to think about is you wrapping those gorgeous, long legs around me. But I respect you way too much to have made a move on you when we were back at your house. Shit. Taking you to the fair was just as much to distract me as it was to help you find a little happiness today. But when you kissed me… Well, let's just say, I'm not so sure how much longer I can be a gentleman."

"Good."

He chanced another look at her. "What?"

"Good," she said, louder this time. "I don't want you to be a gentleman right now, Gabe Dawson."

Ah, Christ.

He glanced around, getting his bearings. They were still fifteen minutes from her house. A good thirty from his. At the moment, they were surrounded by farm fields and woods. A few yards up the road, a service access road obscured by overgrowth caught his eye and he jerked the wheel, impulsively turning off onto it. He recognized the road in an instant. It led to an abandoned church that had fallen into disrepair years before, after the congregation had disbanded.

"Where are we going?" Elle asked, as he carefully navigated the unpaved rural road.

"Church," he ground out.

"Sorry, *what*?"

"The place is long forgotten," he explained. "We don't even have to check it out from time to time to shoo away kids or squatters anymore. Nobody even remembers it's back here."

Even so, he pulled the Charger around to the back of

the structure, just on the off chance that anyone would drive back here after taking a wrong turn, and turned off the engine.

"Gabe, what—"

Elle didn't get a chance to finish her sentence. Gabe reached across the space between them and grasped the nape of her neck, his mouth crashing down on hers. Her lips instantly parted, accepting his kiss with abandon. Needing to get her in his arms before he lost his mind, he broke the kiss abruptly and shoved open his door.

She was already out of the car and standing beside it by the time he got around to her side. She was trembling a little, her green eyes wide as she glanced around the darkening woods. For a moment, he wondered if stopping out here was a good idea, but then she took a step forward to meet him, her arms going around his neck and pulling him down to the bliss of her lips.

Emboldened, his hands began to roam, slipping under the hem of her T-shirt to smooth over the soft skin of her back. She sighed as he left her lips to press kisses along the curve of her throat. When he made it to the sensitive area where neck and shoulder met, she gasped but grasped his head on either side, keeping him where he was.

"Should we get back inside?" she asked, breathless.

Before he could even respond, she was opening up the door and climbing into the massive backseat. He didn't hesitate to follow, slamming the door behind him. The moment he was inside, he reached for her, pulling her onto his lap so she was straddling him, and found her lips again. His hands smoothed over the creamy skin of her thighs, loving the way his touch made her moan and shiver as she kissed him hungrily.

And then, holy hell, she left his mouth to trace the line of his jaw with her tongue until she reached his earlobe, which she nipped lightly, making him groan. The little minx chuckled at his reaction and pulled back enough to grin at him. Then, bless her sweet heart, she grabbed the hem of her T-shirt and pulled it over her head, tossing it onto the seat beside them.

He wanted to say something seductive and charming, but the breath had left his lungs, making it impossible to speak.

When she reached behind her, unfastening her bra to let it slowly slide down her arms, all he could do was swallow hard as he took in the beautiful, perfect breasts before him. He knew he'd caught a glimpse of them the night after Chris had died, but they'd been in his completely darkened room. Now, with the twilight allowing him enough light to see just how beautiful and full they were, Gabe couldn't help the slow grin that curved his mouth.

Careful to take his time and savor the moment, he reached up to Elle's cheek, running the back of his fingers along the curve of her jaw and along her neck, where her pulse pounded so powerfully he could see it beating beneath her skin. Then his fingers traced a path along her collarbone to the swell of her left breast. Elle's head dropped back with a little moan as he reached her already-erect nipple, which seemed to harden even more at his touch.

"Please, Gabe," she whispered.

He didn't have to ask what she was asking for. He lifted her breast and leaned forward to bring it into his mouth. He sucked hard, grazing her nipple with his teeth, causing her to gasp in pleasure. When his tongue swirled against the rosy tip, she moaned and ground her hips against his groin. With a groan, he switched to the other breast, his teeth grazing her skin a little harder as he pulled back, not bothering to hide his grin when she cried out his name.

Then, without a word, she began to fumble with the buttons of his shirt, her brows coming together in an adorable frown when her fingers wouldn't work as efficiently as she'd like. He joined in, making short work of his shirt and tossing it onto the floor, and pulled his T-shirt over his head and adding it to the pile.

Then he dragged her close, until her breasts were pressed against his bare chest, and ravaged her mouth once more, determined to kiss her until she was breathless. When she suddenly broke their kiss and pulled away, they both were panting.

For a moment he thought something was wrong when Elle opened the door and climbed out. But she was smiling when she turned back. "You said no one comes back here."

He wasn't quite sure what she had in mind until she unfastened the button on her cutoffs and slowly slid down the zipper. He gulped, his eyes hungry as he watched her oh-so-slowly slide the cutoffs over her hips to reveal a tiny scrap of white panties.

"Oh sweet Jesus," he murmured, scrambling out of the backseat in an instant, gathering her into his arms and kissing the hell out of her as her fingers worked on the button of his jeans. It popped open and his mind barely registered that the zipper had slid down. But when he felt her slip her hand between them and grasp him, he nearly lost his shit right then and there.

He sent up a curse and squeezed his eyes shut, clenching his teeth.

"Do you like this?" she murmured, pressing kisses to his chest. Her hand slid a little lower, cupping his sac and stealing any response that came to mind. A moment later, she slid his jeans over his hips and shoved them down his thighs. "How about this?"

He opened his eyes and looked down just in time to see her take him into her mouth.

Holy. Fucking. Hell.

His legs turned to jelly and he ass-planted onto the front passenger seat, but that apparently just gave her more access. She sucked him hard, taking him deep, her hand working his shaft at the base. When she drew back enough for her tongue to circle the tip of him, he jerked, an orgasm rapidly building at the base of his spine.

"Elle, stop," he demanded, gently taking her head in his hands. He blew out a harsh string of curses when she merely lifted her eyes defiantly and took him full into her mouth again. He groaned deep in his chest and his head fell back, his hips beginning to thrust. She loved the power she had over him at that moment, the pleasure she saw in his handsome face as he braced himself, gripping the headrest of the front seat with one hand and the dashboard with the other.

Dear God, he was a beautiful man. She'd always thought him devastatingly handsome, but since coming to know him better in the last few weeks and getting beyond the cocky facade he wore like a shield, in her eyes, he was the most beautiful man she'd ever seen.

The muscles in his neck and arms bulged with the effort to keep from coming. When the head of his penis began to weep, the salty taste of him tingling her tongue, she withdrew with one long, hard suck that made him swallow a cry.

In the next moment, he was sweeping her off her feet to switch places with her, tearing off her panties with such haste that she heard the satin tear, but she didn't care. As close as he'd been to coming, she expected him to plunge into her and nearly bowed off the seat when she felt the flick of his tongue against her clit.

"Oh God," she gasped when his tongue teased lightly, tickling and tasting. He pulled back at her words and her eyes popped open to make sure everything was okay, only to find him giving her a self-satisfied grin as he peered at her. "Gabe?"

"I want to look at you," he said. "I want to see your face when I make you come."

She opened her mouth to inquire exactly how he planned to make her come when he was just kneeling there grinning at her, but then she felt a long finger ease into her and his thumb brushed her clit, making her arch. As his thumb moved in a slow, sensual motion, his finger moved within her, searching. And then—

"Holy shit!" she cried as a sensation so intense shook her to her bones.

"That's it," he encouraged as his tempo increased, making her writhe against his hand. "Do you like that, Elle?"

Did she like it? Was he kidding?

"Oh God, yes!" she panted, leaning back on her elbows. Between the onslaught of sensation from the way he was working her clit and stroking her G-spot, she felt like her entire body was about to shatter into a million pieces. It briefly crossed her mind that she shouldn't let go completely, that she should keep her guard up. After all, this could be just a one-time thing, a fling that both of them had been longing for—no matter how much she now realized she wanted it to be more. Even if Gabe's reputation with women had been exaggerated, he was still not one for commitment. But then, neither was she.

But as soon as the thoughts had crossed her mind, the intensity of the pleasure Gabe was eliciting pushed them away, making it impossible for her not to completely give herself over to the moment.

"Don't stop," she managed.

His voice was deeper, his breathing ragged when he said, "Don't stop what, Elle? Say it."

Her head thrashed from side to side as her pleasure began to peak. "Don't stop touching me," she ordered. "Don't stop—"

She arched off the seat as she came, not able to stifle her cry as light exploded in her head.

Elle expected him to withdraw then, but instead he rasped, "Come here."

When she rose up, he leaned forward, taking her breast in his mouth, alternately scraping her nipple with his teeth and teasing it with his tongue as he slipped a second finger inside her, thrusting rapidly.

She was shocked to feel another release building again almost immediately. "Oh God, oh God," she panted. "Gabe!"

He released her breast to capture her lips in a brief,

savage kiss, then ground out, "What do you want me to do to you, Elle? Tell me. I'm not going any further unless you tell me."

She moaned as her stomach muscles tightened, her head spinning, her orgasm seconds away. This time her cry was almost a whimper, the pleasure so intense she wanted to weep.

"Tell me, Elle," he demanded, finally withdrawing and pulling her gently to her feet, then pressing her against the car. He lifted her leg and hooked it around his hip, then took his cock in his hand and rubbed the head of it against her sensitive clit, sending a powerful aftershock through her. "What do you want?"

"I want…" She was panting, writhing, the need to feel him inside her so powerful she couldn't even think coherently.

He positioned himself at her entrance, sliding in just enough to make his presence known. "Do you want this? Do you want me inside you?"

"God, yes!" she moaned.

He pressed in just a fraction more. "How's this? Is this what you want, Elle?"

"More," she gasped, hooking her legs around his hips, urging him on.

Suddenly, he thrust deep, filling her almost to the point of pain. She'd known he was large, remembered from when they'd made out a year ago, confirmed it when she'd taken him into her hand and then her mouth. But she still gasped.

"What now?" he asked, beginning to withdraw, only to thrust hard again. "This?"

She nodded frantically. "Yes. More. Harder."

His fingers dug into her hips as he thrust faster and harder. "God, it feels good inside you."

And yet as soon as he said it, he withdrew. She frowned, confused, feeling suddenly *empty* when he bent as if to pull up his pants. "Gabe?"

When he rose back to his feet, she realized what he'd been doing even before he ground out, "Condom."

Then he was sliding back inside her, joining their bodies again in that savage, passionate abandon that made her mind reel. And then her senses were spiraling out of control, and once more, she shattered apart.

Gabe's tempo slowed, his thrusts longer, more languid now. She opened her eyes—not having realized she'd even closed them at some point—and the heat in his gaze melted her. He was peering down at her with such reverence she suddenly felt unworthy of such admiration.

"You're beautiful," he managed to grind out through clenched teeth, his muscles beginning to bunch as she'd witnessed before. She wanted to touch him, hold him at that moment, feel him pressed against her as he came. Wrapping her legs tighter around him, she slipped her arms around his neck, pulling him close against her, chest to chest, belly to belly as his arms encircled her.

His breath grew harsher, more ragged, and he buried his face in the curve of her neck, in the mass of curls that had come loose from her ponytail. Then he groaned, long and deep, as he finally let go. "God, you're so beautiful."

When he went completely still, she held him, smoothing her hands lightly over his shoulders as his breath sawed in and out of his lungs, hot on her skin. It was only then she realized they were both covered in sweat, the heavy summer air clinging to them, slickening their skin.

Finally, his hold on her eased and she pulled back enough to take his face in her hands and press a slow kiss to his lips. The kiss was languid, unhurried, lips and tongues teasing and searching. When the kiss ended, he traced a finger along the swell of her breast, a slow grin curving his lips.

"That was even more incredible than I'd always imagined," he murmured.

Her hands continued to roam over his skin, loving the feel of him beneath her fingertips. She could've said the same. He'd been the subject of her fantasies even when she'd been rebuffing his advances. But she'd never imagined *this*. Not in her wildest dreams.

"What now?" she whispered, nipping his dimpled chin with her teeth.

He groaned and pulled out slowly, then turned away slightly as he removed the condom and tied it off. "Oh, honey," he chuckled. "I've got a few ideas. But maybe we should head home first."

He bent and pulled his jeans back on, wincing a little as he adjusted his still-erect penis.

"Okay," she agreed as he went to the trunk of the Charger, "but not my house."

He grabbed some tissues and a few other things and came back around. He was frowning as he handed her the tissues so she could clean up some before getting dressed. "My house then."

As soon as he said it, she cringed, realizing she'd totally just invited herself to his place. "I didn't mean to presume," she said in a rush. "I can just go to my aunt's."

He gave her a chastising look. "Seriously, Elle? Do you really think I want to dump you on Charlotte's doorstep after what just happened? I thought we were past that perception of me."

She felt the heat rising to her cheeks and finished wiping herself off, depositing the tissues in a small plastic trash bag he held out before saying, "We are. I am. I just didn't want you to think I have any expectations."

"Well, *I* do," he assured her, dragging on his T-shirt and giving her a pointed look. "I expect for you to give me a shot to prove I'm the kind of man who deserves you."

Her heart sank, realizing how much her misperception had hurt him. "I agree I owe you that much."

"It's settled then," he said with a sharp nod. "You're coming home with me. But mind if I ask why you don't *want* to go to your house?"

"I don't want to be there right now," she told him, locating her cutoffs and pulling them on. She grabbed her bra and T-shirt and put them on before adding, "If I go back there tonight, I'm going to have to face the pictures. And the memories."

He stepped closer, took her face in his hands, and brushed a brief kiss to her lips. "Say no more. You're staying with me tonight. In my arms. And I promise not to let you go until morning."

She snaked her arms around his waist and rested her cheek against his chest, loving the feel of his strong arms as they held her close. "That sounds perfect."

Chapter 15

GABE KEPT GLANCING AT ELLE AS THEY DROVE BACK to his house, still not quite sure he hadn't imagined what had happened outside the old, abandoned church. Was this really Elle McCoy sitting beside him, her head back against the seat, eyes closed, a contented smile draping her luscious, full lips? Even now, he longed to whip the car over to the side of the road so he could lose himself in another kiss.

Her grin widened. "You should keep your eyes on the road."

He laughed. "How did you know they weren't?"

Her auburn lashes fluttered a little as she opened her eyes and rolled her head toward him. She was tired. He could relate. "I can feel you looking at me. I've always been able to feel you looking at me."

He scoffed. "Right."

"Believe it or not," she said with a shrug, "but I've always known when you were near, when you were watching me."

He sent a glance her way and tried not to sound skeptical when he said, "Prove it."

"I can't, not really," she admitted. "Maybe it's like when moms know something is up with their kids. Or when twins know when something's going on with the other. I just *know*. Runs in the family, I guess. Charlotte has the same instinct. Half the time she shows

up to come to my rescue, I haven't called her. She
just *knows*."

"What are you saying?" he asked cautiously. "You
have some kind of sixth sense? Are you going to tell me
you see dead people next?"

She laughed sleepily. "No. Nothing like that. It's not
supernatural." She yawned and when he glanced away
from the road, her eyes were drooping as she murmured,
"It's love."

Gabe's chest constricted, squeezing the air out of
him. But it wasn't panic he felt. It was hope—hope he
hadn't been willing to indulge in until that moment. Was
she saying she *loved* him? How was that even possible?
Just a few weeks ago, she'd been calling him an irredeemable jackass.

But, more importantly, what the hell was *he* feeling?
Did he love *her*? He knew he cared about her, had been
infatuated with her since she was that gawky, wiry teenager she was so convinced was beneath his notice. But
was it love?

Whoa. Slow your roll, dude.

It was a little early to be thinking that way. Right
now, he needed to just focus on the moment and on
keeping her safe. Then, maybe at some point, he could
get a handle on what the hell he was feeling.

When he glanced her way again, she was fast asleep,
her face slack in repose and unbelievably beautiful.
He reached out and took her hand in his, bending over
slightly to bring her hand to his mouth and press a tender
kiss to her fingertips. She shifted a little at the pressure
and twined her fingers with his.

God, he was in trouble…

When he pulled into his driveway a few minutes later, he almost hated to rouse her from her slumber. Odds were good she hadn't slept a whole lot lately—well, judging by his sleep habits of late, anyway.

He came around and opened the door, unbuckling her seat belt and lifting her into his arms. She nuzzled close and mumbled something incoherent against his shirt, then lazily draped her arms around his neck.

"I gotcha," he whispered, easily carrying her up the steps—not so easily maneuvering around until he could unlock the door.

How the hell did the guys manage this kind of thing in the movies, for shit's sake?

The sound of the front door closing roused her enough that she lifted her head and glanced around, eyes still glassy with sleep. "Are we home?"

He hugged her a little tighter. "Yeah, honey. We're home. I'm gonna get you to bed."

She sighed, a sweet little sound of contentment that went straight to his dick. "Mmm. Like the sound of that."

He chuckled but didn't respond, knowing she probably didn't even realize what she was mumbling. But when he gently placed her on the bed and pulled back to help remove her shoes, she was staring up at him with a hungry look in her eyes.

"You should get some sleep," he told her, trying his damnedest to be a gentleman.

Elle glanced toward his bedside table at the clock there. "It's still early." She sat up and grasped the front of his shirt, yanking him toward her. "Besides, I need a shower before I get in your bed."

He couldn't help grinning. "That so? Need any help?"

She slowly got to her feet, her body sliding up his as she stood, her lips finding his in a slow, sultry kiss that left his pulse pounding. "Well, since you asked..."

He wasn't entirely sure who undressed whom as they made their way to the bathroom, but by the time they were there, they were both naked. He started the water, then reached for Elle, capturing her mouth again. But the kiss was brief. As blissful as it was to lose himself in her kisses, he wanted to explore every inch of her peaches-and-cream skin. He stepped back, starting with her fingertips, pressing a kiss to the pad of each one, then her palm, the inside of her wrist.

She gasped a little and shivered when he found her pulse point with his tongue. "Oh God, Gabe," she whispered. "That's too delicious."

He chuckled. "You're telling me."

But he continued his path, kissing his way up her arm to her shoulder, pausing for several moments, loving the way she moaned softly and clutched at him as he teased the sensitive skin there with his tongue and teeth.

"We should get in the shower," she murmured half-heartedly as he kissed his way down to her breasts, her belly, her hips.

He didn't respond. He was more interested in her response as he explored her thighs, the center of her, already slick and swollen with need. He spent a good deal of time there, bracing her hips as he suckled and lathed, not granting her any quarter until she cried out and her knees buckled. Then he kissed his way back up, turning her so he could press another line of kisses along the smooth skin of her back.

As soon as he was standing again, he wrapped his

arms around her, pulling her back into the curve of his body until her bottom was pressed firmly against his groin. "Still want that shower?"

Her head dropped back against his shoulder as he nipped at hers. "Touch me," she whispered. Not waiting for him to respond, she grasped his wrist and guided him to the patch of glossy, red curls between her legs.

"Jesus, Elle," he rasped, grinding his hips against hers. "I want to be inside you. Right. Now."

She bent forward to turn off the water, the sight of her gorgeous, perfectly rounded bottom making him groan. In response, she sent a saucy look over her shoulder. "What are you waiting for?"

He gently grasped her hips, and they sank down together on their knees. She leaned forward, bracing her forearms on the edge of the bathtub as he positioned himself and slid easily into her from behind.

She moaned, pressing back against him, grinding against him, urging him on. He didn't need to be asked twice. He moved with slow, measured strokes, wanting to draw out her pleasure for as long as possible.

"Oh God, yes," she gasped. He could feel her muscles beginning to tighten, close to orgasm already, still sensitive and aroused.

When she pushed up from the bathtub, he sank back on his heels, bringing her back flush against his chest, one hand kneading her breast as the other fingered her clit. Her breath came in gasps as they moved together. When she came, her cry of release echoed in the bathroom, filling his ears and making everything male in him want to pound his chest with pride.

But then he was crying out along with her, his own

orgasm uncoiling in one great release. They continued to move together, thrusting and withdrawing through the aftershocks that left them both panting until she finally collapsed back against him.

It was only then that he paused to get his shit together and realized he hadn't bothered to withdraw before he came, hadn't bothered to stop long enough to put on a condom. He was clean, had never had such a lapse in judgment with anyone else, but he'd let his dick get in the way of being responsible and respectful to *her*.

"Shit, Elle," he spat as they drew apart. "I'm sorry. I shouldn't have been so stupid."

She turned on the water and cast a glance at him over her shoulder. "It takes two to tango, Gabe. I could've stopped you. Should I be concerned?"

His eyes went wide. "Oh, God no! I'm good. Clean bill of health in all regards. I'm more worried about not being respectful to you. I love—" He bit off his words. *Holy fucking hell. He'd almost said he loved her.* He quickly amended, "I love being inside you. Love the feel of you. I've never been that intimate with any other woman. But…I'm just thinking of Joe and Sadie and the baby on the way."

She gave him a nod, then pressed a kiss to his lips. "Truth? I've never been that intimate with anyone else either. But you're right. We should probably be more careful. For now."

Their shower together had been sensual but chaste aside from some very heated kisses as they lathered each other's skin. Dried off and lying in Gabe's bed now, wearing only one of his sheriff department T-shirts as she waited for him to join her, she mulled over their conversation. She hadn't been lying when she'd told him that she'd never been as intimate with any other man. Heck, there were only a handful of men in her history to begin with.

Yet she was completely willing to throw caution to the wind where Gabe was concerned. What the hell was she *thinking*? So maybe her aunt Charlotte had been right. Maybe he went through women so quickly because he realized the relationship wasn't going anywhere. She was willing to accept as truth what he'd said about his reputation being exaggerated.

So why had things been different this time around for both of them? She'd been infatuated with Gabe since high school, had been attracted to him, drawn to him in spite of every inclination to dislike him. The answer hovered at the edges of her mind, defying all logic and reason.

Fortunately, he sauntered into the bedroom, hot as hell as he moved toward the bed, that cocky self-confidence completely justified, she had to say. He slipped between the sheets and slid an arm beneath her, pulling her against him.

"Hey there, beautiful," he whispered, pressing a kiss to her hair. "Feeling better?"

She curled into him, loving the way they fit together, how her head nestled perfectly in the hollow of his shoulder. And he smelled amazing, a heady mixture of soap and shaving cream and aftershave. She took a deep breath, drawing in the scent of him, letting it swamp her senses, then twined her fingers with his. "Much. How are you?"

He chuckled, the sound rumbling deep in his chest, vibrating beneath her ear. "Oh, I'm good. Better than good. Fantastic."

"Thank you, Gabe," she said softly. "I appreciate everything you've done for me today. I'm so much happier to have these memories to associate with this day."

"You say that like a woman prepared to move on," he said, his tone suddenly stiff, guarded.

"That's not how I meant it," she assured him, but his tension didn't ease. "I just don't want to take anything for granted. Let's just take things one day at a time and see what happens, okay? I have a habit of not thinking much about the future. Not since my family died."

He took a deep breath and let it out slowly, then pressed another kiss to her hair. "I understand."

"Do you?" she asked, rising up to peer down into his face, searching his eyes.

He tucked a lock of hair behind her ear. "Yeah, I do." His brows drew together in a frown, as if he was struggling with a decision, then he said, "Did you know I almost got married once?"

For some reason, the thought of him married to someone else was a sucker punch to the gut that made her want to hurl. But she swallowed back the lump in her throat and shook her head. "No, I didn't. I'm surprised Aunt Charlotte didn't say anything about it."

"Charlotte didn't know," he told her. "Most people didn't. My brother Tom was the only one I told—and you know how tight-lipped Tom is. Only guy I know who can actually keep a secret."

"Why was it a secret?" Elle asked.

He frowned. "Just wanted to wait for the right time to tell my dad and the rest of my brothers."

"Who was she?"

"Her name was Audrey Evans. I dated her when you were away at law school. She was finishing up her senior year in grad school and then we were going to get married. She was planning to be a research chemist." His arm around her tightened. "Guess I have a thing for brilliant women."

Elle grinned at the compliment. "So what happened? You said she was *planning to be* a chemist."

He shrugged. "Dunno. A couple of weeks after we got engaged, I came home a few hours later from my shift because I'd had a shit-ton of paperwork that night and we got into a huge argument. I wasn't even entirely sure what she was so pissed about. But that was it. She finally called me a week or so later to tell me why she'd broken things off. Apparently, she'd decided she couldn't be married to someone in law enforcement, couldn't take all the worrying."

"I'm so sorry, Gabe," Elle told him, partly because she'd never thought him capable of ever committing to one woman, let alone being the one on the receiving end of a broken heart.

His expression grew solemn. "Can't say I blame her."

"Bullshit."

He flinched and drew away, giving her a shocked look. "Sorry?"

"She was an idiot if she couldn't see what she was passing up," she told him.

His answering grin was brief, but then he shook his head. "Maybe she was smarter than I'd thought. I've had more than my share of fuckups, Elle." He ran a hand over his hair, his expression twisting with emotion, and she realized this was about more than just one of his ex-girlfriends bailing. Her instinct was confirmed when he said, "I should've checked the battery in my radio before I went into Moe's that day, Elle. I shouldn't have been out in my vehicle when Chris was shot."

She turned his face toward her. "You couldn't have known Derrick Monroe was going to barge into the diner and shoot Chris any more than you could've known Mark Monroe was going to take a shot at me."

His eyes closed, effectively shuttering his gaze from her, but she could sense the turmoil inside him, the survivor guilt that plagued him. Mostly because she'd been feeling it, too.

"I was supposed to have Chris's back," he said, his voice catching. "I should've been there."

She touched his cheek, gently skimming along his chiseled jaw. "Look at me, Gabriel Dawson."

He opened his eyes, his expression still guarded, angry—not with her, she could tell, but with himself.

"You can't protect everyone," she reminded him. "You just *can't*. So you need to cut yourself some slack or it's going to eat you alive. Trust me. I know."

"And what if I hadn't been able to protect *you*, Elle?" he asked softly. "What if another stupid coincidence had kept me from following you out to the courthouse steps that day?" He reached up, smoothing her hair away from her face, and grasped the nape of her neck, pulling her down so her forehead was pressed against his. "What if I'd lost you before I'd ever had the chance to hold you in my arms?"

God, he's breaking my heart.

She had to blink away tears when she pulled back to peer down at him. "But you didn't," she assured him. "I'm here now, Gabe. And there's nowhere else I'd rather be."

He kissed her then, the pressure of his lips so loving and tender, the tears she'd been holding back slipped to her cheeks. And she *knew*. Her heart was telling her everything she needed to know but that her brain wasn't ready to acknowledge. When the kiss drew to a close, she nestled against him, the sound of his heartbeat soothing in its steady rhythm as she drifted to sleep in his arms.

Chapter 16

Elle stretched languidly as she awoke, feeling more well rested than she had in ages. A slow smile curved her lips as she remembered why.

Gabe.

God, what a night they'd had. Because… *Damn*.

She had to admit, Gabe definitely had the skill to back his swagger—he was the most selfless lover she'd ever had. But it wasn't just the mind-blowing sexathon that had her grinning from ear to ear. She'd never felt so safe, so cared for as she had while lying in Gabe's arms, held tenderly against his heart.

Longing for those strong arms around her, she slipped from the bed and searched the ground for her clothes. Not immediately finding them *or* the T-shirt she'd worn to bed—which had been discarded at some point during the night when Gabe had awakened her for a kiss that had quickly and blissfully led to more—she opened his closet and grabbed a long-sleeved button-down. Luckily, he was tall enough that the shirt hit her midthigh.

She shrugged. *Good enough*. If she had her way, she wouldn't have it on long anyway.

But as she padded down the hallway, the house was so quiet, she began to wonder if he was even there. Then she caught the sound of soft music coming from the room he used as his office. She crept to the doorway and peered around the doorframe, her breath catching in her lungs when she saw him.

Gabe stood at his desk, holding a steaming cup of coffee, wearing only a low-slung pair of jeans and a fierce scowl. His bare chest moved in slow, even breaths, but Elle could tell from the way his jaw was clenched that he was furious.

"Band of Horses, if I'm not mistaken," she said, referring to the band playing on the stereo.

His gaze snapped up to her face and the tension in his expression instantly eased. "Well, good morning," he said, a smile breaking across his face as he reached out a hand, inviting her in. "Sleep well?"

She nodded as she came forward, taking his hand and letting him draw her into his embrace. She wrapped her arms around his waist and rested her head against his chest, heaving a contented sigh. "How about you? How long have you been awake?"

He pressed a kiss to her hair. "Few hours."

She pulled back and studied him for a long moment. "Gabe, it's only eight ten. What time did you get up?"

He shrugged. "About five. I wanted to do some more snooping on Monroe. He updates his blog every Saturday."

Now it was her turn to frown. "So you've been reading his blog for over three hours on a Sunday morning?"

He took a sip of his coffee, then set the cup down on the desk so he could wrap his arms around her and draw her closer. "I do my best thinking early in the morning. Of course, that's not all I'm best at in the morning."

She raised her brows, preferring his playful, dimpled smile far more than his pensive scowl. "That so?"

He demonstrated what he meant with a long, slow

kiss that set her mind spinning, his lips alternately gentle and demanding. When the kiss ended, he took her hand in his and spun her in a quick dance step before drawing her close again, swaying slowly with her in time to the music.

"And you can dance, too," she mused, grinning up at him.

"Took a class in college," he admitted. "Thought it'd be a good skill to have, make me more of a Renaissance man."

She pulled back with a skeptical look. "Renaissance man. Right… You sure it wasn't just a ploy to get laid?"

He laughed in a loud burst and pulled her closer. "I can't reveal *all* my secrets just yet. Man of mystery, remember? There's a lot you don't know about me, honey."

She brushed a quick kiss against his lips. "So I'm learning. Guess I'll have to hang out with you more often to discover more of these startling revelations about the real Gabe Dawson."

He brought their clasped hands in close, pressing them against his chest. "It could take a while. You might have to tough it out for a long time before you find out all my deepest darkest secrets."

She drew him down for a brief kiss, then snuggled in close. "I think I'm up for that."

As the next song started to play, Gabe began to hum softly, the sound vibrating in his chest where her head rested. Elle closed her eyes, letting the warmth of him envelop her. She didn't remember the last time she felt so *content*. Or loved. It was in his touch, in his smile, in the way he held her close.

As the song ended, Gabe drew back enough to look

down into her eyes. Then he smoothed her curls, his gaze roaming as if memorizing every curve of her face. "How'd we get here, Elle?"

She frowned at him. "What do you mean?"

He tucked her back under his chin, holding her close. "I mean, up until a few weeks ago, you detested me. And now..."

She pushed back and turned her face up to his, wanting him to see the sincerity in her eyes when she said, "Gabe, I never detested you." Her cheeks grew warm when she added, "In fact, I had a huge crush on you for years."

"Nice try," he chuckled. "But you've spent the last few years turning your nose up at me, rolling your eyes every time I tried to ask you out. Don't try to stroke my ego now."

Unable to resist a little mischief, she slid her hand over the front of his jeans. "If memory serves, it's not your ego that responds best to my stroking."

His breath hitched sharply and he grabbed her hand, bringing it up to his lips to kiss to her palm. "Minx," he rasped, his desire impossible to mask. "You're changing the subject. Tell me about this crush you supposedly had. Because, I gotta say, sweet cheeks, you sure as hell could've fooled me."

"Ask Aunt Charlotte," she insisted. "She still teases me about it, so I'm sure she'd be *more* than happy to fill you in."

"Give me the CliffsNotes version," he pressed.

"Fine. If you must know, I fell for you the day you came to help me move in to Charlotte's," she told him. "You were the most handsome boy I'd ever seen, the golden boy of Fairfield County—or so I was to discover."

Gabe groaned. "God, I hated being called that."

She leveled a gaze at him. "And yet you totally used that perception of you to your advantage. Don't even try to deny it."

He gave her a wicked grin. "Hell, wouldn't you use it if you were an eighteen-year-old kid with a talent for getting his ass in trouble? Between my dad being sheriff and my brother Tom covering for me more times than I can count, I got away with more shit than any other stupid teenager should've. Somebody should've kicked my ass and taught me a lesson."

Elle shook her head. "No one dared! You were smart, charming, handsome, awesome at everything you tried…"

He chuckled. "I notice you're talking in past tense."

"Oh, trust me, I had it bad for you back then, Gabe Dawson. But you didn't even know I was alive."

Gabe grunted. "Oh, I knew."

He kissed the side of her neck, eliciting a little moan of need before she pushed him away. "But you ignored me!"

He kissed the tip of her nose. "Because you were too young for me. My dad and your aunt would've had a shit fit if I'd gone out with you," he told her. "Especially after what you'd been through. Besides, I could tell you were the kind of girl who'd be able to see through all my bullshit. I was too much of an idiot to see that as a good thing. Now, back to this crush… When did it fade away?"

She stood on her toes to give a quick nip to his dimpled chin. "Who said it has?"

He looked down his nose at her, still skeptical. "Since you came back to town, you've acted like you wanted nothing more than to nut-punch me every time we were in the same room together."

She shrugged. "Defense mechanism."

His brows lifted slightly at this. "Come again?"

"Love to," she quipped. When he chuckled, she gave him a saucy wink and draped her arms around his neck, pulling him down to receive her kiss.

"I think you're avoiding the question," he murmured against the corner of her mouth before drawing away.

She sighed a little sadly. "You broke my heart when we were teenagers, Gabe."

"But I had no idea," he reminded her. "You can't convict me for crimes I didn't know I was committing."

"I know, I know," she acknowledged. "I can't explain to you the mysteries of the heart of a teenage girl."

He groaned. "I wish someone had back then. God knows I didn't have a fucking clue. But that was *then*."

"The thing is," she said, searching for the words to adequately explain why she'd resisted him for so long, "I'd heard the stories and rumors from while I was away at college and law school, witnessed firsthand the way women were constantly throwing themselves at you when I returned."

"I'll admit I went a little off the rails when Audrey broke things off," he murmured. "But it wasn't nearly as bad as what I'm sure everyone was saying."

"I know that now," she told him, "but at that point, it's what I was hearing over and over. And I didn't want my heart to get broken again. So I kept you at a distance, constantly telling myself you were a womanizer, a player. I wasn't about to fall into bed with you only to be discarded like yesterday's trash."

He winced at her harsh perception of him. "So what changed?" he asked. "You weren't taken in by any of my come-ons, that's for damned sure."

"You let me see the real you," she explained, smoothing a hand lightly over his chest. "And *I* let me see the real you. That day at the courthouse…I realized I'd not given you a fair chance. Then what you told me during the argument we had after you kissed me… Well, I realize now I never should've judged you by what others said."

"And now?" he prompted, his gaze so tender and hopeful Elle's chest went tight. "You sorry you gave me a chance to prove everyone wrong?"

She took his face in her hands. "Not for a second."

He suddenly lifted her up, wrapping her legs around his waist and peppering her lips and cheeks and chin with kisses.

"What are you doing?" she laughed as he carried her from the room.

"Well, I figure I'd better make sure you don't have reason to regret giving me a second chance." He paused, pressing her back against the wall as his hands slid under the hem of the shirt she wore. "And seeing you wearing my shirt has been driving me crazy since you walked into my office."

She leaned her head back against the wall when his lips sought the hollow of her throat. "Gabe, I think you need to take me back to bed," she said, her voice breathless. "Right. Now."

※

Gabe felt Elle's arms go around his waist and the warmth against his back where she pressed her cheek for a moment before releasing him. "How was your shower?" he asked, turning around to pull her close, disappointed to see her dressed in clothes from the day before. He hadn't been exaggerating about seeing her in his shirt. It'd been sexy as hell.

"Lonely," she said with a melodramatic sigh.

He chuckled. "Yeah, well, last time we tried to take a shower together we got a little carried away."

She pressed a kiss to the dimple in his chin then nipped it with her teeth, and his dick jumped to attention, forcing him to shift a little with a groan. "God, woman, you're gonna be the death of me."

"I don't know that I'll ever get enough of you," she admitted.

Gabe ran his hands through her silky curls, loving the way they slid through his fingers. "That's what I like to hear," he assured her. "'Cause I'm damned sure I'll never get enough of *you*, Elle McCoy."

She glanced at his laptop, then back at him, giving him a questioning look. "Seems like I'm not the only thing you can't get enough of. It's Sunday, Gabe. Give the investigation a rest. You'll make yourself crazy."

He closed the laptop and lifted his hands. "There ya go. Done for the day." But the moment he said it, he knew he'd be back at it later that day. He had to find something, anything, that would implicate Monroe. He wasn't going to be able to rest easy until that son of a bitch was behind bars.

She lifted a brow. "Uh-huh."

"I'll prove it," he replied. She studied him for a moment, those incredible eyes boring into him. "Let's run by your place and get you a change of clothes. Then what comes next is up to you. You call the shots today. Whatever you want to do, I'm yours."

His heart hitched at his words, wondering if she had any idea just how true a statement that was. The way her lips curled into a smile and her gaze softened, he thought maybe she did.

Then her eyes went wide on a gasp. "Oh crap! What time is it?"

He checked his watch. "Going on noon. Why?"

"Teddy's birthday party," she said.

"Teddy?"

"Teddy Andrews," she prompted. Then added, "Chris and Jessica's son. The party starts at two o'clock. I promised Jessica I'd be there."

Gabe shrugged. "Let me grab a shirt and shoes and we'll head out."

"I'm so sorry, Gabe," she said. "I wish we could spend the day together."

"Who says we can't?" he asked. "I don't have a gift for Teddy, though. Would a six-year-old be okay with cash?"

Her brows drew together and her head tilted a little to one side as she studied him. "You mean you want to go to the birthday party?"

"Wouldn't miss it," he assured her. "Like I said, you're calling the shots. Besides, a visit to Jessica is long overdue. I helped out for a little while after Chris was killed, but she said it was too hard to have me around, so I hired a guy to do yard work and stuff for her instead. I haven't been back since." A sudden thought occurring to him, he added, "You think she'll be okay with me showing up?"

Elle took his hand and gave it a squeeze. "I'll give

her a call on the way, but I'm sure she'll be happy to see you."

He hoped she was right, because he'd felt for a while now he'd been letting Chris down by not doing more for Jessica and the kids. And although he wanted to respect Jessica's wishes and not make her grieving any harder than it already was, he'd promised Chris when his friend had gotten married that if anything ever happened, he'd look after Jess.

A few minutes later, they were pulling into Elle's driveway. He got out and did a quick scan of the house and the surrounding area, looking for anything suspicious. Except for a few people out and about working on their yards and some kids riding their bikes, the neighborhood was quiet. A typical summer Sunday.

She came jogging up beside him with a small handful of mail and unlocked the front door. "Make yourself at home," she said, flipping through the mail as she headed down the hall toward her bedroom. "I'll only be a few min—"

A loud thump and a strangled sob made every muscle in Gabe's body tense.

"Elle?" he called as he sprinted for the hallway. She was sitting on the floor with her back against the wall. The mail was scattered all over the floor except for a single letter she held in her hands. And on her lap was a small pile of photos.

"Elle, honey?" he said, crouching in front of her. "What is it?"

She turned her eyes up to him, her expression so stricken, his protective urge made his blood boil with fury before he even took the sheet of paper from her hand. It was a copy of a newspaper article about the car accident that claimed the life of the McCoy family, complete with a photo of the car, torn all to hell by the impact. In the foreground of the picture was a little girl's shoe.

Gabe's hand clenched into a fist and it was all he could do not to punch a hole in the wall. "That *mother-fucker*. I'm going to rip his *fucking* head off."

"Gabe," Elle said, her voice quavering.

He looked away from the letter to see her holding up the photos, her hand shaking so badly two of the photos fell from her grasp and back onto her lap. Frowning, he took them from her and let fly a string of furious curses. The pictures were copies of crime scene photos. The individuals were horrifically injured, but he could still recognize them as Elle's mother and sisters.

"Jesus Christ," he hissed. "How the hell did he even get access to these?"

There was only one answer—someone Monroe knew had somehow gained access to the criminal case against the man who'd killed Elle's family. The photos would've been part of the evidence against him. That asshole Monroe had a connection at a courthouse or law office somewhere.

Elle's quiet sobs brought his attention back to her, and he set aside the letter and photos to take her face in his hands and press a kiss to her forehead. "I'm so sorry, honey," he murmured, his throat constricting with emotion, his heart aching, knowing the kind of pain she had to be experiencing. He moved out of his crouch to take a seat beside her and put his arm around her shoulders, pulling her close. He held her as she cried, kissing her hair, murmuring endearments to her, knowing it wasn't nearly enough.

"Why would he do this?" she asked as her tears subsided. "Why be so cruel?"

Gabe shook his head. "I have no idea. Maybe in Monroe's mind, it's a way to get back at you for the loss of his son."

Elle angrily swiped away her tears. "I'm not letting that asshole get to me," she ground out. Her lips pressed together in a determined line, she got to her feet and stormed to her bedroom. Gabe could hear drawers opening and then slamming shut as he followed her to her room.

He leaned against the doorframe as he watched her tear off her clothes and change into an orange-and-yellow sundress. She looked like a living, breathing flame, the anger radiating off of her magnifying the impression.

"My God, you're beautiful," he told her, his heart hammering in his chest at the sight of her. Was it really possible this fiery, brilliant, breathtaking woman cared for him, maybe even loved him? What the hell had he done to deserve such a gift?

Her expression immediately softened at his words, her cheeks flushing. "The way you say that makes me believe it."

"Good," he said, shoving off the doorframe and walking toward her to fold her into his embrace. "I hope you don't get tired of hearing it because I intend to tell you every single day…if you'll let me."

Her arms tightened around his waist. "I think I can live with that."

He held her for several minutes, offering what

strength he could. Eventually, she eased out of his arms and sighed. "We should probably go."

He lifted his brows. "You still want to go to Teddy's party?"

She nodded, but he could tell she was struggling with the idea of putting on a smile when her heart was aching from what that piece of shit Monroe had done. He could only hope the bastard had finally slipped up and they'd manage to get some fingerprints from the letter or the photos that would allow them to at least bring harassment charges against him.

"I'll let you finish getting ready," he said, smoothing his hands up and down her arms. He gave her a brief kiss, then went back into the hall to gather up the letter and photos. He found a gallon-sized storage bag in her kitchen pantry and slipped the evidence inside, then made a brief call to his brother.

It went to voice mail, so he gave him a quick summary of what had been left for Elle and let him know he'd be dropping it off at the department for the folks there to check for fingerprints.

He'd just hung up when Elle came out of her bedroom.

She'd pulled her curls up into some kind of configuration at the crown of her head, but a few had escaped to frame her face and tickle her neck. He hadn't thought she could be more breathtaking than when he'd first seen her in that sundress, but damned if she didn't look even more stunning now.

She gave him a cautious look. "Gabe? What's wrong?"

He shook his head a little, trying to get his shit back together. "Nothing. I'm good."

But he knew that was a lie. He was far from good. He was in love with Elle. He knew he cared about her, admired her, lusted after her with a need that, instead of being satiated, was even greater now that he'd made love to her. But in that moment, he realized without a doubt that he was absolutely and completely in love with her, and no other woman would ever fill his heart the way she did.

Chapter 17

GABE WAS PALE AS THEY PULLED UP TO JESSICA Andrews's house. He'd been fine on the way to the sheriff's department to drop off the baggie containing the article and photos. But his mood had rapidly darkened when they'd left there to head to Jessica's. And he kept shifting in his seat, sending sidelong glances her way.

Maybe he was just nervous about seeing his best friend's widow after so many months. She'd called to let Jessica know that Gabe wanted to come with her, but she'd gotten Jessica's voice mail and so had had to leave a message asking Jess to call if she would prefer Gabe just drop Elle off.

Of course, his fidgeting could have something to do with the questions they might get showing up together. Maybe he wasn't ready to go public. After all, their sparring over the years had hardly gone unnoticed.

Well, hell. Now *she* was nervous.

Trying to divert his attention, she took a deep breath and announced, "So Aunt Charlotte is pressing me to take a job offer that came my way recently from the women's center where I volunteer."

Based on his startled look, her announcement had had the desired effect. "What? What job? You're thinking of leaving the county?"

"I've turned down the offer," she told him. "But they've asked me reconsider. And Charlotte's just worried after the shooting. She'd feel better if I wasn't with the prosecutor's office anymore."

Gabe sent a sidelong glance her way. "Okay...and?"

"And what?"

His brows came together in a frown. "And what are your thoughts?"

She hardly knew anymore. The more she'd thought about the offer, the more appealing it became. She loved the volunteer work she did. And her aunt had been right—helping women and children to put their lives back together made her feel like she was making a difference. There were times when she was working on a case that she couldn't help but wonder if she was prosecuting someone who was innocent of the crimes with which he'd been charged. And there were times when she knew without a doubt that someone was guilty but couldn't do a damned thing about it.

Not that her volunteer work didn't come with frustrations. Too many women she worked with went back to abusive spouses or came in again later, after getting involved with yet another bad relationship. But the success stories...well, they made all the frustrations worth it.

"I'm considering it," she admitted.

Gabe took a deep breath and let it out slowly. "Elle, you can't let this bullshit with Monroe scare you away from doing something you love. I know how much your job means to you. I could tell even before you told me about why you chose to go into law."

"I was so lost after my family was killed," she admitted. "It was the most horrible time in my life. And if I hadn't had Charlotte to help me through it, I hate to think what would've become of me. A lot of the women

who come into the foundation don't have anyone like
Charlotte to turn to. I can help these people, Gabe. I
wouldn't be abandoning my promise to my family—I'd
just be narrowing my focus."

He reached over and took her hand, bringing it to
his lips. "I'd certainly miss seeing you in action at the
courthouse," he said with a wink. "You're sexy as hell
when you're arguing. Sometimes I just provoked you to
see you get mad."

She laughed. "You're joking!"

He shook his head, a mischievous grin curving his
lips—his *incredible* lips she could never taste enough.
"Nope. You're adorable when you're angry."

She shook her head, so many things about him making
sense to her now. All those times she thought he was just
being a jerk, he'd been baiting her because he thought
she was cute when she got mad. "You're incorrigible."

"Guilty."

She slid a glance his way, the mention of his seeing
her in court suddenly giving her pause. "Gabe, do you
realize that if…if things continue between us, I'd have
to recuse myself from any of your cases. And probably
your brothers' cases, for that matter."

He glanced away from the road to send a frown her
way. "Okay. Would that be so bad? It's not like there's
a shortage of crime in Fairfield County."

She blew out a breath, trying to figure out how to
answer that question. "No, but it would dramatically
affect the kinds of cases I get. Let's face it—you and
your brothers tend to get the big ones. If there's something major going on, the Dawson boys are typically on
the other end of it."

"Don't make a career decision based on me," he said. "Or *us*."

Elle's stomach sank. God, what had she been thinking? Of course it was way too soon to be thinking in the long-term where she and Gabe were concerned. They were supposed to be taking things slowly, day by day. That had been her own suggestion. Now she'd just made it sound like her entire career would be decided by her relationship that was all of about two days old.

She closed her eyes, feeling the heat of her embarrassment flooding her cheeks. "Gabe, I didn't mean... I wasn't implying..."

Damn it!

She couldn't even figure out how to dig herself out of this one. She totally sounded like one of those clingy, desperate women who started planning their weddings after the first date and then went psycho when the guy turned tail and ran.

He chuckled. "Hey, Elle?"

She groaned. "Yes?"

"It's okay. I know."

She dared to send a glance his way. "You know what?"

"I know you want me." When she laughed and smacked playfully at his arm, his grin widened. "Ow! Hey, it's okay. I know I'm adorable, too. You just can't help yourself. Don't worry about it."

"Have I *mentioned* you're incorrigible?" she shot back, grinning, glad he wasn't going to make a big deal about her reference to a future.

He cocked his head as if considering her question. "Nope. Don't think so." Then he offered her a wink.

For several minutes, they rode in comfortable silence, hands clasped. Then he said softly, "Hey, Elle?"

"Yeah?"

"I want there to be an us," he told her. "I just don't want us to be what makes you decide whether or not to take a job. I want you to do whatever's going to make you happy. I just hope whatever you decide that maybe…*maybe* that future will include me." He shifted in his seat, his neck growing red. Then he coughed, clearing his throat before adding, "Anyway, thought I'd throw that out there."

Elle didn't know what to say. Her heart swelled with so much joy and panic at the same time, she wasn't sure exactly how she felt. Okay, actually, that was a lie. She knew exactly how she felt.

She was in love with Gabe Dawson.

Her girlhood infatuation had evolved over the years, in spite of her own efforts to keep her feelings in check. And now, after allowing herself to peek behind his cocky, self-assured facade, she knew without a doubt she was head over heels in love with the man beside her.

But after her earlier gaffe, there was no way in hell she was going to admit it right then. Instead, she settled for leaning over and pressing a kiss to his cheek and left it at that. It was actually a relief when they arrived at Jessica's house.

But when she unbuckled her seat belt and reached for the door handle to get out of the Charger, she realized Gabe wasn't moving. Concerned, she took his hand in hers and gave it a squeeze. "Are you sure you want to go inside with me? You can just drop me off and I'll catch a ride home with someone else."

He frowned. "What? Why would I do that?"

"I don't know… I just…" She forced a smile. "Never mind. Let's just go."

Gabe got out and came around to open the door for her, keeping her hand clasped firmly in his as they made their way to the front porch. She twined her fingers with his as he raised his other hand to knock, but the door swung open before he had the chance.

~~~

Jessica Andrews had been crying, her dark eyes puffy and swollen. On a sob, she threw her arms around Gabe's neck, hugging him tightly.

"Thank God you came!" she sniffed as she ushered them in. "I didn't realize the police had called you."

"They didn't," Gabe informed her, his head still reeling from the conversation with Elle in the car and now the added mystery of why Jessica was clearly upset. "We came for Teddy's party. Elle left you a message…"

She cast a glance between him and Elle, her eyes widening a little. "Oh God, the party. Of course! I'm sorry. It's just been… Everyone's out in the backyard. My sister's handling everything. I just… I couldn't."

Elle put her arm around Jessica's shoulders and led her to the sofa. "What's going on, honey?"

She snatched a Kleenex from the box on the side table and dabbed at her eyes. "I got a letter in the mail yesterday, but I was so busy getting things ready for Teddy's party I didn't open it until this morning."

Gabe had a feeling he knew what was coming.

"All that was inside was a copy of a newspaper article about Chris's death," she continued. "But someone had typed a Bible verse at the bottom."

"Do you still have it?" he asked, struggling to keep the fury out of his voice.

She shook her head. "No, I sent it with Mike Dandridge when he came by this morning. You remember Mike, right?"

Gabe nodded. "Sure. He's a good guy and fantastic cop. And he was a good friend to Chris. I've worked with him a few times on cases. How about I give him a call and see if they've processed the letter for prints?"

Jessica nodded and sniffed, wiping at her eyes. "Thanks. I appreciate that."

Gabe sent a questioning glance to Elle, and when she nodded and turned her sympathetic smile to Jessica, he got up and slipped outside to the porch and dialed Officer Mike Dandridge. The officer answered on the second ring with a cheerful, "Yo."

"Hey, Mike, how's it hangin', man?"

Mike groaned. "Dude. Just got off my shift and have to go sweat my balls off directing traffic at the megachurch on Harding so I can pay my friggin' bills. Same shit, different day. Whaddup?"

Gabe cringed, knowing well that most of the officers he knew had to work side jobs, doing security at concerts or taking traffic details just to make ends meet. He'd certainly done his fair share of shit work a couple of years earlier, when he'd secretly been paying some of his brother Joe's bills while Joe was recovering from the wounds he'd received in Afghanistan.

"Sorry, man," Gabe told him sincerely. "I won't keep you long. I was just following up on the letter Jessica Andrews handed over to you this morning. Was wondering if you'd been able to get any prints off it."

"Nah," Mike told him, clearly frustrated. "Whoever sent it did one helluva job keeping the letter clean. And it wasn't mailed, so there's nothing to go on there. You at Jessica's now?"

"Yeah, stopped by for Teddy's birthday party and found out about the letter," he told his colleague, scanning the sun-drenched suburban street. It was too hot at that point in the afternoon for many people to be out and about working on their yards or washing their cars, but there were a few. "You talked to the neighbors already? They see anybody?"

"Nobody we talked to saw anyone dropping off anything in Jessie's mailbox," Mike assured him. "Neighborhoods aren't like what they used to be, man. People aren't paying attention to what's going on around them anymore. Makes it a helluva lot harder to canvas the neighbors."

"I hear ya." Gabe ran a hand over his hair, irritated the local PD hadn't had any better luck than they'd had in nailing Monroe. "Jess wasn't the only one to get a letter like that. Elle McCoy got one, too."

"That blows," Mike said. "You know who it is?"

"Can't prove it," Gabe admitted, "but I have a feeling it's a guy named Jeb Monroe."

There was a slight pause before Mike ground out, "That's the fucker whose son killed Chris."

Gabe's chest tightened at his words. "Yeah."

"What do you need from us?" Mike asked. "I'll talk to my captain, let him know what's going on. We'll give you whatever assistance you need to bring down that bastard. You just say the word, Gabe, and you got it."

Gabe felt that familiar warmth that had nothing to

do with the summer heat and everything to do with the brotherhood that existed in the law enforcement community. The various departments sometimes had their differences, but when it came down to it, he always knew he could count on the others serving behind the badge. "Thanks, Mike. Just let me know if you get anything at all or if you hear of any other suspicious incidents."

"You got it, man."

When Gabe went back inside, the blast of cool air that greeted him was a welcome relief. Jessica's and Elle's gazes snapped toward him, their expressions questioning, hopeful. "Mike's going to keep me posted, but right now they don't have anything."

Jessica's expression fell and she fought back tears. "Thank you, Gabe. I appreciate you trying."

He resumed his seat and reached out to take Jessica's hand. "Anything like this happens again, I want you to call me. You know you could've called me this time, too. I would've come right over."

She lifted a brow. "Oh really? You *would've*? Because you've been *so* concerned about us since Chris was killed? I know I told you that I needed some time, but it's been a *year*, Gabe! You haven't even *called*." As soon as the words came out of her mouth, she seemed to regret them. "I'm sorry. That was a shitty thing to say. I heard about what happened at the courthouse a few weeks ago." She glanced at Elle. "To both of you. I'm sure it's been rough for you."

"No, you're right, Jess," Gabe admitted. "I promised Chris I'd look after you and the kids. I haven't done such a great job lately. And I'm sorry for that. But I want to fix it. So anytime you need anything, you call me. I'm here."

Her eyes welled up, tears slipping to her cheeks as she nodded. "Okay."

"Honey," Elle said gently to Jessica, "you mentioned a Bible verse that was on the note you received. Do you remember what it was?"

She sniffed and pulled a folded sheet of paper out of her shorts pocket. "I wrote it down."

Gabe took the note and read aloud, "'I myself will be hostile toward you and will afflict you for your sins seven times over.'"

"Sins," Jessica echoed, her voice thick with tears. "Can you believe it? What the he—" She bit off her angry words and glanced over her shoulder toward the sliding glass door that led to her backyard, where the sounds of happy chatter and laughter could be heard. She resumed in a harsh whisper, "What the *hell* is this sick son of a bitch talking about? What *sins* would Chris possibly have committed against this person? He was the best man I've ever known! What *sins* could the kids or I have committed?"

Gabe took a deep breath and shared a glance with Elle. "Jessica, honey, the guy we think is behind this has some very extreme views on the government, law enforcement in particular."

She looked at Gabe with a mixture of confusion and anger. "You know who it is? How?"

"I received a letter, too," Elle told her. "But we only have suspicions. Nothing concrete."

"It's someone from Derrick Monroe's crazy family, isn't it?" she demanded, her fear quickly replaced by fury.

Gabe sent another glance Elle's way. "I can't say—"

"Why haven't you arrested him?" she demanded. "Why are you letting him torture my family? For Chrissake, Gabe—Chris was your best friend! And you're just going to sit there and let this bastard treat us this way? Why aren't you *doing* something?"

"It's complicated," Gabe assured her. "We don't have any evidence linking him to any of the harassing messages we've received."

Jessica went completely still, staring at him in disbelief. Then her eyes narrowed, her lips trembling when she hissed, "Then find some."

Elle cleared her throat. "Jessica, I promise—we're doing everything we can. Even if we find evidence linking him to these threats, if we don't do things by the book, he could walk on a technicality."

Jessica began to shake with fury. "Screw 'by the book'!" she spat. "How long has this been going on? How long have you known this bastard would be coming after my family?"

"We had no idea," Gabe told her, keeping his voice level. "I never thought—"

At that moment, the sliding door slid opened and a little boy with dark hair and wide, brown eyes bounded inside, the Batman cape he wore billowing out behind him. "Mom! Are you coming outside yet? You're gonna miss the whole party!"

"I'll be out in a minute, Teddy," she assured him, wiping at her eyes and forcing a grin for his benefit.

"Uncle Gabe!" the boy cried, running toward him.

Gabe swept the boy into a bear hug. "Hey, there, buddy. Happy birthday."

"How come you haven't come over for a while?" Teddy asked. "Are you staying for my party? Mommy got me a Batman cake and there's even ice cream!"

"That sounds awesome," Gabe told him, forcing a grin. "I wouldn't miss it."

"Cool!" Teddy then sent a cheerful smile Elle's way and waved. "Hi, Miss Elle."

But before Elle could even reply, Teddy turned on his heel and raced back outside to join the fun.

Gabe felt like the world's biggest asshole for staying away for so long. He didn't realize how much he'd missed Chris's family until that moment. Chris had been like another brother to him, and his children might as well have been Gabe's nieces and nephew. Teddy had grown like a weed since Gabe had been by to see them and had apparently lost a couple of teeth. And he'd missed it. Missed it all.

"I need to get outside," Jessica informed them, shoving to her feet, her back straight, her chin held high. "And you're welcome to stay for the party, Gabe, for Teddy's sake. But then I want you to leave."

Gabe was taken aback by her coldness toward him. He'd known Jessica for over a decade and had treated her like a sister the entire time. All he could manage was a startled look.

Elle, of course, was far more articulate. "Jessica, I know you're upset and frustrated. We all are. But Gabe's right. There's nothing he can do until we have a reason to arrest this person. All we can do is try to keep an eye on him and hope he slips up and gives us something to work with."

Jessica glanced between the two of them a couple of

times before laughing bitterly. "Oh my God, I'm such an idiot! No wonder you're taking his side—you two are *sleeping* together! I should've figured that out when you arrived on my doorstep at the same time."

"That has nothing to do with anything," Elle assured her. "I'm telling you the truth as deputy prosecutor."

"Right," Jessica spat. "God, Gabe—this is so typical! When the hell are you going to grow up? Chris always talked about you like you were some kind of freaking *legend*, like you were his hero or something. Well, you know what? Chris was *my* hero. And now he's gone."

Gabe reached out to her. "Jess—"

Jessica snatched her hand out of his reach and shook her head before storming off and slamming the sliding door behind her. Gabe got up to go after her, but Elle put a restraining hand on his arm. "Let her go. She's scared and angry, Gabe. She didn't mean what she said."

Gabe shook his head on a sigh. "Yeah she did. And she's right. I'm my father's son, for shit's sake. When the hell did *he* ever give a damn about doing anything by the book? The man's a goddamned legend because he always gets his man, no matter what."

"That's not fair, Gabe," Elle assured him. "You're not the renegade your father was at your age, sure, but the climate has shifted. The kind of crap he and your grandfather used to pull wouldn't fly today. Not by a long shot."

"Maybe not," he agreed, "but I guarantee neither of them would've been sitting around with their thumbs up their asses while a murdered cop's widow received threats!"

Elle leveled a stern look at him, and when he tried to look away, she stepped into his line of sight, forcing him to face her. "You're not sitting around with your thumb up your ass, Gabe. You're still recovering from nearly being killed. There's a big freaking difference. Jessica's still grieving. But she had no right to say any of the things she did."

Gabe shoved his hands deep into his pockets. "Yeah, she did. I shouldn't be here, Elle. I should be out there right now, hunting down Monroe's ass and making sure he confesses to tormenting all of us. Instead of…"

He bit back his words, realizing they would only make things worse.

"Instead of what?" Elle prompted gently. "Instead of spending time with *me*?"

Gabe ran a hand over his hair in frustration. "God no! That's not what I was going to say. Spending time with you…" He took a deep breath and let it out slowly, bringing his anger and frustration back under control. Then he took her face in his hands, his thumbs tenderly caressing her skin. "Being with you is the only thing that makes all the rest of this bullshit bearable, Elle."

The look in her eyes made him feel twelve feet tall, and she pressed her hands against his chest before coming up on her toes to brush a lingering kiss to his lips. "Then stay. Stay here. With me."

Chapter 18

Jᴇʙ Mᴏɴʀᴏᴇ ʜᴀᴅ ᴍɪsᴄᴀʟᴄᴜʟᴀᴛᴇᴅ. Hᴇ'ᴅ ꜰᴜʟʟʏ anticipated receiving a visit from one of the Dawsons after his most recent messages to the dead cop's widow and the whore who was spreading her legs for Gabe Dawson. What more did he have to do to force them to play into his hands?

He frowned down at his workbench, where he'd laid out the various parts for assembling the guns he'd later sell to his neighbors a few miles down the road. The Feds could keep him from selling *completed* firearms without a license, but there was nothing that could keep him from cutting the metal on his own and partially assembling them to sell the parts to those he knew who also believed in the cause. Those tyrants in Washington could limit someone else's firepower, but he'd be ready when the revolution finally began.

"I'm going to town."

He glanced up from his work at the sound of his daughter's voice, but then turned back to his the weapon in his hands. "You don't need anything. Supplies came in a week ago."

He heard the girl swallow hard, knew she was working up her courage to defy him. "I need to buy...feminine things."

He grunted, not bothering to lift his gaze. "Your brother will get them when he's in town."

That should've been the end of the conversation, but she didn't turn to go. Instead, she heaved a frustrated sigh. "I am not a prisoner here. You can't keep me from leaving!"

He slowly raised his narrowed gaze to meet hers. The only thing that kept her from getting a hand across the mouth was the fear he saw in her eyes. She was terrified of him.

Good.

"You'd better check your tone, girl," he growled. "Don't make me say it twice."

She took a deep, shaky breath and let it out slowly. "Give me a job, then," she said, her voice quaking. "The boys have gone to town for you. Why can't I?"

"Because the boys don't sass me every time they open their mouths," Jeb drawled. "Now, I'm busy. Go tend to your chores."

"They're finished," she shot back, daring to raise her chin at him.

But when he slowly got to his feet, his patience at an end, he was gratified to see her shrink into herself a little, cringing.

"I can take her to town before dinner, sir."

Jeb sent an angry look over Sandra's shoulder at his son Jeremy. "Don't believe I was talking to you, boy."

"Sorry, sir," Jeremy said. "I have to go anyway to pick up the parts you need before the hardware store closes. I can drop her off on the way and pick her up when I'm finished."

Jeb stared at his children, inhaling and exhaling with long, measured breaths. He didn't like this one bit. It was one thing to send his sons to town without him, but his daughter… The girl was barely twenty-two and hadn't been around others much except at church. He'd never bothered sending any of the children to school— his wife had taught them all at home with a curriculum *he* approved, not with the government's indoctrination that passed for public education these days.

"Really," Jeremy said with a shrug, "it's no trouble."

Jeb narrowed his eyes at the both of them. "Alright then," he relented. "You go with your brother, Sandra. But I find out there's something more to this, you're both going to get the strap."

Sandra gave him a relieved grin before turning and hurrying off to get ready, but Jeremy lingered a few moments, looking more than a little nervous. He shifted from one foot to other as if he had something to say.

"What is it, boy?" Jeb finally demanded, tiring of the boy's indecision. Mark and Derrick were never so wishy-washy. They acted—without worrying about the consequences. He didn't always agree with their decisions, but at least they'd had the balls to do what needed to be done.

Jeremy cleared his throat. "I think maybe Sandra is going to town to meet someone."

Jeb's hand clenched into a fist, but he managed to say evenly, "And you offered to give her an escort down the road to sin, is that it?"

"No, sir," Jeremy said quickly. "I thought I'd find out who it is. Figured you'd want to know who she's seeing on the sly."

Something twisted in Jeb's gut—a strange mixture of irritation and relief. "She's not seeing anyone," he spat, getting back to work. "When would she meet anyone? Only people she's around are at church, and I know all those boys—so do you. None of them would dare to touch a hair on your sister's head."

Jeremy looked a little skeptical, giving away what he was thinking before he said, "I think there are a couple of boys who are more interested in the sins of the flesh than concerned about what might happen to them if they lead Sandra astray."

Jeb's relief was quickly replaced by fury. He punched his fist down onto his desk and ground out, "Who are they?"

"I don't know," Jeremy admitted, edging back toward the door. "But I've heard her talking to some of her friends when she didn't think I was listening. Some of the things they're telling her..."

Jeb nodded. "Well, we'll put an end to this. You tell me who you see her talking to, and I'll make sure they're dealt with."

―᷈ᵃᵛ―

"Gabe?"

Gabe looked up from the plate of sushi he'd picked part, meeting Elle's gaze, his brows lifting by way of response.

Elle sighed. Clearly he'd been a mile away, as she'd suspected. "I'm sorry to say you haven't been a very lively date this evening."

He reached across the table and took her hand in his and brought it to his lips, pressing a kiss to her palm. "Sorry. Just going over everything in my head, trying to piece it all together, figure out something we might've missed that would implicate Monroe."

She loved his doggedness, had always admired his

inability to back off when he was on a case. It was what made him one hell of a deputy. But she'd suggested coming to the sushi place near her office so they could have a quiet dinner after the party, just enjoy being together like they had at the fair.

"You're off the clock, Dawson," she reminded him.

He gave her a terse nod. "You're right. What can I do to make it up to you?"

She gave him her best sultry look. "Oh, I think I can come up with a few things."

Without missing a beat, he signaled the waiter for their check, making her giggle. *Giggle?* She was hardly in the habit of giggling, but, yep, that was the effect the man had on her. Well, that and other very naughty, pleasurable effects she couldn't wait to delve into once they got back home.

Gabe paid for their dinner and then clasped her hand, leading her out to the car. She shivered at the sight of it. Good lord, that *car*... Never in a million years had she ever dreamed of making out in a car, let alone making love in one. Or against one, for that matter. But she had a feeling there were lots of things she'd never dared to dream of before. And when they reached the car and he pulled her into his arms for a heated kiss, she had no trouble letting her imagination run wild.

When the kiss ended, he pressed his forehead to hers. "So where we headed?"

She grinned, ready to suggest they stay at her place this time around, but then she gasped and pulled back. "Crap! I almost forgot—I have to pick up something at my office. I have to depose a witness first thing tomorrow morning."

"No problem," he told her. "It's cooled down finally. Why don't we just walk to your office and get what you need, then I'll drop you off at your place."

She felt the heat rising in her cheeks as she said, "Thanks, but I wasn't suggesting that we call it a night so soon. I just need a couple of minutes to grab a file."

His grin spread slowly, his eyes darkening with desire. "Good thing," he murmured, pressing a hand to the small of her back and guiding her toward her office. "Because I think a few minutes is about all I can wait."

They didn't talk the few blocks to her office, nor on the stairs that led up to the third floor of the historic building that housed her office. He was silent as a grave as she rummaged around on her desk, looking for the file she needed, her thoughts so distracted she had to pause on several occasions just to remember what exactly it was she was looking for.

Elle's thoughts were so distracted, in fact, she didn't even hear him when he came up behind her and put his hands on her hips. She started, making him chuckle as he pressed a kiss to her bare shoulder, covered only by a thin strap of her sundress.

She moaned softly as she leaned back against him and rested her head on his chest. "Keep doing that and I'm going to be in trouble."

His hands slipped around her waist, pulling her flush against him, feathering kisses along the side of her throat before whispering in her ear, "I'm up for a little trouble."

"What?" she gasped. "Here?"

When he responded by slipping his hands beneath the straps of her sundress and sliding them down her arms until it began to peel her dress off, she sidestepped out of his reach and pulled the bodice of her dress back up to cover her bare breasts. "Gabe!" she said with a chuckle. "If we get caught, I could lose my job!"

Grinning, she shook her head and turned back around to grab the file from the top of her desk, but clearly that was a mistake. The next thing she knew, his strong hands had slipped beneath the hem of her dress and were sliding lightly up her legs.

She shuddered, her breath catching in her lungs at his touch. "Gabe," she gasped as his hands reached her thong.

He hooked his thumbs under the elastic and slid her panties down her legs until he reached her ankles. Then he gently lifted one foot and then the other, divesting her of the scrap of an undergarment. "Should I stop?" he murmured as his hands drifted back up her legs.

She knew she should. She opened her mouth to tell him so, but all that came out was a loud moan as one hand slipped between her legs. His finger delved insider her, caressing gently, tenderly. *Maddeningly*.

"Oh God," she gasped. She bent forward, bracing herself against her desk as the pleasure of his touch overtook her.

He withdrew slowly and a moment later, cool air hit her skin as he shoved her dress up around her hips. In the next moment, she felt his tongue on her, delving between her folds, tasting and teasing as his fingers resumed their caress.

Her breath quickened as her release rushed up on her, and she no longer cared about someone walking in, didn't care about the fact that she was violating pretty much every office policy imaginable. Her thoughts were only for the maddening pleasure that had her writhing and panting and shuddering with a loud cry that filled her office.

She'd not even finished before Gabe had managed to put on a condom and thrust into her. Her moan blended with his guttural groan.

"God, yes," she panted as he began to thrust, hard and fast, all gentleness having vanished as his skin slapped against hers.

His hands grasped her hips, his fingers digging into her skin where he clutched her tightly, the pressure adding to the intensity of her pleasure as the world began to spin.

His tempo increased as her muscles spasmed; then he thrust once more, long and deep, with a hoarse cry. She thought he would withdraw, but then he was thrusting again, his breath hot on the back of her neck, and a moment later they were shuddering together for a second time.

Finally, he pressed a kiss to her shoulder, to the back of her neck. "Sorry. I had a few ideas of my own."

She rolled her hips against him with a breathy chuckle. "Gotta say, lover, I think I like the way your mind works."

He brushed feathery light kisses along the back of her neck again before finally withdrawing, then snatched several tissues from a box on the corner of her desk and handed them to her.

When she'd discarded the tissues, she let the skirt of her dress fall back into place and started to pull the straps back up over her shoulders, but he stilled her hands. "Allow me."

He bent, taking her breast into his mouth and teasing

the already-hard bud before switching to the other. Then with a resigned sigh, he pulled her straps back up to her shoulders. "I've got to get you home. These clothes are just getting in the way."

She wrapped her arms around his neck and kissed him long and deep, assuring him she was thinking the same thing, then pulled back, giving him a grin. "Why don't you go get the car and come back to get me? I don't think my knees could carry me the few blocks back to where you parked."

He chuckled, the sound sending a shiver of need through her. "I'll meet you downstairs in five minutes."

—⁓—

Gabe tossed his keys up and caught them midair, not bothering to hide what had to be a stupid-looking grin. Hell, as happy as he was at that moment, he could've skipped down the sidewalk, tossing fucking flowers up in the air or some ridiculous shit.

Even being away from Elle now in the few minutes it was going to take for him to walk to the car and pull it around to pick her up was too long. All he wanted to do was hold her in his arms, feel the incredible warmth of her body pressed into his, and never let her go.

He gave himself a quick mental shake, wondering what the hell had happened to him. He'd never felt like this with anyone—not even Audrey.

But Elle, what he felt for her... Well, hell—it defied explanation. He almost felt like if he even tried to put it into words, whatever came out of his mouth would just cheapen what he was really feeling because he wouldn't even be able to come close.

The intensity of it made him want to run down Main Street, whooping and shouting and thumping his chest, but it also scared the shit out of him. Because she was *it*. At least for him. But he had no guarantee that she felt the same way, no matter what she might've admitted to when she was half-asleep.

When he reached his car, he took a deep breath and let it out slowly. Damn. He was a fucking mess. He chuckled quietly and shook his head.

"Excuse me."

He'd been so in his own head, he started at the sudden, quiet voice behind him and turned so quickly that the woman who'd spoken leaped back a step, her eyes wide.

"I'm so sorry," she said softly, her eyes darting about like a frightened doe's. "I didn't mean to scare you."

Gabe shook his head, his brows coming together in a frown. "It's okay. Can I help you?"

She swallowed hard and her eyes darted around again, her anxiety immediately putting Gabe on edge. "Are you Deputy Gabe Dawson?"

He straightened, studying her more closely now. There was something vaguely familiar about her. She was young—college aged if Gabe had to hazard a guess—and pretty in a very sweet, wholesome way. Her thick, golden-blond hair was pulled back in a braid that came down to her waist, and she was dressed in a long sundress that obscured her figure. She had *innocent* written all over her.

Yet she held a bag that contained a small box of what Gabe would've guessed were condoms from what he could see through the thin white bag from the pharmacy.

When she saw him glance at what she was holding, she quickly wrapped the bag around its contents and shoved it deep into the pocket of her skirt. Based on the way she flushed, he'd been dead on about her innocence—but it looked like she wasn't planning to stay that way.

"Yeah," he finally replied to her question, his tone cautious, "I'm Deputy Gabe Dawson. Who's asking?"

She took a quick step forward, grasped his arm, and said in a tumble of words, "I recognize you from the photos. You have to be careful. You and the woman. He's planning something. I don't know what, but he's making my brothers do things, and they're going to get killed! You have to stop him. Please—you have to save my brothers. Brian's only thirteen—he doesn't understand what he's doing!"

"Whoa, hold on there," Gabe said, holding up his free hand. Realization sent a cool shiver down his spine even as he asked, "Let's start with your name. You okay with telling me that?"

"Sandra Monroe," she whispered, glancing around frantically.

"Jeb Monroe's daughter."

She nodded, her eyes darting again.

Damn, he hated being right all the time.

"He'll be back soon." She whimpered ever so slightly, as she added, "I can't be seen with you. My father will kill me if he knows I've told you anything."

Gabe's hackles were up in an instant, his protective instincts in full force. "Get in the car, Sandra," he urged, opening the door for her. "I'll take you to the sheriff's department where you can give a statement. We can protect you."

She shook her head vehemently. "No! I can't. I have to protect my brothers."

Gabe took a cautious step toward her and gently grasped her upper arm, keeping his voice even when he said, "Sandra, the best way to protect your brothers is to come in with me and tell us what you know. Then we can do what's necessary to remove them from your father's house."

She lifted wide blue eyes to his, silently pleading, clearly torn. God, the woman was completely terrified. What kind of father terrorizes his own daughter, for fuck's sake? Gabe was gonna wring that bastard Monroe's neck when he got his hands on him.

"I…I don't know," she stammered. "I need to think. This was a mistake."

Gabe bent his knees slightly so that he was at her eye level. "It's never a mistake to do that right thing, Sandra." He took out his phone and dialed his brother's number, planning to give him a heads-up that he was bringing in Monroe's daughter, but she snatched the phone from his grasp with a strangled cry and hung up.

When she handed the phone back to him, her hand was trembling and she seemed to curl into herself, as if she expected him to lash out at her. "Please don't tell anyone I said anything," she pleaded. "If he finds out…"

Gabe shook his head. "I won't say a word."

"Not even to the woman, the attorney," she insisted. "I don't want her to get hurt. My father can't suspect she knows anything or it'll force his hand."

Gabe's blood chilled. "What's he planning, Sandra? I love that attorney you're talking about. Very much. If anything ever happened to her…" His throat constricted

at the thought, making it impossible for him to finish
the sentence. He leveled his gaze at Monroe's daughter. "Tell me how to protect Elle, and I promise I'll do
everything I can to protect your brothers."

She closed her eyes for a moment, and he knew
he'd gotten through to her. "Okay. But not here. My
brother will—"

"*Sandra*."

The woman practically jumped out of her skin at the
harsh bark behind her. Gabe's eyes snapped up to meet
the furious gaze of Jeremy Monroe.

"Get away from my sister," Jeremy growled, his
hands balled into fists at his sides.

Gabe immediately took a step back. "It's okay. It's
not what you think."

"Liar!" Jeremy yelled, taking a menacing step forward, shaking with rage. "I know all about you, *sinner*!
Leave my sister alone. You already have a whore."

It took every bit of Gabe's control to not deck the
little shit for calling Elle a whore. He clenched his jaw
and shoved his finger in the kid's face. "Watch your
mouth, Monroe. If I didn't know you were just parroting
your father's words—"

"What?" Jeremy shot back. "You'd shoot me like you
did my brother? Kill me here in the middle of the street?"

"I didn't kill your brother," Gabe told him on a sigh,
now feeling sorry for the kid more than angry. "And
I'm not putting the moves on your sister. She's worried
about you and your younger brother. Your father has
brainwashed you, Jeremy—"

Gabe saw Jeremy's fist coming in plenty of time to
block it. He grabbed the kid's arm and twisted it behind

his back in one swift motion, frog-marching him across the sidewalk and pressing him against the wall of the pharmacy.

"I'm going to pretend that didn't happen," Gabe ground out, hoping cutting the kid some slack would help persuade Jeremy that Gabe could be trusted. "I'm not the enemy, Jeremy. But you take another swing at me, kid, and I'm throwing your ass in jail. You get me?"

Jeremy nodded, but when Gabe released him, he took a step back out of Jeremy's reach, just in case. The kid was glaring daggers at him, his face white with a mixture of fear and fury. Without taking his gaze off of Gabe, Jeremy grabbed his sister's arm and shoved her ahead of him toward a pickup truck double-parked a few yards away.

Sandra sent one more pleading look at Gabe over her shoulder before climbing in the truck. Her brother quickly scurried around to the other side and peeled away, nearly taking out the front-end of another car in the process.

Shit!

Gabe ran a hand over his hair in frustration and cursed a blue streak. He'd been *this close* to convincing Sandra Monroe to come with him before her brother had shown up. Now he wasn't sure she'd ever give him the information they needed. And part of that information included an unknown threat to Elle. Fear squeezed his lungs like a vise, making it hard to breathe.

Forcing himself to get his shit together, Gabe got into the Charger and headed back to Elle's office to pick her up, using the two-minute drive to shake off the apprehension worming its way under his skin.

When he pulled up to the curb, Elle's smile was exactly what he needed. As soon as she slid into the seat, he leaned over and captured her lips in a long, slow kiss.

"Is that an apology for taking longer than five minutes?" she murmured with a grin. "If so, you can be late as often as you'd like."

He kissed her again, briefly, then pulled away from the curb and reached over, clasping her fingers and giving them a squeeze. "Sorry. Took a bit longer than expected."

"What happened?" she asked, reading him better than he liked at the moment.

He opened his mouth to tell her about Sandra Monroe, about what she'd been trying to tell him before her brother's sudden arrival, but his gut twisted with dread. He'd taken it on faith that Sandra's story was genuine, that she'd reached out to him in a genuine cry for help. But even if that was the case, he hated to think how her father would react if—hell, he might as well be honest—*when* he found out she'd spoken to someone he considered an enemy.

But Sandra's warning echoed in his head, making him bite back the truth. Instead, he shrugged and forced a smile. "Nothing. Just trying to help somebody who was lost. But promise me you'll be careful, okay? If you see one of the Monroes, just walk the other direction."

She frowned at him. "Yeah, okay. What's going on with you?"

"Seriously, Elle, promise me," he demanded. "I'm worried as hell about what Monroe's up to. If anything were to happen to you…"

She nodded and squeezed his hand. "Okay. I promise."

groan. He pulled Sandra to her feet, dragging her out of the room. She flailed and punched at him, screaming at him to let her go, which only increased his rage. Didn't she realize what he'd done to protect her over the years? What lengths he'd gone to to keep her safe from the lascivious eyes of the corrupt and sinful who would defile her innocence?

Society had grown too lax. The government had ruined the youth of today with their interference. All *he* had ever done was try to keep his daughter safe from these modern-day Sodomites. And the ungrateful little bitch thanked him by running headlong into the arms of the very sinners he was trying to protect her from.

He opened her bedroom door and shoved her in, locking her inside. "You're staying in there until you're ready to give me a name. You hear me, girl?"

The only answer was incoherent screaming as she pounded her fists on the door.

His chest heaving, Jeb strode back into the living room to deal with his traitorous wife. She was lying on the sofa where he'd left her, not moving. He felt a slight twinge of guilt at having knocked her unconscious, but he shoved it aside. She'd brought it upon herself. If she'd just shut her mouth and let him handle things instead of coddling Sandra when her sins were laid bare, then the woman wouldn't be in such a state now.

He left her where she was and stormed into the kitchen, where he'd banished the boys. Brian made a swipe at his eyes, trying to hide the fact that he'd been crying. Jeb made a mental note that he'd need to toughen that boy up if he was going to carry on the cause. But right now, he had a bone to pick with his other son.

Chapter 19

"Jezebel!"

Jeb Monroe's fury stoked a fire in his veins that threatened to burst forth at any moment and blaze brighter than the pits of Hell. He charged toward his daughter where she cowered on the sofa, wrapped in her mother's embrace, tempted to smash her pretty face with the hand he'd balled into a fist.

"Who is he?" he roared, throwing the box of condoms at her. He'd been waiting for her to return and had forced her to empty her pockets and show him what she'd purchased. Her cheek was still red and swollen where he'd struck her. "Who's the boy you're spreading your legs for, you filthy little *whore*!"

"No one!" she cried through her sobs. "I've not been with anyone yet!"

"Yet!" he shouted, seizing upon the word. He grabbed her hair and wrenched her head up, forcing her to look him in the eyes. Through clenched teeth he demanded, "You give me a name, girl. You tell me right now or I will take a strap to you until you bleed."

"Leave her be, Jeb!" his wife screamed at him, digging her nails into his hand, trying to pry his grip loose. "She's done nothing wrong."

Tired of his wife's interference and coddling, he swung his free arm, catching her in the temple, barely sparing her a glance when she fell to the side with a

"Brian, get to your room," Jeb ordered. "I need to talk to your brother."

Without a word, Brian launched to his feet and ran from the room. As soon as he was gone, Jeb pegged his son with a pointed glare. "Give me a name, boy."

Jeremy swallowed hard and glanced in the direction of Sandra's screams, his eyes wide with fear.

"You want to help your sister?" Jeb asked. "You want to keep her safe from harm?"

Jeremy nodded. "Yes, sir."

"Then you give me a name, boy," Jeb ordered. "You tell me who it was your sister was meeting in town."

"I saw her talking with someone," Jeremy admitted. "But I don't think... I mean, I'm not sure anymore... She said nothing happened."

"And you're going believe her?" Jeb demanded. "When she lied to me about why she wanted to go to town? When she was planning on lying down with devils?"

Jeremy flinched at a tremendous thud that sounded like Sandra was trying to batter down her door. "Please, sir," he said, his voice breaking. "Please let her go. She's going to hurt herself."

Jeb pulled out a chair and sat down across the table from his son. He kept his voice low, even, when he said, "You tell me the man's name, boy, and I'll let her go."

Jeremy licked his lips, still looking torn, but then rasped, "Gabe Dawson."

Jeb nodded slowly. He should've known. It was the ultimate betrayal. Mac Dawson had already stolen Jeb's land for the government. Had taken two of his sons. It only made sense that the sheriff would send his favorite son to steal away Jeb's only daughter too.

"I saw them talking," Jeremy added. "I don't know if he's the one she's been meeting, though, Dad."

Jeb slowly got to his feet. "You did the right thing telling me, boy."

"What're you gonna do?" Jeremy asked, his voice quaking. "You're gonna let Sandra out now, right?"

Before Jeb could answer, he heard hurried footsteps behind him and turned to see his youngest standing in the kitchen doorway. "I told you to go to your room!"

"It's Mom," Brian said. "I can't wake her up."

Jeb heaved an irritated sigh and strode back into the living room. As if he didn't have enough to deal with. "Get up, woman," he ordered. "Your son's convinced something's wrong with you." When she didn't respond, Jeb grumbled under his breath and strode to the sofa, grabbing her shoulder and roughly shoving her back. "I said—"

He bit off his words when her head lolled, her mouth agape. He dropped to his knees to put an ear to her chest.

"What's wrong with her?" Brian demanded, frantic. "What's wrong? Mom, wake up!"

Jeb lifted his wife's limp body from the sofa. "Look what they made me do," he growled, carrying her to their bedroom, his sons in tow. "Look what those bastards made me *do*!"

Brian was sobbing, screaming for his mother.

"Stop crying, boy," Jeb snapped as he put his wife on the bed. "She's alive."

He smoothed her hair. "*They* did this. You see that, don't you? They made me do this."

Jeremy shook his head, backing out of the room, dragging his little brother with him. "Who, Dad? Who *the hell* made you do anything? You're totally fuck-ing crazy!"

Jeb was on his feet in an instant, storming after his sons as they rushed down the hall. "Don't you talk to me that way in my own house, boy! I'll tan your hide!" Through the haze of his anger, Jeb heard Jeremy press-ing buttons on his phone. "*Hang up that phone.* Jeremy! Hang up the phone!"

Jeremy halted and turned back to face him, his face twisted with anger of his own. "Mom needs an ambu-lance. I'm calling the police."

Jeb snatched the phone from his son's hand and flung it against the wall. "Like hell you are."

Jeremy shook his head. "I'm not doing this anymore."

When Jeb took a step toward his son, Jeremy shoved his younger brother behind him and lifted his chin in defiance.

So it had come to this, then.

"You do what I say, boy," Jeb hissed. "Don't make me tell you twice."

Jeremy adjusted his stance like he was spoilin' for a fight. "No. What are you going to do if I don't? Kill me too?"

Jeb narrowed his eyes. "I should've known you couldn't take your brothers' places at my side. You're *useless*. I'll handle this myself."

"After you let Sandra go, right?" Jeremy said as Jeb strode from the room.

Jeb scoffed. "She's not going anywhere. And if I catch either one of you boys trying to get her out of her room or sneaking food to her, you'll end up the same way." He glared at his youngest son. "Brian, go use the kitchen phone and call your uncles. Tell them I'm calling a family meeting."

———— ∿ ————

Elle rested her head on Gabe's chest and grinned as his fingers lightly smoothed up and down her spine. "That was incredible."

He pressed a kiss to the top of her head. "Incredible is an understatement."

She took a deep breath and let it out slowly on a long, contented sigh. "Why didn't we do this sooner?"

He chuckled. "It wasn't for lack of trying on my part, let me tell ya."

She kissed his chest, loving the way he groaned with need. She was beginning to recognize that particular sound and what it meant, and that knowledge made her shiver as he rolled her onto her back and captured her mouth in a hungry kiss.

When the kiss ended, he raised his head and peered down at her, brushing her hair away from her face. The look in his eyes was so filled with emotion, her throat constricted. "Gabe, is something wrong?"

He shook his head. "No. In fact, everything's *right*. It scares the hell out of me."

"Why?" she asked, confused. "Do you regret what's happening between us?"

"God no!" he assured her. "Not for a second." His fingertips trailed along the curve of her face as his gaze took her in.

"Then what is it?" she prompted, the gravity of his mood worrying her. "Something's on your mind, I can tell."

His gorgeous, full lips curved up into a grin. "Making love to you all night is the only thing on my mind right now."

He was lying. *But why?*

She lifted her chin, granting him access to her throat as his lips explored her skin, arching into him as his mouth teased her breasts, holding him close as he made love to her again, slowly, languidly, as if savoring every moment.

But when he would've withdrawn from her, she wrapped her arms and legs around him, keeping him where he was. "All night long?" she whispered. "Is that your plan?"

He nodded, nuzzling near her ear. "Every night," he murmured. "If you'll let me."

Her heart began to pound, fluttering against her chest. "Gabe—"

He stopped her words with a kiss, then lifted his head to meet her gaze. "I love you, Elle."

Her breath caught in her lungs. She'd longed to hear those words since she was a teenager, had denied herself even the smallest hope of *ever* hearing them. And now she couldn't quite believe them.

She shook her head a little, clearing away the blissful haze that always descended upon her when she was in Gabe's arms. "What did you say?"

"I love you," he repeated. "I know it's probably too soon to say that. But—"

"I love you, too," she said, the words coming out before she could stop them. "I always have."

His breath shot out of him on a sharp exhale, and he pressed his forehead to hers. Then he was kissing her

again, his fingers spearing into her hair. But there was
something off in his kiss, something in the way his lips
clung to hers, that made her search his gaze for answers
when he at last drew the kiss to a close and got up to
dispose of the condom. When he returned to bed, he
pulled her back into his arms without a word, holding
her close to his heart as if afraid to let her go.

"What is it?" she pressed gently. "Gabe, there's
something wrong. I can feel it." When he tried to turn his
gaze from her, she took his face in her hands and forced
him to look at her. "Gabe Dawson, I *love* you. With all
my heart. But you have to *let* me love you. Don't shut
me out now—not after what you just confessed."

He closed his eyes for a moment as if considering
her words. "I'm worried about Monroe, about what he's
going to try next. I've got to stop that son of a bitch.
When I think about him trying to hurt you again… God,
Elle, I just want to keep you here in my arms and never
let you go."

"Oh, Gabe…" She brushed a kiss to his cheek, his
brow. "Do you think I worry about *you* any less? You're
the one who told me we can't let Monroe get to us or
he wins."

He shook his head. "It's different now."

"Why?" she pressed. "Because we're lovers?"

He clenched his jaw, his chiseled features appearing
even sharper. "Something like that."

She lifted the silver Saint Michael's pendant from
where it lay just below the hollow of his throat and
rubbed her thumb over the image of the archangel, his
sword raised against the cowering Satan at his feet.
How many times had she prayed for Saint Michael's

protection for Gabe and all the Dawsons? Too many to count.

"Nothing's different for me when it comes to being afraid for your safety," she insisted. When he gave her a questioning look, she continued, "Since you became a deputy over a decade ago, I've prayed every day I wouldn't get a call that you'd been hurt. Or killed. Just because I hadn't told you I love you, Gabe, it didn't make my fear for you any less real."

"But this is my *job*," he reminded her. "I accepted the risks when I signed on. Every man in my family has been in law enforcement since before Fairfield County even *was* a county. There were no rose-colored glasses when I decided to follow in my father's footsteps. But you're an *attorney*, for Chrissake. You shouldn't ever have to be in the crosshairs, Elle. Not like this."

Elle offered him a halfhearted smile. "You might not be seeing *your* career with rose-colored glasses, Dawson, but you're certainly using them to view *mine*. I prosecute the bad guys you're arresting, remember? You don't think any of them or their family hold grudges? There's a reason my address isn't listed in the phone book, Gabe."

He sighed—which she immediately recognized as a sign that he was about to capitulate to her rather than actually confide what was bothering him. Yeah, well, that tactic might work for some people, but she wasn't about to let him off the hook that easily. After all, hadn't he said one of the things he admired most about her was her ability to see through his bullshit?

"What are you keeping from me?" she asked, narrowing her eyes at him. "And don't tell me nothing. That would just be insulting."

He ran a hand over his hair and she could tell he was considering his words carefully. "I think Monroe is about to make a move—worse than what we've seen up to now. I think up to this point, he's just been toying with us, trying to make us paranoid until we didn't have a moment's peace. But I think whatever else he has brewing is the real deal and that scares the shit out of me. The fact that I don't have a single fucking clue what he's planning to pull makes it that much worse. I don't know any more than that, Elle. I really don't. I tried to find out more, but it was a no-go."

She leaned upon one elbow, peering down at him. "You have a source?"

He nodded, but it was hesitant. "Anonymous."

"We need to bring this person in," she said, her words coming out in a rush. "We need to find out what he knows, get a statement. It could be the break we were looking for."

"Yeah, well, like I said, it was a no-go," he reminded her. "The informant was afraid of Monroe and was reluctant to make any waves. I mean, hell, can you blame them? Billy Monroe decided to cooperate with us and inform against his uncle, and now they can't find enough of him to even bury."

Elle heaved a frustrated sigh. "Well, this person came to you once. Maybe he will again."

Gabe shook his head. "Something tells me that won't be the case."

"Give me a name," Elle pressed.

"Elle—"

"I'll look into it myself," she continued, "see if I can convince the person to meet with me."

"Let it go," he said, his tone sharp. When she pulled back a little, taken off guard by how adamant he was, he closed his eyes for a moment before saying in a much calmer tone, "I go back to work tomorrow. I'll see what else I can dig up while I'm there."

"And you'll share what you find?" she prompted.

He gave her a terse nod. "Scout's honor."

She arched a single brow at him. "You are a lot of things, Gabe Dawson. But a boy scout is *not* one of them."

The next thing she knew, she was flat on her back and Gabe was grinning down at her. "Thank God for that."

Chapter 20

GABE STOOD IN FRONT OF THE MIRROR AND STRETCHED one arm across his chest and then the other, the new uniform he'd been issued feeling a little stiff. Or maybe it was just the fact that he hadn't been in his Class A's for several weeks. The material felt coarser, scratching the back of his neck; the weight of his gun belt felt heavier somehow.

Then Elle appeared in the mirror behind him, her gorgeous hair pulled back into a low ponytail at the nape of her neck, her tailored charcoal-gray pantsuit accentuating the tantalizing curves of her figure. Her eyes caught his in the mirror and an adorable flush flooded her cheeks.

"Wow," she breathed. "I'd almost forgotten how good you look in a uniform."

He laughed and turned to gather her into his arms. "And here I was thinking I looked like a tool. You're good for my ego, Elle McCoy."

She tapped his chin with her index finger. "I don't think your ego needs any help, lover. But I'll go ahead and tell you that you look seriously hot anyway."

He pressed a kiss to her jaw near her ear, loving the soft little sigh she made, wishing the workday wasn't calling them away from bed so soon. "You have plans this evening?"

Her arms went around his neck, pulling him closer. "Mmm-hmm. And they involve a hot bubble bath."

"Yeah?" he murmured, nuzzling the curve of her throat. "Want some company?"

She pulled back enough to give him a sultry grin. "Sure. Know anyone who'd be interested?"

He bent his head and captured her mouth in a slow kiss, deepening it when she nipped at his bottom lip. When his watch alarm started beeping, they both sighed in disappointment, then chuckled. He pressed his forehead to hers. "We should probably go."

She reluctantly pulled out of his embrace. "Guess so," she agreed as she turned to leave the bathroom. "Give me a ride to the office?"

Although a ride to the office wasn't the kind of ride he had on his mind at that moment, he was happy to give her a lift since her car was still in the shop. "Only if you agree to accompany me to my brother's tonight."

She slung her laptop bag over her shoulder and grabbed her handbag. "Sure. For what?"

Gabe turned on the house alarm and followed her out onto the porch, locking the door behind him before responding. "Abby and Kyle wanted to throw a dinner party at their place. Back to work celebration for me or something, I guess."

She offered him a smile. "I'm glad to see you and Kyle trying to get along better."

Gabe shrugged. "I love the little shit—I hated having that tension between us. But once he lost the massive chip on his shoulder over everything that happened when Mom was sick, we were able to bury the hatchet."

"Well, then, dinner would be great," Elle mused as she headed to his department Tahoe. "So...maybe we should invite Charlotte. Unless you think Kyle and Abby would mind."

He gave her a sidelong glance, noticing she was trying just a little too hard to appear nonchalant. "She's always welcome, of course. But why do I get the impression you have ulterior motives beyond just wanting to include your aunt? What are you up to?"

She shrugged. "Nothing. I just thought it would be nice. I assume your dad will be there?"

"I guess so." He eyed her for a moment before starting up the Tahoe and pulling out of the driveway. "Where are you going with this?"

She cleared her throat and tried to look casual, fiddling with the hem of her suit jacket as she said, "Nowhere. Not really." But when he let silence hang between them she cracked like an egg. "Well, okay—I just thought maybe it would be nice for them to finally go public, for crying out loud. I mean, it's got to be tough sneaking around—"

"Sneaking around?" Gabe sent a startled glance her way. He'd had no idea what she was thinking, but he sure as shit hadn't anticipated an implication his dad was banging Charlotte on the sly. "What the hell are you talking about?"

The look she gave him was equally incredulous. "You didn't realize…? Oh boy."

"What?" he demanded. "You think there's something going on between the Old Man and Charlotte?"

She gave him a disbelieving look. "Seriously? You haven't noticed? He calls her *Charlie*, Gabe. No one else ever calls my aunt that."

He shrugged, suddenly feeling uncomfortable with

the conversation. "So what? They've known each other their entire lives."

"It's not like they were just passing acquaintances," Elle pointed out. "They were high school sweethearts and have remained close friends all these years—more than friends for a while, I'm guessing. Have you really never even entertained the possibility that they'd rekindle their romance?"

He shifted in his seat, wondering why the hell the thought of his dad having a secret girlfriend was pissing him off. Especially when it was a woman who'd been like an aunt to the Dawson boys their whole lives and had often been a surrogate mother to them when their own mother had gotten sick. Was it because Mac hadn't bothered telling any of his sons he was seeing someone after all these years? Or was it because it somehow felt like it was a betrayal to Gabe's mother?

Or maybe he was just predisposed to be irritable because he was returning to duty, only to be parked behind a desk, thanks to his elder brother's newly discovered cautious behavior. Regardless, he left Elle's question unanswered and sulked the rest of the way to her office, only rallying from his piss-poor mood when she leaned across the seat to give him a good-bye kiss and whisper an "I love you" against his lips.

But his mood continued to darken as he drove to the department and pulled into a parking spot. He sat behind the wheel for several moments, psyching himself up, trying to tell himself being a desk jockey was just temporary, that Tom would come around after a week or two and he'd be back out on the road. And if that didn't work, he'd go over Tom's head and take his thoughts on the matter straight to the Old Man.

Their father had made it clear from the moment he'd promoted Tom to the executive deputy position that he was their boss. No questions. No bullshit. If anyone had a problem, they'd have to take it up with Tom. But screw that noise. Gabe had never backed down from anything. He sure as hell wasn't going to now, when his career was on the line.

Setting his jaw and squaring his shoulders, ready to take on whatever bullshit he was going to encounter once he walked in the door, Gabe got out of the Tahoe and strode inside. He was so determined to appear unconcerned with his temporary desk duty that he didn't at first notice the cautious, anxious stares from his colleagues. But after catching the eye of more than one deputy who quickly looked away or offered only a slight jerk of the chin in response to his nod of greeting, his purposeful strides slowed until he came to a halt in the middle of the room.

Gabe hadn't expected a surprise welcome-back party—he wasn't quite the egomaniacal dick people seemed to think he was—but a fucking hello would've been nice.

What the hell…?

He sent a frown toward his brother's office. Tom's door was closed, but his light was on, so Gabe knew his brother was there.

Shit—when wasn't *Tom there these days?*

"Welcome back."

Gabe turned his head to see Deputy Abby Morrow—the sheriff department's digital forensics investigator and his brother Kyle's girlfriend—sitting at her desk. She offered him a grin that looked forced. "It's good to see you up and around again."

"Thanks," he muttered. "What the hell's going on this morning? Someone piss in the coffee?"

Abby sent a glance toward Tom's office, then leaned forward a little and tucked a wisp of shoulder-length blond hair behind her ear. "Tom wants to see you—and you might want to wear a flak jacket."

His brows shot up. "What? This involves *me*? I've only been in the office for two minutes. I haven't had time to piss off anybody yet."

"Your dad got a call this morning," Abby explained, keeping her voice low. "Don't know what about, but we could hear him yelling at whoever it was from all the way out here. He called Tom into his office afterward. Tom stormed out a few minutes later and demanded we send you in as soon as you got here, then slammed his door."

Gabe grunted. "Well, that's encouraging. Where's the Old Man?"

"Left," Abby informed him. "No clue where he went, but he looked like he wanted to kill someone."

Shit.

Gabe knew that look well. The last time he'd seen it was when the Old Man had caught him and Joe sneaking in after curfew coming home from Eric Malone's party, where they'd consumed at least a case of beer between them—probably more. To make matters worse, Gabe had still been completely blitzed when he'd driven his younger brother home.

That was the first and last time Gabe had ever driven after drinking. He'd learned his lesson. The Old Man had made damned sure of that when he'd put both boys into the back of his patrol car and driven them to the jail to sit in the drunk tank overnight. Gabe still remembered dozing off on the cell bench and waking up to some boozer lying on the floor at his feet, puking all over his shoes.

Yeah, no way in hell was he ever gonna go through that shit again. Even if he hadn't become a deputy, that experience alone would've kept from getting behind the wheel when he was trashed and putting someone he loved at risk. Now he either caught a ride home or took a cab. Period.

He frowned, wondering who was on the receiving end of the Old Man's fury now. And why. "And that's all you know about what's going on?"

"Sorry," Abby said on a regretful sigh. "I wish I could give you more to go on before sending you in."

He shook his head. "Yeah. No problem. Thanks for the heads-up." He rapped his knuckles on her desk and donned his most unconcerned smile. "Well, guess I'd better get my ass in there before Tommy throws another tantrum."

Based on the way Abby grimaced and suddenly became very interested in what was on her laptop screen, Gabe suspected he'd already lingered too long. When he turned to see Tom standing in his office doorway, arms crossed over his chest and looking like he was barely keeping a lid on his urge to go completely apeshit, that pretty much confirmed it.

Gabe didn't even wait for Tom to say a word. He headed into his brother's office and dropped down into the chair in front of the desk. As soon as he heard the door close, he drawled, "So, thanks for rolling out the red carpet, Bro. You all really know how to welcome a guy back."

Tom took his seat behind the desk and ran a hand through his dark hair before heaving a harsh sigh. "How do you know Sandra Monroe?"

Well, fuck.

"I don't," Gabe said, his stomach sinking even as he said it. "I met her yesterday on the sidewalk outside of the pharmacy on Fulton. She came up to me and asked if I was Gabe Dawson. Then she told me she was afraid her dad was planning something. She didn't know what, but she was worried for my safety and Elle's. And she was worried about her brothers getting hurt. I tried to get her to come into the department with me to make a statement, but her brother Jeremy showed up and made her leave with him."

Tom pulled a hand down his face and gave Gabe a pleading look. "Please tell me you didn't have your hands on her when her brother got there."

Gabe closed his eyes, his shoulders sagging. He cursed under his breath, dread clenching his gut as he realized where this was probably going. "Of course not. But you know it's going to be my word against theirs."

"Jesus, Gabe," Tom hissed. "Are you fucking *kidding* me? Jeb Monroe's *daughter*!"

Gabe shot to his feet and jabbed a finger at his brother. "Now just wait a goddamned minute! I didn't do anything more than talk to her. And *she* approached *me*. What exactly are you accusing me of?"

Tom shook his head, his jaw clenched tight. "It's not me who's doing the accusing. It's her father. He's saying you assaulted her."

Gabe straightened, his jaw falling open in his shock. "What?"

Tom shook his head, looking sick at having to even say the words. "Monroe is claiming you made an advance on Sandra, tried to force yourself on her, and when she refused, you roughed her up."

"That's fucking crazy," Gabe breathed, dropping into the chair. "You know I'd never lay a hand on a woman, no matter who she is. And I've never even seen Sandra Monroe before yesterday. Not only that—we were in the middle of the sidewalk. Check the pharmacy's security cameras and you'll be able to see what happened."

Tom nodded. "Already working on that. What am I going to see, Gabe? Anything I need to worry about?"

"I had my hands on her upper arms," Gabe explained, shaking his head in dismay. "She was shivering with fear. I was just trying to convince her she'd be safe if she talked with us. I was trying to console her."

"How hard were you gripping her arms?" Tom asked.

Gabe's brows came together in a confused frown. "Not at all. She was so skittish, I was barely even touching her."

Tom turned his laptop around to show Gabe the screen. "These are photos Monroe sent to the Old Man this morning."

Gabe cursed a blue streak when he saw the images before him. The pretty little blond he'd met the evening before was a bruised and bloody mess. Her arms bore heinous black and yellow and purple bruises. Her bottom lip was split, blood covering her chin. Her left eye was swollen shut. And a close-up of her hands showed broken and bloodied fingernails and other wounds that made it appear she'd put up one hell of a fight.

"I didn't do this," Gabe rasped. "Jesus, Tom. You know I didn't."

"Where did you go after you met her on the street?" Tom asked.

Gabe was so disconcerted, he shook his head, needing to stop and get his thoughts in order before answering. "Uh…I went back to Elle's office to pick her up. We'd had dinner, and I dropped her at her office so she could pick up a file. I was getting the car when Sandra approached me."

"And then?"

Gabe leveled his gaze at his brother, growing angry that the incredible night he'd had with the woman he loved was turning out to be an alibi. "We spent the night together. And before you even ask, yeah, it was the entire night. Give her a call and ask her. I dropped her off at her office this morning."

Tom dropped his gaze. "She's dealing with her own issues right now."

Gabe felt rage building in his chest and had to tamp it down in order to grind out, "What the hell do you mean?"

Tom looked up, his expression guarded. "How long have you and Elle been sleeping together?"

Gabe was on his feet in an instant. "What the hell business is it of yours?"

"Turns out it's going to be everyone's business soon," Tom informed him. "Monroe's planning to ask that Derrick receive a new trial. He's claiming that Elle should've recused herself as prosecutor because you were the lead investigator on the case and she was having a sexual relationship with you at that time."

"That's bullshit!" Gabe raged. "Elle and I didn't get together until after I was shot."

"Nothing ever happened before that?" Tom prompted. "She'll confirm that?"

Gabe paced a tight path in front of Tom's desk. "Of course! You know what our relationship has been like. She wouldn't give me a chance—" He came to an abrupt halt. "Ah, fuck."

"When?" Tom demanded. "*When* did something happen between you two prior to the trial? And who knows about it?"

Gabe laced his fingers behind his neck and leaned his head back, squeezing his eyes shut. "The night Chris died. The bartender at Mulaney's called her. I was shit-faced and she came in to encourage me to leave. She gave me a ride home and one thing led to another."

"Goddamn it, Gabe!" Tom roared, coming out of his chair.

"We didn't sleep together," Gabe fired back. "We just… Christ, why am I telling you any of this? I don't have to explain myself to you, you sanctimonious dick!"

"Yeah?" Tom retorted. "You'd better tell me every single *fucking* detail, Gabe. Do you have any clue what it'll do to Chris's widow if we have to go through another trial? If Derrick Monroe walks?"

Gabe shook his head. "We did everything right in that investigation. Derrick won't walk. There're no holes."

"Except the big fucking crater where Billy Monroe's house used to be," Tom shot back. "You know as well as I do that the evidence Elle presented against Derrick wasn't ironclad. The eyewitnesses from the diner were a little hazy on some of the details. Only two of them could positively ID Derrick at all. Elle did one hell of a job in that trial and the jury made the right call. But there's no guarantee another jury would."

Gabe dropped back into the chair and put his face in his hands, his thoughts racing. He lifted his gaze to his brother. "Where's Dad? Abby said he stormed out before I got here. I need to talk to him, make sure he knows this is bullshit."

Tom heaved a sigh. "He knows it's bullshit just as much as I do, Gabe. You think Dad would ever think you're capable of doing something like this? The Old Man has his faults, but he raised us better than that. In fact, he's on his way to Phil Murray's house to try to get to him before Monroe does."

Gabe nodded. "Judge Murray's not gonna let Monroe get away with this."

Tom sat down on the corner of his desk. "Gabe, even if that's the case, this is going to come out. Even the *allegation* of something of this nature is going to affect you and Elle. There'll have to be an investigation."

"We need to get Sandra Monroe in here somehow, get her side of the story," Gabe muttered. "She can set the record straight."

"Her father's bringing her in later today to make her statement against you," Tom told him. "And he's bringing her brother as a witness."

Gabe stared at Tom for a long moment, suddenly numb.

He was done. Tom was right. This story was going to hit the media and even though it was patently false, it wouldn't matter. He'd be convicted by public opinion even when it was later proven to be just a fabrication of

Jeb Monroe's deranged mind. Gabe's dream of someday taking over as sheriff was over. Everything he'd worked for all these years, all the good he'd done for the community…it was now tainted, sullied.

"I'm going to have to put you on paid leave until after an investigation has been conducted," Tom told him, his voice strained. "You know that, right?"

Gabe nodded, still in a daze. "Yeah. I know."

Tom's expression was pained as he said, "If there was anything else I could do…"

Gabe stood and glanced around the room, momentarily forgetting where the door was. "Yeah."

The next thing he knew, his brother was hugging him. "We're not going to let this son of a bitch get away with this, Gabe," he ground out, an edge in his voice Gabe had never heard before. "I swear it."

The grim determination in his brother's voice snapped Gabe out of his stupor. He returned the hug for a moment, but when his throat grew tight with emotion, he tapped out and strode from Tom's office, keeping his eyes forward, not daring to meet any of the questioning stares he felt trained on him.

Right then, his only concern was getting to Elle. He'd be damned if he'd let her go down for his mistakes. He'd take the fight to Monroe personally before he'd let that happen. Fuck protocol. This shit was about to get real.

Chapter 21

ELLE SAT IN A DAZE BEHIND HER DESK, STILL UNABLE to believe what she'd heard. There was no way Gabe had done what he'd been accused of. It simply wasn't possible. Even if she'd heard the ludicrous allegations before she'd known him—before she'd fallen in love with him—she wouldn't have believed it for a moment. Now that she knew him like she did, had seen the depth of his heart, the limitlessness of his kindness and compassion, the mere thought of someone making an accusation like this infuriated her.

But what she couldn't understand was why he'd not told her about Sandra Monroe. She'd been unable to completely refute Monroe's allegation of assault against his daughter because she hadn't known anything at all about the encounter. Why the hell hadn't Gabe thought to mention it? Why had he withheld that information?

"Elle?"

She glanced up to her office doorway to see Gabe standing there, his expression so forlorn and haggard he looked far older than his thirty-six years. "Looks like I might be reconsidering that job at the foundation after all."

He closed the door and came toward her, his hands balled into fists at his side. "They *fired* you?"

She shook her head, still trying to process it all. "No. Well, not yet anyway. I'm being put on paid administrative leave and have been given the option of resigning in order to save face. But odds are good that even if we're cleared of any wrongdoing, this will follow me wherever I go."

Gabe ran a hand over his hair in agitation, his frustration and anger at the situation a palpable force in the air around him. She hadn't asked what he'd encountered when he'd arrived at the department, but the fact that his strong, proud shoulders had bowed under the weight of the situation was a pretty good indication his morning had been as sucktacular as her own.

She wanted to go to him, put her arms around him and comfort him, feel his arms around her and know a little comfort of her own, but her shock was quickly edging toward anger. "God, Gabe," she said on a dejected sigh. "Why didn't you tell me you ran into Sandra Monroe last night? When confronted about it, I'm sure I looked like a deer in headlights. I couldn't defend you against something I had no knowledge of. The only thing I could give my boss was the truth about us being together all night. And let me tell ya, that led to quite the interrogation!"

"I'm so sorry, honey," he said, coming around the desk and reaching out to her, but she held up her hands, avoiding his touch. His face fell at her reaction. "I fucked up, Elle. I get that. But I was trying to protect Sandra, protect *you*."

"*Protect* me?" she repeated, pushing back from her desk and getting to her feet. "How is keeping me in the dark *protecting* me? We had a deal, Dawson! We were supposed to be in this *together*. You were supposed to keep me in the loop on *every*thing. And yet you decided this would be a good little tidbit to keep from me? Great idea!"

Gabe clenched his jaw, averting his eyes. Then his shook his head before turning his gaze back to hers. "Yeah, Elle, I decided to keep this one from you. Sandra is convinced that you're in danger, and that little 'tidbit' has me scared shitless, okay? The thought of anything happening to you..." His words trailed off, and he abruptly looked away again, his jaw clenched so hard she could see the muscle twitching in his cheek.

"Well," she said quietly, "I guess you were right about Monroe making a move. I'd say this certainly qualifies."

"I don't think this is the end of it," Gabe told her. "Something tells me that trying to ruin our careers, our reputations, by claiming I assaulted his daughter wasn't part of the plan."

"Jeremy was following me. He saw us together at the fair," Elle reminded him. "You don't think he told his father?"

Gabe shook his head. "He might've had something up his sleeve regarding our relationship, but Sandra running into me was a coincidence. It wasn't planned—she was at the pharmacy buying condoms from what I could see in the bag she had. She had no idea I'd happen to be walking by just then. I think he pounced on our encounter and used it to cover his own ass."

"He beat his own daughter *just* to pin it on you?" Elle said, not bothering to hide her doubt. Any decent prosecutor would shoot that theory full of holes in an instant. "Seems a bit extreme even for Monroe."

"No, I don't think he beat her just to make me look bad," Gabe spat. "I think he beat the shit out of her for whatever reason and then decided to use it to his advantage. And he has her so fucking scared that she's willing to come in and give a statement supporting his bullshit story."

"What the hell are you going to do, Gabe?" Elle asked, finally coming toward him, closing the gap between them, her concern for him trumping her anger at that moment. The thought of him losing his job as a deputy, his entire future in law enforcement potentially destroyed, was heartbreaking enough. But the possibility that he could end up being convicted of a crime he didn't commit had her barely holding her panic and dread in check.

"I'm not taking this shit lying down, I can tell you that," Gabe assured her, a dangerous edge to his voice.

She eyed him warily, her dread taking on a new slant. "Please tell me that by that you mean allowing your father and brothers to conduct a full investigation and clear your name."

The look Gabe gave Elle made her stomach drop, and his words pretty much confirmed her fears. "I'm not letting that asshole destroy us, Elle."

"Gabe, this is not the time to confront Monroe," she insisted. "Don't talk to him. Don't talk to anyone he knows. If you see him or any of his family on the sidewalk again, you cross the street and don't so much as glance in their direction."

"Like hell," Gabe spat. "I'm not just going to slink off with my tail between my legs like I've done something wrong. I refuse to let that bastard win!"

"I'm not telling you this as just the woman who loves you and wants to have a future with you, Gabe," Elle hissed through clenched teeth, damning that stubborn Dawson pride. "I'm telling you this as an attorney. You confront him and you'll just give him more fuel for the fire. You know that!"

He took her face in his hands, his expression fierce. "I'm not going to make the same mistake I made before. I'm not letting anything happen to *you*."

Seeing him so emotional made Elle's chest constrict. But if they were going to make this thing between them work—and that seemed like a pretty damned big *if* at the moment—there was one thing he was going to have to understand about her. "I'm not helpless, Gabe."

Gabe's hands dropped away, a dark scowl on his face as he took a step back, putting distance between them. "What the hell is that supposed to mean? I realize that."

"I don't need to be rescued," she insisted. "But *you* might need to be if you don't listen to me. Right now I'm more concerned about keeping you out of prison, for crying out loud! So would you stop being a knight in shining armor for one goddamned minute and try to be reasonable for once?"

"*Reasonable?*" he retorted, his voice filling her office. "So you want me to just bend over and take it? Let Monroe get away with ruining both of us? With hurting *you?* Fuck. That."

Elle huffed. God, the man could be infuriating! "That's not what I'm saying."

"Yeah? Well, it sure as hell sounds that way," Gabe barked. "You might be perfectly happy to just throw your hands up in the air and give up without a fight, but that's *not* the Elle McCoy I know, *not* the woman I fell in love with."

Elle straightened, hurt that he'd think she wasn't pissed as hell and determined to do her damnedest to fight back. Did he really think she'd give up that easily? That she'd give up on *him* that easily? Her throat was tight as she said, "Maybe you don't know me as well as you thought."

He stared at her for a long moment before giving her a sharp nod. "Yeah. Maybe I don't."

With that, he stormed from her office, slamming the door behind him. Elle stood watching the door for several moments, half expecting him to come back in and take her in his arms, to whisper an apology and assure her they'd get through this, they'd figure it out. But when he didn't return, she dropped back into her chair and put her face in her hands.

She desperately wanted to either burst into tears or punch a hole in the wall. Maybe both. Just get it out of her system so she could clear her head. And that wasn't going to happen while she was at the office.

She fished her phone out of her handbag and brought up her recent call list. She briefly considered calling Gabe to make sure he was okay, but just as quickly discarded the idea, deciding they both needed a little time to cool off before they talked things over again. Instead, she hit the number below it.

When the call connected and she heard the familiar voice on the other end, the tears of anger and frustration Elle had been holding back spilled onto her cheeks.

———

Elle slammed down the shot glass and motioned to her aunt Charlotte for another. "One more."

Charlotte gave Elle a disapproving look as she removed the upside-down glass from the counter and wiped up the tequila that had spilled out. "That's your fourth, baby girl, and it's just noon."

Elle ran a hand through her hair, which had to be a frizzy mess by now. Her aunt had picked her up from her office three hours earlier, but when she'd pulled into Elle's driveway, Elle had realized she didn't want to be at home, didn't want to think about the blissful moments she and Gabe had shared there, didn't want to smell his aftershave on her couch—or her clothes.

So she'd ditched her pantsuit for jeans and a T-shirt and had joined Charlotte at the pub, filling in her aunt on all that had taken place with Gabe, with Monroe, with the colossal clusterfuck that was her career at that moment. She'd thought it would help ease the ache in the center of her chest that had been there since Gabe had stormed out, but the wound was rawer now, the ache more intense. The shots of tequila had done nothing at all to dull it.

She glared at her aunt, but there wasn't much ire in it. "I'm barely buzzed. I think I deserve a bit more than that, don't you?"

"I think there's a lot you deserve, Elle," Charlotte said on a sigh. "But one helluva hangover isn't on the list."

Elle scoffed. "I haven't had a hangover since my twenty-first birthday." She made a grab for the bottle, but her aunt calmly moved it back to the shelf.

"Call Gabe," Charlotte ordered when she turned back to the bar, sliding Elle's phone toward her hand. "You know you're just going to sit here and torture yourself over everything until you do."

Elle shook her head. "I'm the last person he wants to hear from right now."

"You sure about that?" Charlotte drawled. "Maybe *you're* the one trying to avoid a conversation."

She rolled her eyes. "Don't be ridiculous. I'm not avoiding anything."

Charlotte's brows lifted. "No? Sounds to me like you might regret a few of the things you said."

"Are you taking his side?" Elle asked. "Seriously?"

The bell on the door jingled as the beginnings of the lunch crowd started coming in. Charlotte lifted her hand in greeting. "Be right with ya, folks." She then turned her attention back to Elle. "I'm not taking anyone's *side*. Jeb Monroe is a son of a bitch and what you and Gabe are going through because of Jeb's bullshit has me ready to march up to his front door and punch that bastard right in the balls."

Elle laughed, getting a mental image of her aunt nailing Monroe in his family jewels. She had no doubt Charlotte could've made the man sing soprano without any difficulty, too.

"But," Charlotte continued, "my point is I love you and Gabe both and want you to be happy. The way I see it, your chances at happiness are better if you're fighting against *Monroe* and not each other."

Elle sighed. "I know. I just…I want this to work, Charlotte. I love him. I'm *in* love with him. But he can't keep treating me like I'm helpless."

"Well, I think you made that pretty clear," Charlotte told her. "Now maybe it's time to give him the chance to prove he got the message."

Elle glanced at her phone. Charlotte was right.

As usual. Maybe Elle *was* avoiding calling Gabe. But her phone hadn't exactly been ringing off the hook either. "If he calls, I'll talk to him."

"And if he doesn't call?" Charlotte prompted.

Elle shrugged. "He invited us to Kyle and Abby's tonight for dinner. I'm still going—they're my friends, regardless of what's going on with Gabe and me. I'll just talk to him then."

Charlotte shook her head and grabbed her notepad and pen to go take her customers' orders. "Sometimes it takes a little courage to set aside pride and be the first to apologize, baby girl," she said. "Doesn't make him any less wrong for what he did or what he said. Just means you're opening the door for him to come crawling in on his knees."

Elle laughed again, earning a good-humored wink from her aunt. Then she picked up her phone and purse, stuffed a twenty into her aunt's tip jar when she was sure Charlotte wasn't watching, then headed out front to call a cab to take her home.

But before she could place a call, her phone began to ring. She glanced at the number, not recognizing it. Frowning, she answered, "Hello?"

"Ms. McCoy?"

Elle's frown deepened. The voice was soft, hoarse, as if the woman on the other end was whispering. "Yes. Who's this?"

"Janice Monroe."

Elle's blood turned to ice water in her veins. *Jeb Monroe's wife*. She'd never spoken to Mrs. Monroe, had only seen her in the courtroom during Derrick's trial, her eyes red and swollen, her slight frame curled forward in sorrow and hopelessness. "Mrs. Monroe," Elle said. "How did you get this number?"

She hesitated a moment before answering, "My husband has the addresses and phone numbers of everyone who works for the county. He's had them for quite some time."

Elle's mind raced with the implications of what she'd just heard. "How did he get that kind of information?"

"I don't know," Janice stammered. "I just know he does."

Elle pressed her lips together in frustration. The woman knew more than she was admitting, but she kept her voice level when she said, "Mrs. Monroe, you shouldn't be calling me. I'm sorry, but—"

"Please don't hang up!" the woman cried. Her voice cracked pitifully when she added, "I…I need your help."

Elle's grip on her phone tightened. Gabe had thought Monroe's daughter was on the verge of talking. Maybe his wife was eager to talk as well. The poor woman sounded terrified. "Call the police. I'm sure they can assist you."

"He'll kill me if I go to the police," Janice told her. "I need you to go to them for me."

Elle pressed the heel of her palm against her eyes. *Great*. She was half-popped from tequila and Janice Monroe wanted her to call the cops for her. "Mrs. Monroe, could you meet me somewhere in about an hour? Somewhere public, of your choosing. I'll help you if I can, but I'm unable to drive at the moment."

There was hesitation on the other end of the line before Janice finally said, "I'll try. I have a concussion, I think. He hit me—Jeb did. And…oh my God, my

God—my baby girl!" She began to sob. "What he did to my baby girl!"

The fear and anguish in the woman's voice made Elle's blood boil with outrage. Women like Janice Monroe were exactly the kinds of victims Elle assisted through her work at the foundation, the very women she had vowed to protect and help wherever and however she could. The woman was desperate. If anyone needed Elle at the moment, it was Janice Monroe.

"Where's Jeb now?" Elle asked. "Is he there with you?"

The woman sniffed, her voice shaky as she said, "No. He's at the sheriff's department, making a complaint against Deputy Dawson. He took our son Jeremy and daughter Sandra with him."

Elle nodded to herself. That could take a while. If they moved quickly, she could get a cab to the Monroe farm and get Janice to the sheriff's department before Jeb made it back home. She'd just have to make sure to time it right. She'd made a promise to Gabe about staying safe and avoiding any of the Monroe men after all.

"Mrs. Monroe," she said, "I'm coming to pick you up. But it's imperative that you be ready to go when I get there."

As soon as Elle hung up, she called the cab, then placed another call.

"Deputy Abby Morrow."

Elle was relieved to catch her friend at her desk. "Hey, Abby. It's Elle."

"Hey, sweetie," Abby said. "How're you holding up?"

Elle groaned. "Been better. I was wondering if you could do me a favor."

"You know I will," Abby responded without hesitation. "What do you need?"

"I need you to give me a call as soon as Jeb Monroe leaves the department to head home."

"Okay…" Abby replied, drawing out the word in her wariness. "Why?"

"Just want to keep track of his movements," Elle said, flagging down the cabbie as he pulled into Mulaney's parking lot. "I'll explain it all later."

"Should I tell Gabe you called?" Abby asked in a rush. "He's in with Mac, but I can tell him when he comes out."

Elle hesitated as she opened the cab door. If he knew what she was doing, he'd come racing out to the farm, probably just in time to confront Jeb. That's the *last* thing he needed right then. She'd give him a call as soon as she had Janice safely in the cab and they were on their way back to the sheriff's department. He'd definitely want to be there to listen in as Janice gave her statement.

"No," she finally replied to Abby. "I'll give him a call as soon as I can."

Elle hung up and glanced at her phone as she got into the cab. Her battery was nearly dead. Her window of opportunity for getting Janice Monroe and her children to safety just got a little smaller.

Damn it!

"Miss? Where to?" the cab driver prompted.

Elle rattled off the address to the Monroe farm. She wasn't surprised at all that she still remembered it. After looking through Derrick's file so many times, searing every fact into her brain for the trial, she doubted she'd ever forget any of it. Even the parts she wished she could.

Chapter 22

GABE SAT IN THE CHAIR IN HIS FATHER'S OFFICE, GRIPPING the wooden arms so hard in his rage that his knuckles were white. "You've got to be *fucking* kidding me."

Mac's brows lifted in a look of slight disapproval. "Care to rephrase that?"

Gabe gave his father a defiant look. "You've got to be *fucking* kidding me, sir?"

Mac jabbed his index finger at his son. "I'm not the enemy here, Son."

Gabe took a moment to collect himself before he managed to grind out, "Judge Murray owes his entire career to your influence, and the one time you go to him for a favor, he tells you to piss off?"

"It's an election year," Mac muttered, rising from his chair and pacing over to his office window.

Gabe waited for the rest of an explanation for several moments before he realized that was all he was going to get. "This is bullshit," he spat. "You know this, right? I didn't do any of what Monroe is claiming."

Mac gave him a terse nod without turning away from the window. "I know that, Gabriel. But it doesn't matter a damn what I believe. My influence only goes so far in this county."

"You wouldn't have said that twenty years ago," Gabe shot back.

At this, Mac did turn to give him a questioning

look. "What the hell is that supposed to mean, young man?"

Gabe meant that twenty years ago, if someone had tried to pull this kind of shit on one of Mac's deputies, Mac would've been paying the bastard a visit to make it clear he wasn't about to let a move like that go unanswered. There was no way in hell he would've taken no for an answer.

"I'm just wondering who else might be worried about an election year," Gabe admitted.

Mac's normally stoic face went stormy. "You think I'd let you go down because I was worried about keeping my ass in this chair? You think I'd *ever* put my career over you boys?"

Gabe immediately felt like an ass. Only a few months earlier, he'd been defending the Old Man to Kyle with the same argument, knowing full well what lengths Mac would go to for family after having witnessed his unfaltering devotion to their mother in her illness. He'd sacrificed everything to try to save her life only to fail in the end.

The guilt didn't end there. Mac had been forced to deplete the boys' college funds to cover medical bills. Tom and Kyle had managed on scholarships and student loans. Gabe had gone to school part-time, working his way through. But Joe had joined the National Guard, and during one of his deployments, they'd nearly lost him. Gabe knew their father blamed himself to this day, berating himself for not providing better for his family. He saw it in his dad's eyes every time he caught Mac looking at Joe.

The one time he'd worked up the nerve to ask his dad what was going through his head, he just got a terse, "It'd kill me, losing one of you boys."

Finally, Gabe heaved a sigh. "Of course not, sir. I'm sorry. I just don't know what the hell I'm gonna do."

Mac came around to the front of his desk and sat on the corner, looking so much like a twenty-five-year-older version of Tom, Gabe had to suppress a grin.

Mac narrowed his eyes at Gabe for a long moment, then gave a nod as if coming to some decision. "You're gonna man up, Gabriel, and keep your head high. And when we clear you of these bullshit charges, you're gonna bring that son of a bitch down. Is that clear?"

Gabe gave a terse nod that mirrored his father's. "Yes, sir."

<hr />

Jeb Monroe led his daughter by the arm, holding her gently, as if she might break. He didn't miss the way the deputies he passed on the way into the sheriff's department looked away, as if they might be considered guilty by association.

So the story was already out…

Good. It was the first nail in Deputy Dawson's coffin. And, by extension, that of his father. The Dawson family was about to feel the fury of his wrath as demanded by the judgment of the Great Almighty himself.

Jeb had realized the night before that it was time to act, time to make his move on the Dawsons and their whore in the prosecutor's office. And what he had planned would be just the sort of incident that made the papers, galvanized other righteous people like him who prepared for the revolution that was coming. They'd know it was time to act, time to take up arms and declare independence from tyranny.

"I can't do this."

He halted abruptly, his daughter's cowardice snapping him out of his dreams for the future. He sent a quick glance around and jerked her arm, making her whimper and shrink away from him. "You *can* do this," he growled. "You *will* do this. Is that clear? You know what's at stake."

Her chin began to tremble. "But it's wrong."

He narrowed his eyes at her, his grip on her arm tightening until she cried out. "Is rising up against tyranny ever wrong? Is following the will of God to rid the world of hedonists ever wrong?"

She didn't reply, merely stood there trembling. And well she *should* tremble for fear of the world and how Satan had sunk his claws into the godless. She should be very afraid her own soul was at risk. But soon she'd be delivered of the horrors of this world. She would serve as a martyr for the cause and be forever spoken of with reverence among the righteous. It would be his final gift to her. He would save her from turning her back on the cause before her betrayal was known to any others.

But first she had a vital part to play.

Jeremy stood off to the side of the door, hands in his pockets, his head hanging. Jeb had yet to determine what to do about his son. The boy had betrayed him as well, had called him crazy. But weren't many of the great men of history considered crazy until they were proven right? Jeremy was misguided, led astray by his traitorous mother. But he would soon have him back on the right path.

"Get inside," Jeb snapped, dragging Sandra forward. "Now both of you remember what I told you. You say exactly what we rehearsed on the ride here."

When Jeremy nodded, Jeb pulled open the door and strode straight to the front desk. "I'm here to see Sheriff Dawson," he announced. "You can tell him Jeb Monroe is here with his daughter."

———

Gabe felt something in the air shift and the hair on the back of his neck prickled. His instincts told him Monroe had arrived even before he turned in his seat to see who his father was glaring daggers at.

"Here we go," Mac ground out. "You can listen in, in the observation room."

Gabe nodded and waited until one of the deputies ushered Jeb and his children to the conference room, then squared his shoulders and strode out of his father's office, not bothering to meet the curious gazes of any of his colleagues. But just as he was entering the observation room, his phone began to buzz.

His heart leaped up into his throat. Expecting it to be Elle finally calling him, he snatched it from his hip and answered without even checking the screen display. "Hey, I'm sorry—"

"Is it true?"

Shit.

"Jessica," he said, slipping into one of the other conference rooms instead. "How are you and the kids?"

"Pretty damned pissed, Gabe," Chris's widow hissed. "Is it true you screwed up the investigation? Is Derrick Monroe getting another trial? And did you assault some woman? I know you've always been a player, but did you *seriously* stoop to something so brutal?"

"Jesus, Jess," he interjected when she finally paused

to take a breath. "You know I didn't! I would never treat anyone that way. It's all bullshit. How did you even find out?"

"Are you serious?" she laughed. "It's all over the news."

Gabe's head suddenly felt like it was about to explode. He pinched the bridge of his nose and squeezed his eyes shut, trying to focus on something other than the pounding in his head. "Of course Monroe would go to the press. Why am I surprised?"

"And the trial?" she continued. "What about that?"

He heaved a frustrated sigh, wishing he could give her such an emphatic denial on that one. "I don't know. We're fighting it. Dad talked to Judge Murray, but with the climate not being particularly friendly to law enforcement right now, Murray's treading lightly."

He heard her mutter a curse. "That man can*not* go free, Gabe. He just *can't*. I can't go through that again. The *kids* can't go through that. Teddy's old enough now to understand what's going on. I don't want him to hear all the details of how his father died."

"You know we did everything by the book in Chris's case," Gabe assured her. "You *know* we did right by him, Jess. I loved the guy like a brother."

"Yeah, well, what would you do if it was one of your *real* brothers, Gabe?" she demanded. "If you cared so much about Chris, then you make sure that son of a bitch sitting in prison for his murder doesn't get out."

She hung up before he had a chance to respond. It was probably just as well. All he could do was make empty promises anyway.

Speaking of empty promises…

He checked the call list on his phone, hoping that maybe he'd missed a call from Elle, but no such luck.

He'd been an ass to storm out of her office like he had earlier. All he'd wanted to do was take her in his arms and hold her, tell her how much he loved her over and over again and hope it still meant something to her.

It was killing him that they'd left things the way they had. He'd almost called her a few times since then but had thought better of it, not wanting to make the situation worse. He checked his watch. Several hours had passed. *Shit*. He probably should've at least *tried* to call sooner… Even if she'd told him to go to hell, she would've at least known he wanted to talk.

He hit her number before he could talk himself out of it and listened to the phone ring until it went to her voice mail. Even the sound of her recorded voice made his heart race.

God, he had it bad…

"Hey, it's me," he said. "I just… I was just hoping to talk. I'm sorry I stormed out earlier. Just…call me, I guess."

He returned his phone to his hip, an undercurrent of apprehension creeping beneath his skin. He had the sudden urge to claw at himself to dig out the sensation.

It was ridiculous. Elle was fine. She was probably just busy. Or still pissed. Either one was completely plausible, all things considered.

And yet he couldn't help feeling that something was off. Something just didn't feel right. His instincts were telling him he needed to get his ass moving—but where? Why? Was it just the fact that Monroe was sitting just a couple rooms down, spouting lies so ridiculous they'd already starting spreading like wildfire? Or was there something more?

He gave himself a hard mental shake and tried to tamp down the restlessness plaguing him, then charged toward the observation room to try to catch some of the bullshit Monroe was slinging.

He slipped inside, closed the door softly behind him, and jerked his chin at his brothers who'd gathered there as well.

"Hey, Joe, Kyle," he said. "Come to enjoy the show?"

"Tom called us," Kyle told him. "Thought we might want to be here. Nobody's seriously buying this shit, are they?"

"Apparently so," Gabe replied. "Got a call from Jessica Andrews a few minutes ago—she heard it on the news."

Joe cursed under his breath. "Media doesn't miss a beat, do they? Never mind that this son of a bitch is a total whack-job."

Kyle shook his head as he watched through the observation glass while Sandra Monroe told her story to the deputy Tom had assigned to take her statement. "Look at her body language," Kyle murmured. "She's clearly been coerced. I can see that even without knowing the backstory. And you can tell she's been coached by the *way* she's telling the story. Every time Adam asks her a question to clarify a detail, she turns to look to her father for approval."

"I don't think Monroe cares that we know she's lying," Gabe told them. "Just planting the doubt against Elle and me serves his purpose, even when we're cleared later. This is just a diversion."

"From what?" Joe asked.

Gabe shook his head. "Wish I knew."

Tom jerked his chin toward the glass. "Jeremy's up."

Gabe narrowed his eyes as he watched and listened to Jeremy's account of Gabe's encounter with Sandra. There was just enough truth in it to be believable.

Joe grunted in disgust. "He's pretty damned twitchy. Wonder what Monroe threatened to do to them if they didn't lie for him."

"Considering what he did to his daughter just for talking to me, God knows," Gabe murmured, wishing like hell that he'd been able to persuade Sandra to get into his car. Seeing her in person was even worse than what the pictures showed. He fisted his hands at his sides, forcing himself to stay where he was and not charge in there and beat the shit out of Monroe for treating his own daughter with such brutality.

A loud scraping of chairs on the tile floor jolted Gabe from his thoughts. "They're finished? It's only been half an hour."

"Guess that's all you need when you're lying out your ass," Kyle said.

Gabe started for the door, but Tom intercepted him, covering the doorknob with his hand before Gabe could reach for it. "No way. You stay here until they've cleared out. The last thing you need is that bastard causing a scene in front of half the department."

Gabe clenched his jaw, furious at having to hide like a fucking coward, but he raised his arms and took a couple of steps back to let his brothers leave. A few minutes later, Joe opened the door and stuck his head in.

"All clear, but I'd go out the back," he said. "News

cameras are out front. Monroe's giving them quite the statement."

"I'll bet." Gabe jerked open the door and stormed down the hall toward the back entrance.

"Oh, hey, Gabe!" Joe called after him.

Gabe halted. "Yeah?"

"Abby said to tell you she tried calling Elle a couple of times to let her know Monroe was leaving, but Elle didn't answer. Went straight to voice mail. You might want to try giving her a call yourself."

That prickling sensation beneath Gabe's skin came rushing back with a vengeance. "Why the hell is Elle wanting to know when Monroe leaves?"

Joe frowned. "Got me. *You* don't know anything about it?"

Gabe shook his head. "No."

He turned back to the door, his pace increasing with each step—as was his concern for Elle and what she might be getting herself into growing. He shoved open the door and dialed Elle's number as he jogged to his Tahoe, wincing a little from his still-healing leg, grateful he was parked off to the side and didn't have to deal with all the damned news vultures.

When Elle's voice mail picked up again, he barked a quick message for her to call him as soon as she could, then tossed the phone into the seat beside him with a curse. He threw the Tahoe into reverse and peeled out, racing in the direction of Elle's house, his heart hammering.

"Jesus, Elle," he murmured. "What the hell are you doing, honey?"

Chapter 23

ELLE SWALLOWED HARD AS THE CABBIE DROVE UP THE long drive that led to the Monroe home. The house was the standard two-story farmhouse that had been so common in the area when the Monroe family moved there several generations ago. The paint on the wood siding was peeling and the porch was leaning a little to the left, but the grounds were impeccably tended, the flower beds beautiful. The fields that stretched out for numerous acres around and behind the house were thriving.

In addition to the farmhouse, there were two enormous outbuildings—one looked like some kind of storage facility for farm equipment; the other might've been a barn for livestock at some point, but now was little more than a glorified garage. Several cars in various states of disrepair and two ATVs were parked in front of the structure.

Elle had to give Jeb Monroe credit. For all his despicable traits, he took a great deal of pride in his land. She could hardly blame him for being so upset when a large portion of the family farm had been seized by the government. If she'd had to give up her family's legacy due to circumstances beyond her control, she would've been furious and heartbroken as well. But that didn't excuse Monroe's efforts to incite his own children to murder or his own brutality against his family.

The cab came to a halt in front of the porch and Elle

took a deep breath. "Could you please wait here? I'll be right back."

"Sure thing, lady," the cabbie said with a shrug. "Meter's running."

She gave him a grateful smile then got out of the cab, taking a quick look around before starting toward the house. She glanced down at her phone. *Dead*. *Shit*. It had taken her a good thirty minutes to get out to the farm. She had time. But not much.

The front steps creaked ominously as she made her way up to the porch, but she suppressed the shiver that snaked up her spine and knocked on the door. Seconds later, the door opened a crack and a woman with graying blond hair peered at her through the opening.

"Mrs. Monroe," Elle said, offering her a tentative smile. "I have a cab waiting. Do you have your things together?"

Janice Monroe opened the door a little wider. "I can't leave here without my children."

Elle fidgeted, ready to be gone. "Mrs. Monroe, Sandra is with your husband. We can't wait for her to return. But we can take the others. Where are they?"

The woman's chin trembled. "Gone. Except for my youngest. He took Jeremy as well."

Elle gave her a wary look. "Mrs. Monroe, Jeb can't find me here. You know that. If you and your youngest child come with me, I promise, we'll talk to the police and do what we can to keep the others safe."

She shook her head slowly, tears spilling onto her cheeks. "He'll kill them. He told me so. He told me if I betrayed him again, he'd kill my sweet babies. I've lost enough. I won't lose any more."

Elle sent another anxious glance over her shoulder, toward the road. "Mrs. Monroe, do you still want my help? If not, I'll leave. But I'd really like you to come with me—for your own safety."

The woman's face twisted in anguish. "I'm so sorry. God forgive me."

The porch steps suddenly creaked behind Elle, bringing goose bumps to her flesh. She spun around on a gasp, her heart leaping into her throat when she saw the barrel of a shotgun leveled at her chest.

"Now, don't you do anything stupid," the man holding it drawled. Some flicker of recognition passed through Elle's mind. She knew him. Had seen him somewhere before. But she couldn't quite place him. "I'm not supposed to kill you before Jeb gets back."

"I'm so sorry!" Janice Monroe sobbed behind her. "He made me call you. I'm so sorry!"

A commotion over the man's shoulder brought Elle's eyes up in time to see another man dragging the cabbie out of his car and shoving him to the ground. Too late she realized what was happening. Her eyes went wide and a scream tore from her throat just as the man fired a bullet into the cabbie.

"Get rid of the body," the man with the gun on her called over his shoulder. "And the car. Don't want anyone finding that here." He glanced at Mrs. Monroe. "Take her phone, Janice." He then motioned with the barrel of the gun for Elle to go inside.

Shaking, she sent one last glance toward the car where her purse sat on the floorboards of the backseat. As soon as someone realized she was missing—

Her heart sank as she backed slowly through the

front door, keeping her eyes on the gun still aimed at her chest. Gabe would probably just think she was avoiding him. Her aunt would probably think she was patching things up with Gabe. Hell, it might be that evening when she didn't show up at Kyle and Abby's before anyone even realized she was missing. Based on what the man with the gun had said, she might not have that long...

"Back there," the man prompted, motioning toward a hallway off of the living room.

"People know where I am," she lied, turning to walk down the hall. Abby knew Elle was keeping tabs on Monroe, but she hadn't told her why. "They're going to come looking for me."

"That's the plan," the man said with a little laugh. "Kill two birds with one stone."

Elle's breath caught in her lungs. *Gabe.* They were planning to use her to get to him. "You bastards," she hissed. "Killing one cop isn't enough for you?"

The man nudged her in the back with the gun, forcing her to stumble into what looked like a little girl's bedroom. When she turned to glare at him in outrage, he just grinned. "Every revolution has casualties. This is just the beginning."

"Do you seriously think you're going to start a revolution?" she spat. "Jeb Monroe is insane! He's just a man with a chip on his shoulder, not the brilliant leader you seem to think he is."

The man shook his head. "Don't underestimate my brother. You think this is just some whim? We've been planning for this for years. The Dawsons aren't the only ones got family connections. Our cousin in the courthouse has been getting us whatever we need."

Elle's stomach twisted into knots. "You're Dave Monroe," she deduced. "I remember you now from the courtroom. You were there during Derrick's trial. And the other man outside—he's also your brother..." She grasped for a name, trying to identify with the man, keep him talking in the hopes he'd reveal something she could use to possibly save her life and Gabe's.

"James," he barked. "James Monroe. You oughta remember his name—you're the same whore who talked his wife into leaving him after he smacked her around a bit."

Elle's breath left her on a gasp. Dear God—that was one of her first counseling cases at the foundation. The woman had been horribly brutalized. "Smacked around" was an understatement. She'd had to have her jaw wired shut. But she'd been too afraid to press charges. That time. Elle had been glad to hear when the woman had at last left him and moved on—hopefully to a better situation.

"And the cleaning lady in your office?" he sneered. "That's my wife. I'll bet you never even knew my Terri's last name. But she certainly knew everything about you. You really shouldn't leave so many personal notes to yourself lying around on top of your desk. We could tell you when you last saw your gynecologist, what you ate for lunch, how your boyfriend screwed you in your office just last night..."

Elle felt her knees grow weak and had to force herself to remain standing. There was no way in hell she was going to let this asshole know he was getting to her, that the knowledge of having her most intimate secrets known to these bastards made her want to hurl in revulsion.

She settled for glaring at him, her lips pressed together in angry silence.

He chuckled and backed out of the room. "You think on that," he told her. "And then when Jeb gets home, you tell him he's not the brilliant leader we think he is."

The man closed the door behind him and Elle heard him put a key in the door to lock it. As if that wasn't enough, it sounded like there was also some kind of latch sliding into place. The second his footsteps receded, she pivoted and went to the bedroom window, but the heavy, double-paned window was nailed shut. She looked around for something to use to smash it, but her eyes went wide as she realized she was standing in a debris field.

Clothes were strewn all over the floor, torn to shreds. Shards of glass and ceramic littered the floor, as if everything of value in the room had been smashed in a fit of rage. But most disturbing was the blood on the frilly, pink bedspread, the splatters upon the wall. And bloody smears were on the door along with deep grooves, as if someone had been trying desperately to claw her way out.

"Sweet Jesus," Elle breathed, her hand going to her mouth to keep the bile down.

This had to be Sandra's room. This must've been where she'd been beaten by her father. And that was just the treatment they knew about. God knows what else she'd been put through. Elle tried not to imagine what other unspeakable horrors she'd endured.

Her determination to escape taking on an even greater urgency, she searched frantically for something big enough to break the window. She finally found what looked like a thick, wooden curtain rod, but was now broken in half, splintered and jagged at one end. The undamaged end had a knob that might be just the thing she needed.

She grabbed a scrap of blanket, wrapped it around the sharp end, and peered through the window, checking to see if anyone was outside. A large maple tree partially obscured her view, but also helped partially hide the window from anyone looking at the house. Seeing no one outside and praying the sound of the glass breaking wouldn't be heard too easily in the rest of the house, she drove the rod against the window. But it didn't even crack.

She cursed roundly and tried again with the same result.

"Shit!" Elle rubbed her palms against her thighs, wiping the nervous perspiration from them, and reassessed the window. Maybe the bottom pane was the wrong way to go. She might be able to get more leverage and power if she went for the upper pane. Readjusting her grip on the curtain rod, she lifted it over her head and drove it toward the window. This time it cracked in just a tiny starburst only about the size of an eraser head.

"You've got to be fucking kidding me!" she hissed. "What the hell kind of glass is this?"

She took a closer look at the window, studying it for a moment. It didn't appear to be ballistic glass—although she wouldn't have put it past Monroe to have installed that in his house in case of an attack. But it definitely wasn't just ordinary, run-of-the-mill glass. It was more the thickness of a car windshield. She realized she was going about breaking it all wrong.

She shook out her hands and turned the rod around to use the jagged end instead when she heard a vehicle approaching and craned to see who it was. She recognized the truck immediately as the one Jeremy Monroe had been driving when she'd seen him following her.

"Damn it." She renewed her assault on the window, her shoulder muscles screaming as she drove the rod against the glass again. The little starburst began to grow larger as the cracks spread. Then with a savage cry, she drove it against the window once more and the glass finally shattered.

Elle's breath shot out of her in a relieved burst. Then she used the curtain rod to knock out the jagged shards of glass that remained so she could safely climb out. The sound of a truck door slamming reached her ears. She quickly unwound the material from the curtain rod, draped it over the bottom of the pane to protect herself from any remaining glass, and put her foot up on the sill, pulling herself up and through the window as she heard voices inside the house.

"Shit, shit, shit," she muttered, throwing the jagged curtain rod onto the ground and grabbing one of the tree branches, pulling herself all the way out of the window. The minute she kicked free, she dropped to the ground and snatched up the curtain rod. Frantically searching for the best escape route, she immediately rejected running toward the road. That would be the first place they looked.

Then her gaze lighted on the cornfield, the corn at its full height. She bolted toward it, her arms and legs pumping.

Gabe pounded on Elle's front door, then paused to listen for any movement inside. Nothing. He walked the perimeter of the house, looking for any signs that she might be inside, but decided she wasn't home.

He got back behind the wheel of his Tahoe and ran though his contacts until he found the number he sought.

"Mulaney's."

"Charlotte?" he said, his voice coming out in a rough bark. "Is Elle there?"

"No, sweetie, she left some time ago," she said. "She'd had a little to drink so she was taking a cab home."

"I'm there now," Gabe said, peeling out of the driveway, not entirely sure where he was heading next but not able to just sit and wait. "She's not home. You sure she was heading here?"

Now it was Charlotte's turn to sound concerned. "That's what she said. Gabe? What's going on?"

Gabe turned out of Elle's neighborhood and onto the main road before he answered, "I guess you know what's going on with Monroe?"

"Yes. Elle told me. I picked her up from her office earlier today and brought her to Mulaney's with me."

"Well, Elle called Abby and asked her to let Elle know when Jeb left the department, saying she wanted to keep tabs on his movements, whatever the hell that means. What's she up to, Charlotte? You need to tell me if you know anything."

"If I knew more than that, I'd tell you," Charlotte assured him. "She's my world, Gabe."

Gabe gripped the phone so hard his hand began to ache. "Mine too."

He disconnected the call and immediately dialed

Abby's number at the department. "It's Gabe," he said when she picked up. "How long would it take you to get me the GPS coordinates on Elle's phone?"

"Not long if I can get a search warrant," she said, her voice taut with concern. "Maybe an hour or so. Why? What's going on?"

"That's what I'm trying to find out," he said, taking a turn without thinking. "Charlotte says Elle left Mulaney's some time ago in a cab to go home, but she's not there."

Abby cursed under her breath. "You don't think she's following Monroe, do you?"

"I don't know what the hell she's doing or why she was interested in tracking Monroe," he told her. "It doesn't make any sense. She was just telling me to stay clear of them and not engage in any way. I just... My gut's telling me she's in trouble, Abby. I gotta find her."

"I'll ask Tom to sign off on a search warrant," she assured him. "I can go ahead and contact her cell provider to save time. Do you know what cab company she used? We can call them and find out where the driver is now. He can at least tell you where he took her."

"Mulaney's has an arrangement with Standard Cabs," he said, knowing their service well. "I'll give them a call."

"I'll call you as soon as I get anything," Abby assured him. "Keep me posted, Gabe. Please call me as soon as you know she's safe."

Gabe dialed the cab company next. "Hey, Frank. It's Gabe Dawson."

The guy on the other end chuckled. "Little early to call for a pickup isn't it, Dawson?"

"Unfortunately, it's not that kind of call," Gabe told

him. "Charlotte Mulaney's niece, Elle McCoy, called for a ride earlier today but never reached her destination. Could you put me in touch with your driver so I can find out where he dropped her off?"

"Sure, buddy. No problem." Gabe heard the clacking of typing on the other end of the line. "Huh. That's weird. Looks like Bobby picked her up all right, but he never checked back in service."

"What was his destination?" Gabe asked, a massive boulder of dread dropping into his stomach.

More typing on the other end. "Uh...looks like some rural address out in Venice. Want the address?"

Fuck.

"No thanks," Gabe replied, his throat constricting. "I know where it is. Do you have the GPS coordinates on the cab now? Is it still there?"

There was a pause. Then, "No. It looks like it's about five miles from there. No address is listed, but I can give you the location if you want to check it out. It's not like Bobby to not check back in service. He's the most dependable guy I've got."

Gabe flipped on his lights and sirens and slammed down on the accelerator. Screw being on administrative leave. Right now, his only concern was getting to Elle. "Text me the information, Frank. I'm on my way."

As soon as he hung up, his phone rang. "Yeah?"

"What the fuck is going on? Where are you?"

Gabe tried not to sigh. The last thing he was in the mood for at that moment was a lecture from Tom.

"On my way out to the Monroe farm," Gabe informed him, his tone clipped. "I think Elle's there."

"What the hell is she doing *there*?"

Gabe slowed as he came to an intersection, checking to make sure the cross traffic was stopping before he blew through the red light. "I don't know, Tom. But I swear to God, if Monroe has hurt her…"

"Joe and I are on our way," Tom said, his voice sounding like he was already on the move. "Joey! Let's go! Gabe, how close are you to Monroe's?"

"I'm about fifteen minutes out," he said, turning onto the rural route that led to Monroe's farm. "There's a cab about five miles from the farm that I'm going to check out on the way. The cabbie never checked back in. I need to make sure she's not there first."

There was a slight pause before Tom said, "We'll be there as soon as we can. And Dad has alerted the local PD. Don't take on Monroe by yourself, Gabe. Wait for backup."

Gabe's heart pounded in his ears, fear for Elle making his chest tight. "Can't make any promises."

"Gabe," Tom said, his tone pleading, "I'm ordering you not to go in on your own."

"I'm not letting you pull rank on me this time, Bro," Gabe insisted. "I love her, Tommy. I'm not going to let that bastard hurt her. If I have to die protecting her, I will."

"I understand that—"

Gabe hung up and tossed his phone into the passenger seat. It immediately started ringing again, but when he saw it was Tom calling back, he ignored it. He understood his brother's concerns, especially in light of what Tom had confided in him about his fears of losing one of them in the line of duty. But Gabe wasn't about to let Tom's fear prevent him from protecting the woman he loved.

Elle could hear shouting behind her and knew she'd been spotted. She ran faster, pushing herself until her arms and legs turned to rubber, her breath ragged.

Almost there. Almost there...

She had no idea what the hell she was going to do once she made it to the cornfield. Hell, they knew the rows and orientation of the field better than she did. She didn't even have any freaking clue where it ended. She could only pray that she'd end up near another house or the road where she could flag down a passing motorist.

The roar of an engine assaulted her ears, making her start. Her heart stuttered in panic and she threw a glance over her shoulder to see two men on one ATV and one on another racing in her direction.

Oh God...

She whimpered softly but kept running, not about to give up now that she was so close. A loud pop sounded behind her as one of them fired off a shot. She instinctively ducked at the sound, losing her footing and landing hard in the grass.

Cursing, she scrambled to her feet, barely registering the blood trickling down her arm from a skinned elbow. She could worry about it later. Right now she was more concerned about the damned ATVs that were right on top of her.

She sprinted forward, finally making the cornfield, and raced down the row, then zagged randomly, hoping to lose her pursuers, who were now crashing through the cornfield after her on foot. Her lungs began to burn, her breath loud in her ears as she continued to run, her adrenaline keeping her on her feet.

The heavy footfalls behind her were growing closer, gaining on her. In desperation, she made another random zag through the rows, but catching a glimpse of someone running parallel to her, she turned again and sprinted forward, praying the man hadn't seen her too.

Another loud pop made her flinch, fully expecting to feel the impact of a bullet in her back. But when she felt no pain, she sent a glance over her shoulder to check for her pursuer.

No one was there. *Thank God! Maybe she'd—*

The sudden impact as she collided with another mass sent her sprawling on her back, knocking the air from her lungs. The next thing she knew, Jeremy Monroe was standing over her, a shotgun pointed at her chest.

"Don't move," he ordered.

Tears of frustration rushed to her throat, choking her, but she closed her eyes, swallowed past them, and tried to slow her ragged breathing. When she opened her eyes, Jeremy was still staring down at her, his brows drawn together as if he was undecided what to do with her now that he'd caught her.

"Let me go," she said softly. "You don't want to do this, Jeremy."

She saw his throat work as he swallowed hard. He licked his lips, then glanced around, checking for others. Then he bent forward, looking anguished as he said, "I'm sorry. I don't want to hurt you, but—"

"Good job, boy," came a rough voice from behind him.

Jeremy instantly snapped upright but gave Elle a

pleading look, silently begging her not to betray him. Jeb Monroe appeared next to his son, a smug sneer draped across his cruel mouth. "Well, now, where do you think you're running off to? It's not very polite to leave without saying good-bye." He then gestured to someone out of Elle's line of sight. "Get her on her feet."

Jeb's brother Dave stepped forward and grabbed her arm, dragging her roughly to her feet. She winced in pain from the cut on her arm.

The men dragged her along with them to the ATVs. "You go on," Jeb said to his son and brother. "I'll bring her up."

As soon as the other two started up the ATVs and drove back to the house, Jeb pulled Elle toward the house. "You're proving more trouble than you're worth."

"Guess you should let me go then," she hissed.

He chuckled, making her skin crawl. "You know I can't do that," he told her. "Not now."

"The Sheriff's Department knows where I am. They're going to realize I'm missing," she assured him. "There's no denying your role in everything this time."

"I have no intention of denying anything." The grin he gave her was chilling. "In fact, I'm looking forward to whole Dawson family showing up—especially Gabe Dawson rushing in here in all his arrogance, thinking he can rescue his beloved whore. His brothers won't be far behind, I'm sure."

The man was a fanatic—that she already knew. But the look on his face told her he was no longer concerned about being cautious. Jeb Monroe was more dangerous than ever.

When they reached the house, Jeb shoved her inside

and motioned at this wife. "Bandage that cut up. Don't want her bleeding all over the carpet."

Janice came forward, her head bowed in deference. The woman was clearly broken. She led Elle to the sofa where Sandra sat, her eyes staring out at nothing as she rocked a little. Whatever the poor girl had been through, her physical wounds were nothing compared to what her emotional wounds must be.

Jeb walked to the window and peered outside, watching the driveway that led up to the house while Janice cleaned Elle's cut with peroxide and covered it with a couple of Band-Aids. At one point, she lifted her eyes and met Elle's gaze, then abruptly shifted her gaze to the left, gesturing for Elle to look that way.

Elle felt suddenly cold in spite of the summer heat.

A boy of perhaps twelve or thirteen years old sat in a wooden chair in the next room, his arms tied behind his back, his feet bound at the ankles, his mouth covered with duct tape. His cheek was bruised and swollen, and his eyes were red, as if he'd been crying recently.

Sweet Jesus.

Now Elle understood how Janice was persuaded to call Elle and trap her into coming out to the farm. Janice had told her Jeb had threatened to kill her children. It appeared their youngest son had been the particular target.

And now Elle had become the bait to draw Gabe and his brothers right into this monster's lair, into the trap he'd set and was ready to spring.

Tears pricked her eyes when she thought of how she and Gabe had left things, how the last words he might hear from her were words of anger. She hoped she'd have the chance to tell him again how much she loved him, how she couldn't imagine ever loving anyone else. She longed to once more feel his arms around her, to know the warmth of his love.

And yet it was that very same love, from the heart of a man whose loyalty and duty were the most steadfast of anyone she'd ever known, that was most likely leading him to his death.

———

Gabe glanced at the speedometer, cursing his inability to go any faster. As he got closer to the coordinates Frank had given him, he studied the edges of the road, searching the fields and tree lines, searching for any sign of the missing cab. Suddenly a blur of yellow among rusted-out shells of various cars and vans in a makeshift junkyard near a copse of trees caught his attention.

He whipped the Tahoe over to the side of the road and drew his weapon as he leaped from the SUV and hurried toward the trees where the car was parked. As he got closer, he slowed his pace, keeping his weapon at the ready as he approached with caution. He was still several feet away when he saw the blood splatter on the driver's side door.

"Shit," he rasped. He hurried forward, searching the interior of the car in a quick glance. No blood inside that he could see, but what looked like Elle's purse was sitting on the floorboards in the back.

Oh God.

He fished his handkerchief from his pocket and used it to try the front door handle. Whoever had dumped the car hadn't bothered locking it. He took another quick glance, then popped the trunk.

Gabe hurried around to the back of the car and took a deep breath, then lifted the trunk lid, having a pretty damned good idea what he'd find. And yet his stomach still churned when he saw the cabbie's body, half his head blown off from a gunshot. *Shit*.

He swallowed and looked about. No sign of Elle.

Gabe ran back to his Tahoe, jumped inside, and pulled onto the road before calling in the location of the cab and the death of the cab driver to dispatch. Then, not wanting to get yet another lecture from his brother Tom, he called Joe instead.

"Joey," Gabe ground out the second his brother answered, "the cabbie that picked up Elle is dead. He's got her, Joe. That motherfucker has Elle."

"Ah, shit," Joe muttered. "We're on our way, Gabe. Just hang tight. Tom and I are on the way. And we were able to catch Kyle before he was too far down to the road. We got your back, Bro."

Gabe hung up and, this time, attached his phone to his hip, gradually decreasing his speed as he drew close to the Monroe farm. He took a deep breath and let it out slowly, getting his emotions under control. He wasn't going to be any use to Elle if he couldn't keep his shit together.

He needed to figure out a game plan. Waiting the fifteen or so minutes it would take for his brothers to catch up could mean the difference in whether Elle lived or died. He couldn't just come up the driveway and knock on the front door. He most likely wouldn't even make it to the porch before Monroe put a bullet in him.

Before he reached the farm, he pulled off onto a small access road used to drive between the fields and went just far enough to obscure the Tahoe from the road but not to tip off anyone at the house that a vehicle was approaching.

Then he slipped out of the SUV and texted his brothers: Doing recon. Will approach with caution.

He wasn't surprised when he immediately got a message back from Tom. WTF? Stay put.

Gabe took a deep breath and let it out slowly, then silenced his phone and his radio. "Sorry, Tommy. See you soon, Bro."

Chapter 24

"GO CHECK THE PERIMETER," JEB SAID, GESTURING TO his brother James.

His younger brother gave him a sharp nod and gestured to their brother Dave. "Comin'?"

Dave looked to Jeb for permission. "Want me to go with him or stay here and keep watch over these?" He gestured to Jeb's traitorous family.

They'd all betrayed him in some way. Even his youngest boy had chosen his mother in the end. But Jeb's brothers were loyal. He knew that for a fact. That's exactly how he knew that Gabe Dawson wouldn't come looking for his whore without bringing his own kin along.

"'For the great day of their wrath has come,'" Jeb murmured. Then he turned away from the window and nodded to Dave. "Go on. I'll be fine here."

He continued to watch from the window until his brothers split up to walk separate paths, then went to sit in the chair across from the whore. She hadn't said a word since he'd brought her back to the house after she'd tried to escape. Now that her hands and feet were tied, she'd just sat there on the sofa, watching him with narrowed eyes.

Well, she could glare all she wanted. Soon he'd be rid of her. He'd planned to give her to his boy Jeremy to enjoy, but Jeremy seemed to have lost the taste for their cause. He'd soon fix that, though. He wouldn't force the boy to take a whore, but he *would* force him to put a bullet in one.

He leaned back to give her an appraising look. She had some fight in her, he had to give her that. It was too bad for her that she chose to serve the tyrants. Now she would pay the price.

"It won't be long now," he assured her. "We'll give everyone a little time to get here, but if they don't show soon, I've got a little message planned. One of the brothers has a pretty little schoolteacher for a whore, as I recall. Pregnant too. Her death would be a tragic loss to the Dawson family, wouldn't you say?"

He chuckled when the whore's eyes went wide in alarm.

"You're a sick bastard," she spat at him, her face twisting in disgust. "If you hurt one hair on Sadie's hair, I swear—"

A sudden commotion outside brought Jeb to his feet, and he missed whatever meaningless threat the whore was spewing at him. He pulled back the curtains to peer outside but didn't see the source of the noise. He muttered a curse, stormed over to his son, and grabbed him by the front of his shirt, pulling him to his feet.

"You keep watch of them," he ordered. "Don't let that whore try to sweet-talk you again, boy. You hear me?"

Jeremy nodded and took his father's vacated seat, his shotgun in his lap. "Yes, sir."

Jeb hesitated for a moment, not sure if he could trust his son to be strong and resist the whore devil's tongue, but he had no choice. He strode to the front door and opened it cautiously, then stepped outside.

—⁓—

Gabe cursed under his breath as he lowered the man's body to the ground and quickly rolled him onto his stomach to cuff his hands behind his back. The guy had come around the corner of the barn and taken Gabe by surprise, but, fortunately, Gabe's reflexes kicked in faster than the other guy's, and Gabe was able to get the drop on him and knock him out cold.

It was only after he'd laid the guy out with a final right hook that he'd recognized the man as Jeb's brother David.

Gabe dragged the unconscious man around to the back of the barn so he was out of sight, then picked up his gun from where it'd landed during their brief scuffle. The son of a bitch most likely had a broken nose and would have one hell of a headache when he woke up, but he was alive.

Gabe crept along the edge of the barn and peered around corner, checking to see if anyone else was patrolling the perimeter. At that moment, another man came into view. Gabe recognized him right away. Jeb's youngest brother, James Monroe. He should've known this asshole wouldn't be far if something big was about to go down.

As soon as James had passed by Gabe, Gabe came out from around the barn, his Glock trained on the center of James's back. "Drop your weapon, Monroe. And turn around slowly."

The man went completely still, his muscles visibly tensing. Then he raised his arms and turned slowly as instructed, his rifle still in one hand. Once he was fully facing Gabe, the man's lips curled into a smirk that sent a shiver down Gabe's spine.

Ah, shit.

The guy was totally gonna go suicide-by-cop on him if he didn't diffuse this situation seriously fucking fast.

"Put your weapon down," Gabe ordered again. "There's still time to walk away from this, James. There's still time to end this peacefully. Don't let your brother drag you down with him."

James shook his head, his chilling grin widening. "You're wrong, pig. Jeb's going to usher in a new day for this country. And it starts today."

Gabe heard sirens in the distance. Odds were it was the local police on their way to what had all the makings of a shoot-out that could end with casualties on both sides of the line.

In the next few moments, time seemed to slow to a crawl. James's gaze flicked toward the road, where the police cars would soon be arriving, then back to Gabe. "'And free those who all their lives were held in slavery by their fear of death,'" he called out, his voice raised. Then his face went blank and he dropped his hands, aiming his rifle at Gabe's chest.

———

Elle started violently at the sound of the gunfire outside the house, her heart in her throat.

Oh God. Gabe.

"Untie me," she pleaded with Jeremy. "Please! You know your father's insane!" She turned her gaze to Janice. "Mrs. Monroe, you have to stop this. Your sons and daughter are in danger! Look what he's already done to you."

Janice blinked at Elle as if she was coming out of a trance, then let her gaze light on each of her children. "You'll help them? You'll make sure they're all safe? That they won't go to prison?"

Elle glanced frantically toward the door. "I can't promise that—"

"Oh my God," the woman moaned plaintively, her arms wrapped around her torso as she rocked.

"—but I'll do what I can to make sure your son gets a fair trial, that they understand what his father has forced him to do."

"Mom, I swear, I didn't want to do any of this!" Jeremy cried, setting aside his gun and coming to his mother's side, dropping down to his knees and taking her hands. "I swear it!"

"Untie me," Elle ground out. "*Please*. Jeremy, you said you didn't want to hurt me. I believe you. Help. Me."

Jeremy swallowed hard. Then he shoved a hand into his jeans pocket and pulled out a pocketknife, making quick work of the rope. Elle was instantly on her feet, desperate to get to Gabe.

She bolted toward the open front door, which had been closed just a moment before...

—~~~—

The same instant Gabe's gun fired, a blow to his back brought him to his knees. But not before he saw James Monroe drop. Another blow to the back knocked the wind from his lungs and sent him face-planting into the grass.

In spite of the pain, he rolled over in time to see Jeb's rifle aimed at him and he kicked hard, nailing that crazy-ass bastard Jeb in the kneecap with his boot. As the man fell to his knees, wailing in agony, Gabe scrambled to his feet and brought up his Glock, relieved as hell that some sick sense of honor must've prevented the bastard from shooting him in the back—or maybe he'd just wanted to see the look of fear in Gabe's eyes before he killed him. Fuck if he knew. But this was ending *now*.

Monroe's hand edged toward the rifle where it lay next to him on the grass. "Don't move," Gabe barked.

Monroe's hand stilled.

Gabe heard the approaching sirens growing louder as the backup got closer but didn't glance away from Monroe to see how close they were. "Leave the gun on the ground and get up slowly."

Monroe took a deep breath, then managed to push himself up to his feet, favoring his knee. "You think this is over, Dawson? This is just the beginning. Now the world will be my audience. My message will spread through the discontent and usher in a new day."

"Where's Elle?" Gabe demanded.

"'Deliver me, my God!'" Jeb called out over the wail of the sirens, ignoring Gabe's question. "'Strike all my enemies on the jaw; break the teeth of the—'"

When Gabe heard the report of the gunshot, for a split second, he thought he'd been ambushed, that this time he wasn't going to be lucky enough to walk away from it. But then he saw Jeb drop.

Gabe's head whipped toward the sound of the gunshot to see Sandra Monroe standing there holding a .22, her entire body trembling, tears streaming down her face. "Sandra, honey," he said, edging toward her, "you need to put down the gun."

In his periphery, Gabe saw several local police cars as well as his brothers arriving, getting into position to assess and assist.

"Gabe!"

Relief washed over him at the sound of Elle's voice, and he sent a glance her way that he hoped conveyed how full his heart was at seeing her alive. But he held up a hand, motioning for her to stay where she was when she took a step forward to come to him, and turned his attention back to Sandra.

"Honey," he said softly, "it's okay now. Let me help you."

Sandra blinked once and finally turned her eyes away from her father's body to meet Gabe's gaze. "Deputy Dawson."

He gave her a slight smile. "Yeah, it's me. I'm going to help you now. You just need to give me the gun."

She stared at him for a moment, then nodded.

He came to her at an angle, holstering his Glock, then slowly reached out and took the gun from her trembling fingers. Then he gently put an arm around her shoulders and led her toward the line of police cars. He turned her over to his brother Tom and gave a terse nod to his father, who was on the radio calling for EMTs. Kyle was on his cell phone, most likely reporting on the situation to the FBI field office.

"Jeb's other brother is behind the barn in cuffs," Gabe muttered to no one in particular, motioning in the general direction of the outbuilding. Joe clapped him on the shoulder as he headed that way.

When he turned back around toward the house, the lawn was a sea of activity as local officers rushed forward to check on Jeb and James Monroe and to intercept Janice Monroe and her sons as they exited the house with their hands raised.

But it was pretty much all a blur. The only clarity in the chaos was Elle's beautiful face as she rushed toward him. Then her arms were around his neck, holding him tightly. He buried his face in her hair, breathing in the scent of her, letting the warmth of her love envelope him.

—∾∾—

"Are you okay?" Elle asked when she pulled back enough to peer up into his face. Her heart was still racing, her head still spinning. He looked okay, but she had to be sure, had to hear him say it. Her voice broke when she said, "My God, Gabe, when I heard that gunshot, I thought—"

He stopped her words with a slow, tender kiss, and her heart was racing for an entirely different reason. When the kiss ended, Gabe took her face in his hands. "I'm fine," he assured her, "now that I know you're safe."

"Where's Joe?" she asked in a rush. "You have to get someone out to check on Sadie."

"Sadie?" he frowned. "Why?"

She grasped the front of his uniform. "Monroe—he had someone at the ready to harm her if luring me here didn't get your attention. Please, Gabe."

He kissed her forehead. "I'll be right back."

When he hurried off to talk with his dad and apprise him of the situation, she leaned back against the nearest car and wrapped her arms around herself, missing Gabe's embrace already. A few moments later, he returned, a deep scowl creasing his brows.

"Dad's sending two cars over right away," he assured her. "And Joe's on his way. Whoever Monroe had watching Sadie better be glad that the other deputies will get to him before Joe does."

"Ms. McCoy?"

Elle turned toward the sound of her name, glad Gabe kept his arm around her shoulders, pulling her tight against him. "Mrs. Monroe."

The woman came toward her, an officer at her elbow, her youngest son tucked close to her side, and took Elle's hand in hers. "Thank you. For saving my children. For saving me."

"I didn't save you," Elle assured her. "That was all you. You made the right decision, Mrs. Monroe."

Janice glanced at Jeremy and Sandra being loaded into the backseats of police cars, but then pressed a kiss to the top of her son Brian's head. "I hope so, Ms. McCoy. My Sandra..." Her expression was pained when she met Elle's gaze. "What he did to her... I hope they'll understand why she did what she did."

Elle squeezed her hand, wishing she'd been able to help the woman and her children sooner, that she'd been able to reach out to them before their situation had come to this. "I hope so, too."

Elle didn't know how much time passed before she and Gabe were able to finally leave, but her head was pounding and it was all she could do to make it to where Gabe had left his Tahoe.

"I need to call Charlotte," she told him as he handed her into the SUV. "Before she hears anything on the news."

He took her hand and pressed a kiss to her palm. "I'll

take care of it. You look completely drained. Just rest while I drive you home."

She nodded, her eyelids drooping as the exhaustion dragged her down. The next thing she knew, she was waking up in Gabe's arms as he carried her into his house and down the hall to his bedroom.

"Hey there, handsome," she drawled sleepily.

"Hey there, beautiful." The dimpled smile he gave her was so sultry, warmth began to spread through her body, pooling in all the right womanly places and bringing her fully awake and alive.

"I seem to recall we had some plans for the evening," she mused.

He lifted a single brow. "Oh yeah?"

She nodded. "Mmm-hmm. I believe there was a hot bubble bath involved."

"I might be a little low on bubble bath at the old bachelor pad," he told her, his aqua eyes growing darker as he peered down at her, "but I think I can handle the hot part."

"Oh, honey," she said with a grin, "I have no doubt about that…"

Gabe set her on her feet, then removed his gun, laying it on his dresser before taking off his gun belt and setting it aside. She watched him with hungry eyes as he removed the clips from his uniform buttons, placing them in a neat little pile.

The pace he was undressing at was maddeningly slow.

"Here," she murmured, stepping closer, slipping her hands beneath his shirt and sliding it off his broad shoulders. "Let me help you with that."

Next was his T-shirt. She untucked it and drew it

over his head, tossing it aside. Then she leaned in and pressed a kiss to his bare chest, grinning at the low moan it elicited.

Then she slid her hand down between them, cupping him through his pants. "I think the bath can wait just a little while," she said, giving him a slow grin. "Don't you?"

Gabe didn't answer. Couldn't. His powers of speech had left him. All he knew was need—the need to be inside Elle, to lose himself in her love, to reassure himself that she was safe in his arms.

He pulled off her T-shirt, then popped the button on her jeans, slipping his hand inside and finding her already slick with desire. And at that moment, any restraint he possibly maintained left him. He captured her lips with his in a savage kiss, his fingers stroking her with demanding caresses as she moaned and arched against him.

When he felt her muscles begin to spasm, he finally broke their kiss and peered down at her, bracing her with his other arm as her release rocked her, loving the way her rapture played over her face.

"Oh God, Gabe!" she gasped, her fingers digging into his arms. "Please."

Seconds later, they had shed the rest of their clothes and were falling onto his bed together in a blissful tangle. He joined their bodies in one rough thrust, making love to her with the same savage, life-affirming abandon. She rose to meet him, drawing him in, clutching at his back, demanding all he had to give.

When she came again, his name on her lips in a

breathless gasp, he let go with a ragged cry. Then his mouth found hers in a slow, languid kiss as her hands smoothed over his skin, soothing him with the tenderness of her touch.

"Mind if I ask you something?" Gabe said sometime later as they lay in his bed, their arms and legs entwined, her head resting on his chest as he held her close. "Why did you go out to the Monroes' farm on your own? Don't take this the wrong way, but what the hell were you thinking?"

Elle explained about the call she'd received from Janice Monroe. "She needed help. Even if it was a ruse to get me out there, her cry for help was genuine at the heart of it. Would you have reacted any differently if she'd called *you*?"

She has a point, but still…

"It's my job to rush in when people need help, Elle," he reminded her. "I'm trained to handle myself."

She sighed. "Well, I've decided helping women like Janice Monroe is where my heart is. I'm taking the job at the foundation."

His brows shot up. "Are you sure? I know how much being a prosecutor has meant to you."

"I went into law so I could make a positive impact," she told him. "After seeing firsthand the terror this family experienced…"

"There are going to be a lot of people you can't help, Elle," he told her, knowing all too well the challenges she might face.

She sighed and shook her head. "If I can help just one

woman have a better life, help one child escape that kind of situation before it comes to what happened today…"

Gabe's heart swelled with pride for the woman in his arms. He'd never known anyone quite as strong or resilient. She'd been through hell, and instead of dwelling on her own trauma, all she could think about was how she might continue to help others.

When she fell silent, snuggling in tighter against him, he smoothed his fingertips along her arm, trying to push away the images of just how wrong things could've gone earlier that day, how close he'd come to losing this incredible woman, how close the world had come to being deprived of the light she brought to the lives of so many.

He sighed, realizing he'd completely underestimated her. "I'm sorry, Elle."

She frowned at him. "For what?"

"For thinking you needed a knight in shining armor." He brushed her hair from her face. "You were right when you said I can't constantly worry that something could happen to you, that I might not be able to protect you."

She rose up on her elbow and scooted up higher on the mattress so that she could look down at him. "You saved my life that day at the courthouse without a moment's hesitation," she reminded him. "And odds are good that you saved my life again today. If you hadn't shown up when you did, I don't know what would've happened. So while it's true I may not need a knight in shining armor, I do need *you*, Gabe Dawson. But I want you as a partner in whatever this is between us, as my lover and my friend—not just as my handsome hero."

"I think I can promise that," Gabe assured her,

tucking a lock of her fiery hair behind her ear. "But you have to promise me one thing first."

She gave him a cautious look out of the corner of her eye. "What's that?"

"That you'll stop referring to 'whatever this is between us' as if you don't know what it is."

She flushed, and her green eyes grew darker as she whispered, "What is this then, Gabe?"

He caressed her bottom lip with this thumb, knowing that, in a moment, he was planning to taste them again and lose himself in the bliss he could only find in her arms. "This is forever," he told her. "I love you, Elle. And I can't imagine ever loving anyone else."

A slow smile curved her lips as he drew her down to receive his kiss. "I love you, too," she murmured against his mouth. "And forever sounds about right..."

Epilogue

"WHERE ARE WE GOING?"

Gabe grinned at her. "It's a surprise."

"And I needed to be blindfolded for said surprise?"

"Yep."

Elle had no idea what to expect. After a year together, Gabe still surprised her. She found herself falling in love with him over and over again every single day.

"What are you grinning about?" he asked. She could tell even without seeing him that he was smiling too.

"How much I love you."

He took her hand and brought it to his lips. "Well, hold that thought for two more minutes. We're almost there."

"Okay, but don't forget we're supposed to be back by noon to meet Jessica and the kids for lunch," she reminded him, having lost all sense of how long they'd been in the car. "You're helping Teddy learn to ride his bike today."

"Haven't forgotten," he assured her. "I have his new bike in the trunk so we can go straight there after your surprise. And I even remembered the helmet, and the elbow guards and kneepads, and the special training wheels that are on springs, and—"

"Okay, okay," she laughed. "You're a wonderful godfather."

"Thanks," he said. "I love those kids—they make it easy. And it's good practice."

"Practice?" she echoed, her pulse kicking up a notch, not wanting to presume too much.

"Yeah, you know, for when I have little monkeys of my own running around some day." There was moment of tense silence before he announced, "We're here."

Elle couldn't mistake the note of relief in his voice. A few seconds later, Gabe stopped the car and came around to her door to take her hand and help her out. Elle frowned when she felt that his hand was uncharacteristically clammy.

Is he nervous?

She felt him take a deep breath and let it out on a short burst. "Okay. Ready?"

When she nodded, he removed the blindfold. Slowly, Elle opened her eyes, blinking as her eyes adjusted in the summer morning sunlight. Then she gasped, her heart fluttering when she realized they were standing on the edge of a meadow of wildflowers, the vibrant green grass dotted with crimson, yellow, white, and lavender flowers that swayed gently in the breeze.

"Oh my God, Gabe," she breathed. "This is beautiful."

He stepped behind her and wrapped his arms around her waist. "I was driving through here yesterday and knew you had to have these wildflowers. But seeing as how I couldn't pick them all and leave them in your locker…"

She turned in his arms to face him, her eyes wide. "It was *you*?"

He smiled down at her and shrugged. "It was me."

Her heart began to pound and she blinked to clear the sudden blur as tears pricked the corners of her eyes. "Why didn't you say anything before now?"

"I was waiting for the perfect place and time." He held her gaze for a long moment before easing down on his knees, his hands resting lightly on her hips as he peered up at her. He chuckled. "I had a whole speech planned, but I've forgotten every damned word. So I'll just say I love you, Elle. And I hope that forever still sounds as right and perfect to you as it does to me. Will you marry me?"

She stared at him, emotion choking her and making it momentarily impossible to speak.

When she didn't immediately respond, he cleared his throat, and continued, "I know I'm probably not the guy you always pictured yourself with, but—"

Elle dropped to her knees and stopped his words with a kiss. When she pulled back, she took his face in her hands. "It was you, Gabe," she breathed. This time there was no question. "It was always you."

*Keep reading for an excerpt from the first book
in Kate SeRine's Protect & Serve series*

STOP AT NOTHING

WELL, SON OF A BITCH.

The little bastard had decided to run. Didn't that just fucking figure? It was at least ninety degrees, and the air was so thick Kyle might as well have been trying to inhale the gumbo that the citizens of New Orleans found so enticing. And now that freaky little shit Harlan Rhodes was sprinting down Decatur Street wearing nothing but a Speedo, tube socks, and glittery gold sneakers.

No one even raised an eyebrow—except for a random tourist or two who hadn't quite figured out that natives of the Big Easy were rarely surprised by anything.

"Dawson!"

Kyle groaned inwardly when his partner, Dave Peterman, called out to him. He could already hear the ass-chewing he was going to get later for pissing on protocol. But screw it—Kyle wasn't letting Rhodes give him the slip. No way in hell. He'd been working this case almost since he'd arrived in New Orleans a year ago and finally had the key witness needed to put an end to one of the biggest human-trafficking operations in the country. Peterman was just going to have to get his ass moving.

Rhodes suddenly darted into the street, sprinting toward Jackson Square, causing cars to come to a screeching halt. Kyle raced after him, ignoring the cacophony of blaring horns and shouted obscenities. Sweat soaked through his shirt. His suit jacket and tie began to feel like a wet straitjacket, restricting his movement. But the adrenaline pumping through his veins pushed him forward.

For all his wiriness, Rhodes was struggling just as much as Kyle in the heavy air, his strides beginning to slow even as he vaulted over a couple picnicking in the grass. The muscles in Kyle's legs were on fire and his breath sawed in and out, but he surged forward in a burst of speed.

When he was within a few feet of Rhodes, Kyle lunged, tackling the other man. They crashed to the pavement, sliding along the concrete path and nearly taking down a bride and groom making their vows before a preacher dressed in a Colonel Sanders-like white suit, string tie, and goatee. Ignoring the couple's startled cries, Kyle wrapped his arm around Rhodes's neck, putting him in a headlock and rolling until the man was on his stomach. Kyle scrambled to his knees and twisted Rhodes's arm behind him. The man bucked, trying to throw him off, forcing Kyle to press his knee into Rhodes's back to keep him down.

"Now," Kyle panted, having to yell as the brass band on the other side of the fence struck up their first tune of the afternoon, "I think you had a few things you wanted to tell me, Harlan..."

"Suck my dick!" Rhodes spat. "I ain't tellin' you shit, Dawson!"

Kyle shrugged, slapping handcuffs on Rhodes and dragging him to his feet. "That's what you think, asshole."

～～～

Kyle popped a handful of peanut M&M's into his mouth just as Peterman stormed out of the assistant director's office and halted abruptly to give Kyle a shitty look. So, pretty much business as usual.

He'd been catching hell from the moment he set foot in the New Orleans office. The other agents treated him like a piece of shit that'd been dumped on their lawn. Whatever. He didn't give a rat's ass what anyone else thought of him personally. He wasn't there to make friends; he was there to do his job. If they felt threatened by that, then screw them.

So instead of kissing their asses to ingratiate himself into their good-ol'-boys' club or slinking off into a corner to lick his wounds, Kyle had fallen back on the arrogance and insolence that had served him so well before. He'd figured out a long time ago how to get under people's skin and turn their own attitudes around on them, thanks in no small part to the decades-long pissing match he had going on with his father.

"You guys have a nice chat?" he taunted Peterman. "Or were you just dropping by to polish Skinner's knob before demanding a new partner?"

"Fuck off, Dawson," Peterman sneered. "I gotta get home to my kid. I don't have time for your shit."

Kyle leaned back on the hand-carved wooden bench that sat in the hallway outside his boss's office, regarding what he figured was now his *former* partner, and feigned a concerned frown. "How *will* I go on? First Hughes and now you? I'm heartbroken, Peterman."

Peterman's already florid face turned an alarming shade of purple. When he opened his mouth to respond to Kyle's sarcasm, Kyle held up his hand. "No, no. Please don't give me the 'It's not you, it's me' speech. Let me spare you the effort. You're right, Peterman—it *is* you. I accept that. And I forgive you."

"Forgive—?" The vein in Peterman's forehead began to pulse. "You're an arrogant prick, you know that?"

"Dawson!"

Kyle hopped to his feet. "Sorry, gotta run. Boss wants to see me." He shivered with mock excitement. "Can't wait to see what he has to say. Our private chats are always so scintillating."

Peterman snorted derisively then stormed away, shaking his head and mumbling something under his breath.

Ignoring the way his gut clenched in apprehension, Kyle cleared his throat and plastered on his most care-free grin before swaggering into his boss's office. "You know, I don't think Peterman knows what *scintillating* means," he said, jabbing a thumb over his shoulder.

Assistant Director Skinner eyed Kyle with his bland, dispassionate gaze and asked on a sigh, "Beg pardon?"

"Scintillating," Kyle explained. "That's how I described our private chats. But it was totally lost on

Peterman. Really, sir, I just can't stay partners with someone who has such a limited vocabulary."

"Well, good thing you won't have to," Skinner replied.

Kyle's brows shot up. "Really?" he said, dropping into the chair across from Skinner's desk. "Sweet! So, who's up next? *Please* tell me my new partner's a hot redhead named Scully."

Skinner blinked.

Kyle gaped at him. "Seriously? You're an assistant director at the FBI who's named Skinner, and you've *never* seen an episode of *The X-Files*? Not *ever*?"

"No, Dawson," Skinner retorted, leaning back in his chair and folding his hands over his stomach. "I'm happy to say I learned how to be an agent from shutting my piehole and listening to the more seasoned agents who knew what the hell they were doing, instead of acting like a self-important, smart-ass prick."

"I thought I was an *arrogant* prick," Kyle corrected. "You and Peterman really need to coordinate your insults better. It's confusing."

Skinner's eyes flashed. "Arrogant, self-important— take your pick. You've been here less than a year, Dawson, and you've already pissed away two partners. No one wants to work with you because you're reckless and dangerous and have no respect for authority or for the badge you carry."

"That's not true," Kyle shot back, his indignation genuine. "I have a *great* deal of respect for the badge."

The muscle in Skinner's jaw twitched, but he maintained his composure. "I knew you'd be trouble the minute you walked in the door."

Kyle's internal shit-storm alarm started blaring loud

and clear, so he took his cockiness down a notch, ready
to play nice. "Sir—"

"Oh, I've heard all about your family, Dawson,"
Skinner interrupted before Kyle could make good on his
shift in attitude. "What'd you think? You could come
down here, do whatever the hell you wanted just because
your granddaddy's got his name in the history books?"

When Kyle merely clenched his jaw, Skinner continued. "Heard all about your daddy too. About his
renegade methods of dispensing justice, how he runs
his county and expects all you boys to follow in his
footsteps. Except you didn't, did you? Well, let me tell
you something, son. If you need to work out your daddy
issues, you can head on back up north."

Kyle's spine stiffened, but he managed to maintain
his blank expression in spite of the mention of his
father, torn between defending his father's unorthodox
but extremely effective ways of fighting the crime that
trickled into their county from Detroit and Chicago, and
distancing himself from the infamous Mac Dawson as
he'd been trying to do his entire life.

"I don't have any contact with my father," he replied,
his words as stiff as his posture. "Not anymore."

Eh—what could he say? Old habits die hard.

"Well," Skinner said, cracking a smile that seemed
rather menacing. "Guess that's about to change."

Kyle's blood went cold. "What?"

Now Skinner's smile was positively smug. "You're
being transferred."

Kyle's stomach sank. "Sir," he said, ditching the
devil-may-care act entirely, "if this is about Harlan
Rhodes and what happened in Jackson Square today, I

had to do what was necessary to bring him in. Peterman and I have never seen eye-to-eye on how to deal with this case, but soon we'll have what we need to—"

"It's not about Rhodes," Skinner interrupted, "even though I've got that little asshole spewing excessive-force allegations against you to anyone and everyone who'll listen. I've already had two phone calls about it—one from that weaselly little bastard who calls himself a lawyer. You're damned lucky Rhodes is spilling his guts, or you'd be even farther up shit creek than you already are."

Kyle shook his head. "Then what gives? I'm one of the best agents you have." When Skinner grunted, Kyle added, "Tell me I'm lying."

"You don't get it, do you?" Skinner said, leaning forward to rest his elbows on his desk and clasp his hands together. "Dawson, you could be the greatest agent of all time, but we have a little thing we like to call the Law around here. And I expect my agents to abide by it."

"Sir—"

Skinner narrowed his eyes. "You waltz in here with your cocky attitude and your blatant disregard for the rules and regulations, and you think you should get a pat on the back for it? Well, that dog might hunt with some folks, son, but not with me. I've been working on eighty-sixing your ass since you walked into my building. I'm just disappointed it took me this long to kick you to the curb."

Kyle's temples began to throb as it hit him that Skinner had been planning this since he'd waltzed— yeah, he'd waltzed, no question—into the New Orleans office. He'd been cocky, complacent, smug.

And he'd seriously fucked up by not playing nice in the sandbox with the rest of the kids.

He'd been shitting on authority for so long just to spite his father that he hadn't considered what it might eventually cost him when he'd decided to walk away from his job as a deputy in Fairfield County and flip the proverbial bird to his father by joining the FBI.

Oh, sure—he'd won *that* battle, showing his dad that the guilt trips and harsh code of honor that had governed their family for generations couldn't sway him. But his heart had been the ultimate casualty. Because in finally breaking away from the Old Man's will, he'd also left *her* behind. Abby Morrow. The woman who'd captured his heart like no one else ever had—and then shattered it into a million jagged pieces. Even thinking of her now made his chest tight with heartache and regret.

He gave himself a quick shake, pushing away the image of Abby's sensual smile, bright cornflower-blue eyes, and flawless fair skin and forcing his attention back to the news that he was being reassigned. He cleared his throat. "Where're you sending me?"

Skinner's lips twitched. "Well, since the apple doesn't seem to fall far from the tree, it seems only fitting that you go fill a spot in one of our northern Indiana resident agencies."

Kyle suppressed a resigned, bitter laugh. The irony of being forced back home when he'd worked so hard to break away was not lost on him. But it was too late to confess that his attitude and brash behavior were all an act, that upholding the law was in his blood—no matter how much he wanted to deny it—and that getting scum off the streets was not just his job, but his calling. Any protestations of the sort would just look like he was a whiny bitch trying to save his own ass.

So, instead, he donned his most unconcerned demeanor and flashed what he imagined was an infuriatingly undaunted grin. "So when do I leave?"

Author's Note

For the purposes of this series, I have created fictional Fairfield County, Indiana. All of the cities, towns, events, and people therein are products of my imagination.

Also, although I have made every attempt at accuracy in writing this story, there may be times when I had to bend the rules of police procedure or when I needed to make a judgment call when said procedures varied or sources conflicted.

Acknowledgments

It is with great respect and gratitude for those in law enforcement that I write the Protect & Serve series. In particular, I owe a special debt of gratitude to my technical advisors: Deputy S., Detective L., and Sheriff B. Thank you for answering all of my questions and for giving me a small glimpse into your world.

In addition, I would be remiss if I didn't thank my incredible team at Sourcebooks, especially my amazing editor, Cat Clyne. And this series never would have come to be without my dear friend and tireless agent, Nicole Resciniti, whose faith in me never wavers. Love you, Nic. Also, huge hugs to my amazingly talented BFF, Cecy Robson, who keeps me sane.

And, as always, thank you to my husband and our darling boys. There's no way I could do this without your love and support. You are my sun, moon, stars.

About the Author

Kate SeRine (pronounced "serene") has been telling stories since before she could hold a pen. When she's not writing, you'll find Kate watching low-budget horror movies or geeking out over pretty much any movie adaptation of a comic book. As long as action and suspense are involved, she's in!

Kate lives in a smallish, quintessentially Midwestern town with her husband and two sons, who share her love of storytelling. She never tires of creating new worlds to share, and is even now working on her next project— probably while consuming way too much coffee. Kate is also the author of the award-winning Transplanted Tales paranormal romance series and the Dark Alliance romantic suspense series.

Connect with Kate at www.kateserine.com, Facebook .com/kateserine, or on Twitter @KateSeRine.

Devil and the Deep

The Deep Six

by Julie Ann Walker

New York Times and *USA Today* bestselling author

A flaming desire with earth-shattering repercussions...

Maddy Powers's life revolves around fund-raisers and charity events—but she can't forget the daring former SEAL and the scorching kiss they shared before he disappeared into the deep blue sea.

Bran Pallidino carries a dark secret behind his lady-killer eyes—one that keeps him from pursuing a serious relationship with Maddy. But when she's taken hostage, he enlists the men of Deep Six Salvage to embark on a dangerous mission to save Maddy.

As they fight her merciless kidnappers, they discover this isn't a simple hostage situation, but something far more sinister. Passion boils between Bran and Maddy, but what good is putting their hearts on the line if they don't survive the dawn?

Praise for *Hell or High Water*:

"Readers will be panting for the next in the series." —*Publishers Weekly*

"Hot men, hot action, and hot temperatures make for one hot romance!" —*BookPage*

For more Julie Ann Walker, visit:
www.sourcebooks.com

Heart Strike

Delta Force

by M. L. Buchman

―᷈᷈᷈―

The deadliest elite counter-terrorism unit on the planet:
- A precision strike force
- The most out-of-the-box thinkers in any military

Rescued from an icy mountaintop by a Delta operative, Melissa Moore has never met a challenge she can't conquer. Not only she will make Delta Force, she will be the best female warrior in The Unit.

Technical wizard Richie Goldman is Bond's "Q" turned warrior. A genius about everything except women, he takes point on the team's most dangerous mission yet. When the Delta Force team goes undercover in the depths of the Colombian jungle, surviving attacks from every side requires that Richie and Melissa strike right at the heart of the matter... and come out with their own hearts intact.

―᷈᷈᷈―

Praise for By *Break of Day*:

"High-octane action, perfect attention to technical details, and sizzling-hot love scenes... If you are a fan of military romance and haven't tried a Night Stalkers book, what are you waiting for?" —*RT Book Reviews*, 4 Stars

"Fascinating technical details and superb sex scenes!" —*Booklist* Starred Review

For more M. L. Buchman, visit:
www.sourcebooks.com

The Soul of a SEAL

West Coast Navy SEALs

by Anne Elizabeth

New York Times Bestselling Author

—⁂—

LOVE MAY BE THE TOUGHEST BATTLE OF ALL

**Captain Bennett Oscar Sheraton
Navy SEAL, the best of the best**

**Dr. Kimberly Warren
Brilliant engineer, founder of secret space program**

When scientists on Dr. Warren's super-secret space mission start dying, Navy SEAL Captain Sheraton is sent in as an astronaut candidate with a hidden agenda—find the person sabotaging the program.

Kimberly and Bennett's instant attraction may prove to be a major distraction—or it might be the key to both of their dreams coming true…

—⁂—

Praise for Anne Elizabeth's West Coast Navy SEALs:

"Anne Elizabeth writes Navy SEALs from the
heart—action-packed, intense, and sexy."
— *New York Times* bestseller Christine Feehan for *Once a SEAL*

"Sexy romance and super-hot concept."
—*RT Book Reviews*, 4 Stars for *A SEAL Forever*

For more Anne Elizabeth, visit:
www.sourcebooks.com

In Safe Hands

Rocky Mountain Search & Rescue

by Katie Ruggle

New York Times and *USA Today* Bestselling Author

———~~~———

As a member of the Field County Sheriff's Department, Chris Jennings is used to having it rough. The Colorado Rockies aren't for the weak of spirit, but he's devoted his life to upholding the law—and to protecting the one woman he knows he can never have. He'll do whatever it takes to keep her safe.

Even if that means turning against one of his own.

Daisy Little has lived in agoraphobic terror for over eight years. Trapped within a prison of her own making, she watches time pass through her bedroom window. Daisy knows she'll never be a part of the world...until the day she becomes the sole witness of a terrible crime that may finally tear the Search & Rescue brotherhood apart for good.

———~~~———

Praise for *Hold Your Breath*:

"Sexy and suspenseful, I couldn't turn the pages fast enough."
—Julie Ann Walker, *New York Times* and
USA Today bestselling author

"Chills and thrills and a sexy, slow-burning
romance from a terrific new voice."
—D. D. Ayres, author of the K-9 Rescue series

For more Katie Ruggle, visit:
www.sourcebooks.com

Way of the Warrior

A romance anthology to benefit the
Wounded Warrior Project

Eight passionate love stories about amazing military heroes by bestselling authors:

Suzanne Brockmann	Julie Ann Walker
Catherine Mann	Tina Wainscott
Anne Elizabeth	M.L. Buchman
Kate SeRine	Lea Griffith

—∿∿—

**To honor and empower those who've served,
all author and publisher proceeds go to the
Wounded Warrior Project.**

The Wounded Warrior Project was founded in 2002 and provides a wide range of programs and services to veterans and service members who have survived physical or mental injury during their brave service to our nation. Get involved or register for programs and benefits for yourself and your family online at www.woundedwarriorproject.org.

—∿∿—

For more information, visit:

www.sourcebooks.com

Stop at Nothing

A Protect & Serve Novel

by Kate SeRine

—⁓—

When a high-profile investigation goes wrong, FBI Agent Kyle Dawson is transferred back home where he is forced to confront his demons...and the only woman he ever loved. Three years ago, Kyle and Abby Morrow shared a wild, passionate summer—then Abby broke his heart.

Now she needs his help

Kyle never stopped loving Abby. So when Abby uncovers evidence of a human-trafficking ring, leading to her sister's kidnapping, he swears he'll stop at nothing to bring her sister home and keep Abby safe. Caught in a lethal game of cat and mouse and blindsided by their own explosive desires, they must set aside the past before it's too late.

—⁓—

"Heart-pounding action and steamy sexual tension. This series is a must-read!" —Julie Ann Walker, *New York Times* bestselling author of the Black Knights Inc. series

For more Kate SeRine, visit:

www.sourcebooks.com